TERMINAL GENESIS

Book 1
The Progenitor's Stratagem

KEVIN OLMSTEAD

The characters in this book are fictional. Any resemblance to real persons is purely coincidental or used in a fictional manner. The setting and situations depicted do not represent any real events or actual places, and any similarities noted is unintentional. This book is purely a work of fiction.

ISBN-13: 978-0692479841
ISBN-10: 0692479848

DEDICATION

This book is dedicated to my wife, Kristina. This book is a realization of a seed planted by her, that I could be something more than I was. She planted the seed with a suggestion, cultivated it carefully through encouragement and patience, and watched it blossom into the ultimate realization you have selected to read.

CONTENTS

ACKNOWLEDGMENTS

I would like to acknowledge several people from the website fiverr.com. The user *pawxy2000* was inspirational in preparing the vivid planet and background scenery for the cover. In addition, user *mdw_jason* created the character for the cover and he did an excellent job of capturing my character. Additionally, I would like to thank *adamleavens* for proofreading and editing my book. He did an excellent job ensuring my vision became fully realized. His attention to detail was impressive.

1 INITIATION

On any other occasion, the sight would have been awe inspiring and humbling. Young and old citizens alike cheered as the motorcade made its procession from Andilusia Attack Base through the Capital to the Hall of Authority. Never had a lowly Commander rated such an honor as to meet the High Authority himself. They cheered for the announced victory over their mortal enemies...the Paclids...that secured a small moon that circled a neighboring planet. If the crowd only knew what they had ordered him not to say. As his motorcade pulled up to the Grand Entrance to the Hall of Authority, the sickening feeling inside grew. The greeting from the High Honor Guard Commander interrupted his thoughts.

"Welcome to the Hall of Authority. The High Authority awaits inside."

"Thank you for this honor," he replied.

"The *honor* is all yours," sarcasm and contempt were dripping from the word. The Commander knew the reality of the situation. He bowed and offered his hand to steady the descent from the motorcade. The crowd roared in response.

"Rarely does one such as *yourself* receive these accolades," again, sarcasm punched the word. The sickening feeling was deepening in his gut. He did not like the ruse he had been forced into portraying. He just was not sure how high the ruse went. *Could the High Authority himself be involved?* He pondered these thoughts as the Commander escorted him up the steps to the entrance of the Great Arch Way. If the High Authority were involved, what would that mean? He would know soon enough.

The Great Arch Way was magnificent. It was a long corridor down the center of the Hall of Authority, leading to the High Chamber, where the High Authority bestows an audience to the privileged. Gold gilded the pillars, and the carpeting was the deepest, luxurious shade of red he had ever seen. He smiled at the sight because it was his wife's favorite shade of lip coloring. The carpet gave way to his heavily armored body as he was in his recently donned full battle dress, leaving deep depressions as he walked. Two Honor Guards stood next to each pillar holding shield and laser spears in silence, one relic of millennia long past and one of highest technology. Their laser spears angled inward toward the ceiling, the slight hum and faint crackle of a powered laser spear was unmistakable. They might have been mistaken for statues, but every so often, you could see slight movement as they stood in their statuesque poses.

His thoughts returned to the ruse that had been forced upon him. *How could he determine if the High Authority knew?* The High Executrix himself interrupted that thought.

He bent low and whispered into the Commander's ear. "Do you have your scripted responses memorized?"

The Commander nodded and said, "Yes," in a similar hushed tone.

Backing away, the High Executrix loudly said, "Excellent! I am glad that you enjoyed your ride from the base." The High Executrix bowed low and extended his arm towards the High Authority. "Commander, come with me, and meet your High Authority." The Commander stepped forward, and bowed, lowering his head as well to acknowledge the High Authority's presence.

"Commander Andorin Wilcon, thank you for the formality, but the conquering hero need not bow in my presence." With a wave of his hand, he gestured for the Commander to rise. "Please, tell me how the battle went."

He knew what he was supposed to say. Out of the corner of his eye, he saw the High Executrix slightly lean his head in his direction and made subtle eye contact. He remembered his script.

"Your Highness," he said bowing again for effect, "the battle was fierce. Many Paclid light Zona battle units were destroyed, leaving their heavily armored Aversa units open for attack. With the majority of their zonas destroyed or retreating, our heavy Vauchevis had no trouble engaging their aversas."

The High Authority squealed with happiness. "Was it by flanking the enemy or a direct full on assault of their position that caused their zona units to falter?"

The question caught the Commander off guard; this was not one of the scripted questions. He looked at the High Executrix out of the corner of his eye, and he looked back, offering no help whatsoever. "Your Highness, it was a combination of the two. Our first assault was on their forward zona units that were protecting their aversas. Our light Semoni units attacked, and then feigned retreat to draw their units out of position. Since our force was the smaller force on the battlefield, the Paclids sensed they could obliterate our forces and moved forward to do so."

The High Authority praised the move by saying, "Excellent strategy. Continue."

"Our flanking forces then moved in from both sides, cutting off the zona units from their aversa protection. Their aversas could not fire on the position because they would have to fire on their zona's as well, and could only watch as their zona force was decimated, leaving the aversas vulnerable to attack. Our remaining lightly armored Semoni forces moved within the aversa's minimum distance attack range, unable to target our units forced their Pilosa infantry units to disembark in an attempt to clear out our Semoni light armor and Nahali infantry units. This is when our vauchevis started dealing heavy damage. Our barrages did some damage to their aversa units, but the pilosa units that exited their aversas were flung about like puppets. This left their aversas with minimal operational forces and they could not sustain long firefight operations. Once their fire rates started falling off, our vauchevis destroyed their remaining aversas with ease."

The High Authority was giddy with excitement, stomping his feet and clapping his hands. "I cannot wait to read the medal citations for bravery and heroism. You do have citations ready?"

Again, he was not following the script. "Your Highness, I only traveled from the frontlines to bring you the news of our victory. The mundane paperwork can begin once our initial occupation forces return to our planet. I am sure that there will be many citations and decorations to please your Highness."

"Ah," said the High Authority. "You are right of course. You cannot withdraw your best and brightest from the front lines at the moment of victory."

The Commander bowed again. "Again, the High Authority demonstrates his ability as a military strategist." *That was close to script*, he thought. He needed to get him more on script.

"Well," the High Authority said, "you are here and you can receive an award." He clapped his hands, and two pages appeared carrying red velvet pillows with items on top. "Commander Wilcon, step forward and kneel."

He did as commanded, kneeling before the High Authority. The High Authority held up *The Medal of Authority*, the highest honor a soldier could receive. The High Authority held the medal above his head and slowly turned from side to side as he said, "All here today bear witness to Commander Wilcon. His battle prowess over the Paclid defense forces ensured our victory and continued expansion into the heavens. By his clarity of vision and unnerving battle tactics, he won this battle over our fierce enemies. The Paclids tasted sour defeat this day as our expansion efforts continue. By my authority, I bestow the Medal of Authority onto Commander Wilcon." He placed the medal around the Commander's neck, resting the ribbon on his neck plates. "In addition to this honor," He continued, "I am awarding him the rank of *Low Executrix*, that his keen insight and battle-tested tactics may be put to good use in our war efforts." The High Authority held up the new rank insignia. The two pages removed his old rank insignia, and the High Authority himself placed the new insignia in its rightful place. "From this moment forward you are now recognized as Low Executrix."

Executrix Wilcon took one step back, and rendered a hand salute, which the High Authority returned. "Your Highness, I do not deserve such treatment. I am only a loyal Andlid fulfilling his duty and realizing his place within the military and I must—"

The High Authority cut him off in mid-sentence. "You will do no such thing. No one ever refuses promotion at the personal hands of the High Authority."

"But your Highness—" and was cut off again with a stern look that was very obviously directed toward him from the High Executrix. "I accept your gracious accolades." Low Executrix Wilcon sighed in resignation to the situation and bowed. Getting back on script he stated, "Your Highness, I present you with this," he produced a golden helmet from within a black bag, given to him during the ride to the Hall of Authority. "This is the head piece from the commanding officer of the defeated Paclid forces. I offer this for your growing collection of defeated opponent headdresses." He held it out in front of him and above his head offering it to the High Authority as he knelt down on one knee. One of the pages retrieved the piece and stood next to the High Authority holding the prize on a velvet pillow. The dried blood patches blended nicely with the lush fabric, and punctuated the irony of the situation; falsehood dressed up. It looked very out of place.

"I'll have it cleaned and placed with the others," the High Authority continued, "Executrix Wilcon, I expect big things from you in the future. Our battle strategists are preparing a new assault on another Paclid held moon. I am sure your input would be most welcome. You are now part of the Battle Council."

The High Executrix had heard enough; now the High Authority was altering things in his domain. "Your Highness, I am sure a newly appointed Low Executrix would be better served in other areas." The *Low* had an overtone of thinly veiled sarcasm that only he was able to discern.

The High Authority dismissed this notion and continued, "Nonsense! More minds on the battle planning front will ensure more glorious victories for our race. More victories mean greater opportunities for expansion into our system and, maybe, beyond."

The word *beyond* piqued Wilcon's interest, because he had not heard of efforts to leave the solar system. The High Executrix confirmed this.

"Your Highness, such plans carry the highest classification and

Commander–I mean Low Executrix Wilcon does not have the proper clearance levels," the High Executrix explained.

The High Authority simply stated, "He does now," and continued, "Furthermore, he is now part of the Extra Solar Council. You will brief him and bring him up to speed with our extra solar progress."

The High Executrix seemed extremely upset about this new development. The thinly veiled smile was holding back anger and rage as he bowed and said, "As you command."

The High Authority stated, "That is enough for today." With that, he clapped his hands and the two conscripts took up positions and preceded him as he left the High Chamber.

As soon as the High Authority left, the High Executrix turned to Wilcon and angrily pointed at his chest. "You had better realize that what he just told you will not happen. Furthermore, you are to forget the mention of the Extra Solar Council and extra solar travel." He grabbed the new Executrix's arm and forced him into his armored vehicle. Once the door had closed, he continued.

"You are never going to hold a seat on the Battle Council, much less the Extra Solar Council. You are lucky; I had no idea he was going to promote you at this meeting. His handlers are getting lazy." He spat in anger. The High Executrix realized he had spoken too much at that point and softened his gaze, the gears of thought spinning frantically to hide the reality of his spoken words. He turned back towards the newly appointed Low Executrix and said with a soothing smile on his face, "The High Authority does often visit the Battle Council room and would realize something if you were not there. I suppose you'll have to take a seat on the council. I will have to remove someone..." Wilcon could see the wheels spinning again in his head. "I have just the person in mind," he said smiling wily. "As far as the Extra Solar Council goes, you need to forget that for now, although I would imagine we will need you to be engaged in some fashion from time to time as well. Even though you now wear the title Low Executrix, you will still be treated as the Commander you are."

The vehicle stopped at a random intersection and the High Executrix opened the armored vehicle's door and said, "This is your stop."

LE Wilcon exited the vehicle. Finally, he was able to be alone and piece together what had just happened. The vehicle motorcade sped off leaving him to his thoughts. He walked aimlessly towards his home many blocks away. He thought about hailing a cab because his vehicle was still at the base where he left it, but realized he needed the time to process what he just heard and experienced. He now understood that the High Authority was not involved in the cover up he had been forced into portraying. The High Authority believed the battle actually took place because he asked for blow-by-blow details, as it were. This also made sense, because had the

High Authority truly been involved, he would not need a script of ready-made questions, nor would he have received the highest honor possible, nor have been promoted. Obviously, the High Authority had no knowledge of what was actually going on. At that moment, he realized that neither did he. He had only been drafted to play a part: talk to the High Authority, explain the battle. He had no notion that he was going to get promoted, and neither did the High Executrix. *He is apparently involved in this as well, whatever 'this' is.*

A hapless resident stopped LE Wilcon in mid-thought. "Soldier, Soldier! I have the greatest respect for the military, your sense of honor and duty; they are the glue that holds our society together."

LE Wilcon simply smiled back and said, "Thank you," and continued walking. The citizen's words echoed in his mind. Could he live with himself for what he had just let occur? At that very second and sleek black vehicle pulled up to the curb.

The door opened and a dark figure said, "Get in the vehicle." It sounded more like an order.

Will this day never end? He thought to himself.

Inside the vehicle was dark and dimly lit, enhanced by the dwindling daylight from the setting sun. The windows were tinted beyond legal levels, so the person who owned the vehicle must be very powerful. The figure sat silently as the vehicle moved through the city. The vehicle seemed to be heading back in the direction toward the Hall of Authority, but instead sped by it without much fanfare. The vehicle started to slow a few blocks past the Hall of Authority and entered a parking garage. It came to a stop in front of an elevator were two additional dark figures were waiting. The figure inside the vehicle opened the door, and one of the figures outside gestured for him to get out and move to the elevator. The door opened in silence, and the three people stepped into the elevator. The person closest to the control panel produced a key reserved for emergency personnel and inserted the key into the appropriate lock. They operated the key in a very particular manner: first the right to upper right position then back to the upper left position, then to the space at the bottom. The elevator proceeded downward, a strange sensation because this was the bottom floor. He then removed the key and secured it in his pocket.

The elevator opened on a long corridor where a small electric vehicle was waiting. The person with the elevator key produced another key to operate the vehicle. The other motioned for him to sit in the back seat. Again, they drove in silence. At the end of the corridor was yet another elevator door. The second person produced a key that called the elevator to that floor. Once inside the same figure operated the controls in a different manner and pushed three floor buttons at the same time. All the lights on the panel went blank as the elevator ascended. Once it stopped the back panel of the elevator opened to reveal a door. It was another corridor. The two dark figures led him down a hallway to an empty room with a three chairs. The room was windowless, and they motioned for him to sit in the chair. They closed the door behind them as they left the room.

Shortly after that, he heard a familiar voice as the door opened. "Low Executrix Wilcon, thank you for meeting me like this. Welcome to my secret meeting room." LE Wilcon nearly fell out of his chair as the High Authority entered the room. He immediately stood at attention.

"Come now Mr. Wilcon we have now entered a higher level in our new found relationship. Well, new for you, since we have never met before today. Anyway. How much of this did you take part in?"

He replied, "Sir, I have no idea what you are talking about."

"Really? You had no idea that I went off script, and did things no one thought I would? Or did you think I did not see the High Executrix look you down when you tried to turn down my promotion. It was at that point I realized you were just one of the many pawns in the little game we are playing."

Wilcon sat frozen in his chair. It was much worse than he thought. The High Authority knew he was being manipulated, and worse was actively resisting their attempts. *What had he been drawn into?*

His Highness continued, "Now, I know you have many questions, but before we get started I need the answer to one question. This one question will either end your military career...and maybe your life or you will become my latest weapon in the game we are playing. Will you act as my agent inside their organization? Now, I know you think you are not involved, but I will make sure that they involve you. They have to involve you in the Battle Council now. I made sure of that. This is where all their acquisitions are planned. Did you know we bought that moon you supposedly invaded and defeated a well-armed Paclid force? I am not supposed to know this, mind you, but I do. Like them, I have my spies as well. Where did you get your story about the battle? That was not part of your scripted answers." He gazed hard at Wilcon.

LE Wilcon sat in utter fear and disbelief. This was not the man he had met in the Hall of Authority earlier. This man was cunning, quick-witted and forward thinking whereas the man earlier seemed dim-witted, and easily manipulated. He was not sure which answer would lead to his death. However, he knew something was amiss, and he did not like portraying this falsehood. He started with the truth, "I will answer your second question first. I made it up on the spot. I knew you were a military buff and studied ancient military tactics, so I made up the story about separating their forces by a direct assault and feigned retreat to draw their forces out, and then finish them off with two flanking elements. I hoped this would be enough to draw your attention away from my true intent."

"Interesting point. Do you even know what your *intention* was?"

Wilcon lowered his head and said, "No."

"I did not think so. You did not seem that willing to play the game. Moreover, after I promoted you on the spot, and you attempted to turn me down, I knew 100% that you were not involved. When I placed you on the Battle and Extra Solar Councils, did you see High Executrix's face? I thought he was going to implode. Whew! That was quite a show. I can't imagine how he took that little bit of news. What did he say to you during your very short ride? Oh, that's right; you have not answered my first question. What do you say? Do you want to work for me? Before you say anything, ask yourself this question: Do you think either side will let someone see the inner workings of their operation and then let them live? You are either going to join my team or their team. I prefer both. If you don't join my team, well...you can imagine. They also will make a similar proposal as well, leaving you little room for saying no."

Ice water was now pumping through his arteries. He had never been so terrified in his life. He wished he were back on the battlefield he had envisioned for the High Authority and had died there. He would be in a far better place had that happened. However, that battle never happened, and everyone in that room knew that. He could no longer take a passive role in this. At that moment, he chose.

"I will work for you. I feel best about this option. I was trying to figure out on the way from the base whether or not you were part of the plots I am forced to take part in. I did not like myself very much for what I was doing at that moment, but there was no way out for me either; I had to comply. Now I have a new option, I believe secretly serving you, our nation will be far better in the long run."

The High Authority smiled and said, "Excellent. Forces will now be pulling you in many directions seeking to ally you to their cause. I have to bring you up to speed on the Extra Solar Council. We are currently researching technology that we can use to leave our solar system. The fact is that we are in a struggle with the Paclids over dwindling resources, though it is never the battle portrayed in the media. We are in various phases of development of starships and the various supporting technologies, and I have the least visibility over this program. I need you on this project. Take this data processor. Here are the credentials to access the data. The first attempt to access the data that does not use these specific credentials will destroy the data disks. If the device is disassembled, the data will also be destroyed."

At that moment, two technicians entered the room, took his battle armor off of him, and secured the data processor to the inside. They replaced the armor back on his body, hiding the new processor within its confines. It was much tighter now, but still livable. As those technicians left, another technician entered the room dressed in medical garb. The High Authority sensed Wilcon's trepidation and put him at ease, "This person will insert a data transfer cell under your exoskeleton leaving very little scarring. She will select an appropriate existing scar and make that the insertion point. You have many scars that are viable insertion points." The tech selected one and inserted the cell under his exoskeleton. She applied a salve that seemed to cause it to scar immediately, and he could not discern any difference in the scar. "Now to test the device. The device runs off your body's electrical processes and, therefore, will not run out of power. The device communicates with specific receptors via non-wired interfaces. Both doors leading to the Battle Council chambers have scanners to detect and read this device. I will install another near your workspace, but not in your office...some place close by. The transfer is noiseless, but you may notice a slight vibration, acknowledgment that a transfer is taking place. Learn to overlook this discomfort."

The technician pulled out a device and then Wilcon felt the vibration the High Authority had described. The effect was a little disconcerting, but he could not hear anything. The tech smiled at the High Authority and then left the room.

"The procedure is complete. The transfer will take only a few seconds and walking through one of the doors is sufficient time to read any data files after this initial transfer. The Tech loaded all relevant data onto your implant, and when you connect to the processing device, it will upload the data immediately and initialize the system once activated. After that, you will use the device to record your findings and data gathered. Do you understand?"

"Yes," replied Wilcon, bewildered. This was all moving much too fast for his liking.

"Good. Now it is time to place you back in the wild, as it were." He smiled turning away and heading for the door.

"Wait, I have no idea what I am supposed to be looking for. How can I help if you don't give more specifics?"

The High Authority paused momentarily, raised his head slightly in contemplation, and then turned toward Wilcon and said, "Well, I would not need you if I knew that...now would I?" He departed without another word.

Immediately, the two dark figures opened the door he had entered the room through and motioned for him to exit the room. They followed the same path they had getting to the building, and exited into the parking garage. They entered the vehicle and it drove off. The path the vehicle took seemed to lead toward his house, but not quite. They stopped a few blocks away from his street and one figured opened the door closest to the sidewalk, ushering him out. The door closed behind him. The window rolled down and the dark figure said, "Make sure the dark blue vehicle three doors from your house sees you walk by, but do not look directly at the vehicle, just notice it."

Now he only had two blocks to clear his head before he had to, somehow, face his family. *His Family! Can they know? Could he tell them? His life may be in danger...is theirs?* All these questions were running through his mind, reeling from recent events. His only conclusion was this: He had been dragged into a shadow war between two factions of the government. One faction supported the High Authority, and was led directly by the High Authority himself; the other by unknown leadership that seemed to be at the highest levels of military leadership, but which ones? Who specifically? Based on recent events, he knew that the High Executrix was involved for sure. His thoughts subsided as he approached his house. He noticed the mysterious dark blue vehicle mentioned by his Highness' minions. As he walked past, he looked straight ahead, resisting the urge to look into the vehicle. The windows were darkly tinted, and it was impossible to see through with the last rays of sun the day offered reflecting off of the glass. He walked past and continued to his house, walking up the steps to his three-story home.

The exterior was similar to all the others on the street, the familiar brown, sandy color made by workers through a process of secretion and packing. The workers secreted various chemicals that worked as a binding agent to bind the individual grains of sand and other building materials into a workable clay like substance. Once dried, it was nearly as hard as solid granite. The workers are very efficient; when working as a unit, they can build an entire block of buildings in a few days. The older construction was roundish on the insides, even if the outsides looked angular. Newer houses with metal reinforcing mesh could have walls that were more angular because the granite-like substance could hold in place attached to this mesh.

Wilcon lived in a newer house. He liked the angular features of the house. The older houses made you feel like you were still living in tunnels like their prehistoric relatives. One could still see their ancient ancestors toiling away moving this grain of sand from here to there. They build their tunnels like round little straws.

He could not imagine living like their closest genetic relatives, toiling for days and weeks nonstop before simply dying. They had evolved to a much higher level. Beyond the need for one Queen to lay every egg, they had moved to a point where any female could give birth. That one change caused their species to evolve rapidly. They were no longer strapped to a genetic monolith of the Queen's lineage. The species started outpacing their rivals. Soon, they were the apex predator. Nothing stood in their way. This simple change had started an evolutionary cycle that led to where he was, at this moment in front of his house heading in.

2 FINAL BEGINNING

Once inside, he rested his head on the hard metallic door, a soft crunch sounded from his exoskeleton hitting the door. He closed his eyes, inhaled deeply, exhaled slowly, and started to sense the pheromones left by the rest of his family over the course of the day. Most of what he sensed was happy. However, Gilphon and Helphan were at it again, fighting over something. He could only sense the raw emotions released by the two. He then sensed his wife's soothing pheromones attempting to calm the situation between the two bickering brothers, the eldest, Gilphon, always seems to keep the upper hand until either he or Miliki interceded. *Ah, Miliki*, he thought, *how I love her scent*. He searched the air, inhaling deeply for more of her scent. He needed her reassuring scents right now. His contemplative thoughts were broken by his wife's sweet voice.

"There you are. I thought I sensed you." She had a wide smile on her face with sheer delight at seeing her husband. "How was your day at work?" She asked innocently.

He had no idea how to answer that question. His day at work had started out normal enough, but had then flown out of control and he was now trapped in webs from multiple plots, all of which he knew very little of. Being at home, his control over his own pheromone release relaxed, and he could not hide his sheer terror. Even with his chemically suppressed pheromone system, he was producing enough pheromones for ten Andlids at this point, and some escaped past the suppression implants. Being in battle was much less stressful. He watched as his wife's expression changed from delight to fear as she picked up the faint scent.

"What happened today? What's going on? Why are you so scared?" She asked with trepidation.

He owed her something of an explanation, but what could he tell her? "Where are the kids?" He asked her.

"The two boys are outside playing with Felici, and Stranaya is upstairs in her room, but that did not answer my question. What happened today?" She replied.

He attempted a smile and said, "I know it didn't, but I needed to know where everyone is." He motioned for Miliki to join him in the front study. He closed the doors behind him and started the pheromone filter to remove the scents from the air.

"Why did you start that thing? I hate it. It is so noisy, and the air smells funny afterward. What in *The Divinity's* name happened today?"

"Honey, I am in a bad situation at work. Did you see the news at all today?"

"No, I was busy with the children and errands. The city was clogged for some stupid parade the High Authority thought was necessary. Honestly, sometimes I regret voting for him."

He sheepishly smiled and said, "That parade was for me."

"For you!" She gasped, and it was then that she noticed the new rank insignia, "You got promoted! When were you going to tell me? I could have been in the parade with you!"

"Trust me, you would not have wanted to be with me this afternoon. I did not want to be with me this afternoon. It's all very complicated."

"Well go on, explain it to me."

"It was a normal morning until I was summoned to our LE's office. I was ordered to participate in a briefing at the Hall of Authority. That is where everything went haywire. Once in the motorcade, which seemed very odd at first, I was handed a packet of information. It outlined very specific responses I was to provide the High Authority regarding a secret mission. I was supposed to represent the commander of the forces and that I was personally involved in this battle that took place."

"You were not in any battle. You left the house at the usual time this morning," she chimed in.

"I know, right? Once we arrived, I was presented to the High Authority himself. He asked questions that were not on the briefing I was given. He wanted explicit details regarding the battle and how I won the battle, which was not in the briefing."

"What did you do?" She gasped.

"I improvised. From his election campaign, I knew he was a battle historian buff, so I made up a story about feigned retreats and flanking attacks. It probably never would have worked in an actual battle, but he seemed to eat it up. Then he promoted me to Low Executrix on the spot. I attempted to decline the promotion."

"You did not!"

"I did, but he interrupted me and said no one turns down a promotion by the High Authority. Then he placed me on two councils, the Battle

Council, and something dealing with outer space."

"Outer space? What do you have to do with that?"

"I have no idea. He was very vague on the topic, but because of this, I was also given a higher security clearance just to deal with it. So I am not sure at this point how much if anything I'll be able to talk to you about that."

"I am used to your compartmentalization of information. I ask just to share with me what you can."

"I will, you know I will."

She smiled at him and then paused and said, "That still does not explain why you are so scared."

"No, it does not. I have not gotten to that part yet."

"Oh, you saved the worst for last," as she smiled briefly.

"Honey, this is beyond *worst*." He paused for a second before starting in, "When I got back in the motorcade with High Executrix Slithneigh, he was seething with anger. He pretty much told me my rank is just for show, and I would still be treated as if I hold my old rank." He continued, "He also said I would not participate in the councils identified by the High Authority. He finally reconsidered on the Battle Council, as he would have to explain my absence from it. Nevertheless, he still said I was not going to take part in the space stuff. He mentioned that the High Authority was not doing what he was supposed to be doing."

"What did he mean by that?"

"Well I think there was a script for him to follow as well that mirrored my script. It probably had very specific questions to ask, that matched my specific answers. Then he left me on a street about thirty blocks from our house. I decided to walk to think things through. Shortly after, another car pulled up, and a dark figure ordered me into the vehicle."

"Did you get in?"

"This person looked like the kind of person you just do not say no to. Yeah, I got in the car. The car sped through downtown back towards the Hall of Authority and pulled into some parking garage. The two figures escorted me to a secret location without another word." He could see her eyes widening as he progressed through his story. "Finally, I was shown to a room, where I met the High Authority again, although this time was much scarier. He informed me that I had just been drawn into a secret struggle between two opposing sides and that either I get to keep my promotion," pausing to swallow hard, "or I could lose my life."

"He threatened you!" She gasped bring her hands up to her mouth. "Who does he think he is!"

"Honey, Honey! Calm down. Now you know why I turned on the air filtration unit. We don't what the kids to sense this hostility or fear."

"Fear? There is more?" She said with a bewildered look on her face.

13

"Yes, this is the scary part. I am now one of his agents." He took off his armor and removed the data processing unit. Her eyes went very wide, and she froze in place.

"What...what is that thing?" She struggled to say.

"The less you know, the better. I have to update him via a secret channel using this device and an implant they put inside my exoskeleton."

"They put something inside you?!" She looked repellent and backed away from him. "Are they listening right now?"

Looking down, as he rubbed the injection site, and he said, "I don't think so. I was told it was a data transfer device, but I guess I'll find out soon enough."

She suddenly gasped. "Are the children safe! Am I safe? What happens now?"

He looked at her long and hard and simply said, "I don't know." After a brief pause, he continued with a low sullen voice, "I don't know the answer to any of those questions."

Now she started pacing back and forth exuding fierce panic pheromones, "Oh No! Oh No! We have to leave. Oh No!"

He grabbed her shoulders and held her gaze to his, "Honey, I don't think you should, at least not yet. There is still more I have to tell you."

"More?" She gasped as her shoulders drooped in defeat. "I don't think I can handle more at this point."

"You have to. The High Authority said the other side was also going to recruit me and force me to work for them with a similar threat. If you leave, you may tip them off that something has happened, and that would endanger everyone."

She started sobbing and put her head on his shoulder and said, "Why is this happening to us? We were so content, and everything was going great. Why now? Why us?"

He patted her head in an attempt to soothe her. His emotional pheromones had been suppressed chemically by the military, so he was completely ineffectual. He said, "I don't know either, but we need to make the best of it. Somehow I got pulled into this, and there is no way out that I can see."

"I know," she sobbed on his shoulder.

He continued, "And, it is still not over. I have not even met the other side yet, well...except HE Slithneigh. I am sure that will go much the same."

She continued crying on his shoulder for a little while longer as he patted her head still attempting to soothe her. Without his emotional pheromones there was little more he could do. Slowly, she stopped crying. As she settled down, her pheromones were starting to diminish.

"We have to tell the kids something," she finally said.

He sighed and said, "We don't have to tell them anything. You are starting to get your control back and soon everything will seem normal. The less the kids know at this point, the better."

Wiping the tears from her eyes, she pulled away and said, "I know."

Attempting to change the subject and lighten the mood he said, "What's for dinner?"

"Dinner? You have the nerve to ask me about dinner?" She paused for a long second and then said, "Dinner! I left it in the oven, and it only had a few minutes left to cook when this all started," as she made her way out of the room and to the kitchen.

Following her he said, "So, what is it?"

"I'll tell you after I determine if it is still edible." She said as she opened the oven door and the room filled with succulent odors with a faint over seared tinge.

"So...what is the verdict?"

"Well, it is over cooked in a few places, but the meat fared well and is mostly edible. We can cut out any unsavory parts. The vegetables are also slightly overcooked, but passable. Not my best meal by far," she said with a slight frown on her face.

"Honey, after what I just told you, we're lucky it is not a charcoal briquette," he said with a devilish smile on his face.

"Darling, would you be a dear and finish setting the table while I get everything ready?" She asked her husband.

"Sure thing," he replied and proceeded to set the table. He took the plates from a nearby cupboard and placed them neatly on the table. He arranged the plates so he and Miliki would sit at opposite ends of the table and would only be an arm's length away from any child seated at the table. Dinner was sometimes a raucous event. After the plates, the glasses and utensils were next. Finally, he placed linen napkins at each place setting folding them into little pyramids on each plate. Most other families in the neighborhood had moved to disposable variety napkins. However, his wife still liked the feel of linen napkins and was willing to put in the extra time to launder these. Of course, he was not one to argue with her, on this matter anyway. She was just bringing the meat to the table as he finished the last napkin. Folding them today took a little longer because he was so on edge. He did notice that Miliki had stopped exuding any emotions from their prior conversation, and it presented what the kids would expect as normal.

Miliki asked, "Please go get Stranaya from upstairs in her room and I'll get the kids from outside."

He started up the stairs, moving towards Stranaya's room, and heard her playing quietly in her room. She was making motor sounds, like she was driving a vehicle. He peeked into her room and saw her moving her toys around and smashing them into one another. It brought a smile to his face to watch her play so innocently. Finally, he broke the silence and said,

"Little One, it is time for dinner."

She immediately dropped her toys, turned toward him and screamed at the top of her lungs, "Daddy!" She ran to him and squeezed him as hard as she could, for an almost three-year-old. "I missed you, Daddy," she said, her voice muffled by the hug.

He feigned choking and said, "You are getting so strong, Little One."

She looked up and him and smiled saying, "I know. One day I'll be in space, just like you Daddy."

He smiled down at her and said, "Well I hope not just like me."

"No, not just like you, but I did have a dream last night I would see the stars. It was like I was floating in space, and the stars were all around me."

"That is a beautiful image Stranaya. But that day is a long way off yet, you have to go to School, join the military, and then flight school and then yes, you could see the stars like you imagined."

She simply said, "No Daddy, that is not how it will happen. You'll see."

It was then a chill went up his back carapace and his senses heightened as if he was in danger. He suppressed that feeling as much as he could. He remembered a month or so ago when she had congratulated him on his promotion and said the same thing. *You'll see.* He had forgotten about that until just this moment.

"Sorry I was not at the door to greet you, but you needed to talk to Mommy first today." She said with barely any visible emotions about the situation.

"Why did I need to see Mommy first today?" He asked with trepidation.

She looked up and said, "You know why. I am not supposed to know yet."

He smiled down at her and patted her on her head and said, "You are right of course. How much do you know?"

She smiled deeply and said, "I know more than I should. It will be alright in the end, you'll see."

She took his hand and started downstairs saying, "Your new rank looks good Daddy."

As they walked down the stairs it was getting harder to suppress the chills running through him. As they entered the dining area, the rest of the family was already seated.

Miliki said, "What took you so long?"

"Stranaya was telling me about her dream she had last night. That she was going to be in the stars with me."

Gilphon snorted with derision and said, "They don't let little girls go fight like Daddy does. Right, Daddy?"

He was just about to chastise Gilphon for such a callous remark when Stranaya chimed in saying, "I never said I was going to fight like Daddy. I just said I was going to space like Daddy was. They let girls do that all the time."

"Not little girls they don't." Gilphon quipped back.

"Gilphon, watch your mouth. It is not your sister's fault she is slightly smaller than the others for her age." He looked sternly at him.

Gilphon looked down and said, "Sorry Father. But they don't let little girls go to war."

"Gilphon! Enough of that! Your sister is entitled to her dreams and you will not crush them. Do you understand?"

Gilphon looked down at his plate again, exuding placating pheromones and said, "Yes Father."

"Andorin, be a dear and bless this food so we can eat," Miliki said, with a pleading look in his direction.

"Everyone please grasp hands. Oh, Divine One, bless this food we are about to eat. May your spirit guide and watch over us."

Stranaya chimed in at the end and said, "Don't worry Daddy, she does. You'll see. Doesn't Daddy's new rank look good on him, Mommy?"

Miliki dropped her spoon, and it sounded like a thousand utensils at that moment as it careened off her plate, against her chair and then finally the floor. She slowly looked up to meet Andorin's gaze and said, "How does she know these things?"

Helphan said, "Daddy got promoted? Why were we not there? We have been at all your other promotions." As he looked towards his father for an answer.

He slowly put his utensil down and said, "This time was different. I did not even know I was getting promoted today. The High Authority–"

"The High Authority!" Gilphon interrupted. "You met him today? He promoted you personally?"

"Yes, Gilphon, he promoted me."

"You should have called us to come and see it. As it was, I got pulled out of classes today to go stand on the road while some stupid motorcade drove by taking someone to see the Hi..." his voice trailed off as the realization of what he was saying came across his face. "That was for you?" He asked. "We were told it was some battlefield commander getting recognized for his victory over some Paclid forces."

"Yes, Gilphon, I was in that motorcade and I did meet the High Authority himself. The promotion was spontaneous and was not planned in any manner. I do not even think the High Authority himself knew, before that moment, he was going to promote me. He just did it on the spot." Andorin tried to explain.

"You were getting a motorcade. How could he not know he was going to promote you?" Gilphon asked inquisitively.

"You know son, I do not know either, but I am sure if it was planned more people would have been there to witness the event. You know how he likes the Video Feeds. So I have to imagine it was spontaneous because it did not happen that way. There were no VidFeed devices present."

"Daddy are you telling me that you got a motorcade to see the High Authority, but it was not recorded by the media?"

"No, son, it was not."

Gilphon continued his line of questions, "So Daddy, why did they say you were returning from a distant battlefield that you were fighting the Paclids on? Aren't the Paclid's moons days travel away?"

"Son, all you need to know was that I was promoted. You should not tell people how, where or who promoted me. If anyone asks for particulars, just say you don't know, which you really don't."

"This is crap. My dad gets promoted by the High Authority himself and I cannot tell anyone?"

"No, you can say only that I was promoted. I know it's hard son, but you need to do it. Please, for my sake."

"Yes Father," Gilphon said as he lowered his head in defeat.

"Thank you, Gilphon. Meeting the High Authority was not what I expected it to be like."

"What was he like?" Gilphon asked with renewed interest.

Andorin thought hard about what he should say next and settled on, "He is an imposing man with a lot of responsibilities for the position he holds." He continued, "Enough talk about me and my day, Helphan how was your day at school?"

"Fine Daddy, we did art projects today. We had to use ordinary foodstuffs to create pictures or sculptures. I made a picture of our house and family." He said with youthful innocence.

"That is great, can I see it?"

Helphan lowered his head and said, "Something happened, and it got destroyed."

Stranaya chimed in, "A classmate ripped it up, threw it on the ground and stomped on it."

Helphan's eyes went wide and screamed, "You don't know! You weren't there! You can't know!" He started sobbing.

Miliki reached out and stroked his head as she exuded calming pheromones. The effect started to affect Helphan instantly, and he began to calm down.

His head was lowered now and in soft tones all he said was, "How does she know?"

Miliki sensing he was calming down said, "She just guessed based on other incidents you had in the past being bullied by your classmates." She flashed a stern look towards Stranaya.

"Sorry Mommy," she said.

Andorin finally said, "Helphan, you can make another one for me tonight, here. I am sure we have everything you need."

Miliki looked lovingly at her wonderful husband as Helphan brightened up and said, "Really?"

"Sure! After we finish dinner and clean up, you can start work on it." Andorin said.

Helphan asked pleadingly, "Will you help me? Please?"

Andorin smiled back at him and said, "Yes, it will be fun to help you."

At that moment, Stranaya stood up, and declared, "I will go upstairs and get my things."

Miliki and Andorin exchanged questioning looks but thought nothing of it. A few minutes later the door chime sounded.

Andorin looked at Miliki and said, "Are you expecting anyone this evening?"

Miliki responded, "No, are you?"

Andorin now seemed concerned. As he stood up the door chime sounded again. He moved to the door. Upon reaching the door, he asked through the door, "Who is it?"

The voice on the other side of the door seemed very calm. "I am Doctor Fillingraph. I am here to talk to you about your daughter, Stranaya."

Miliki was now at his side and sighed in relief and said, "That is Stranaya's doctor, What is he doing here now?" She wondered aloud.

The Doctor's voice was still calm on the other side when he said, "I just need you to open the door."

Andorin said, "Sure thing." He reached for the door. As turned the knob, the door swung inward, he was flung back by a force pushing from the other side. Struggling to get to his feet, he heard the distinctive click and spin up of laser spears to full power. He looked up to see two of the largest Andlid soldiers he had ever seen holding the spears. One was pointed at his throat, and the other was on Miliki's throat.

"Comma...I mean *Low Executrix* Wilcon." The Low Executrix was punctuated with sarcasm as a voice spoke from outside the house. "Please do not struggle. We would not want any unfortunate *accidents* to happen." As he spoke, the soldier holding the laser spear moved the tip closer to Andorin's throat. He could feel the energy surging through the spear tip. He had seen battle damage from one of these devices. They cut through flesh and light armor like butter. Worse, it destroyed whatever it touched, and cauterized the wound leaving a gaping hole in the victim, already seared closed on both sides. He had seen people live from limbs being severed because the spear sealed the wound as it cut the limb off. A gruesome weapon in the wrong hands. These weapons were definitely in the wrong hands.

Andorin looked over at his wife and could see the absolute fear in her eyes. Her eyes glinted from the glow of the laser spear at her throat. She looked beautiful, even in that grotesque light. He attempted to reassure her and said, "Kids stay there at the dining room table, do not move from the room. Everything will be all right. Honey, it will be okay. Just do not make any sudden moves. "

"Yes, that would be unwise." Doctor Fillingraph agreed, and both spear holders turned the spear tips slightly supporting the doctor's response. "Tell your children to go to their rooms."

"Helphan, Gilphon, and Felici, go to your rooms. Everything will be all right. Do not come out until I come and get you." He said in a stern voice.

Felici replied, "Daddy, I am scared."

"I understand, darling. Everything will be okay as long as you go to your rooms."

"Okay." They all replied.

Andorin strained as he watched them leave and go to their rooms. A few seconds later, Stranaya appeared.

"I am ready Doctor Fillingraph." Stranaya said at the bottom of the stairs.

"Ah, my star patient. You do not disappoint me. You are the only one who was ready to leave."

"How can I disappoint you? I knew you were coming. I just had to get my bags, they were already packed under my bed." As she moved between her parents pinned down by the tips of laser spears, she said to the doctor, "This was unnecessary."

"I know you think so," Fillingraph replied. "I have found that parents do unpredictable things when confronted with the reality of the situation."

"My parents do not know the reality of the situation."

Fillingraph said, "They know enough to cause them to lash out in an attempt to stop me. Tell me the scenario that would have transpired had I not come with these soldiers."

She thought for a second, and turned, looking back into the house at her father. "My father would have killed you where you stood. He would have broken your neck and thrown your dead body aside like yesterday's garbage...which you are."

The quick flash of anger on Doctor Fillingraph's face showed she had hit a nerve. "You should not speak to me in such a manner."

"Why? There is nothing you can do to me. You said it yourself: I am your star patient. Without me your plans will fail. *Everything* will fail. I have seen it."

He smiled down at her and said, "Sometimes, I forget what you can do."

As they walked out the door, Stranaya looked back at her parents and said, "I love you. It'll be okay, you'll see."

"Stranaya! Stranaya!" Andorin screamed. He moved to get up. He would sweep the laser spear from his throat, and attempt to kill the massive soldier standing in front of him.

Being battle-hardened, the soldier sensed this and slightly turned the laser spear into the exposed flesh between his neck plates, the sizzle was unmistakable.

Andorin screamed in anguish as the tip seared his exposed flesh.

The soldier looked down and smiled saying, "You're lucky I have orders not to kill you. It seems someone has special plans for you." He called to someone outside and three additional soldiers entered the house, two of which were of normal size like himself, the other was larger, like the two already inside. However, a fourth person entered and Andorin's breath caught in his throat because they looked just like Stranaya. Even the slight pattern of her exoskeleton was the same, which was impossible. Each Andlid had a unique exoskeletal pattern. No Andlid is the same, even twins had slightly different patterns.

The guard holding the spear to Andorin's throat motioned to the other huge soldier. He moved between Andorin and Miliki, facing the duplicate of Stranaya. "Like the others, the girl first." He said to the smaller soldiers.

All three powered up their spears. The two smaller guards took up a position behind the girl as the third larger guard directing their actions said, "On my signal—Go!"

What followed was horrific. The two smaller guards thrust their laser spears into the girl. No sooner had their spears entered the girl then the third guard moved. He was swift and deliberate. He thrust his spear into the smaller soldier to his left. As the tip entered the body, he rotated the tip and moved in a sweeping arc that cut a large part of the soldier's midsection, cutting out vital organs as the tip traveled through its body. The arc of the spear ended as it left the body and passed through the neck of the other soldier, killing him instantly. The entire motion lasted only two or three seconds. It had been well planned where everyone was going to stand and how they were going to be killed.

Miliki screamed and fainted at the sight. She had never seen anyone die, especially at the hands of a laser spear. Oddly the girl did not make a sound. She died instantly.

The guard holding the spear to Andorin spoke, "Did you see how they were killed?"

He replied, "Yes."

"Good, because you killed them. We were never here. Make no mention of your daughter still being alive. The authorities are on their way." He looked down at Andorin, smiled and said, "Also, they did this to you." With that, he raked the spear tip down his chest plate and superficially cut his exoskeleton in a diagonal fashion upper right to lower left. "A mark to remember me by," he said with a deepening grin.

He motioned for his companion to withdraw out the door first, and followed. The last one moved to the door, and he pulled papers from his armor and threw them to the ground around the fallen soldiers. He backed out, powered down the spear, and threw it to Andorin saying, "You all have a lovely evening," closing the door behind him.

As the door was closing Miliki started waking up, she moved to Andorin. She grabbed him and said, "Are you all right? You're bleeding."

Although the pain was intense, it was superficial. He pushed her aside and ran to the door in time to see a large transport vehicle leaving with what looked like dozens of children aboard of similar ages. The trailing vehicle pulled away and Andorin noticed the outstretched arm pointed directly at him as it sped away and watched as the arm was drawn back into the vehicle and the window closed. He knew this clearly was a warning.

From behind he heard Miliki scream again, "They killed her! They killed Stranaya!" She was weeping over the body holding it to her. Andorin turned back toward his wife leaving the front door wide open.

Andorin was perplexed, because she had watched as they killed this girl. She must not remember that it was not Stranaya. *This is better in the long run. She will be able to deal with the loss easier.* He watched as she rocked back and forth holding the body to her, weeping in anguish over her loss.

She sat like this for a long while, crying and rocking, grief consuming her. It was nearly fifteen minutes before she noticed the two dead soldiers and asked, "Did you kill them?"

"Yes, Honey I killed them," he lied. He had to keep the story intact.

"Good, I hope they suffered." She replied.

"No, they died very quickly, almost instantly."

"Dead is dead," she said in a low, barely audible voice. She looked directly at the body of the girl that was supposed to be Stranaya. "Dead is dead," she whispered, lowering her head closer to the body.

"Yes," he paused and said, "Dead is dead," while thinking, *Dead is not always dead, especially in this instance.* He heard the sirens getting closer as the Tactical Response Unit drew near. Realizing what this was meant to look like, Andorin had to act quickly. "Miliki, do not mention Doctor Fillingraph's involvement, only that there were soldiers. Do you understand?"

"Yes," she said faintly, barely coherent.

3 AFTERMATH

Less than a minute later, an officer appeared at the top of the stairs and peered through the open door. His weapon pointed into the room, and he quickly surveyed the scene. As his gaze fell on Andorin, he asked, "Are there any more in the house?"

Andorin looked over his shoulder and said, "No, all the attackers are dead."

The officer turned and said, "Clear," as he entered the room slowly, lowering his weapon, taking in the scene. He noticed the two soldiers and the dead girl. He looked at Andorin and said, "What happened here?" Three more officers entered the house with weapons drawn, but lowered them as they entered, finding no additional threat.

Andorin sighed. He had felt this more often today, than any other time in his life. He was forced to play the role others had thrust upon him, and he did not like it one bit.

"They entered the house, they said they were delivering flowers." He replied. "Stranaya was excited to have flowers delivered and rushed to the door with us. When I opened the door, they burst into the room and killed Stranaya instantly. I grabbed my laser spear and cut through this one where he stood, and decapitated the other."

"How is it that you have a laser spear?" The officer asked.

"I am Low Executrix Andorin Wilcon, 1-15-128, First Commander," he replied. He noticed the other officers starting to collect the papers from the floor. They started to review them.

"Ah," The Commander said. "They picked the wrong house today it seems."

"Sir, sir!" One of the other officers said, holding up some of the papers.

He grabbed the papers and started reading, slowly at first, but the more he read, the less he looked at each page. It seemed he was only focusing on

23

specific information on each of the pages. He sorted the papers as he read, making two stacks. Finally, he looked up and said to Andorin, "Looks like we have a hero here."

Andorin, perplexed, yet not surprised, said, "Why is that?"

The officer replied as he walked around the dead soldiers' bodies, "These papers seem to outline the families they were going to attack this evening. This stack," he said as he held up a few papers, "outline other families attacked in a similar manner. Everyone in these places died from laser spear wounds," he motioned to the girl's dead body, "much like your...daughter?"

"Yes." Andorin lied.

"This other stack looks like it represents the remaining families they were going to attack this evening. There are at least twenty families on this list," he continued.

Andorin asked, "Do you know why these families...why *we* were targeted?"

"We have no idea. Do you know why these people would target you?"

Andorin's skin crawled at this question, but he replied, "No, I have no idea why they would target my family." Inside, he knew this was to hide the abduction of children, a lot of children, but he could not share this information.

"I will need to take statements from any witnesses." The officer said.

"I am the only person that witnessed the actual attack."

"That is okay. We will still need to take her statement too."

Andorin noticed one of the officers had moved to Miliki, and was talking to her.

The first officer addressed Andorin, recording pad in hand. "LE Wilcon, please walk me through the events as they happened."

"Like I said, the doorbell rang, and we...my wife and I...went to the door. As I opened the door, they forced their way in and killed Stranaya...my daughter, who had rushed up behind us...almost instantly. I grabbed my spear from beside the door and killed both soldiers. One of them got a lucky slash with their spear, but I was able to dodge back far enough to only get a glancing blow down my chest plates. I decapitated that soldier for his efforts to kill me and my family."

"When did these papers get dropped?"

"I am not sure. I did not notice them until they were flying in the air. I believe the last one may have been holding them when he died. His body landed on the floor as the papers flew about."

"Anything else you want to add to your statement?"

"No, I believe that about covers it," he said to the officer, who had turned toward another officer who had spoken up.

"Sir, we may have a problem."

"What is it?"

"The woman says there may have been more attackers."

"More attackers?" He turned back to Andorin. "LE Wilcon, can you shed any light on this?"

"Officer, I am battle tested and I am used to making decisions and acting under extreme circumstances. My wife had just witnessed her daughter's death, and then she fainted because she is not accustomed to death as I am. I wallow in it on the battlefield. Her memory is tainted by that image of her daughter dying, and trying to reconcile how someone could die so quickly."

The officer's radio chimed in, "Sir, we have the vehicle."

Andorin's heart leaped at what he heard, until the conversation concluded.

"It is a small vehicle, left running apparently waiting for a quick exit. The Investigation unit is taking the vehicle into evidence."

"Keep me posted and send in three body bags for the victims inside."

Andorin noticed members of the unit documenting the bodies, taking images of the scene for evidence.

The officer turned back to Andorin, "LE Wilcon, I would like you to reenact what happened here. We will have some officers stand in as the attackers and for your daughter."

"Okay. Have two officers stand outside and one stand here as my daughter. My laser spear was here," he pointed to a spot on the wall near the door. "Now, have your two officers rush into the room. I was knocked to the floor, and they threatened me with their spears. As they turned to kill my daughter, I jumped to my feet, grabbed my spear and wheeled it around in an arc catching the one to my left on his left shoulder. As the spear struck, I rotated the tip and dropped it through his body cutting a huge portion of his midsection out. As I moved it through the body, I changed its direction. By this time, the second soldier saw what was happening and moved to attack me. His spear did this to me," Wilcon again indicated the scar on his carapace, "and my right hand instinctively let go to allow their spear to clear the area, after which my spear completed its arc with only my two left arms sweeping through the neck of the last soldier."

The officer looked around as the story unfolded. Finally he said, "It appears your description matches what the bodies are saying."

"Officer, If my wife is correct, and there were more soldiers, how can we be alive? They would have surely killed me as I killed these two and then they would have finished the job killing my family. Since that did not happen, there could not have been any other soldiers."

"Clearly, you are correct." The officer agreed as he motioned to the officer recording the entire crime scene as it was being processed. They moved to record the bodies being processed.

"We are almost done here," the officer said, as he watched the bodies placed into the body bags. Stranaya was first, and they moved towards two soldiers next. Then he turned to Andorin and said, "Don't you have other children?"

Horrified because he realized that they might be the weak point in his story he replied with a sigh, "Yes."

"Where are they?"

"They are in their rooms."

"How many surviving children do you have?"

Andorin said, "Three, Helphan, Gilphon and Felici."

The officer motioned to three officers, "Go get their statements." They stopped putting the soldier's bodies into the bags and headed towards the bedrooms.

Andorin's mind was racing at this point. *What had the children seen? What would they say?* He did not hear the officer speaking to him.

"Did you hear me?" The officer said for a second time.

"What?" Andorin said dazedly.

"I asked what did the children see?"

"They only saw two soldiers. Miliki and I were on the ground."

"Did they see Stranaya get killed?"

"No," he replied, "they only saw two soldiers." He was panicking inside. His battle suppression system prevented him from displaying his true feelings though. If the kids said they saw two huge soldiers instead of just soldiers, there would be a huge problem.

One by one, each officer returned with the children in tow. The children moved to their mother for comfort. They reported a similar scene, two soldiers, then being ordered upstairs. Andorin was calming down because they were mirroring his story. After Gilphon finished his report, the Officer turned towards Andorin again.

"The picture is clearer now. Your children only saw two soldiers, which matches your story exactly. Your wife's story could be an aberration of her memory in how she is dealing with the loss and her grief overpowering her." He watched as the bodies were carried out of the house. "The Laser Spear is an amazing weapon," He continued. "There is no clean up like other shootings or stabbings, no blood or other fluids on the floor to remove. I wish every crime scene looked this pristine after we removed the bodies. At least you will not have any lingering stains on your floor to remind you of what happened here. Unfortunately, your memories are another story. I will tell you what I have told other victims: these events will fade over time...but it will take time." Speaking to his unit he said, "Finish bagging the bodies."

"Thank you for your words, Officer…"

"Soltag, Tactical Response Unit, Commander Soltag."

"I am sorry, I did not address your rank, Commander."

"Officer Soltag is fine. I am not military like you are. Commander is my title, not my rank."

"Oh, I see. I did not understand."

Officer Soltag smiled at him and said, "It's all right, after this night you can call me anything and I would understand."

Andorin attempted a smile, but it turned out feeble. He watched as the last of the officers filed out of the house carrying the last body bag with Officer Soltag as last to leave.

Finally Commander Soltag said, "On behalf of the city and my unit we extend our deepest sympathies for your loss. Good evening."

Andorin moved to the open door and watched the unit and various support vehicles depart, driving away with their sirens silent and lights off.

Miliki joined him at the door and wrapped her arms around him from behind and said, "What are we going to do now?"

"Daddy, Mommy, Daddy," the other children clamored as they rushed to the door and hugged their parents from various angles.

"Where is Stranaya?" Felici, the eldest daughter, asked as she looked up pleadingly.

Andorin stroked her face and said, "She is dead. The soldiers killed her. We are going to live. That is what we are going to do," answering Miliki's question.

"How can we? They killed my little girl, killed her dead." She paused and in a lower voice said, "Dead is dead."

"I know they did, but we are alive, and will live on. Stranaya will live in our memories." He was silent as he thought to himself, *I will find out who did this and what they did with Stranaya. No one can come into my house, take my child and leave me holding the bag for more deaths.* He ended his thought with a staggering rage, "NO ONE!"

It was only after Miliki looked at him did he realize that he had actually screamed that last part, "No one...what?" Miliki asked still wiping tears from her eyes.

Coming to his senses, he said, "No one will get away with this. I will find out who did this I will make them pay for taking my daughter."

"Taking?" Miliki asked.

"Yes," replied, "In killing my daughter, they took her from us," quickly fixing his misspeak. He realized he would have to be more careful in the future.

"Yes," she said, "Dead is dead. I just thank the Divinity that the children did not witness her death like I did. I can still see her go limp as they killed her. I don't remember much else," Miliki said.

"That is more than you should remember."

The other children gripped them tighter. Felici looked up and said, "We don't want to lose you, Daddy. I was so afraid when those soldiers came in I thought we were going to die. But you said it would be all right and now Stranaya is dead. How is this all right, Daddy?"

"Honey, I know I said that. It will be all right. We are alive. Stranaya may not be, but we are." It was then that Andorin looked down and realized he had three other children that needed his attention right now; Stranaya would have to wait, which she seemed more than capable of doing. He looked down at his children and was thankful they were still alive and untouched, maybe traumatized a little, but everything would work itself out. He hugged his family back and said in a low voice resigning to the situation, "Let's go back inside."

Slowly, each of the children broke away and went back inside. Helphan was the last and looked up and asked, "Are they going to dead me too?" A tear rolled down his face.

"No Helphan, I do not think so. If they were, they would have done so this evening."

Helphan still looking up said, "But I want Stranaya back. I miss her already."

"I miss her too," Andorin replied, "I miss her too," looking down the road where the vehicle had pulled away.

Finally, Helphan left the embrace leaving only Miliki and Andorin at the door.

"What are we going to do?" Miliki asked again.

"Right now? We have to plan her passing ceremony," he said in a calm voice.

"I do not want to do that. It will mean she is actually dead. I do not want her to be dead." She pleaded, tears welling up in her eyes as she struck his chest plates with her fists.

He looked at her and stroked her head, wishing he could exude calming reassuring pheromones, but he could not. He only had his words, and his words tonight seemed empty and hollow in light of what had just happened.

"It could be worse," he said calmly.

She beat his chest again and said, "How could it be worse than this?"

He calmly looked into her eyes and said matter-of-factly, "We could all be dead."

She froze in mid-strike to his chest and fear filled her again. "Dead? Could they have killed us? I am glad you killed them. But you could have saved Stranaya." She beat his chest harder.

"We both had laser spears to our throats, you have seen what those things can do. It is not pretty, so yes we could have easily have been dead. Luckily, I was able to kill the guards once they were...distracted. Also, the one guard said he had orders not to kill me. So again we are alive because someone else has other plans."

Miliki buried her face into her husband's chest and said, "Will this day ever end?"

"Yes, dear, it will end soon enough. Let's go inside," he said in calm, reassuring tones. They moved into the house and Andorin paused to looked down the street both ways. He noticed smoke billowing up from multiple locations around the city, but it did not draw much concern. It could have easily have been chimneys spewing out smoke from houses trying to fend off the cool from the changing seasons. He went inside and closed the door and helped Miliki clear the table. He said, "Forget about washing them tonight, they can wait until morning."

"Tonight, tomorrow, they still have to get done. Better I do them tonight, and get them out of the way. Besides it will give me something to do."

"I was just trying to help," he replied.

"I know Dear, and it was sweet, but I need to keep busy to forget this evening happened," she replied.

"Daddy," Helphan called tapping on his lower leg, "Daddy, can we make my picture now?"

He looked down and replied, "Son, it has been a long day can we wait until tomorrow?"

Helphan looked up and said, "But you said we could do it tonight, after dinner. I want to do it tonight," he said starting to cry.

Andorin realized Helphan also had needs. "All right, get the paper and food items from Mommy, I'll go find some glue." He heard Helphan ask Miliki for the items and she also tried to dissuade him from doing it tonight, and she also failed. It was for the better anyway. Andorin found the glue and moved to the table they just had eaten dinner on. He wanted to protect the table from the glue so he asked, "Helphan could you go ask Mommy for an extra trash bag." If they got glue on the bag, they could just throw it out.

Andorin sat at the table with his youngest son while he worked on his picture.

Miliki left the kitchen and as she walked into the living room said in passing, "I am done in the kitchen. I am going to turn on the news to see what is going on. I see everything is going well."

"Okay, I'll be in when I am done," he replied.

The picture was coming along nicely when Andorin noticed he only placed five people in the picture. He asked Helphan, "Why did you only put five people in this picture, I thought this was a picture of our family?"

Helphan replied, "It is. Stranaya is not with us anymore, so we don't need six people, only five."

"Helphan! That is no way to think about your sister, she is still part of this family, she will always be with us."

"No she will not. They came and deaded her." Helphan replied.

Andorin steeled his response and said, "Yes, but she will always be with us, in *here*." He pointed to Helphan's heart.

Helphan conceded, "Okay Daddy, I'll put her in the picture, but not with us."

"All right, where do you want to put her then?" He asked his son.

"Stranaya should be with the Divinity. Right, Daddy?" He asked innocently.

"Yes son, she is." He said, lying to his son.

"Then I will put her floating in the sky way up here, away from us, like she is now." He proceeded to glue the food items to the picture to show Stranaya in the sky like a bird. "There!" He exclaimed. "Done."

Andorin, choked back his tears, affronted by the picture that reminded them Stranaya was taken from them, but he could not let Helphan see what he was feeling. He turned slightly to the side and wiped at his eyes.

A scream from the living room broke the calm. "Andorin! Come in here quick!"

"What's wrong?" He moved from the table and headed for the living room.

When he got in the room, he could see his wife covering her mouth with one hand and pointing at the monitor with the other hand. It was a news announcer with a breaking story in the city.

"We have reports coming in that as many as twelve homes are ablaze at this time. Fire crews are working as fast as they can to fight the fires, but the sheer number of blazes around the capital make it impossible to fight all of them. Some are being left to burn." Off screen, the announcer was handed a sheet that he started to read. "We have reports of severe injuries to some of the occupants. Fire crews recovered some bodies that had ...what?"

The announcer paused and looked off screen to someone else for reassurance. "Yes, we have confirmed that some of these victims did not die in the fire. A few had laser spear wounds, gaping holes through their chest and back plates. One individual crawled outside, and was spared any major fire damage, which was amazing because he was missing his two right arms. Ultimately, he succumbed to his injuries before rescue crews could arrive. The laser spear wound completely cut his right side of his body away. Somehow he managed the will to crawl outside. His family was not so lucky. Some have called this an act of terrorism." Another paper was handed to him. "We now have reports that the first fires are out, and investigators have moved in, their preliminary findings support what we have reported earlier. These people were murdered by laser spears and fires set to hide evidence of the crime. Never before have we witnessed such atrocities within our peaceful community. These scenes look more at home on a battlefield than in the capital city." He was handed yet another paper." We're now going live to a news conference being given by the Peace Commissioner himself."

The scene changed to a briefing hall with the Peace Commissioner standing in front of many recording devices.

"Citizens," he began, "there is no need to fear. The incident is over. We have identified the perpetrators, who were killed in the act of their last attack at 6:35 PM this evening. These were known members of the Society for Andlid Purity (SAP). They were killed at the last crime scene, where they attacked a seasoned battle officer of the Imperial Army, Commander Wilcon."

They displayed a file photo they had on record from a number of years ago that still had his old rank. "He acted heroically, preventing more deaths. It seems they had many more families targeted for an attack that evening, and had they not been stopped, we would be talking about a much worse and far reaching tragedy. The City Mayor has announced Commander Wilcon," The announcer received a paper from off screen. "Correction, *Low Executrix* Wilcon will be honored by the Mayor in a ceremony tomorrow where he will be awarded the Highest civilian decoration available, The Star of Distinction. It is rumored that the High Authority will also be in attendance and will present the award himself. Notes left at the last victim's residence outlined their victims' tainted past with distant Paclid bloodlines. SAP will not stand while the Paclid race infiltrates Andlid society." The announcer continued, but was heard by neither Andorin nor Miliki as they exchanged looks.

Miliki was clearly terrified again. "When you said *we* could have been dead I thought you were joking to lighten the mood. I did not actually believe that it was possible. Thank the Divinity you killed them." She punctuated the *we*, because she did not understand how they were alive, while everyone else visited that night was dead.

He looked at her and said, "This may sound weird, but hear me out. I think it is because I got embroiled in the conflict between these two shadow factions. The High Authority's side wants me alive to help them. The other side, I do not know well. I think I just met the second player, Doctor Fillingraph. He is obviously involved because they did not speak of anything about Andlid purity. But this other side must also want me involved as well."

"How do you know this?" She asked.

"I think," he paused, processing the thought. "because we are still alive."

4 PRESSURE POINT

The High Divinity sat in his office reading papers. His office was ornately adorned, with gold inlay and accents throughout the entire room. Many pictures hung on the wall, many were priceless works of art. His desk was intricately carved wood made by master craftsman ages ago when working without the aid of machinery was commonplace. The desk was easily one hundred years old, if not older. He liked the desk because it was imposing. He sat in front of a huge, bowed window that looked across a long garden and park space open to the public that looked upon the High Authority's great Hall of Authority. The placement of his office was not an oversight or luck. It was deliberately placed to let the people know that the Government, the High Authority, rules them, but the High Divinity also governs them. He is charged with guiding the race based on religious teachings. Often, as it is with the Government and Religion, they do not see eye to eye. This is one of those times in history.

A loud knock broke his quiet contemplation behind his desk. "Enter," he said loudly. The door opened, and a dark figure walked in. The High Divinity smiled and said, "Ah, Doctor Fillingraph. Did your candidate recruitment exercise go well?"

"Yes, Exalted One," he said as he formally bowed low, showing his devotion.

"I saw the news reports. I see my SAP group is responsible. How did you manage that?"

"The less you know, is the less you know." He said with a slight smile and a subtle bow.

"Ah, I love the devoted, Doctor Fillingraph, I truly do. I am glad my creation has aided our cause. It is so good to have a fictitious group of people to lay blame at its feet. You cannot trace people back to a group that does not exist. I love it."

"Exalted one, I do have one question. Why did you want Low Executrix Wilcon alive? We should have killed him like the others. He will not let this go. I could see that in his eyes. His daughter said he would have killed me, and I believe her."

"You believe her? Why do you believe her Doctor?"

"Her regimen includes psychotropic drugs and DNA alterations. Her senses have opened to the highest extremes. She is precognitive, and knows many things before they happen. She is the only one that survived the enhancement protocols. We wanted to treat their other children as well, but they were too old and they were already past the first molting." He paused slightly and continued, "She said Wilcon would have broken my neck, and when I looked into his eyes, I could see she was right. The genetically engineered shock troops we created kept him in line. I think they were the *only* thing that kept him in line. Then when we were leaving, she called me *Yesterday's garbage*."

"Honestly, you do not need to be prophetic to see that Doctor, which is why I like you so much." He said with a smile and looked up from his papers for the first time and made eye contact with Doctor Fillingraph. He could see the doctor recoil from the intense look, "Make no illusion doctor. You are expendable, as all the families you killed this evening, and if it is even traced back to you, you will be."

"Your exaltedness," he said dropping to his knees, "We took every effort to hide who we are. The only one alive who knows for sure is Wilcon. That's why he should die."

"NO!" He screamed at him. The doctor fell forwards from the forcefulness of the High Divinity's words. "I told you, I have plans for him and he is not to be touched. From the reports from the VidFeeds, he is sticking to the cover story you apparently created for him. He is proving himself very useful to our cause...even if he does not know what that is yet."

"Yes, yes your Exaltedness. Yes, I understand. As you will, so shall it be done."

"Good," he said and smiled deeply as he finished, "I will tell your wife while she beds me tonight that you are obeying. Of course, you know she does not *have* to be with me." He emphasized *have* to remind him that she was collateral to ensure his compliance. *Moreover, he is collateral to ensure her continued service in his bedroom.* He smiled inwardly as he thought, *How she loved her position...all of them.*

"No your exaltedness, my possessions are yours." Fillingraph said bowing even lower.

"As long as I see results, you both are safe. If either fail me, you both shall pay dearly." *Although*, he thought inwardly, *it would be hard to find another woman with such passion for servicing another man.* He mused how much women would do when their existence is threatened. *It helps when they watch their predecessor dispatched before they start their service.* Now his thoughts turned towards the future. *Could he get rid of him and keep her? There has to be a way, eventually.*

"Doctor, stand up."

"Yes, Exalted one."

"Ah, you were crying. I am sorry," he said sarcastically. "Is the image of your wife and I too much for you to bear? Well it is not always I, you understand. I have dignitaries and others that need convincing. She is very good at convincing." He said smiling again. He could see the Doctor shaking with frustration.

"Now that I have your attention, explain your timeline doctor."

He looked up and said, wiping his eyes, "The transformation process will take many years. It has already begun at least for the mental aspect. There are a few more tweaks remaining for each candidate, but the Wilcon child is most promising. With her abilities, we could advertise functionality for anticipation of crew needs."

"Whatever, Doctor. I am looking for timeframes in the future. When will Phase Three begin?"

"Phase One just ended this evening," Fillingraph replied.

"I know this, but the Phase Two timeline is rather vague."

"There is no way to calculate how long it will take. We took these children because they were heading toward their first molting. Most Andlids have only five moltings before the body solidifies forever in its end state. We need these five moltings to achieve the results we are looking for. We have also developed an ability to initiate a sixth molting if needed, but we have to move quickly because the first molting is the only one that can be repeated." He paused then continued, "The time between moltings varies by different aspects of development. While we have tested this planet side, we have not tested this space side."

"What are you waiting for then, Doctor?"

"Phase Two to start."

"AND?" The High Divinity said losing patience.

"The children are on the launch pad right now as we speak. The launch will be in three hours, and they will be delivered to my development teams as a secret research arm under SpaceCon Industries. From this point forward, they will be referred to by their designation codes. The codes have already been assigned and stamped on their uniforms, which are genetic amplification suits."

"Who will have access to the Name/code list?"

"Only us." He walked forward and presented the Exalted One with the translation table and the data ampoule that contained the file.

"Good. How many copies of this file?" *When you are dead I will be the only one who knows, and I will enjoy what your wife will do when she fears she is next. A* slow evil grin formed on his face.

"Only yours. I do not need their names any longer. I am leaving for the launch pad right now," he said. Fillingraph bowed, and started to leave.

The Exalted One said, "Don't you want to say goodbye to your wife?"

"I can see her?" He asked with glee in his voice.

"Of course." The High Divinity replied. He pushed a button, then heard an audible whoosh as a panel moved out of the way.

Fillingraph's wife was staked out on a bed, arms and legs strapped down with a chain around her neck, gagged. She could barely move. She struggled when she saw him. He ran to her, crying, and cradled her head. Her eyes closed.

"Doctor, say your goodbyes," the High Divinity said.

He was weeping again as he said, "Goodbye, my love. I will try to get you out of this, I promise. I am so sorry. Please forgive me. I have to go now."

"Goodbye, Doctor." The High Divinity said loudly.

When the Doctor cleared the threshold of the room, the High Divinity pressed the button to close the door. It whooshed down right in front of the doctor's eyes.

"The door is over there doctor, get moving," he said getting short with him taking his time. Seeing her staked out like that got his blood boiling again and his passion was rising, and he needed satisfaction. She was always best after she had seen him, and he could not wait any longer. He screamed, "Get out doctor! NOW!" He concluded with, "Lock the door before you leave."

The doctor locked the door before he closed it behind him.

Finally! He pushed the button again to raise the panel, and he started walking to her again. As he entered the room, he asked, "Did you enjoy seeing your husband still alive?" He watched her head nod slowly. As he approached the bed, he let his robes drop to the floor and as he drew closer to her, he pushed the button to close the panel.

"Are you ready to show your gratitude?" The panel closed, locking tight. No other sound was heard from the soundproof room.

5 TERMINATION

Doctor Fillingraph stood outside the door, straining to hear what was happening on the other side. No sound came through after the door had closed. He was not sure whether that was a blessing or a curse. He missed his wife terribly, but there was little he could do now, other than fulfill his part of the plan. He started walking down the hallway toward the elevator. The two guards were still at their post, and barely acknowledged his passing as he pressed the button to call the elevator. He silently got into the elevator and pressed the button for the ground floor. The elevator jarred slightly as it started descending towards the ground. He sensed the increase of speed as the elevator reached halfway down, and he felt it decelerating before stopping on the ground floor. After a few seconds of the elevator matching the floor heights, the door opened and he walked out into the lobby. Two guards were watching reports of the attacks that had occurred around the city. As he approached, he could overhear their conversation.

"Can you believe the nut job that did this?" The first guard said.

"I heard he was in some paramilitary organization."

"Yeah, thought he was ridding the world of inferior Paclid stock."

"Everyone knows the Paclids and Andlids share a common lineage."

"What! You are one of those that believe that the Paclids and Andlids are one in the same?"

"No! We are not the same. How can you say that? We are reddish brown, and they are bluish black."

"Then why would you say we have a common lineage?"

"Well it is a fact that we do, otherwise how do you explain the occasional blue Andlid?"

"Blue Andlids?" The other guard laughed in a mocking manner. "Blue Andlids are not real they are a myth. They never occur..."

The rest of the conversation was lost when he exited the lobby and headed toward the waiting staff vehicle. His lab technician met him and opened the door for him.

"Sir, the cores have been prepped and ready for transfer."

"Good. Driver, go to the corporate launch facility. How did the procedures go?"

"Three of them rejected the first procedure."

"Three? That many? I was expecting no more than one...if any at all. Wait. Which ones? Any of the girls?"

"No sir, they were all boys."

"Good. Our continuing research shows boys have a higher rejection rate than the girls, but they make far better military craft. This is why we need more of them. Luckily, we took 50% more than we needed because of these little setbacks."

"Yes, sir." The technician responded, "If you could tell me where they come from, perhaps I could help select more suitable subjects."

The doctor smiled and asked, "How long have we worked together Stalig?"

"Many years. At least five, perhaps more."

"Yes, it has been a long time. Driver, stop the vehicle." The vehicle slowed and finally halted on a darkly lit road.

"Stalig, I need some fresh air could you get the door for me, please?"

"Sure thing, Doctor." Stalig moved to the door, opened it, stepped out and breathed in deeply. He slowly stepped away from the vehicle, making room for Fillingraph to exit as well. He said, "Yes sir the air sure is cris—" The weapon's blast tore through his head, killing him instantly.

"Drive on," Doctor Fillingraph spoke, as he closed the door and stowed the weapon back in the compartment beneath his seat. The vehicle sped off again towards their destination. The corporate launch facility was barely visible on the horizon. However, the ascent transport was clearly visible on the launch pad, even from this distance. It towered above the facility. The doctor watched, as the launch facility slowly got larger. Finally, the vehicle stopped at the security checkpoint. One guard moved to the driver where he reviewed the security credentials of the driver. The other guard approached his door. The doctor lowered the window.

"Present your credentials." The guard said in a deep, authoritative tone.

"Here." The doctor said as he handed his security token to the guard.

The guard first used his light to look at the credentials. Then he produced two different attachments, one that was ultra violet and one that was infrared. The two additional lights displayed the different secret information on the credentials. It was at that moment that he knew he had made a mistake. He should have collected the security token from Stalig's body.

"Doctor Fillingraph, I have been told to direct you to preflight staging."

"Yes, I am aware that I am scheduled to depart."

"Everyone has checked in except Technician Level 5, Kothil Stalig," the guard continued. "We were told that he would arrive with you."

"Ah yes, Stalig. Unfortunately, there was something he was just dying to get out of his head before we left. Something he just had to take care of. I am sure he will be along presently. We cannot hold up the launch just for him. Contact me when he reports in."

"Yes, sir. How can I reach you?" The guard inquired.

"Contact me at launch command and they will patch me through. However, if he shows up too late, he will be a liability. We cannot have liabilities just lying around unaccounted for. Do you understand what I am saying?"

"Yes, sir. What time frame should I look for him?"

"If he does not show up in the next thirty minutes, then he never showed up. Understand?" The doctor said with a smile, thinking that he tied that up nicely.

"Lethal force authorized?"

"Yes, after thirty minutes."

"Sir yes sir! Please place your hand on this pad to authorize the order." The guard typed a few words, and then presented his BioMetric scanner pad for the hand scan required.

The doctor did not even acknowledge the pad and slowly looked up at the guard and said, "This order is off book." He started to close the window and then continued, "Either you follow the order, or you might go off book as well." The window closed just after he finished the last word. The guard staggered back a few steps from the force of what he had just heard. The doctor waved his hand forward and said, "Drive." He knew of course that Stalig would never show up so it was an empty threat, but the guard did not need to know that. The vehicle sped off towards the Preflight Processing Center. As the vehicle navigated the facility, he contemplated his story about Stalig's absence. Then he thought, *If the driver gives the right answer to this next question, why would I have to come up with anything?*. The doctor lowered the partition between the driver and passenger compartments and asked, "Was Stalig with you when you picked me up?"

The driver calmly replied, "No, I have no idea where he is. He never showed up at his pickup point."

"Thank you." The doctor smiled and then continued, "I know I should have asked you when I first got in, but I was a little preoccupied."

"That is all right sir, completely understandable. We are almost at the PPC sir."

"Thank you, I can see that. How long has this vehicle been in service?"

"A few years, I think."

"Ah," the doctor replied pausing in contemplation, then continued, "I think this vehicle has outlived its usefulness."

"Yes, sir. Orders?"

"Decommission this vehicle by smelting it down. After you drop me off, drive to the smelting facility and personally see to its destruction. I expect it completed before liftoff."

"Yes sir, I will personally see to its destruction. I will need high-level authorization to get them to smelt this vehicle before its true decommissioning date."

"Yes, you will. Present your pad." The driver handed over his biometric scanner pad. The doctor typed the order, *Decommission the vehicle presented immediately; override End of Service Date required.* "Wait. Driver, what is the vehicle inventory control number for this vehicle?"

The driver responded, "TD798000-3245-77AA-33570"

The doctor changed the word *presented* with the VICN to ensure that only this vehicle could be destroyed by this order and placed his hand on the BioMet pad. Paranoia was his strongest personality trait. The striations of his hand were recorded, granting the order; the authority needed to destroy the vehicle. He handed the pad back to the driver.

He looked at it and said, "Yes sir, everything is in order. It will be done before your launch. How would you like confirmation?"

"Send me an InCorp Transmission/Communication that says, *Sorry, I forgot to say goodbye.* Then I'll know."

"Yes sir, I will take care of it," as the vehicle pulled up to the PPC. The door that Stalig exited was facing the building. The doctor was feeling a little trepidation because he did not know what the outside of the vehicle looked like. However, it was too late now; the vehicle was already on the VidFeeds. He calmly exited the vehicle he placed his briefcase down when he got out. He got out, turned around and looked back into the vehicle and thought, *I am glad this vehicle will be destroyed.* He backed away and closed the door, which gave him an opportunity to survey the outside of the vehicle. There was no visible evidence that anything had occurred just outside of it. He sighed and thought that the advancement of forensics would turn up microscopic evidence of what had occurred, even if nothing obvious was seen. This was the true reason to destroy the vehicle, to ensure no one ever knew Stalig had been in that vehicle with him. If it were found out, there would be only one suspect. Then that is when it hit him, *The VidFeeds.* Stalig was outside the vehicle waiting for him; the VidFeeds would clearly show that he did get in the vehicle. Fillingraph reeled and fell against the departing vehicle, but was knocked out of the way and was not seriously injured.

The vehicle stopped, and the driver got out and asked, "What is wrong? What happened?" He asked as he helped the doctor up from the ground.

"The VidFeeds! I forgot about the VidFeeds." The doctor said with breathless words as a panic attack was starting.

"Sir, the VidFeeds here are fine," the driver replied.

"Not here. The VidFeeds at the office of the High Divinity...they will clearly show Stalig outside and getting in with me."

The driver helped the doctor up off the ground and said, "Yes they will, and also where I picked him up at."

"Space will not be far enough away to prevent them from reaching me," the doctor said. As he regained his senses, a plan formulated. I need you to go back and get Stalig's body and credentials. Act quickly, and get the guard to check him into the facility. Once you get through the gate, go straight to the smelting facility and destroy everything."

"I will but I need to leave quickly," the driver replied.

"You know...I do not even know your name." The doctor said.

"It's Rengalo sir," the driver replied.

"Rengalo. Very good, Rengalo, very good." The doctor said as he brushed himself off and started towards the PPC.

6 SECOND DEATH

Rengalo sped off back to where Stalig's body was left. He was planning everything about how it would work at the gate. He was not sure how he would get Stalig in without being alive. He was pondering that as he approached Stalig's body. Since this was a corporate road, not many vehicles would be passing this way. That was a good thing. His body was where they had left it, untouched. The site was horrific. A hole was blown through the right side of his head; it was completely missing. However, the left side looked untouched. This might work for him since the guards check the Security credentials from the left side. *This just might work*, he thought to himself. He loaded Stalig's body into the vehicle, slumped him over and made it look like he had passed out. He took his security credentials and headed back to the facility. As he approached the gate, he slowed again and stopped for the first guard. He handed his and Stalig's security credentials to the guard.

The guard looked at his and said, "That was fast."

"Yeah, the doctor forgot something, and I had to go and get it," Rengalo said to the guard.

The guard finished with his credentials, and selected Stalig's. Rengalo could see something was wrong. The guard looked at his watch, and then the credentials.

"Is there a problem?" Rengalo asked.

"I am not sure," he said, as he stepped away from the vehicle.

Rengalo exited the vehicle and walked up to the guard. "What is the problem?"

"I...I don't think I can tell you." The guard replied.

"Then we *do* have a problem," Rengalo replied.

The guard stepped further away and motioned for Rengalo to follow. He leaned close and said in a low whisper, "I have a terminate order for this person if he showed up thirty minutes after Doctor Fillingraph. It's now forty-five minutes past his arrival."

Rengalo could clearly see that the guard was not up to the task, but then he had a flash of insight. He said, "Then do it."

The guard recoiled from him with horror on his face and said, "I cannot do that."

"Can't? Or won't?" Rengalo pushed harder.

"Can't!" The guard screamed and then whimpered, "I can't, I can't. I just can't!"

"Who gave the order?"

"Doctor Fillingraph." The guard replied.

"Show me the order," Rengalo demanded.

"I...I can't." the guard stammered. "Doctor Fillingraph said it was *off book* and would not sign the order and said that if I did not do it then I might go *off book* as well."

Rengalo shook his head and asked, "So, what are you going to do?"

"I just can't," the guard said, now crying knowing he was signing his death sentence. "I have a family to think about."

Rengalo just laughed and said, "You are pathetic. Give me your weapon and BioMet pad."

"I cannot give you my weapon and BioMet pad," the guard replied.

"Fine, you kill him." Rengalo pushed him towards the vehicle.

"I told you I cannot."

"I know! Give me your weapon and BioMet pad!" Rengalo demanded more harshly.

Reluctantly, the guard handed him his weapon and pad, hands trembling. "What are you going to do?"

Rengalo smiled and quickly walked towards the vehicle. He looked for the VidFeeder farthest away from the vehicle pointed in his direction. That one presented the most problem. He peeked his head around the corner of a tower and took it out with the guard's weapon. The second guard moved to stop him but the first guard, fearing for his life, stopped him and dragged him out the VidFeed's line of sight as well. Rengalo noticed the two VidFeeds near the gate. He fired at the one furthest away destroying it, then shot the next one closest to him that looked down on the gate. He looked around some more, found the one back behind the vehicle cordon and shot that one. He moved and turned looking for the fifth one and saw it on the corner of a tower behind the gate entrance and shot that one. With the VidFeed down, he proceeded to the vehicle and opened up the door. He quickly fired, hitting the left side of Stalig's corpse. Blood flew everywhere inside the vehicle. It could easily be seen from the outside of the vehicle. He reached in, grabbed Stalig's arm, and placed it on the pad.

The pad responded, *Identity confirmed.*

He slammed the door shut and said, "Done. Now check him in, and get out of my way." Rengalo threw the gun and pad back at the guard.

"How did you do that?" The guard asked.

"I did not do anything. You destroyed the VidFeeds. You killed him, unless he is not checked in." Rengalo looked directly into his eyes and the guard shuddered.

"He is checked in. He is checked in," the guard said as he recoiled.

"Good, keep it that way. Now send whatever confirmation was required." Rengalo said as he closed the door.

He drove directly to the smelting facility and delivered the vehicle for destruction. Delivering vehicles was not unusual, but ahead of the scheduled decommission date was. He moved to the passenger compartment and removed the weapon Doctor Fillingraph had stowed there. He produced the signed order and the process began. A huge claw smashed into the vehicle, hoisted it overhead and dropped it into a vat of superheated slag. The combustible parts ignited almost instantly. The metal parts slowly started heating and warping until they reached their melting points. A fire broke out from inside the passenger compartment, but that was not unusual either because the seat covering burned easily. The smell was horrible, but the workers did not seem fazed.

Rengalo asked, "Is that smell normal?"

"Yeah," the operator replied, "if the seat coverings were animal hides of some kind. From the looks of it there were a lot of animal hides in that vehicle."

Rengalo sighed then asked, "How do you get used to the smell?"

The operator smiled, looked at him and said, "What smell?"

Rengalo laughed at that and smiled back at the operator. With that, the vehicle let out a final gurgle and submerged completely, incorporated into the smelting liquid, leaving no trace.

Rengalo started walking back to the PPC and sent, *Sorry, I forgot to say goodbye.*

7 PREFLIGHT

Doctor Fillingraph just entered the pressure suit room when the intercom chimed. *Doctor Fillingraph, you have an incoming InCorp TransCom. Please proceed to the nearest intercom terminal for final connection.* He approached the comm device on the wall, picked up the hand held interface and said, "Fillingraph, route incoming connection."

"Sir, this is Security Technician Mildo," said the guard in a shaky hesitant voice.

"Who?" Doctor Fillingraph replied.

"Sir, I am the guard at the main gate who you—"

"Yes, yes, yes! Do not discuss the details over this channel. What news do you have for me?" He asked, his interest piqued. *There should be no reason he should call me about anything. Stalig was already dead, so he cannot be killed again.*

"Kothil Stalig arrived forty-five minutes after you," he paused after his voice was breaking in an out.

"Spit it out! I do not have time for this." Doctor Fillingraph demanded.

"Everything occurred as directed," the guard finally said.

Now he was thoroughly confused. *How could my directive be carried out and the guard not realize Stalig was already dead?* He stated, "Very good. Thank you for your cooperation. Did you take care of this personally?" The doctor probed.

"No your driver checked in Tech Stalig. I-I-I just could not—"

"Enough! I get the idea," Doctor Fillingraph broke in again. Rengalo was very resourceful he thought, *getting a dead person checked into one of the highest security level facilities outside of the military was no minor task. Very resourceful indeed.* Fillingraph proceeded to don his pressure suit for the launch to the Zero Gravity Ship Construction - Primary Facility commonly referred to as *ZCon Prime.* This facility handled the vast majority of military space vehicles that entered the Andlid service fleet. It was so gigantic that it could house

44

the construction bays for a multitude of ships, from small interceptor and fighter craft to the massively huge dreadnaughts. All were constructed in a highly secret process, however, the ships created at this facility were far superior to those created by any other ship production facility. The ships created here had heightened reaction times, near instantaneous decision-making and advanced Artificial Intelligence that was far ahead of its time. Corporate rivals did not know how they were achieving such success or technological advancements; they were always sending spies to find out. Doctor Fillingraph reasoned that, *Stalig may have been one of those spies*, and then thought, *This might be a problem later on if someone were to inquire as to his whereabouts. However, at least now his trails ends at the facility with the highest civil security level which should make it difficult for anyone to investigate anything.* He smiled to himself and he pulled the suit up around his body and thought. *It's all coming together now.*

Doctor Fillingraph was just finishing donning his spacesuit when his pad sounded saying he received an InCorp TransCom. He read the predefined message and sighed a huge breath to read what it said. However, now he potentially had a new problem, SecTech Mildo. He quickly formulated a plan. Smiling, he sent back, *Security seemed lacking this evening. Take care of it.*

8 SANITATION

Rengalo's pad chimed with a response, one that he had not been expecting. He pulled up his pad and read the message. *Yes*, he agreed *the guard was a weak point.* Had there not been two guards there, he would have killed the one on the spot and shoved him in the vehicle with Stalig. Now, he would have to get more creative to take care of this matter. Once he arrived at the PPC, he contacted the motor pool and arranged for a junk vehicle well past its scheduled decommissioning date. Luckily, the motor pool had a few in stock; they always kept a few of those things around for spare parts, and dirty jobs that needed doing. He selected one that was massive but had a powerful engine, allowing it to move quickly. This was exactly what he needed. He ordered the vehicle delivered to the PPC right now.

While he waited, he needed to do some research. He proceeded inside the facility and found a tech on duty. She was cute and not unattractive, he being in a similar situation, decided to use that to his advantage. He approached the tech and said, "Hi," in a soft pleasing tone.

The tech looked up from her terminal and flushed a little and said, "Oh, Hi to you too."

He said, "I noticed you when I came in, and thought to myself, 'I have to meet that girl' and so here I am," he said smiling.

She giggled softly at the attention and said, "Well I did not notice you until you interrupted me, but I don't mind that."

"What do you do when you do not work here?" Rengalo inquired.

"Not much, mostly I stay in the dorm. I don't have much of a social life," the tech looked down, embarrassed.

"Now I cannot believe that. There has to be plenty of guys breaking your door down to be with you," Rengalo laid on more flattery.

"No. Most people seem me as Tech, Level Three and not as Simlana Jilcon," Simlana replied.

"Well then let me fix that. How about you and I get together this evening, and I take you to dinner...I mean breakfast. When do you get off shift?"

"I can't. I live at the corporate dorms, strict entry and exit procedures," Simlana replied.

"There has to be some way?" Rengalo replied.

"Well I do live on the first floor. That makes entry and exit a little easier."

"I have an idea!" Rengalo blurted out. "Since you live on the main floor, you could check into the complex, and then slip out your window and meet me. I'll wait outside in my vehicle."

She said, "I don't know about that. I could get in a lot of trouble."

Rengalo grabbed her chin, pulled her close to him, flashed a devilish smile and whispered, "I hope so."

She breathed deeply, expecting something that did not happen. Rengalo backed away and said, "I surely hope so, but you have to come to me for it to work," he grinned.

She sighed, "But I am just not sure."

"Has anything like this ever happened to you? What is the worst that could happen? They catch you sneaking out and levy administrative sanctions on you? What I am offering will be with you for the rest of your life, just one night free of the rules and limitations. Come on you know you want to." He said leaning closer to her again. He could see her breathing quicken, and he knew he had her.

"Yes," she whispered, "I will meet you."

"Good! Now that that is out of the way I have a favor to ask you. Could you look up the personal information for a few people?"

"Wait. What?" Simlana said seeming confused.

"I have a few people I want to find out about and I need your help, that's all," Rengalo said in soothing tones. "They were very helpful to me this evening and I want to ensure that I take care of everything," he smiled to her again.

"Okay," she replied grudgingly and he inquired about twenty various techs on duty, two of which were the guards at the gate that had checked them in. He got their shift end times. Both were getting off shift within an hour of each other. The first one was the pathetic guard he dealt with, the other was off shift later. He thought to himself *this is working out perfectly*. He also found out the vehicle registered to each: make, model, color and vehicle tag number.

When he was done, she asked, "You *are* going to be there when I sneak out, right?"

"Of course I would not leave you unattended to," Rengalo soothed again.

"Good," she giggled again, "I cannot wait."

"Me either. Oh, and remember avoid the VidFeeds otherwise you'll get caught and then we cannot be together."

"I know a way. This is not the first time I have snuck out of my dorms. Why do you think I asked for the ground floor?" Now she flashed him a devilish grin.

This may become interesting, he thought to himself, "Oh, I see. You're a little risk taker."

She smiled again and leaned in closer and whispered, "I give as much as I take...and I take a lot. But it looks like you can handle me."

Wow, this was going to be really interesting, "Now you have got me," he said.

"You had better be there!" She said to him as he headed towards the door.

"Oh, I would not miss this," he said over his shoulder.

He planned the evening's events while he waited for the vehicle to be delivered. When the vehicle got there, he was very pleased with the choice. It was time to put the plan into motion. First, he headed to the motor pool and talked to the vehicle control officer.

"I am taking this heap you gave me to the smelter for decommissioning." Rengalo said abruptly.

"Hey, I gave you what you asked for."

"Yeah, but I didn't think it was going to be some pile of junk held together by sheer will of thought." He quipped.

"You get what you get," the officer replied.

"Well take my name off it, and mark it decommissioned." Rengalo firmly stated.

The vehicle officer stated, "I do not think I can do that."

"You know you are not supposed to have this kind of junk lying around. It should have been decommissioned years ago." Rengalo countered.

"Yeah, but then you wouldn't have it for what you wanted to do. Right?" A sinister grin appeared on his face.

Now Rengalo knew what was going on, "All right. How much will it take?"

"Six thousand credits," the officer replied calmly.

"*Six thousand?*" Rengalo seethed. He whipped out the doctor's weapon, grabbed the officer by the neck and placed the barrel in the chest of the officer. "What will stop me from blasting a hole in your chest, changing the order myself and smelting your body with the vehicle?"

"Whoa, whoa, whoa," the officer gurgled out. "There is no need for that. Calm down now. I can see you're a man of means," he slowly slid the weapon to point away from his chest. "Can't blame a guy for trying, can you? Please, just calm down."

"Make the change and sign the decommissioning order." Rengalo demanded, and watched closely as he completed both tasks, his name was removed from the vehicle roster and now it stated the vehicle was to be decommissioned.

"There, see? All done," the officer replied.

Rengalo moved in close and whispered into his ear, "If you breathe a word to anyone, your entire family will *disappear*. Your children, your wife. Your brothers, sisters, mother, father, and everyone else, until there is no trace of your bloodline and you'll be the last one to go. You will watch as your family perishes one by one. Do we have an understanding?"

"Yes," the vehicle officer said as he looked away from the intensity of Rengalo's gaze.

"Good. Don't make me come back here to finish what I started." Rengalo intoned with ill intentions.

"No, no, that will not be necessary. Everything is fine," the officer replied and sighed, "Everything is fine."

Rengalo exited the office with him still mumbling, "Everything is fine," he had that effect on people.

He drove to the vehicle parking lot and located all the VidFeeds. He started from the outer ones and cut the feed wires to them. As he was moving from VidFeed to VidFeed, he also searched for his targets' vehicles. After he had cut the VidFeed lines, he made his way to the first vehicle. He got under the vehicle and started bending the feed tube to the hydraulic braking system. Finally, the tube cracked and hydraulic liquid seethed from the gap. He was going to repeat this for all of the assemblies, but that might look suspicious. One would be enough for his needs.

He moved to the second vehicle. He was going to be more creative with this one. In fact, he had decided to do nothing mechanically to this vehicle. He had formulated another plan, one which tied everything up neatly.

He exited the facility, waiting along the dark expanse of road heading towards the city. There were ravines along the road that lead to the corporate complex. He watched the gate intently. Finally, he saw the pathetic guard's vehicle leave the facility. Without using lights, he made his way onto the road and followed him slowly gaining ground on him until they were approaching the ravine. As they approached the first corner of the ravine, he sped up and pulled alongside the guard's vehicle as if he was passing him, but then did not move from the spot. The guard thought nothing of it until the sharp corner loomed closer and realized something was wrong. He feverishly pumped the brakes, trying desperately to stop. Rengalo removed his foot from the accelerator, jamming his foot on the brakes. His vehicle stopped fine, well before the corner. Even removing his foot from the accelerator, the guards' vehicle was still traveling too fast. Rengalo watched as it crashed through the ravine railing and plummeted over the edge, exploding as the fuel ignited from the crash.

One down, Rengalo thought. He turned his attention to the second guard, that would be coming by later. He decided to wait by this first crash site. Luckily, very few people lived in the city; most were required to live at the facility. The guards were civilians under contract, and were allowed to live off facility. This worked to his advantage. He noticed light approaching off in the distance. It was about the right time for the second guard. He got out of his vehicle and started waving his hands. The vehicle slowed as it approached.

The guard lowered his window and asked, "What happened?" The guard asked.

"I don't know. I saw this vehicle crash over the ravine and explode," Rengalo replied, attempting to shield his face. He pointed with his left hand and reached in with his right, grabbing the guard's neck.

"What the—" The guard exclaimed. His sentence ended with the loud crack of his neck plates, killing him instantly.

Rengalo pushed him over the edge, drove the vehicle quite a ways and hid it from the view of the road. He looked at his watch and saw that it was almost time to meet Simlana. He smiled, because he was so looking forward to that. He hiked back to where is vehicle was.

He pulled up to Simlana's dorm area away from all VidFeeds, where she said she would be. When he saw her, his eyes almost popped out of their sockets. She was amazingly beautiful. *Wow*.

She climbed into the passenger seat and said, "What is this thing?"

"It's a loaner," he replied calmly.

She slid over next to him, placed her hand on the inside of his leg, started rubbing, and said, "I hope you have something special planned, because I cannot wait to get started. I'll start right now if you want me to," she said with a smile that would start even a dead person's heart.

"I have just the thing. I thought we would drive out into the desert and have our fun," Rengalo smoothly replied.

"Ooh!" She replied, "I love it under the stars. I can't wait, I want to start now, we'll finish when we get there," as she moved her hand higher on his leg.

"Well we have to get there, and with you doing that I doubt we'd make it."

She smiled again and said, "But it would be fun right?"

"Oh yeah, it would be fun. But it would be more fun to get there in one piece and the freedom to do whatever we wanted, not bound by the confined space of this vehicle," Rengalo said. They were approaching the point where the vehicle was stashed and he turned off the road.

Simlana said, "Ooh we're here, we're here," and she started taking off her clothes. Then she stopped, and said, "Someone is already here," in a sad voice.

"Actually, it was a surprise I had planned for you," Rengalo said in a soft, low voice, "I arranged to meet this guy here–" Rengalo started to say.

"Ooh! Yes, yes! Let's go." Simlana squealed in excitement as she got out of the vehicle and scrambled to the passenger side of the other vehicle.

Rengalo followed close behind as she was pulling him by the arm to get there. She opened the door and saw a dark figure in the driver seat as the interior lights did not turn on. She turned around and said, "Looks like we might not have enough room."

Rengalo replied, "There is enough room look again," as she turned, again Rengalo reached out and broke her neck cleanly killing her instantly. He sighed, because she was a rare gem that, at another time, he would have polished intently. *Not today, however.* He stuffed her dead body into the vehicle and drove it to the area where the first car went over. He drove it right up to the edge and left it there running in neutral to allow it to be easily pushed. He arranged them in their seats to look like they were together, a couple. He hiked back to where his junker was parked. He drove that back to the other vehicle and approached it from behind, slowly. Once the vehicles made contact, he floored it and pushed the vehicle over the ravine. The fire from the first vehicle was not out yet and ignited the second vehicle's fuel, causing another explosion.

He drove back to the gate and entered the facility. Once inside, he took the junker to the smelter to decommission it and threw the doctor's weapon into it. He watched the entire process to ensure everything was gone. When he was done, he decided to walk back to his on-call room to get some well-earned sleep. On the way, he keyed the message, *Security tightened,* to Doctor Fillingraph. His thoughts turned to the vehicle officer. *Since he attempted to blackmail me, then he knew the rules of the game and maybe played as well. I doubt he will become a problem.* Once he checked into his room, he called his wife, "Hey Babe, how are you?"

"I am fine," she replied. "Just waking up. Where are you?"

"I am on facility, my on call room, I am just getting to bed," he replied.

"Oh, you're not coming home then?" She asked.

"No, not until I get some sleep. It has been a long day," he stated.

"Good," she replied, "I am glad because there seems to be an accident on the facility access road."

"Accident? What accident?" He replied feigning surprise.

"It seems two vehicles crashed in the ravine outside of the facility. They have an aerial vehicle on site, taking feeds."

"Really? I wonder when that happened? I have not heard anything about it yet," he replied.

"They say no one knows for sure, but it looks like they crashed through the railings into the ravine. They think it was odd that two vehicles crashed at the same spot at almost the same time. They said they would investigate further," she told him. "Although they did say that the fire will hamper their investigation because it destroyed all most everything. Oh, my!" She exclaimed, "They found three bodies."

"Hon, I am sure the authorities will sort things out. I am tired, and I need to get some sleep," he said.

"I am just glad you are not driving on that road right now, it could have been you out there," she said back to him with concern in her voice.

He thought to himself, *She would not be so concerned if she knew I put them there.*

"Bye, dear. See you later when you come home." She said as she ended the call.

He placed his pad down on the table next to him, closed his eyes and quickly fell asleep.

9 FRUITION

Doctor Fillingraph left the pressure suit room and headed towards Preflight Staging. Walking the corridor, he was not sure what or how Rengalo would take care of things but he had shown himself useful. He would just have to wait and see. He entered the room and saw all the techs awaiting transit. The cores would be secluded and carried in a separate area of the craft that only a few knew about. He left the room again and headed down one level. He had to show his credentials and provide biometric scans to enter the area.

Once through the checkpoint, he proceeded to the Classified Cargo Loading Area. The CCLA required all cargo be fully sealed in self-contained modules. This module was slightly different in that it had life support connections to the main life support systems of the ship. It also had limited self-contained life support functions, only used for transport of highly infectious viruses and bacterium. There were many different kinds of research conducted on the space station. He approached the module and peered inside. He could see the cores, heavily sedated and strapped into their protective pods in preparation for the trip.

The mooring preparation pieces were firmly implanted in the cores' mouths. Currently, it slightly hindered speech. When fully integrated into the mooring point, it would serve as the main connection point and nutrient delivery station to allow the cores to fulfill their design function. All communications and control commands would occur through the moorings once fully seated into the mooring positions. Neural links directly connected to digital interchanges would completely replace vocal communication; this enhancement would increase communications output to subsystems to near light speed. Interaction with technical staff would be limited to visual reception and responses via the digital interchange.

Once he was satisfied with his cargo, Doctor Fillingraph made his way back to the less secure passenger area. He arrived with only about five minutes prior to lift off. As he strapped himself in, a crew staff member hurriedly approached him.

"Doctor Fillingraph. Doctor Fillingraph! We may have an issue. Technician Level Five, Kothil Stalig has not reported to preflight, nor can he be located. We have a record that he checked in at the front gate, but he cannot be located. What should we do?"

"We cannot stop the launch for one person. I do not know why he is not here. I will attempt to contact him on his BioMet." With that, he pulled his pad and typed a message *Launching in five, where are you? Get to launch ASAP!* He looked back up at the crew member and said, "There. I have sent him a message, but we are too far along and too many deadlines must be met by the current launch window. We cannot delay. Proceed as scheduled."

"This is highly irregular. No one misses a chance to go into space. No one." The crew member said. He talked into a hand communicator, "Proceed with count down ten minutes start on my Mark...Mark."

Shortly after this, the ship-wide communication channel opened and said, "Launch in ten minutes. Make all final preparations, and all crew members strap in."

To which Doctor Fillingraph leaned into the crew member and asked, "I thought we were launching in five minutes?"

"We delayed the countdown in anticipation of Stalig's arrival," the crew member responded.

"I want that person, and their supervisor, in my office one hour after station docking."

"B-b-but sir. I thought we were helping you by waiting for him?"

"I have cargo that is very time sensitive and must be in place at very specific intervals, even this five minute delay could jeopardize years of preparation and planning." Doctor Fillingraph lied. He continued, "I simply need to know who will pay for the failed research and development if these sensitive requirements are not met. This could be millions of credits."

"M-m-millions?!" The crew member stammered with surprise.

"Maybe billions," Doctor Fillingraph added for dramatic effect. "I mean, I am the highest ranking official on this mission and in charge of these delays. I should have been consulted before such a delay was considered, which I was not. I just need to know who will pay for anything that is destroyed."

The crew member walked away frantically talking on his communicator. A few seconds later, another ship-wide announcement came over the intercoms. "All hands, prepare for immediate departure. Strike prior departure window. Launch window now three minutes and counting. All crew take immediate action to secure passengers and cargo. Seal outer and inner hull doors. I say again launch window now two minutes, forty-five seconds and counting."

Doctor Fillingraph smiled to himself and motioned for the crew member to come back to him. When he got close, he grabbed his pressure suit, pulled him in close and said, "I still want the person who authorized the change and their supervisor in my office one hour after docking."

"But sir it was corrected!" The crew member stammered.

"It was, but that does not change the fact that someone overstepped their authority," Doctor Fillingraph growled menacingly and shoved the crew member to the floor.

He stumbled to get into his chair when the announcement came over the intercom, "Two minutes and counting. Final launch preparation completed. Awaiting final launch clearance."

Doctor Fillingraph watched the crew member strap in. Secretly, he had hoped that he would not be strapped in on time so he could watch his body squish on the floor from the launch forces.

Shortly another announcement followed, "Final launch authority received. On schedule departure. Launch in one minute. All passengers and crew brace for launch."

The next announcement was, "Launch imminent. Ten seconds. Nine, eight, seven. Engines engaging. Lift buildup commencing. Three, two, launch!"

The engines roared as they spun up to full thrust. The cabin started vibrating, and the pressure was starting to increase. The specifically designed seating absorbed and cushioned the forces of lift off without cracking or breaking any carapaces. The pressure suits also provided support and stability in resisting launch forces. As the vehicle increased speed through the atmosphere, the pressure was increasing, pushing everyone deeper and deeper into the cushioning material of the seats. Slowly, as the ship gained altitude, the pressure subsided and was eventually replaced by the feeling of weightlessness as it moved into the outer atmosphere, getting further beyond the full gravity of the planet.

They were still an hour or so out from the space station. It was in high orbit at the outermost edges of the planet's gravitational field in geosynchronous orbit. It stayed in place by gravitational forces and station thrusters that fired at a thousand different points around the station to ensure orbit stability. This ensured that the gravitational effects had minimal fluctuations. The fluctuations could have disastrous effects on core development if they changed drastically at a critical juncture. This could lead to core stress fractures, core implosions, core warping or core disintegration, all of which would result in decommissioning of the effected core. Unfortunately, they did not have the time to restart, so that much of what he told the crew member was true. It was critical that core development proceeded on schedule.

Doctor Fillingraph sat weightless in his pod as the transport moved toward the Ship Production Orbital Platform. He noticed a crew member walking, in what seemed in his direction.

"Doctor Fillingraph?" The crew member asked tentatively.

"Yes," he said perplexed, "can I help you?"

"I hope so. I was told to come and get you. I was even told what pod you would be in," the crew member stated.

"Told you? Who told you this?" He asked.

"Well," the crew member began, "I don't remember talking to anyone. I just know I was told to come and take you to the Secure Cargo Area."

"How did you get into the SCA?" He asked.

"I did not go anywhere near it. I work in the engine room. I just remember being told, but I can't remember who it was that told me. I can't even picture their face. I cannot even remember if they were a man or a woman. I just know I was told."

As the crew member was finishing their statement, Doctor Fillingraph noticed over their shoulder another tech that seemed like they were heading towards them in a purposeful manner.

"Doctor Fillingraph I was told to find you and that you would be talking to another crew member. You need to go to the Secure Cargo Area, right now," the second crew member stated.

"Who told you this?" He asked the second crew member.

"I have no idea. I just...I had to get you to go to the SCA."

Doctor Fillingraph noticed a third tech that seemed headed in his direction as well and finally he said, "Fine! I'll go there now."

The two crew members said, "Thank You," almost simultaneously. He noticed the third technician stop abruptly and shook their head slightly. They looked around trying to get oriented to where they were and then they turned and started back from where they came.

Doctor Fillingraph heard part of their mumblings as they walked away, "How did I get..." was all that he was able to discern before they moved out of hearing range. On a hunch, he asked, "Technician, did you tell me everything you needed to?"

The tech replied, "Who are you again? Why did you interrupt my duties? Wait." The tech paused and continued, "How did I get here? I don't belong here. I'll get another fine for being away from my post."

"It's all right. Go back to your duties," Doctor Fillingraph said.

"But how did I get here?" The tech asked.

"You walked, of course." Doctor Fillingraph quipped.

"I did?" The tech said still confused, "I did." They conceded, but questioned their motives, "But why?"

"Because you had something to tell me and you did. Now you go back to work." He told them.

"Okay." The tech said as they moved away, still shaking their head a little.

Doctor Fillingraph unstrapped himself and started to float upwards. He cursed to himself, because he always forgot to turn on his GravBoots. He reached down and flicked the switch on. His boots hummed to life.

The boots created a magnetic field that fluctuated with the intensity matched against the readings from the movement of his feet to allow walking. When the boot sensed upward movement, the magnetic field decreased allowing the boot to lift away from the floor plating. As the foot applied downward pressure, the magnetic field increased and *pulled* the boot towards the floor plating. The flooring was a magnetic substance that allowed the boot to exert forces: either attracting strongly to pull the boot down, or weakening to allow the boot to be lifted easily. The boot controlled the magnetic field. However, it still took some getting used to.

He started towards the SCA still trying to get the feeling of the GravBoots. He always had this problem in space, at least for the first day or two. Although, this stint in space will be much longer. *Stranaya, I mean IG-3725-001, could become a problem.* He thought to himself. *Her powers are growing beyond what I had hoped or even dared to dream.* What scared him the most was that he had no idea where they would stop, or even if they would stop. *She was obviously controlling the techs. She could control and manipulate people.* That was a scary thought. He would have to find out more about this, maybe even find a way to counteract it. He did not want to be mind controlled. As he approached the SCA Access port, he heard.

I would not control you. The voice was eerie and seemed to come from everywhere and nowhere.

He spun around to find no one, even in the corridor nearby; there was no one there with him. He asked, "Who is there?"

You know who it is, Doctor, the voice said again.

"Am I actually hearing you?" He asked.

No and Yes. It is thought. Your brain makes sense of what I am thinking and you hear it as speech. Though it is not spoken aloud, your brain thinks you hear what I am saying.

Now Doctor Fillingraph understood why the techs were so confused and disoriented. It sounded so real, but was not a sound at all. It had no directionality; it sounded like it came from everywhere. He would definitely have to fix this.

No, you do not, came the reply.

"Yes, I do. And stop that!" Doctor Fillingraph replied, almost back to the viewing window of the SCA pod. What he saw shocked him, everyone was still sedated, even her. Now this was frightening.

Do not be afraid, replied the voice, *you said we would be friends.*

"I did, but not like this. Not with you reading people's minds... controlling them."

I did not control them. I just told them to do something and they did it. Just like what good little technicians do when they are told to do something, the voice replied.

"Why did you not contact me directly?" The doctor asked.

Because you were out of my range. I could not sense you yet, came the reply.

Good. There is a range. I can work with that, he thought.

I have a range for now.

A chill ran up his back carapace.

You do not have to fear me, doctor, the voice stated, attempting to ease the doctor's fears.

Unfortunately, the more that he *heard* the voice, the more fearful he got. He pushed a button to remove the anesthetic from the air, and replaced it with a mild stimulant. Slowly, the cores started to display movement.

We will talk again, doctor, said the voice.

"When?" He asked as he peered through the window and saw everyone now awake. Some had foolishly unstrapped themselves and were now floating around the pod. "When?" He repeated louder.

"When what?"

He heard a woman's voice from behind. He spun around and noticed a tech standing behind him. "When" he said quickly, "will you people ever learn?"

"What do you mean?" The tech replied.

"You do not have the clearance to be here," the doctor stated.

"Yes I do," and produced her badge and showed him.

He looked at it intently, perplexed; he then looked at his badge. They were identical aside from the name and identification images. *How is this possible?* he thought. He looked back up at her and now noticed what looked like military style clothing sticking up from her pressure suit, barely visible, but still there.

"I am Low Executrix Kolana, Tilkani Kolana. I am the military oversight in construction and delivery of the ships your company contracted to provide. We have received many ships from your company and others as well, but your company's ships are far superior to any other companies' ships. We, the military, wanted to see the manufacturing process first hand."

Oh crap. Oh, crap. Oh crap! He thought to himself *No one outside of a few people are supposed to know the entire process. No one is supposed to know the true source of the ships, the true reasoning why their ships are so much better. No one can know. No one.* "LE Kolana, is it?" The doctor asked.

"Yes," she replied.

"Why don't we meet up after we dock? Let's say two hours afterward?" The doctor asked.

"That is not how this is going to work doctor," she replied.

"What do you mean?" The doctor asked.

"It means that from this point forward, I follow you everywhere," she stated.

Oh this is not good, not good at all, he thought to himself. He reached up and pushed the button to deliver the anesthetic to sedate the cores again. He was concerned about some of them not being strapped in. He hoped they would float harmlessly until they pulled the pod and they relocated the cores into their holding areas.

That was sooner than I thought, the disembodied voice said again.

"Stop that!" The doctor said angrily.

"Stop what?" LE Kolana said matching his tone.

"I was not talking to you," he said without thinking.

"*Careful,*" said the voice.

"Who were you talking to just then?" The puzzled LE asked.

"I-I-I...myself. I was talking to myself," he said quickly.

Now she thinks you are craaazzzyyy, the voice said trailing off in a high pitch.

"Do you often talk to yourself, Doctor?" The LE asked.

"I've been doing it a lot more lately," he replied. *True, to a point.*

Wow, she does not like you at all, the voice said.

"Quiet!" He tried to say in a hushed tone.

"I didn't say anything," replied LE Kolana.

Oops, said the voice.

"I know, I know. I was talking to myself again," Fillingraph replied, in part to Kolana and in part to the voice.

"That is a bad habit you have," Kolana commented.

"I know. I am not used to being with people," the doctor said.

"What? Aren't you a doctor?" The LE asked.

"Yes, I am a geneticist, not a medical doctor," he replied hoping to clarify the matter.

No. You are not very good with people, the voice added.

"I don't work well with others," he said answering both conversations.

You know doctor. You do not have to talk to me, you can just think it and I'll understand, said the voice.

"That was very helpful," he said aloud.

"What was that?" LE Kolana asked, somewhat puzzled.

"Ah, that you think I am a doctor," he replied.

She replied quickly, "I will not make that mistake again."

You are not a very good doctor of anything, the voice stated.

He thought, *No one asked you,* and then asked LE Kolana, "What can I help you with? Why did you come down here?"

"I saw you leave your seat and I wanted to see what you were doing. I also wanted to see any materials you might be using in the manufacturing process."

"I see. The materials are mostly in the raw state, and we combine and create the unique compounds on the station for the ships."

"The military is most interested in how you develop your Artificial Intelligence Operating Systems and your sleek, seamless hull designs. Your corporation is leaps and bounds beyond any other systems fielded or in development by your competitors."

"Thank you for saying that. I will pass on those words of high praise. Nevertheless, you must understand we cannot divulge proprietary trade secrets to anyone outside our corporation. Doing so would severely harm our ability to stay ahead of our competitors. So, I am sorry, I cannot help you in this manner."

"I am sorry, that is my fault," started LE Kolana, "I should have never let you think you had a choice in the matter. You do not. Your compliance is necessary, and I will have full access." She stated in her full military authoritative voice.

"I cannot allow that." Fillingraph said sternly.

"Good thing it's not your decision then. These orders come directly from the High Authority himself; no room for negotiations. How do you think I got this badge?" She paused for effect. "I was given the same access as you for a reason. I will go where you go."

You are in deep trouble, the voice chimed in.

He thought, *I know,* and said, "We'll see about that!"

"Doctor?" Kolana asked.

"Yes?"

"Explain to me why a geneticist is leading the ship production on this space station."

Oh, crap! He thought to himself, *think quickly.*

Yes, think quickly, goaded the voice.

"Well, the state of our AI is so advanced, that it mimics that of a living organism. So much so, that code snippets are much like genetic material used by organisms. A geneticist is in the best position to understand how an AI is affected, much as if they were inserted into a living organism. Hence, I head the team."

I almost believed you, said the voice.

"It sounds plausible, but I am not convinced." LE Kolana replied.

Uh, oh, replied the voice.

"I am sure it will become clearer as you see the entire process."

"I am sure it will," LE Kolana said with a stern gaze.

She does not believe you either, said the voice.

I know, he thought. He said, "I am sure, if given enough time, I can convince you. How long is your stay this time?"

She replied coldly, "How long is yours?"

"Ah, I see you're here for the long haul, just like me," replied the doctor with a smile.

She forced a thin smile in return and said, "Well, hopefully not just like you."

I take back what I said earlier. She is disgusted by you," said the voice.

He thought, *Her presence here will make it very difficult to get things done.*

I think that was the point, chided the voice.

The doctor smiled a little despite himself and thought, *I like a good challenge.*

I think this will be more of a challenge than you can handle, said the voice.

Quiet you! I'll deal with it, he thought.

Good luck with that, said the voice.

"Low Executrix Kolana, we may have gotten off on the wrong foot. Why don't you get settled in, and I'll meet you in my office in about an hour and a half after docking. I have an administrative matter that came up during this lift and I will be dealing with that for about an hour after docking. What can I do during this transport anyway?"

"Okay. A hour and a half after docking, I'll be at your office door. Then you can start the tour and show me the initial manufacturing process phase. You do have your base cores on this transport, correct? I want to see them and how the go from basic core to a fully fledged AI."

"See you then. Everything will become clear." He said to her. He watched as she flicked on her GravBoots and clanked to the floor plates and thought, *That is how she snuck up on me. She did not have her GravBoots turned on.*

She is a sneaky one, the voice said.

I know, he thought, *I will have to do something about that.*

What about us? The voice asked.

We are moving forward as planned, he thought.

That will be difficult with LE Kolana around. The voice said.

Not for much longer, he answered, and planned out exactly what he was going to do.

She will not go for that, the voice answered.

She'll have to, or we are done, he thought.

I do not want to be done. I want to be in space, just like my dad, the voice said in somber tones.

If what I have planned doesn't work then they will shut this operation...all our operations, down. You will not go any further into space. You will, most likely...be destroyed as a failed project, he thought. He did not mean to think that last part, but having his thoughts not private was very disconcerting. He would have to fix that.

I might die? For real? The voice asked mimicking a sheepish tone.

Yes, was his only thought.

I do not want to die. I want to travel among the stars like my dad, the voice said with a forlorn tone.

"I promised you I would get you there and I will do my best," said the doctor aloud.

Can I help? The voice simply asked.

You want to help? You want to help deceive the military, the very organization your father works for? You would be willing to do that? Thought the doctor.

As long as what I do does not hurt anyone, yes.

The doctor could not help his thoughts as they drifted onto Stalig and how they parted company.

No, I could not, I will not do anything like that, came the emphatic response.

Will you get out of my mind? Replied the doctor angrily.

I am not in your mind. Your thoughts project outwards. I am close enough to hear them. Your thoughts are energy in your brain after all. I can discern the different energy patterns from a distance, and in this way, I hear what you think. I communicate by creating energy patterns that you pick up and process as if it was speech, the voice corrected.

Can I block the signal? The doctor thought.

I would think so. I have limited range right now. So maybe, came the reply.

It was then that the doctor realized that the voice he was hearing was his voice, not someone else's.

That was why everyone was so confused after I 'talked' to them because they thought they had chosen to do something but could not remember the 'why' they were doing it.

Now that LE Kolana was clearly out of the area, he pushed the button to activate the cores, clearing the sedative and releasing the stimulant into the compartment. The cores slowly started to activate again, and he thought, *Will you help me find a way to block my thoughts?*

Sure I would be happ– The voice cut off mid-thought.

Hey, he thought, with no response. *Hey!* He thought louder, if there was such a thing, but there was still no response. That was curious. They were not done talking, but apparently, they could not finish their thought. He would have to conduct more research to find out more.

The intercom sounded, *Docking Imminent.*

Good, he thought, *I can finally get everything started.*

He opened the SCA pod and entered. He could still faintly detect the anesthetic used to sedate the cores, but it was not high enough in quantity to affect him. However, the stimulant had a powerful effect on him. His heart rate increased dramatically. He felt so alive, invigorated.

The cores started coming around him as he made his way to the core marked IG-3275-001.

"How long have you known that you could do that?" The doctor asked.

Still dazed by the after effects of the anesthesia, they replied, "What? Do what? I do not know what you are talking about," as they released themselves from their pod and started to float slightly upwards.

"Talk to people with your mind."

"I can't do that," IG-3275-001 replied and asked, "Is that even possible?"

"Apparently," he replied but thought to himself, *IG-3275-001 was the best candidate to display those kinds of abilities. However, if not them, then who? It had to be in this room, again but whom?* He looked around and surveyed the room no other candidate stood out as capable of demonstrating this kind of ability, except for IG-3275-001. *That had to be it.* Then he remembered they had discussed their father being in the military. The only candidate taken from a military family was IG-3275-001. *It had to be her, but how? How can they use it but not know it? More research was required into this effect and blocking his thought patterns as well.*

The intercom sounded, *Docking complete. Pressure equalization in progress. Equalization complete. Open docking hatches, prepare for disembarkation. Have a pleasant stay.*

He brought up his BioMet, toggled a few settings and said into the microphone, "Reception teams report to Transport SCA for core arrival. Repeating. Reception teams report to Transport CSA for core arrival.

The responses were almost immediate. "Team Alpha en route." "Team Epsilon acknowledged." "Team Beta entering Transport." Finally, all teams reported in, and one by one, they collected their core and escorted it to their respective areas. He would personally escort IG-3275-001 to her core development center in the Team Prime area just outside his office.

They walked out and then the doctor was jarred out his thoughts when IG-3275-001 asked, "Will the process hurt?"

They continued walking, and he looked down at that little thing that floated beside him and said, "I do not think so we will be using an anesthetic to place you in an unconscious state. You should not feel anything."

"I am a little scared now. This is all so real and not what I was expecting," IG-3275-001 replied.

"You have nothing to fear. Everything will be all right. You'll see." The doctor said in an attempt to calm IG-3275-001 down and return their emotional state to that of being calm.

They approached the core processing area in Team Prime's location. They looked directly down on the planet 40% of the time, the other 60% was a viewing of interstellar space. He opened the door to IG-3275-001's core development room, and the core stopped at the sight. The room was enormous. Many huge buildings could fill this room, and there would still be vast amounts of space. The outer wall was nothing but a force field, and almost the entire planet was visible from this vantage point.

IG-3275-001 said, "Wow, this is huge. Why so large?"

"It needs to be this big for the size of the ship we will create. The largest ship ever built will launch out of this room. It will be the crowning glory of all our technological and genetic achievements of our species. It will take us to the farthest reaches of our galaxy and maybe even beyond. This class of ship called *Progenitor*, will be capable of intergalactic travel. The ship that leaves this room will travel further than any other ship; it will be the first of its kind with the ship designation of IG-3275-001."

"Hey, that is my number. I'll be that ship? Thank you! Thank you! Thank you!" IG-3275-001 hugged Doctor Fillingraph, maybe for the last time.

They looked out over the planet's horizon and watched as the sun rose over the planet to mark the start of a new day. IG-3275-001 said, "I love this room. Thank you again, Doctor Fillingraph. Today is a good day."

With that, Doctor Fillingraph's BioMet chirped indicating he received a message. He opened it and smiled when he read, *Security Tightened.* "Yes," he agreed, "today is a good day indeed." He paused for a second and then said, "I have to go now. I have to see to some things before I can get some rest. The room is set up for your comfort right now. There is a sleeping pod over there, and any biologic functions can be taken care of in that room there. This small room is dismantled as the need dictates. Your development team is heading this way now and will be here very shortly. My office is close by so I'll be able to keep a close eye on your progress. We will be able to talk more often."

He walked out of the room and closed the door behind him. Once closed, the door could not be opened from the inside. He had many things to take care of before his two meetings. He proceeded to his office. He held his security badge up to have the scanner read the credentials from the card. He typed in his security code and placed his hand on the embedded BioMet. The device scanned his handprint and granted him access to his room. He sat at his desk, picked up his intercom device and said, "Security Chief." After a few seconds, the security chief answered.

"Security Chief Orlund. How can I assist you Doctor Fillingraph?"

"I need new security badges like the one I have already, but at a higher level."

"The one you have is at the highest level already."

"Yes, but I want another level created that is higher than this one, this level badge downgraded to specific areas."

"The new badge is the easy part, upgrading the security system will take some time. What color did you want the badges?"

"Clear."

"Clear? No color at all? I am not sure we have the correct source materials in stock to make clear badges."

"No clear, huh? How about platinum."

"Platinum we have. You want solid platinum or micro-bonded platinum?"

"I'll take solid platinum of course. Make one for myself immediately. Downgrade the old ones to only common areas: no labs, processing centers or other areas marked sensitive or restricted."

"Why not just use the lower badges we have for those areas already?"

"If I have to explain it to you, then you won't finish my new badge on time. Also restrict access to my office to this new badge and use my security profile you already have on file to initialize the badge. Once that is done, remove the old level from accessing my office and Prime Team all together. Only the platinum level badge gains entry to my office from now on. Create and deliver the badge, and then update the security protocols and access levels. Then ensure my teams get their platinum badges and updated security profiles, keep the old badges, just downgrade their access to common areas as specified earlier as you move through my teams."

"You want how many? I was thinking we were just going to do one or two, not droves of people."

"My badge is the top priority, have that in my office in thirty minutes. Then complete Team Prime's badges before lunch today. The others can begin tomorrow. Replace the badges by team, downgrading the old badges as each area is processed."

"I guess we can handle a phased implementation."

"All teams need to be upgraded in six days. After Prime, start with the military areas, and with the civilian projects last."

"I'll have your badge on your desk in thirty minutes."

"Good. See you then." He ended the transmission and the intercom silenced.

"Legal, Highest Level." He said into the device.

"Legal Department, Technician Welkoni, Can I help you?" A dainty female voice said.

"Yes, I need a lawyer. Highest Level Security. Now." There was a pause while the transmission was passed to a lawyer.

"Yes, what legal concerns do you have?"

"I need a standard Non Disclosure Agreement, with military and Maximum Penalty riders attached. Also, ensure you include that all military communications, classified, 'off book' or any communication outside corporate channels to anyone, trigger the maximum penalty."

"Maximum Penalty? I have not seen that in a military NDA for a while. Is that really necessary."

"Are you a lawyer or a therapist?" Doctor Fillingraph quipped.

"All right, just checking, no one comes back from the Maximum Penalty being imposed."

"That's the idea, now you got it. Have the name read Tilkani Kolana and ensure the military rank structure cannot serve as protection under Maximum Penalty."

"That's the standard military rider."

"Just making sure, I need that on my desk in about an hour."

"That is not a problem Doctor Fillingraph. This is a standard document just have to add the name. Oh, and what is the NDA being signed for?"

"Include everything and anything on this space station, from lift off to their eventual touchdown planetside. Everything." He smiled and thought, *Everything was coming together now.*

"Not leaving much for wiggle room are you."

"No. Digitally send it to me when complete," he said and then ended the transmission.

10 LEGALITIES

Doctor Fillingraph stood up and stretched; he was very tired after the events of last night. He was emotionally drained, and needed to get some sleep. He had two things to take care of and then he could finally sleep.

While he sat at his desk, he looked at the real-time status updates of core progression. Two cores had already entered the nutrient bath to soften their exteriors. This process submerged the cores into a solution that softened the individual cells, allowing the cells to grow slowly to elongate them, allowing them to be enlarged. The military cores were engaged in extensive reprogramming to elicit minimal or no response to stressful situations. This process would take many months to complete, and would harden the cores into unstoppable juggernauts unabated by their inherent emotions. Only IG-3275-001's progress did not display, which was fine because they needed to slow the process down considerably. A hull of the size and scale needed was immense, and any minor mistakes now would be catastrophic later on. This core's development would take many years to reach the size and durability needed for such a craft. IG-3275-001 was one of a kind, and not easily replaced; extreme caution was warranted.

His door sounded. He said, "Claudette, external view." His security system, code-named Claudette, showed him an image of the person outside his door. "Claudette, door comms." A communication channel opened. "State your business."

"Technician Jendpour, Security. I have your new badge as requested."

"Very good." "Claudette, open the door." With the command, the door opened and the tech walked towards him. When Jendpour reached his desk, he held out the new platinum badge.

"Wow, that looks great," he reached out and took the badge from the tech and they started to leave, "hold on there a second, I have to test it first." "Claudette, security level check," as he held up his old badge to the scanner.

Claudette answered, *Common access only, secured areas restricted.*

"Claudette, specify if this specific badge or all level badges are downgraded."

All badges in badge group affected.

"Claudette, security level check," Fillingraph said, as he held up his new platinum badge.

Highest level, unrestricted access, every level, came the reply.

He looked at the tech and said, "You may go now. Tell your boss that this is excellent work."

"Thank you, sir." They turned and left the room.

Security is taken care of. Two more tasks to take care of, and then I can sleep.

He glanced at the core status area with little changes, as he expected. The beginning of Phase Two was taking shape. The nutrient baths could last for days or weeks at a time, perhaps months in IG-3275-001's case. The process was completed before each molting stage. This would allow the core to shed the old exoskeleton and replace it with a new one. In these cases, the new ones would have enriched elements added to ensure maximum strength. Only the strength would increase after each molting. The size was created before each molting, hence the nutrient bath to allow the alteration. IG-3275-001's molting was fast approaching, and they needed to get the first stage size limits met prior to the molting. IG-3275-001's enlargement factor would be exponential, not just merely a linear progression (doubled, tripled, quadrupled, etc...). This was the only way they could get the size needed.

His door chimed again. "Claudette, external view," An image of the tech from the transport displayed clearly. "Enter," Fillingraph said as the door opened for the tech. He held out his hand and said, "Give me your badge. And where is your supervisor?"

"He would not come because he has heard what happens to people in your office. Here is my badge," replied the tech as he handed his badge over.

"Claudette, scan badge." He held up the badge for the security scanner. "Contact Personnel Resources. Note demotion of this tech, one level, reset promotion criteria and strip any special privileges. Place demerit on permanent record, Authorization Fillingraph, Prime Lead. Also, demote supervisor of record, decrease pay by 10%—no 20% for failure to show. Place note on record stating as such. Authorization Fillingraph, Prime Lead."

"Thank you sir." The tech said.

"You understand, next time I am throwing you out of an airlock, naked."

"Yes sir, Thank you, sir. I am sorry sir."

"Just get out of my office and stop breathing my air," he said harshly.

He heard the tech inhale deeply and start to run out of the room.

Doctor Fillingraph screamed, "Did you just breathe my air? Claudette, seal door!"

He watched as the tech slammed headlong into the sealed doors. The harsh crack of his exoskeleton echoed in the room as his body slumped down to the floor. "Ooh, that had to hurt," Fillingraph said aloud. He walked over to the tech and kicked his body. The tech groaned in response. "Claudette, dispatch MediUnit."

MediUnit dispatched, Claudette replied.

The unit arrived a minute later. Noticing the body on the ground, he asked, "What happened here?"

"He tried to run through a closed door." Doctor Fillingraph said. "As you can see, that did not work out so well."

"No, it did not." Replied the MedTech.

"Just get him out of my office."

"I will in a minute. I'm securing him to the body board for safe transport to the MedCenter."

As the MedTechs carried his body away, LE Kolana walked in. "What happened to him?"

"Head and door do not mix well," replied the doctor.

"I can see that. He has a cranial crack. That is a nasty wound. I've seen many on the battle practice field," the LE commented, "they never seem to heal right."

"You're a little early Low Executrix Kolana." Doctor Fillingraph smiled.

She smiled back and said, "I pride myself on discipline, Doctor."

"A good aspiration to strive towards," the doctor noted. He noticed he had received the document from Legal and started the print job.

"When does the tour begin?" Kolana asked.

"Ah, straight to the point, I like that. We should get along fine, after today," he said with a thin smile. " I have some business for you that we need to settle." He pulled the NDA off the printer and presented it to her. "You need to sign this before I give you any tours or show you any technology. We cannot let our proprietary secrets out into the public. We would lose...our competitive edge. I am sure you understand."

"I do not agree to any of this. I have reports I have to file which detail specifics about your processes, safety measures, protocols, and AI programming."

"You have to agree," he simply stated. "You have no choice."

"I have the same access rights as y–" she stopped as she noticed his badge hanging around his neck. "What is that?" She asked as she pointed to his badge.

"You *did* have the same access rights as I did, but now you do not. All those badges are in the process of being downgraded to a much lower level...only common areas. In a few days, you will not even be able to access this level."

"But I *live* on this level."

"I would move, and quickly," the doctor smiled seeing his plan in action.

"I was ordered to keep close tabs on you, to be involved in every level of development, and to understand how you produce such a higher quality product than anyone else."

"See? That is the problem. No one will ever know without signing one of these, and after you do, you can see the entire process. However, you may never tell a single soul what you see, what you've learned or what you know about this facility...ever...even through covert or secret military channels. You are bound from that moment forward for everything you have seen since lift off. You must comply. Otherwise we are legally allowed to administer the Maximum Penalty."

"You do not even specify what the Maximum Penalty is."

"Of course not. We cannot put that we are going to kill you, legally, on a piece of paper. Now can we? Why do you think our process is completely unknown to anyone outside our corporation? That is because there is no one alive outside our corporation that knows about anything that goes on here."

She stood up and moved towards the doctor. "Are you threatening me?" She intoned in a menacing manner.

"On the contrary. I am just enlightening the extent our security measures will go. It is not a threat, it is a matter of fact. This fact is also bound by the NDA. If you tell anyone about this, well, you'll never leave this station alive. In fact, that part of the NDA is in effect right now," he smiled.

"What do you mean?" She asked.

Read the last paragraph right above the area for your signature. Read it aloud, please. "Claudette, record."

"By reading this and not signing, the Maximum Penalty will be in force and immediately put into effect. Failure to sign the form will constitute acceptance of the Maximum Penalty and concurrence with its implementation. The room in which this form is presented is where either the form is signed, or the Maximum Penalty is carried out."

"Claudette, engage Maximum Penalty Protocol for Tilkani Kolana."

Protocols engaged. One minute timer started. Four particle cannons descended from access ports in each corner and pointed directly at her.

"Disengage timer," the doctor ordered. "We don't want Low Executrix Kolana to feel...*rushed*...into her decision," He said as he slowly sat down in his chair.

"You cannot do this! It is against everything our government stands for.

Everything our *civilization* stands for."

"Not everyone feels the same way, Low Executrix."

"I am not signing this!" She said emphatically.

Claudette sounded, *Protocol activated: three–*

Doctor Fillingraph yelled, "Stop countdown! Disengage all timers except for Maximum Penalty Protocol."

Countdown suspended. Secondary Protocols enacted. Tertiary Protocol -Maximum Penalty Protocol, is pending.

"What the? You had better control your weapons doctor."

"See the thing is: I can stop the countdown one more time. The tertiary protocol is unstoppable and will be carried out unless the Maximum Penalty Protocol is negated...by a signed form. So please, until you sign it, and you will, do not say that you will not sign it. That will trigger the next phase in the protocol."

"I am–"

"Careful what you say," said the doctor. He continued, "I am just going to step out right now while you decide. Here is a pen. I would not talk much or make any move towards the door until you sign the form. I'll be right outside. I don't want to get your blood all over me if you decide not to sign." He waved at her as the doors slid shut. He was half expecting to hear the blasters finish her off. A few moments later, she was at the door.

"Here is your form signed," and she thrust it into his chest. "My superiors are going to hear about this."

"Yeah," Fillingraph sneered. "No, they are not, the Maximum Penalty you just agreed to will be legally enforceable. You forget every communication to and from this facility is monitored, even the covert ones you don't think we know about. Any encrypted data packets will be considered as communication that violates the NDA, and the Maximum Penalty will be enforced. Even embedded ciphers and other means to hide messages will be considered violations as well."

"Fine! I signed the form let's get on with this so I can see how screwed I really am."

"As you wish. Right over here we have the best candidate for the Intergalactic vessel, Progenitor Class, core designation IG-3275-001."

"Ah, this is the core that–"

"Yes, this is that core."

As they approached the door, she asked, "Why are we going to what seem like crew quarters?"

"This is the production bay where core IG-3275-001 will be developed."

"Where are the programmers, the engineers?"

"In due time. You wanted to see the core material, well here it is," he said as he pushed the button to open the door. She entered the room followed by the doctor. She looked around and saw slightly larger living quarters than her own, but opened to a massively huge bay of the space station. She noticed the body nestled in the sleeping pod but thought nothing of it as she surveyed the room.

"Where is the core development station? I need to see the core in its first development stage."

"This is it, I assure you, and you have already seen it."

"You are joking, right?"

"I think introductions are in order. IG-3275-001, please come over here and meet Low Executrix Kolana. She is very interested in the Progenitor class of ship."

IG-3275-001 slipped out of the sleep pod and pushed off towards the Doctor and LE Kolana.

"What? You use kids to program the cores? I find that sickening."

"You'll see."

IG-3275-001 floated closer. LE Kolana stepped backward, seeing the number *IG-3275-001* on her suit. Fillingraph grabbed Kolana's arm and said, "Low Executrix Kolana, meet core IG-3275-001. Core IG-3275-001 meet Low Executrix Kolana. She'll be staying with us for a while, I think."

"Did you come to watch me turn into the largest, most advanced ship our civilization has even produced?"

Kolana broke free of Doctor Fillingraph's grasp, and only made it a few steps toward the door before she vomited everywhere. She was choking and coughing, trying to make sense of what she was seeing. The vomit floated in little pools and globules.

"What is the matter?" IG-3275-001 asked.

Kolana vomited again, and she was finally able to choke out, "You can't do this! This is horrifying. I have never seen anything so disgusting in my life...even on the worst battlefields I have never seen something so despicable." She wiped the vomit from her mouth.

"Ah, and now you know why we just cannot let people run around with our secrets. The military doesn't care they only care about results. Which, by your admission we have the best AI...well...what you *think* is AI." He chuckled.

"How long?" She gagged.

"Every ship we delivered is of the same process. We used the same construction methods. IG-3275-001 volunteered to undertake this transformation."

"Volunteer? Volunteer! She is not old enough to make those kinds of decisions."

"I would disagree. How about you IG-3275-001?"

"I knew exactly what I was doing and what was going to happen to me."

"How? Why? Where did they come from?"

"Did you really think there was an SAP terrorist attack last night? All those families dead; all those *children*, killed? Well, not so much as *dead* as *repurposed* to a higher cause."

"What are you saying? These are those children? That is not possible they found bodies, children's bodies."

"Of course they did. They cannot leave missing children reports left unsolved. We cloned these children. The genetic duplicates left at the scenes allayed any concerns that there might be missing children. Of course, there are no missing children, they are all dead, which also means that if the core fails in any way, well then the matter is already solved they are already dead. It's a pretty nice bow it is tied up in."

She vomited again, this time mostly gastric fluids. "You killed families wholesale, dozens of families, just to cover up this abomination, this horrible act."

"You say killed, I say liberated from their miserable doomed existences. Either way we have the core genetic material to grow the ships we need."

"Grow?"

"Yes, grow. These cores will increase in size; their carapaces will harden and thicken until it becomes the outer hull. Did you ever wonder how our ships had such sleek, seamless hulls with organic lines? It is because our ships *are* organic."

"I cannot take any more of this. I am heading to my quarters to sleep. Can I get there?"

"Your badge will get you there tonight. Tomorrow, I will reinstate some of your access. You will not have access to any of the cores unescorted."

"Fine by me, I do not want to puke anymore." She said as she headed down the corridor towards her room.

"I don't think she approves," said IG-3275-001.

"She'll come around, she has to. She'll have to file reports and mission logs. They did not send her here without expecting progress reports. She will have to come around to our way of thinking."

"Can I go back to bed now?" IG-3275-001 asked.

"Yes, tomorrow is going to be a big day. We start your process."

"Will it hurt?"

"I do not think so, none of the others has complained about any pain. You'll be under sedation and will not be conscious for any operation or the expansion phases."

"Okay. Good night, Doctor Fillingraph." IG-3275-001 said as they moved back towards their sleeping pod.

He left the room and headed back to his office upon entering he said, "Claudette, transmission scan."

One unauthorized channel. Scrambled voice patterns detected.

"Jam signal. Locate the source."

Signal jammed. Source located: Low Executrix Kolana's quarters. A private, unregistered communication device."

"Is the device Video Conference capable?"

Yes.

"Connect to the device, VidCon, my desk," he said as he sat down.

Device connected.

"Low Executrix Kolana, did I not tell you we could find any communication from this station."

"How did you get this number? How did you connect to this device? The device is completely off the network, unregistered and untraceable."

"Who do you think made such a device? Besides there are no access points capable of reaching this station not owned by our corporation. Simply by connecting using our network allowed us to trace your whereabouts, block your signal and connect via this VidCon. Let me be your friend, and we can treat this as a simple misunderstanding and then we don't have to worry about any penalties or the like."

"You cannot do this to me. I have to make reports. I have to communicate."

"Oh, you will. You are not the first military liaison that we had to deal with. I would tell you to ask the others, but alas they are... Let's just say they're out of reach right now."

"How will I make my reports? They'll know something is wrong."

"We have your reports all ready to go. These will outline our new manufacturing techniques to produce the finest alloys and metals for the ship manufacturing process. You'll also report on the advance methods for our AI production and how you will see it progress from simple routines to sophisticated AI's."

"I can't use yours. I have to file my own reports. They'll know it's not me."

"You mean the preassigned code phrases and stenographic techniques used to embed hidden information. You'll find all those phrases and techniques are fully used and completely incorporated to paint the same picture the normal text is saying. There will be no suspicions raised."

"How is that possible? I received those things just yesterday. You cannot know them already?"

"Our operatives in the military developed them. Actually, we developed them and gave them to our operatives to pass along. The military is using the fourth generation removed from what we are using on this station. They think they are using top of the line encryption. They are, if you factor us out of the picture."

"You should not be able to decrypt anything I am sending."

"We don't need to; it will just never go anywhere. Without proper signal authentication codes, you will not get a connection, no matter what channel you use. The last operative tried to use the neighboring satellite, not ours, to make the connection."

"How do you know that?"

"Sometimes you can still see his body floating around the station. Seems he fell out of an airlock or some thing like that. I don't know what happened; the VidFeeds were deactivated."

"You killed the last liaison?"

"No, of course not. As I said, he fell out of an airlock. It's much more common than you might think, especially around here."

"How can I talk to my family?"

The doctor swiped his BioMet and said. "Come now LE Kolana, you're not married, no children, an only child and look! Both parents, and all grandparents are dead. You don't have any family."

"How did you get that information? It's not correct. I have a mom who lives in the capital, and my dad lives in the country farming algae."

"Sure, your *cover* family does, but that's not your real record."

"You cannot know that!"

"We do! Who do you think handles the secure data storage for the military? We do, of course. We have the most advanced AI, after all," he chuckled. "Consider this a warning. If another unauthorized signal, communication or anything that generates power is detected, your room will be jettisoned into space. Or, hadn't you noticed, you're on the outside of the space station, three walls, ceiling and floor open to space. Any misstep on your part and the one side that is attached to the space station will simply fall away, causing rapid decompression, a tragic accident or something like that." He paused to let what he said sink in. "Now you get some rest. Tomorrow, you have reports to file," he said with a wretched smile. He ended the VidCon. "Claudette, establish monitoring three-hundred-foot radius centered on Kolana, full signal blackout, nothing in or out without proper station coding attached."

Perimeter established, linked to Low Executrix Kolana, full spectrum blackout. Window polarization initiated refraction pattern created. Signal lock down complete.

"Good."

Unauthorized signal detected, Low Executrix Kolana. Protocol blocking initiated. Blackout effective.

She is persistent, I will give her that, he thought to himself.

Jettison living quarters? Claudette asked.

"No, not yet. We need her longer than the last one this time. Authorize jettison only on my verbal, hand scan and security card authorization."

Security protocols updated. Jettison disabled, except on your authorization.

"Good. Now that is done, I think I can get some sleep. Claudette, prepare sleeping quarters," With that, a door opened, and the lights in the office started to dim as the lights in the sleeping quarters brightened slightly to mark the way.

Environmental levels set to your presets. Good night Doctor Fillingraph.
"Goodnight Claudette, Secure all external points to office and quarters."
Secured. Claudette replied.

11 INITIALIZATION

Andorin slowly rose to a sitting position on the bed. He rubbed his eyes trying to get the sleepiness out of them. As he moved around and he put his feet on the floor, he thought to himself, *That was the worst nightmare I had ever experienced.* He spoke out to his wife, "Honey, you will not believe the horrible nightmare I had last night." He paused for a long moment waiting for a response and then asked, "Honey, did you hear me?" Again, he paused, waiting for a response, which none followed. Finally, he turned towards his wife's side of the bed and said, "Honey?" At that moment he went into panic mode because his wife was not in bed. She was never up before he was. His senses heightened. He heard the faint sounds of muffled crying. He sprang from the bed and followed them to Stranaya's room. He started to get a sinking feeling in the pit of his stomach. As he slowly opened the door, the reality of the situation hit him full force. Miliki was sitting on the floor in the middle of the room holding some of Stranaya's clothes to her face. The bed was neatly made, awaiting its occupant, which would never come again. He now knew his nightmare was real; Stranaya was actually gone. He moved to Miliki and wrapped his arms around her and gently said, "Honey, I know it's hard, but we have to start letting go."

"She can't be dead, she can't be dead," Miliki whispered.

Andorin started stroking her back and said, "I know it's hard to accept, but she is gone. There is nothing you or I can do about that." He knew that was a lie, however. She was alive, and he was going to find her–somehow. The *somehow* got him thinking. His new position as spy may now work to his advantage. He lowered his head to hers and said, "I know it's hard, but we have to move on, for the sake of our other children who did survive."

"I can't," she reeled and pleaded. "How can you?"

He thought long, searching for the best answer, and finally settled on, "Because I *have* to." He emphasized the *have* for effect. "Things are going to be expected of me, and I doubt either side will care much for what just happened to me, to *us*. They will expect me to behave in a certain manner. I also have my military training. It taught me to deal with death on a massive scale. This is harder to handle than any battlefield death, this is my daughter, and it was in my, in *our* house."

She looked up at him with a look between horror and anguish and said, "I can't do that. I don't think I could ever do that."

He looked at her sweetly and wished he could release soothing pheromones, but he could not, and said in a low, soft voice, "I know, but you have to...eventually. You have to live the rest of your life. It may not be today, tomorrow, or even next week, but it will happen. You will move on. It will just take time."

"I just can't right now. I can only see she is dead." She said sobbing into his arm.

"I know, but we have three other kids that may be experiencing similar feelings. We need to help *them* now, worry about them. There will be time for us after they are taken care of." He said soothingly as he could muster.

Grudgingly she conceded, "You are right. But I don't know how I am going to get through today."

Attempting to get her engaged and occupied with something to keep her mind off Stranaya he said, "I think the kids will be up soon and will want something to eat. Making breakfast might keep you occupied."

"I don't think I can," she replied in a low whimpering voice.

"You need to try, for our other children." With that, he helped her to her feet, and started guiding her towards the door. He finally got her into the hallway. After a few steps of leading he stepped backward, and let her keep walking on her own and said. "Honey, I need to do something important."

She robotically moved down the hall and said, "I'll see what I can do."

"Okay, I'll be in the bedroom working," he told her.

"You are already working!" She exclaimed. "You have not even left home yet."

"I know, I know. But it's important."

"Okay, fine!" She stated sharply. "I'll let you know when breakfast is ready."

"Great!" He moved back into the bedroom. He moved to where he stored his armor and removed the data device. He located the power switch and powered it on for the first time since he received it. He panicked for a moment, as he could not remember his logon credentials. After a few seconds, his military conditioning took over. His mind cleared, and he remembered what was required to log on to the device. At the system prompts, he entered his logon credentials using the attached key pad. The device came to life and words started appearing on the black screen:

Initializing Device
First Use Detected
Locating Slave Drive,
The device imbedded in his arm started to vibrate.
Drive Located
Loading
(4) Active Investigations
Investigation Files Updated
Operative Code Name: Specter
User Interface Loading,
With that, the screen flickered off and then filled with light as the operating system took control of the device. The system displayed four topics: Society for Andlid Purity (SAP); Space Program; Shadow Faction; Weapon   Anomalies.

The Shadow Faction intrigued him and using the arrow keys he moved the selection cursor down onto the topic and activated it. The screen changed, displaying information about what it was. He read that it consisted of officials that act autonomously, but against the established goals of the legitimate government, with their own purposes and agendas in mind. It also listed multiple keywords:
Goals: UNKNOWN
Key Personnel: UNKNOWN
He thought that maybe High Executrix Slithneigh might belong here.
Personnel Strength: UNKNOWN
Activities: UNKNOWN
Andorin selected *Activities* even though it read unknown. He was simply interested in seeing how the system worked. As he expected, a blank screen appeared with the keyword *New* to create a new activity associated with the Shadow Faction. He backed up to the Shadow Faction area.

He selected, *Key Personnel* and selected, *New*. A box popped up with an input area. By Name: he typed *HE Slithneigh* and selected *Enter*. Another box popped up that said *Explain*: He typed *Was in limo, gave me script, and talked about happenings in an unfavorable manner*. He selected, *Enter*. and then moved back to the Main Menu.

How was he going to make this position work in his favor? He thought. *There has to be a way to work for the High Authority and find out what happened to Stranaya.* On the Main Menu, at the bottom of the keywords, *New* was listed. At that moment, he decided to open a new investigation into his daughter's apparent death. He selected *New*

A screen popped up and asked for a title. He wrote *Terrorist Attacks – Abductions* and pushed the *Add* button to create the investigation. A new screen popped up with the title he had just entered and it required a description of the investigation he just created. In this box, he outlined his daughter's abduction - even as it seemed willingly. A duplicate replaced the abducted to *account* for the *dead* child. Presumably, all attacks had the same results, abduction of children, and deaths to cover everything up. Multiple children were seen in a transport.

In another area, it said *Key Personnel* and while he did not know if Stranaya's doctor was key, he did know he was involved—and directing the soldiers. In the box, he typed in his name: *Fillingraph, Horace, Doctor* In another box it said simply *Personnel.* In that box, he decided to put *Military.* A little note box popped up that said *Explain.* He typed in: *Three exceptionally large soldiers, unmarked uniforms, but military trained.* He closed the box and made another entry in the *Personnel* area. He typed *Dead Terrorists.* The *Explain* box opened again, awaiting information. *Two normal sized military looking, not well trained, personnel. Killed to leave* no questions *about who did the killing.* He finished with *need more information* and closed the box.

Again, he navigated back to the Main Menu and found the keyword *Upload.* He was sure that this would load the data onto his drive in his arm. He activated *Upload.* The device in his arm started to vibrate. When the vibrations stopped, the system screen shifted to black and said:

Slave Drive Updated

Upload Verified

Powering Down, Secure Device

Good-Bye

With that, the device powered off. Now he needed to find a place to store the device. Miliki already knew about the device; he was only concerned about the kids. He was afraid they would find it and attempt to enter the logon credentials and then the device would stop working. He ultimately decided on the closet. He placed it under a blanket that was stored there. He carefully lifted up the blanket, placed the device under it and then lowered the blanket back down on it. It looked exactly the same, and hid the device very well. Someone would have to look for it to find the device.

With that taken care of, he decided to get cleaned up and ready for work. He started the shower and removed his bedclothes. He adjusted the temperature of the water; he liked it much hotter than Miliki did. He entered the streams of water shooting out of the ceiling panel. Once he was wet, he pulled a lever to add soap to the spray. The soap bubbled up and scoured away any buildup that had occurred on his exoskeleton, it only took a minute or two. He closed the lever and clean water flowed over his body taking the soap and grime with it. He stood there for longer than normal; he was replaying last night's events. He was looking for anything he could remember that might help him find Stranaya's abductors and find her. However, it did strike him as odd that, one: Stranaya knew she was leaving, and, two: seemed to welcome it.

He was a little hurt by that last revelation. Had Stranaya been that unhappy that this had been her only way out and the reason why she had left? He knew it had been rough for her; even her siblings made fun of her at times. He could not bring himself to think it was that. If not that, then what? The water pounded against his face. Then it came to him—Space! This must be linked to her going to space. He had not heard of any soldier programs that started training at such an early age, but that may be it. *They have selected her for some elite soldiering program that requires constant training from an early age.*

As soon as he thought it, he dismissed it. Other elite programs were highly competitive and very public events; selection was a great honor. He had heard of no such publicity surrounding this event. In fact, it was the opposite. He realized they had taken Stranaya in secret, and that they had to cover it up. His eyes flashed open as he cut the water off. He flicked another switch and jets of air blew off the water droplets. He turned several times to ensure he was dry. He moved to the closet and grabbed a uniform. Belatedly, he realized it had the wrong rank on it. He grabbed the uniform from yesterday, took the insignia off and replaced the one on the uniform from his closet. He proceeded to get dressed. He would have to buy more rank insignia.

His chest armor seemed much looser today after carrying the device yesterday. It reminded him of his younger days, and he managed a little smile thinking of those simpler times. Reality removed that smile just as quickly. He moved out of the bedroom towards the kitchen area. As he approached, he heard Miliki talking to the children as they ate breakfast. He paused just outside the room to gauge the mood of everyone.

Felici asked, "Mommy, do we have to go to school today?"

Miliki just said, "Yes," in a low voice

"But we should not have to because Stranaya was killed last night," Felici said.

The glass bowl Miliki was holding smashed to the floor. "I know she is dead. I was there. I watched her die. It was horrible," as she broke down in tears again.

Andorin came in, held her and said to Felici, "This has been hard on everyone, especially your mother. Why don't you want to go to school today? Is it because you are too sad or is it something else?"

"No, I am not too sad. I know she died, but she was weird. She answered questions I was thinking, but she did not seem to know that she was answering me; she just spoke the response. She also knew things she was not supposed to know as if she knew what was in my diary. So I will not miss those things."

Gilphon chimed in, "Yeah, she creeped me out too. I am glad she stayed in her room most of the time. All the kids at school called her *Freak Feelers*"

"Did you stop them?" Andorin asked.

"No, I did not want anyone to know I was related to her!"

"Gilphon, you should have stood up for her. She was little and needed your protection," he chided.

"Dad, she could take care of herself. One time, someone threw something at her and it hit her...not hard...but it did hit her. She turned toward him and asked him to say he was sorry. Of course, he said, 'No way Freak Feelers.' She asked again, and he just laughed. Then she said something. She said 'he was a frightened little Momma's boy who still wet his bed.' The boy screamed 'Stop lying. I do not.' She said, 'You do and will say you're sorry now or shall I continue?' The boy said, 'You are a liar, and I will never say I am sorry.' Then she said, 'Fine have it your way then. Your Daddy likes to dress up like a woman and walks the street looking for men. You mom is disgusted, but cannot leave him. You wet the bed because you are afraid you are more like your father than your mother.' Then he screamed again and started to run away. You could see the ground get wet as he ran because he was peeing his pants as he ran away. That kid never came back to school, and after that day, no one called her any names...to her face anyway. So, no Dad, I don't need to take care of her."

"When did this happen?" Andorin asked.

"A few months ago, everyone at school is afraid of her...even I was afraid after I saw that. I am kinda glad she is not here anymore, but I did not want her dead." Gilphon stated.

Miliki raised her head and said, "I told you about it, but you said it was an exaggeration and dismissed it."

"Wow! Okay, I am sorry for not listening." Andorin conceded his fault.

Helphan spoke softly, "I miss her. I want to be with her. She was never mean to me," as tears started rolling down his face.

Miliki moved to Helphan, wrapped her arms around him and said, "I know Baby. I know. I miss her too."

Helphan started crying more and said, "Why? Why did they do this?"

Andorin, taken aback by such a simple question, thought for a moment before he answered. "Well, they believe different things than most people do." Helphan was still crying while he continued. "They believe it is okay to harm other people to get what they want. Most people in our society believe the opposite; life is important and must be protected. This is why we have laws protecting life."

Helphan wiped a tear from his eye, looked at his father and asked, "Do you kill people Daddy?"

Andorin paused again and thought about his response. He realized that he had to answer carefully but decided on truthfulness. "Yes. I have killed people."

Helphan said, "The officers said you killed the soldiers."

"Yes." Andorin lied.

"How are you different from them? Are they going to lock you up?"

"No Helphan, they are not going to lock me up. I acted within the law because I was protecting you," He continued the lie he has been forced to perpetrate. "Since they were in my home...*our* home, threatening my family... you, I am allowed to protect us." He paused then continued, "I could not save Stranaya," thinking to himself, a*t least not yet anyway*, "but you, Mom, all of us were saved, and other families too, because they died here, before they could do more harm."

Helphan blinked his eyes at his father, wiped more tears from them, looked deeply at his father and asked, "Other families?"

"Yes, Helphan other families. Our house was not the first, nor the last of the houses they intended to visit."

"How many families?" Helphan asked.

"I am not sure of the exact number, but quite a few I would suspect." Andorin said.

"What happened there?"

"Well," Andorin paused deciding on what to tell his now youngest child. "What happened at the houses before they got to this one would have happened here, had they not been killed."

"What do you mean Daddy?" Helphan inquired.

"They are all dead." There was no other way to say that, to soften the blow.

Helphan's eyes went wide as he grasped the realization of what could have happened to him. He ran to his father, grasped his legs and said, "Thank you, Daddy. I am sad Stranaya is dead, but I am glad that I am not," and he squeezed his father's legs harder.

Andorin tried to lighten the mood by saying, "You are getting really strong."

Helphan smiled up at his father and said, "I want to be big and strong like you when I grow up."

"You will be, son. You will be." Andorin replied as he bent down to hug his son.

Helphan then asked something unexpected, "Daddy, do our bodies shrink when we die?"

Andorin looked at his son with puzzlement and said, "No son, they do not shrink."

He said, "Okay, Thank you, Daddy," and he started to move away.

Curiosity got the better of Andorin and he asked, "Why did you ask?"

"Those soldiers looked much smaller after they were dead."

Andorin's heart skipped a beat or two as he froze in place.

Gilphon piled on as well, "Yeah, they did look much smaller on the floor."

Andorin had to think fast to stop this topic before it got out of hand. "Well, it might have been an illusion on your part."

"What do you mean? How can it be an illusion?" Gilphon asked.

As a demonstration, Andorin picked up two glasses that were of similar design and color except one was taller than the other and said, "Here I'll show you what I mean. See these two glasses?"

"Yes," Gilphon replied slightly puzzled how two glasses would explain anything about dead bodies.

Andorin then motioned for Miliki to join him and said, "Here, hold these," and he handed her the glasses. "Gilphon, close your eye." He moved close to Gilphon's vantage point to gauge what he would see. "Miliki, hold the glasses with the bottoms toward you and the tops towards me. Okay now tilt them down a little. Too far. Up a little. Okay...there. Hold it. "Now Gilphon, open your eyes. What do you see?"

"I see mom holding two glasses."

"Okay, which one is the larger one?"

Gilphon was looking at the glasses from the top down. From this perspective, he could not tell which one was taller. Andorin watched as he strained and squinted to help him see the taller one finally he said, "I can't really tell."

"And that is what you experienced with the soldiers," Andorin explained.

"Okay," Gilphon conceded but continued, "but that does not explain why they looked like they had the air let out of them."

Andorin smiled to himself and thought, *He is getting smarter*, and tried, "It is a similar illusion and let's just leave it at that."

Gilphon said, "Okay."

"Now go finish getting ready for school," Andorin said light heartedly.

All the children headed towards their rooms. Andorin turned his thoughts back towards his children's observation of the different sized soldiers. He thought it might not be a problem because they gave their statement before they saw the bodies and the investigators did not follow up their statements with more questions about the soldiers. The children saw two soldiers and there were two dead soldiers. His thoughts were broken when he realized Miliki was talking to him. He heard just enough to formulate a response.

"I was just trying to figure out how I was going to get through this day," he replied.

"Can't you just stay home today?" Miliki pleaded.

"You know I can't. I have military responsibilities. Taking the day off is just not an option." He said.

"You could take some leave then. How could you not? Your daughter was killed last night." Miliki said sternly.

"I know, that is exactly the reason why I need to go. At least for a little while, I have something, a report that must be filed, so they know the truth about last night," he said.

"The Truth! What truth? Everything was on the VidFeeds. Everyone should know what happened," she quipped back.

Then he remembered. She did not remember the true events from last night. Now was not a good time to tell her, if he was ever going to tell her. He had to think fast now to come up with some new *truth* he needed to relay. He got it. "They do not know about Stranaya's doctor being involved. As the VidFeeds tell it, there were only two soldiers. We know differently."

"Yeah, why did we not tell the investigators about him?" She inquired.

Andorin decided on a half-truth, "While you were unconscious, I traded our lives for secrecy. We live so long as we keep the doctor out of it," *Officially, anyway*, he thought, knowing the doctor was neck deep into this whole business, whatever it was.

"We can't tell anyone?"

"Not now. Maybe eventually. It depends on how things develop and what I learn from my new position. You remember?"

"Yes, your new *position*," she said sarcastically.

"Yes, and that same position might also protect us." He replied.

"I don't see how," she stated.

"Because I'll be in a position to find out information about who killed Stranaya," he said, trying to convince her it was a good thing.

"We already know who killed her...you killed them."

"And that is what the world thinks too. However, do you really think they were working alone? Or, did they have others, that maybe planned it out and let those soldiers take the blame. And what about the doctor? They knew eventually, they would have been caught. Honestly, it worked better for any other conspirators because these dead agents can't talk or tell their stories, protecting everyone else involved."

"I never looked at it like that. I thought they were just two crazy lunatics that lost it like the VidFeeds said. I did not consider that they might be working with others," she voiced.

"There are many possibilities that might come into play, which is why I need to go to work today." He reasoned to her.

"I understand," she said with resignation in her voice.

"I don't want to go in. I *have to* go in." He overemphasized the *have to*.

"I know, I know," she sighed, "I know."

"I'll get to the bottom of this." He said reassuringly. He kissed her on the cheek and headed out the door. He almost forgot he had to take the Commuter Express back to the base because that was where he left his vehicle yesterday when this whole ordeal had started.

When he stepped outside to catch the express, he was surprised to see his vehicle where he usually parked it. *How did that get there? Who did that?* He thought to himself. He pulled out his fob and unlocked the vehicle. *They must have towed it somehow*, he thought. The engine started up.

12 IDENTITY CRISIS

The internal combustion engine ran on raw methane gas. Everything in society ran on methane. It was a natural by-product of their everyday lives. Most waste products either turned into methane or created methane. This was harnessed over the centuries as the chief energy source. Everything seemed to use methane in some fashion or another.

Andorin was fascinated by methane and could not imagine their lives without it. It permeated everywhere and everything. It was one of the most abundant gases on their planet. Water, on the other hand, was very expensive. He just realized that he spent a lot of money taking his shower this morning. He had let the water run for how long? He could not remember, but it had to have been expensive. Luckily, that water would be recycled, and placed back into the system. The city bought back the wastewater at a much-reduced price, but still that would not be near enough to pay for that shower this morning. Miliki was always getting on him for his showers. It wasn't his fault that blood and grime took a long time to dissolve off of him. She kept insisting that he use the showers at work for that. He kept telling her "They do not let us use the showers because of the cost factor." Water was a scarce commodity to say the least. Only a few elements were more expensive; gold, platinum, iridium and other rare elements cost more than water did. This made it hard on most of the society, with a third of its income spent on water alone.

Something had to be done about the water, at least from a societal standpoint. He had heard that they had started mining asteroids and other moons to gather water to bring back to the society. However, it would never be like centuries past when water flowed on the planet freely and pooled into huge bodies of water. That era had long past when they started using hydrogen as a fuel source. Everyone thought it was renewable, and it could not be *consumed* because the by-product was heat and water. Why no one ever did the math to see amount in versus the amount out when burned, was unforgivable. It is not the same. Over time, they consumed almost 40% of the planet's reserves of water before they realized what was happening. It had been too late. The damage was already done. The planet was now dying; they needed to get water–from anywhere–just to stay alive as a species.

He often used his drive to work to contemplate such issues. Most were not as depressing as today, but depressing as it was, it still did not even come close to the events in his personal life. In that sense, it was a lighthearted look at a centuries old problem. However, he realized he was approaching the Andilusia Attack Base main gate. He approached and waited in line for the other vehicles to file into the massive entrance complex. The gate had six incoming and outgoing lanes to meet the sheer number of vehicle that entered every morning. Even with a staggered reporting time, it was still mass chaos getting into work every morning. Today was no different. Only thirty minutes into the initial reporting time, and it looked like there were already twenty vehicles stacked up in each lane. He had hoped he could get in before things got messy. Then he thought, *It must be because of the heightened security because of the attacks last night. Everyone must have to report in early to get things sorted out.* He waited in line like everyone else. When he finally approached the initial gate guard, he lowered his window and followed the guard's direction into a specific lane for processing. He proceeded directly to the identified gate for security screening.

"Security badge," said the guard and reached out his hand as he had done a hundred times already that day.

"Here. Having a good day?" He asked. Which he thought he had probably heard that fifty times today already.

"Well as can be expected here, but today is worse," the guard replied before pausing. "Sir, we have a problem. Your rank is incorrect on your security badge."

"Yes, I know, I was just promoted...yesterday as a matter of fact. I was off base when it occurred, and I could not make it to the Security HQ to get a new one made with the proper rank."

"Sir, you know the rules. You now need clearance to proceed." He talked into his BioMet, "Reception Control, MG Guard thirty-eight. We have a Verification Issue, Rank. Please advise."

The response was swift, "Secure hold, await Verification Protocol."

The guard motioned to the gate keeper to hold vehicles, on his line and then talked back to LE Wilcon, "Sir, I need you to back up your vehicle and park inside the red box in front of this guard post," He pointed across and behind the vehicle. "Do *not* exit your vehicle until told to do so. Do *not* drive outside the red box." The not's were emphasized to ensure compliance.

"But I was just promoted yesterday. Can't I just go to security and get a new badge?" He pleaded.

"Normally, yes you could, sir. Not today. We are dealing with every security issue outside the base, not inside. Back your vehicle into the red box right there. Do *not* move. Do you understand, sir?"

"Yes." Andorin said, he did as instructed and moved his vehicle into the red box that looked as if it had been hastily painted onto the ground. Once there, he waited. He looked around and noticed three or four other vehicles in a similar fate, all stuck in red boxes awaiting some presence, which he did not yet see. Finally, a group of people, four guards and one tech–all heavily armed, left a small building to the right of the vehicle processing area. He watched as they moved to the first vehicle. The guards took up position around the vehicle, pointing their weapons at the occupant. The tech instructed him to exit the vehicle. Andorin watched as the tech questioned the driver. Finally, they pointed to the building and the driver left their vehicle walking towards the building and entered. The group made their way to the next vehicle and he watched similar events unfold. Then they made their way to the next and things started again.

The driver moved towards the tech in a threatening manner. Neither the guards nor the tech made much of his posturing until he punched the tech in the jaw and sent him sprawling to the ground. Four shots sounded almost instantly, and the driver spun around from the force of four heavy impact projectiles that slammed into his body. The driver's right middle arm was completely separated from his body and the other three slugs struck various parts of his thorax. After the driver had slumped to the ground, he did not move again. One of the four guards motioned to someone out of sight. The group started moving towards his vehicle.

The tech approached his window as the four guards took up their positions. The tech said, "Security badge."

Andorin handed his badge to the guard and said, "Here."

"Ah, yes, boys. What we have here is someone that thinks they got promoted." The guard quipped after he checked his BioMet.

"I did get promoted, yesterday."

"Oh that's funny. The base didn't have no promotion ceremonies yesterday, so you couldn't have been promoted."

"I was, and it was off base where I was promoted." He said trying to control his temper.

"There ain't no such thing as an off base ceremony. Those just don't happen. It's a Blue Andlid boys!" The guards laughed.

"They do if you are promoted by the High Authority himself in the Hall of Authority." He seethed starting to lose all patience.

The tech started laughing outright and spoke to the closest guard, "He thinks he was promoted by the High Authority himself. That's rich. Can you believe these SAP spies?"

"Did you just call me a SAP spy?" He seethed.

The guard's voice changed to directive and said, "Guards positions." Then spoke to Wilcon, "Get out of the vehicle." The guards all pointed their weapons at him.

LE Wilcon replied, "You don't want me to do that."

"Yes, we do. You are under arrest for impersonating an officer, *Commander* Wilcon, if that is your name. Now, get out of the vehicle!" The tech demanded.

Andorin had lost all patience by that point, and vented on the tech. "How dare you. Do you know who I am? Do you even know what happened last night? What happened to me, to my *family* last night?"

"What we know is why we are here today. To stop people like you from sneaking on to the base to cause more terror. Now, get out of the vehicle!"

"Uh, sir?" one of the guards said, "I think I recon the name Wilcon. Not sure where though, but I heard it recently, I think. I dunno, for sure."

"What? Are you a conspirator as well then? You two, take him into custody. You watch him." Pointing to Wilcon he said, "Get out now!"

"Do you know that my daughter was killed in those terror attacks last night? In fact, it ended at my house. Do you really want me to come out there right now and end this too?"

"That's what the last guy said. See where it got him?" the tech chided and continued, "Which is where you'll be heading soon if you do not get out the vehicle right now."

"I assure you I am not that last guy. If I do get out, the last thing you'll see is that guard's head on the ground. You had better get your supervisor out here. Right now! Because if I get out of this vehicle, that guard won't save you."

The tech backed away a step or two and then spoke into their BioMet. "Supervisor Requested, lane four, first Red Zone. Situation Hostile." Then he spoke back to Wilcon, "Now you have done it, he has authority to shoot you in your vehicle. You are gonna die in that can, *spy*," he laughed.

Andorin watched as the tech danced and rubbed his hands together, waiting for his death. From the small building another figure appeared, much older, more methodic in their movements. He slowly approached the scene. He shook his head as he passed the scene of the prior shooting. He had a look of bewilderment as he approached. Two guards guarding the third guard and the fourth training his weapon on the vehicle. He called out to the tech, "What's going on here? Why is that guard in custody?"

He pointed at Andorin and said, "He's a spy." Then he pointed to the guard and said, "he was trying to cover for him and get him on or something. He is a co-conspirator."

The supervisor frowned and said, "I highly doubt that."

"You'll see," squealed the tech. He said, "I am so getting promoted over this," to anyone who was listening, but mostly to himself.

The supervisor approached the tech and said, "Credentials."

"Here they are," and he handed them to his supervisor.

The supervisor looked intently at his BioMet.

"See? See?" The tech pointed at the data on the screen. "Wrong rank. He even said he was promoted yesterday, off base even, can you imagine? Off base! I so have a promotion." The tech was giddy with excitement.

The next thing anyone heard was a loud scream, "YOU IDIOT!" The supervisor backhanded the tech so hard he flew backward off his feet to the ground. There were two crunches, one from the hit and the other when he landed on the ground, hard. "How many times have I told you to keep your BioMet on Constant Refresh? You did not have the latest security feeds." The tech was unconscious at this point and did not hear anything after the blow to his head. He pointed to the two guards, "Let him go."

The supervisor approached the vehicle and said, "Low Executrix Wilcon, I am terribly sorry for this unfortunate incident. I humbly offer my apologies for the manner of your treatment. My tech has been a little overzealous in carrying out his duties and today was the last straw. He'll be escorted off base...after he regains consciousness. We have a military escort that has been tasked to transport you from this gate to Security Headquarters to finalize your promotion to Low Executrix at the Hall of Authority and then they will escort you to your unit cordon." He motioned towards the far guard who motioned towards someone unseen.

"I am just glad that cooler heads were allowed to prevail. He called me an SAP spy. It was lucky you came along, because I was going to do worse to him," Andorin stated.

"I am glad that you did not. We have snipers that would have taken you down if these guards failed. I would like to extend my personal condolences on the death of your daughter. I have not experienced such a thing, but a parent should not outlive their children. As the first reasonable person to greet you, I have been instructed to extend the entire base's condolences as well. I am also glad for another reason, much more personal. Sir, please allow me to shake your hand," He extended his hand into the vehicle.

Andorin grasped it and shook it as requested, "What is this for?"

"This is for my son and his family. His was three houses past yours on the list. You saved them, and I am deeply sorry for how my people mistreated you today. It should not have happened. This is not how I wanted to meet you." He said, voice breaking and a tear starting to run down his face. He wiped it away quickly and continued, "I am glad that I did meet you, and I can never repay you for the service you have done to my family, city, and nation."

"Ah, but you have. Don't you see? You prevented this whole incident from ending up like that guy over there." Andorin pointed to the dead person on the ground. He also wanted to move away from thinking about him doing the *saving* when he knew he was not. The lie was perpetuated further.

"That should not have happened either. Again, another reason why we are letting that tech go...if he regains consciousness that is. I hit him pretty hard."

"Honestly, from the looks of you I did not think you had that kind of strength in you," Andorin joked.

The supervisor smiled and said, "You know, I wasn't always old." As the escort vehicles approached and took up lead and trailing positions. "I can do one more thing," he said.

He raised his hand and clenched it closed. Vehicles stopped entering the base. All guards extended their arms toward the oncoming vehicles and they stopped the vehicles. All of the vehicles stopped. His escort started pulling away with him and he heard, "HAND SALUTE!" The supervisor's voice was louder than when he had screamed at the tech.

Andorin thought, *Wow, I did not think he could get louder.*

All the guards faced his vehicle, saluting as he passed. Another lie he must carry, or it could be for his daughter, but alas another lie as well. On the other hand, he could pretend it was for him trying to find her. He could live with that, even if they did not know what that salute meant to him. The escorts made their way to the Security Headquarters, pulled up to the front of the building and parked in reserved spaces. He thought to himself, *Normal rules must be suspended today.*

The driver of the lead escort vehicle exited and moved towards his. They opened the door for him and held it open while he exited. The other people exiting the building stopped and stared as both escort teams led him into the building. He could only imagine what they were thinking. It almost looked like he was under arrest with two guards lead the way followed by two guards behind in a box pattern. They approached the entrance to the Credentials area, but then turned to an unmarked door where they entered. This led to an area behind the main customer service area, visible from the door. There had to have been hundreds of personnel waiting to get new credentials issued. They approached the lone occupant of a desk in the far back corner of the room.

As the group approached the clerk said without looking, "I am afraid you will have to find another clerk. I am waiting for someone specific."

The lead guard, Squad Leader Oost spoke, "He *is* the someone specific," pointing to LE Wilcon.

Finally looking up, the clerk said, "Ah, I can see that now. Have a seat please." He pointed to the empty chair next to the desk. He continued, "It's not often that we get someone promoted by the High Authority, in the Hall of Authority."

"Yes, it was a surprise to me as well," said Wilcon, smiling as he placed his helmet on the clerk's desk.

"Really? I find that hard to believe," the clerk commented sincerely.

"I cannot give you much of the details," he said not sure what he could or should say at this point.

"Don't worry, I have the VidFeed from the promotion ceremony. I just cannot believe you tried to turn him down. I almost fell out of my chair." The clerk said.

"You have the VidFeed? How do you have the VidFeed? I did not see anything recording."

"Every promotion has to have VidFeed evidence to support the action. Without the VidFeed, you would not be receiving this new rank. Credentials please," as he held out his hand.

Andorin gave the clerk his credentials. The clerk scanned the credentials with his BioMet.

"Congratulations on losing your Diamond Crest, Executrix Wilcon." The clerk said.

Instinctively Andorin looked down at his left arm where his crest had been micro laminated onto his armor. The crest was the numerical standing of his progress through the ranks of the military. He had never thought he would make it to Low Executrix so soon. There were only two hundred and sixteen people in this position.

"Uh, oh. We might have a problem. It seems there are no open Low Executrix slots to put you in, which will not do." The clerk said with disdain.

"What's the matter?" Squad Leader Oost asked.

"I just told you what the matter was,: there is no slot for him," The clerk quipped back.

"Fix it," said SL Oost.

"I cannot just fix it; these are real people we are talking about they all have their slots. He does not have one though," answered the clerk.

"We came to you because you are the Lead, the Level One, for this unit. You need to make it happen."

"Well, there is an option that has not been used for over fifty years. As this situation might warrant it, I will research it now."

"Research!" SL Oost seethed, "You were told we were coming, why we were coming, you should have researched this earlier, so the answer was available now." He took a menacing step closer to the clerk.

"What do you think I was doing when you got here? I just have not found the answer yet."

"Look faster," SL Oost replied, as he stepped back to his original position.

"Ah, I think I may have found it. Promotions, Special Circumstances, Position Allocations Exceeded. Yes, yes. This will do nicely. We have the answer." He turned to LE Wilcon and said, "Congratulations on your Promotion to Low Executrix, which can now be officially recorded."

"If you do not mind my asking, what was the solution?" Andorin asked.

"See, there are only two hundred and sixteen Low Executrix's allowed in the rank and file. You are the two hundred and seventeenth. A rarity that has not occurred in the last fifty years," replied the clerk.

"But you just said that I am getting promoted. How is that possible?" Andorin asked.

"It is possible because the Promotion Edicts allow such an occurrence, but only at the hand of the High Authority himself. Only he has the power to exceed any promotion limitations that suits his needs. But that brings up another point," as he looked directly at Andorin's crest.

Andorin looked at the crest too, but could not see anything. "What is the other point?"

"Where to assign you in the hierarchy, I have to research some more. Please be patient."

The clerk started flicking through various edicts looking for his answer. Every so often, he would say, "Interesting," "Huh," or, "Hmm." Finally, he said, "I think I got it! And now I understand why this is so rare."

"What's the solution?" Andorin asked.

"Since you were promoted by the High Authority, you're outside the rank structure at the moment. Everything is geared toward the structure of one High Executrix, six First Executrices, thirty-six Second Executrices, and two hundred and sixteen Low Executrices"

"Yes, everyone knows that."

"The problem is that you now do not belong in that structure anymore...you are outside of it," the clerk explained again.

However, this did not help Andorin understand it any better, "What do you mean outside of it? Am I still in the military?"

"Yes, you are but, not inside a command structure. Here, maybe the graphic of your new Rocker Crest will help you understand." He turned his display so Andorin could see his new Crest.

Andorin stared in disbelief and said, "Why does it look like that? The 1st and 2nd Low Executrix positions are empty."

"See? That is what I was trying to tell you. You are outside of the rank structure and report to no one. I have never seen this before. I have no idea how this works, but this is your new Rocker Crest. I am sending it to Fabrication to apply it to your armor, weaponry and gear. Please deliver your gear to Fabrication for rebranding," stated the clerk.

SL Oost spoke again, "His gear is already in Fabrication awaiting the crest template."

"Great! Now that your Crest is taken care of, I can issue your new credentials," the clerk stated. Then he asked, "Any color preferences for your credentials?"

"Preferences? I get to choose?" Andorin asked.

"Yes, I should think so in these circumstances any way?" The clerk said.

"What is the rarest color badge issued?" Andorin asked.

"All the LE's want Gold or Platinum, but I have one blank that I have never used before: Diamondnyte. It has been held in reserve for just this occurrence. The Edicts are quite specific," the clerk said.

"Diamondnyte? What is that?" Andorin asked curiously.

"Diamondnyte is a composite blend of diamond and platinum where the platinum is infused to the diamond. When the diamond material is forged under intense heat and pressure, the Diamondnyte material is formed. The crystalline structure of the diamond is reinforced by the platinum molecules that allow the diamond structure to form but not be brittle like true diamonds are. Diamondnyte is nearly indestructible, slightly flexible, and must be laser etched. We have the equipment over there." He pointed to an old machine partly covered by a tarp covered with layers of dust.

"Does that thing still work?" He asked, thinking he knew the answer already: *no*.

"Yes, I think so. There is only one way to find out. I will have to print the template first because this machine is not networked. That is how old it is."

"Not networked? How old is that thing anyway?" Andorin asked.

"I don't know. What I *do* know is that it has not been used since the last 217 Low Executrix was promoted. The 217's get the Diamondnyte."

"I thought I had a choice?" Andorin asked.

"You do. Choose Diamondnyte." The Clerk gave a big smile.

"I was," Andorin said.

"I agree. You have," the clerk said. He moved to the template printer, pulled the template off and walked towards the Diamondnyte Etcher. He reached down and plugged the device into the power junction box. He flicked the device to, *On*, and then he heard the device power on.

Almost instantly, every clerk in the front of the room turned to see who had turned that machine on. No one ever turned that machine on. They all knew the machine's use, but had never seen it used. They all wanted to be the one to use that machine. All they could do was watch.

The clerk pulled out the Technical Manual on the machine's operation. He placed the Diamondnyte blank on a tray. He pushed a button and the blank moved into the machine. The machine made many very loud noises: grinding, chewing and sputtering. Finally, another tray opened and the clerk placed the template on the tray, and watched as the machine pulled the template in as well. The machine now made loud cracks and pops as it worked on the blank. After a few minutes the machine quieted down and the first tray slid open again, followed by the second. The clerk reached down, pulled out Andorin's new credentials along with the template printout and said, "Wow!"

"What's wrong?" Andorin asked.

"Oh, nothing is wrong. I was just admiring your new credentials. They are nice...really nice."

As the tech walked back towards his desk, the credentials slipped out of his hand. The credentials hit the slate floor with a resounding, 'Spang,' and bounced on the floor a few times before coming to rest. It sounded like silverware dropping on the ground.

"Oh! Whew." Andorin said, seeing the credential hadn't been broken, "I know you said they were nearly indestructible, but it just does not look like it. It looks like glass."

"Clumsy me. And yes, nearly indestructible, like I said," stated the clerk. When he got back to the desk, he handed Andorin his credentials saying, "Here it is."

"I do have a question. How long do I get to keep my Diamondnyte credentials?" Andorin asked.

"The rest of your life," the clerk replied.

"The rest of my life?" Andorin questioned.

"Yes, the rest of your life. Even when you retire, you will still keep this credential material. If you lose it, Diamondnyte will be used to replace it. That is why most LE's want Gold or Platinum. Some retirees, *lose* their credentials every so often, especially the Gold and Platinum recipients. Those metals pay top premium on the black market." He continued, "There is no appreciable market value to Diamondnyte, but it sure does look nice. Doesn't it?"

"Yes, it does. My picture is etched onto the face of the card? What about the BioMet scanners and other devices? How will then read they information off of this card?" Andorin asked.

"The devices use a mixture of bar codes and magnetic media; both can be read by any BioMet."

"Will everyone think this is real?" Andorin asked curiously.

"They should, the BioMet scanner should read it, the holo lights will display the image imbedded into the Diamondnyte as your image. The lights will allow a hologram to be generated when viewed by security personnel using the holo lights."

"Is he done here?" SL Oost interjected.

"Yes, I should think that he is done. Any more questions Low Executrix Wilcon?" The clerk asked as he turned his gaze toward Andorin.

"Fabrication is next?" Andorin asked the clerk.

Oost replied, "Fabrication is next. Let's move."

Andorin reached over, shook the clerk's hand and said, "Thank you for helping me today."

"It was my pleasure, and I learned something interesting that I had not known before. So all in all, it was good." The clerk cheerfully replied.

Andorin stood up and grabbed his helmet that had the familiar crest with the Diamond Element still there. After today, his crest would look completely different. He looked down at his security credentials. They looked odd because they had only the Rocker Crest with only one number, 217, which was his new ranking. That he did not have a 2nd and 1st Executrix to report to was going to be odd. He had always had numbers in that upper Rocker Crest. Losing the Diamond Crest was not a surprise, he had known that was coming, but not having higher elements was something he had not considered. The procession made its way back outside and to the vehicles. The trailing guard made his way to Andorin's door, opened it for him and then proceeded to his vehicle. The vehicles pulled out one after another in succession. The lead vehicle headed towards Fabrication. Slowly the motorcade made it way towards the Fabrication Compound. They drove through the front gate and made their way to the Field Units Bay. They made their way to the *Combatants* window.

"Credentials," said the technician.

Andorin handed him his new credentials.

He looked at it and held it up to the light, then held it under his BioMet scanner. "I ain't never seen nothin' liken this before," he said.

"It's new to me too," replied Andorin.

The clerk replied, "The ReCrestin' order has been received. I'm awaitin' Gear delivery."

SL Oost motioned to the other two trailing guards who then left the area.

The tech continued, "Sir, please remove your arm platin' and hand me both your'n helmet and arm platin'. Now, let's havin' a look at the new Crest. What? We's gots a problem. There's somethin' wrong with that there Crest design. It's missin' numbers."

"No, those number are not missing they are left off by design. Look at my credential again. I am LE 217."

"LE's don't go that high. There is somethin' missin'. Your credentials are that way too?" He said back to Andorin.

"My credentials are fine. I just came from Security HQ," replied Andorin.

"They're fine," said SL Oost. "You got the order directly from Security. Run the ReCresting routines on his armor pieces here first."

"I gots to be reconfigurin' the run to only do these pieces, and then doin' the same when the other'n items are a gettin' here," the Tech said.

"Good. Now we understand each other," the Guard replied.

"Why's I always gettin' the hard ones?" the tech mumbled.

Andorin watched as he placed his helmet piece and arm plating in predefined location on a large rack. He watched the tech punch in some information into the machine. Andorin watched as the machine worked on his armor. He watched the removal of his old crest. Slowly there was nothing remaining of his old crest designation. The machine then restored the slight desert camouflage pattern removed during the process. With the camouflage repaired, his new crest was applied. It looked funny and it was going to take some getting used to. It was unnerving not having upper reporting echelons. *I guess that this is going to be new for everyone.* As the process was winding down the other two guards showed up with all the rest of his gear, weapons, other armor pieces, and tactical gear, anything assigned to him was marked with his crest. Most of the items would be easier now because he only had the Upper Rocker Crest instead of the full Diamond Rocker Crest combination. The machine automatically scaled the Crest to the specific items branded.

The tech turned around when he heard the other gear crash to the floor, "Nows yous a gettin' here with all that other'n stuff," the tech said, stating the obvious.

"Just be glad we did not make you go and get it," said SL Oost. "Remove the armor, reset the machine and load these items in there."

The tech removed the armor and handed it to Andorin, "Here." Then he moved to pick up the items on the floor and precisely placed the objects into predefined spaces designed to hold the items at the proper angle to update the Crest. When all the items were in place, he entered some information on the computer control panel for the equipment and the process began again. Soon, all his gear was rebranded showing his new Crest. The tech emptied the rack and the other guard picked up the gear and transported it to the vehicles. They placed all the gear and armor in Andorin's vehicle.

Element Leader Puzar, second guard in lead vehicle said to SL Oost, "Sir, it's getting close to the time. We need to report in."

Oost looked at his watch and said, "Yes, it is getting close, but we'll make it there on time. Let's move out."

13 TRUTHFULLY

Andorin followed SL Oost as he led him out the Fabrication entrance, towards the main gate. He watched, as the lead vehicle turned their vehicle's lights on. As he made his way through the exit gates, no one stopped the vehicles in the motorcade. They made their way back towards the city traveling at a speed faster than the posted limit. Andorin could only think to himself *If these guys did this every day, getting to work would be easy*. He still did not know what was happening or where they were going. He just knew they were heading back towards the Capital Area. The motorcade made its way through the city, heading to the dreadful spot where this had all started– The Hall of Authority. The lead vehicle slowed and stopped right in front of the building. The driver got out, and walked over to let Andorin out.

"Take your helmet; leave all your other gear in your car." Andorin took his sidearm and leg holster. He attached the leg holster to his upper thigh so his second right hand could easily reach, and holstered the weapon.

"You're not going to need that." SL Oost said.

"I'm taking it anyway," replied Andorin.

"Suit yourself," Oost replied.

The trailing guard, Element Leader Loh moved up and got in Andorin's vehicle and drove it away, leaving SL Oost there with him. They made their way towards the main entranceway and veered right, to another door. As they approached the door, Andorin felt a vibration in his right arm. He looked down in spite of himself. *I'll have to work on that*, he thought. Nevertheless, he knew his information had been delivered. He breathed easier and could now cross that off the list. However, he still did not know why he was here. "Why are we here?" He asked the guard.

"We are here because you have to be here," replied SL Oost.

They moved towards two very large doors. Andorin could hear muffled talking coming from the other side, but he could not make out what was being said. He noticed the guard at the door held up three fingers, then two then opened the door and Andorin heard, "Here he is. Low Executrix Andorin Wilcon," the High Authority said.

Andorin watched as every VidFeed in the room turned towards him, journalists with BioMets taking notes and stills of the scene. The door guard ushered him towards the stage, and he noticed a vacant seat with his name on it. Andorin moved onto the stage, his guard staying on the floor near the stairs, looking at the audience. He walked on the stage and sat down, moving his sign to the floor. As he looked up, he saw his family in the front row and he wondered *How did they get here?* He made eye contact with his wife and lifted his right inside finger of his lower arm as a slight wave. She smiled back and made a more obvious waving motion with her right middle arm. He had not been paying much attention to the speech, but he decided he had better.

"Citizens, the events of last evening were heinous beyond measure." The High Authority was saying. "We know little about the motives of the attackers. The VidFeeds have painted a picture of these two as mentally unstable or part of a fringe organization. These stories are just conjecture, with no facts to sustain them. One thing I *am* going to do right now is talk to you about the man who stopped this tragedy: Low Executrix Wilcon. It is a little-known fact that I promoted him in a secret ceremony yesterday, before these events transpired. I could not have known such events were possible in our society, let alone carried out in such a brazen manner. Now, I have the opportunity to publicly promote Andorin Wilcon to the rank of Low Executrix. LE Wilcon please rise, and step forward." The High Authority pointed to a spot next to him. Andorin rose, and took his place.

"It is with great honor that I officially promote you to the rank of Low Executrix," The High Authority tapped each insignia on Andorin's shoulder pad where he had personally placed them yesterday. "Congratulations LE Wilcon." He turned back to the assembled crowd, and Andorin stepped back toward his seat. "LE Wilcon single-handedly stopped that attack last evening. Unfortunately, he could not do so before the loss of his daughter, Stranaya Wilcon. I ask for a moment of silence for her and the other victims that were taken from us last evening." Everyone bowed their heads. No sound came from the massive audience in attendance. "Thank you," The High Authority said after a minute. "Many of you here today also feel the sting of loss as well. You know someone personally lost in the attack, or you know someone who knows someone. The extent of this is far reaching. Then still there are the people who were not affected because of the actions of this one man, Andorin Wilcon. He stood up to the attackers and slayed them with his laser spear. Many of you from the list of names after the Wilcon's want to extend their thanks as well. However, it is not possible for everyone to do so and as your appointed leader, I shall thank him from everyone. As your elected official, you have granted me special powers and privileges. One such privilege is the award of various citations, like the one I have here. LE Wilcon, step forward again, please." Andorin moved forward, and the High Authority handed the citation to a staff member.

"This is the Citation to accompany the ward of the Star of Distinction, the highest award that can be presented by a civilian authority. Today, let it be known that Andorin Wilcon acted selflessly, and without hesitation. He acted quickly and decisively to end a rampage of terror that would have affected dozens more families. It is these selfless acts and willingness to do what was required that places him above others. These actions both known and unknown merit this award. This is not awarded to LE Wilcon, but rather, to Andorin, without rank or other military distinction. His actions bring great distinction upon himself, this city and our people. Let it be remembered from this day forward that Andorin Wilcon has distinguished himself through heroism. Let this symbol be the reminder and our token of thanks for all he has done."

With that, the High Authority moved forward, raised the golden enlaced ribbon up over Andorin's head and slowly lowered the ribbon in place around his neck. The gold medallion gleamed in the light as it descended down to rest in the center of his chest. The High Authority smiled at Andorin and leaned in and whispered, "And now the fun part." He moved back to the podium and Andorin moved back to his seat. The crowd cheered and clapped in a raucous manner for quite some time honoring Andorin's well-deserved award.

Andorin was perplexed. *Fun part? What was he talking about fun part?* he thought to himself.

The HA raised his upper and lower arms in an attempt to calm the audience down. When the audience finally subsided, he began. "For as much as we know about last night, we know that there is far more that must be learned. The media has made the case for lone actors. The truth of the matter is that we do not know. That is the frightening part: We do not know. We have to know everything about that evening. Did they act alone? Were they part of the group known as The Society for Andlid Purity...The SAP...as suggested by the media? Again, we do not know. There is only one way to know. We must shine a light in every dark corner of this incident and bring everything out into the open. The people must know! If they acted alone, then we can let the fate stand as is. The guilty were brought to ultimate justice for their crimes. However, if they did not act alone, and were merely pawns, then we will move against the group or groups responsible for these events. Is it SAP? Little is known about this organization, but that will be investigated as well. To that end, I have decided to create a multi-departmental task force to investigate the issue. It was brought to my attention that my actions have created a situation unique to our times, one that I will rectify. You see, my promotion of Andorin

Wilcon to LE has sent waves through the military because I have exceeded the hard upper limit of LE's in the force. He is out of sorts with his military structure, which was not my intention. To alleviate the military of this concern, I am assigning him to lead the newly created task force, to investigate the facts about last evening's attack. Some may say he is too close to the investigation. I say he has more motivation to find the truth as only the other victims of last evening would have, if they lived. He will be their voice. He will be their champion. He will find out what happened. He will know the truth!"

The crowd rose in another cheer and started clapping. The High Authority let that go on for many seconds and then raised his arms again, asking for silence and everyone took their seats again.

"LE Wilcon will be lead investigator and part of the military, but he may not be fully versed in investigative techniques. Therefore, I am appointing our top civilian investigative unit to this task force. The unit has already met LE Wilcon, as they were the unit that was on scene at his home. This firsthand look at many of the crime scenes will be invaluable to the investigation. I expect full cooperation with this new Task Force Totus Veritas. The TF-TV will be charged with every aspect of the investigation, and will operate out of the Hall of Authority. We have offices in the sub-basement designed to handle such matters. Let it be known that officers of the TF-TV will have the powers and authority stemming directly from me, and my authority. Please, as citizens of this city, cooperate with these investigators, and answer the questions they pose, for it may be your answer that provides the vital clue to solving this crime. It is at this time I would like to open the floor for a few questions."

There was an immediate rush of correspondents getting up from their seat to have their question heard. They were all waving hands, notebooks, and BioMets trying to get noticed. However, one hand caught The High Authority's eye. It was a little boy in the front row. The High Authority pointed to him, and the correspondents settled down. An aide brought him a microphone and Andorin was horrified to see it was his youngest son, Helphan, now holding the microphone. "Son, what is your question?" The High Authority asked.

"Will my Daddy have to kill anyone again? Because he should not have to," Helphan asked innocently.

"Son, your Daddy acted bravely, and you should be glad for what he did. To answer your question, though, I should think that he might not need to. You have to understand your father is trained to do such things, and if the situation warrants such action, I have faith your father will do what is necessary."

"Thank you," Helphan said.

With that, the clamor of voices rose again wanting to be noticed. The

High Authority chose another correspondent.

"Filino Carpundi, Daily Times Paper. Do you not believe the fliers left at the Wilcon crime scene...that clearly outline the SAP was the main perpetrator in this attack?"

"I am not disputing what was found at the crime scene. I am merely suggesting that it is not all that it may seem. For instance, if it said...let's say...*your name* instead of the SAP. Would that make you feel better? And would you truly be involved? For all we know, this was another organization pointing the finger at the SAP so they, the true culprits, would go unnoticed."

"I...I...err." Filino stammered

"I know you're not involved. I was only using you as an example to prove a point. Not everything is as clear cut as it may first seem," the High Authority concluded. He pointed to another correspondent.

"Anglique Marnloue, Digital Access Magazine. Why will the military allow one of their own be removed from their ranks so freely?"

"It is not their choice. Through my actions, I created a situation where LE Wilcon found himself outside of the organized rigid command structure. Being on the outside, without a higher echelon to report to, he is free to assist his city, his people, this planet by leading the TF-TV. This was never my intention because he was promoted prior to the events of last evening, but since this opportunity has afforded itself, I seized it for the greater good. One final question." He pointed to another correspondent.

"Arlon Makon, the Voice Informational Services. Are we to believe LE Wilcon was promoted, and *then* attacked, and not the other way around? It seems kind of suspicious, him getting promoted for *Classified* reasons and then getting attacked later that evening."

"I assure you, he was promoted in a ceremony in the Great Hall. I will release the VidFeed of the event with the timestamp information on it for your corroboration. The events, no matter how tragic they were, had no bearing on his promotion and were based on other deeds not able to be discussed outside of classified briefing rooms. These will not be made public. So to answer your question, yes indeed it was as you described: Promoted, attacked, and citation today. I would like to thank all of those in attendance. Have a good day," The High Authority stepped away from the podium, and moved off the stage. Slowly, the others followed suit.

Andorin had not noticed, but the lead investigator was on stage as well. The lead investigator made his way to him.

"Sir, we did not meet under very good circumstances. Please let me introduce myself again. I am Officer Soltag, Efram Soltag. I look forward to working with you. I hope my skills and that of my team will help us find clarity in this very dark situation. What of your team? Who will you bring to the Task Force...Totus Veritas, is it? I'll have to practice saying that name."

"I no longer have a team. I am outside the command structure. The troops I commanded yesterday no longer belong to me. No one belongs to me,...from a military standpoint, anyway," Andorin stated plainly with a little sadness in his voice. He continued, "As for the taskforce name, I am just going to call it Task Force Truth."

"I am sure they will place some people under you to assist you," he said.

"I doubt it." Andorin replied.

Squad Leader Oost approached and said, "Sir, we have a meeting with the High Authority, right now in his private chambers."

"Private Chambers, eh,? Sounds exciting," said Officer Soltag.

"Good," Oost replied, "you're coming, too."

"Me? I have other things—" Soltag was cut of mid sentence by a stern look from the guard, "Lead the way," he finished.

Andorin watched as different guards led his family away. Andorin and Miliki exchanged glances. He could tell she understood what needed to happen now, even if he did not understand himself.

They made their way to the office without much talking. The corridors were narrowing as they made the way deep into the inner building. The guard knocked outside a gold inlaid door.

"Enter," A voice said through the intercom system. SL Oost opened the door, ushered Andorin and Soltag inside, and then closed the door, staying outside.

The High Authority was sitting at his desk and said, "That went rather well, don't you think?" He did not wait for a response and continued. "I asked you both here to clarify a few issues. First, there will be a public investigation. LE Wilcon will head it as stated in public. Your talents, Officer Soltag, will be greatly needed to assist him in this investigation. Second, there will be a private investigation that will be conducted solely by LE Wilcon. Only he and I will know the results or findings. He may ask for information or other things from your team, but not offer a reason or explanation for his actions. Whatever he asks should be carried out, without question. It is most likely that the two investigations will result in completely different findings. The public should not know there are two different investigations happening, but only the public investigation's results will be released. Third, LE Wilcon has the authority to bring people into the private investigation, but completely at *his* discretion." The High Authority looked at them both to make sure they were keeping up. They nodded, and he continued.

"Fourth, the information brought by the media was accurate, but was also misleading. We know for certain that the dead soldiers were not acting alone. Until that can be publicly proven, the media story line will suffice. LE Wilcon, please bring Officer Soltag up to speed on that last point."

"Yes, sir." Andorin turned to Soltag. "We know it to be so. The true events of that evening are as follows: Two extremely large soldiers entered the house and pinned Miliki and I down with laser spears. A third person took Stranaya out of the house. They led in two smaller guards along with a genetic duplicate of my daughter, all of which ended up dead,. The two smaller guards killed the duplicate, and my wife fainted as the larger third guard...which had entered with them...killed them both almost instantly. The larger guard left me with the slash wound on a thorax and a warning to 'stay the party line' as it were. I have no idea why my wife does not remember the entire event as it happened; it must be stress induced. The duplicate looked exactly like Stranaya, I mean *exactly*. It was traumatic to watch...even for me, even knowing it was not really her dying. The killings were a cover-up for abductions of the children."

"So what you told me was a complete fabrication?" Soltag asked.

"Not really. Those events happened as I explained, but I did not kill the guards. Their own team killed them to cover their tracks, to leave no one looking for other people. Which is what we must do now," Andorin replied.

"Wow, you did it so well I believed you, and so did my investigators. Do the children know the truth?" Soltag asked.

"No. They were in their bedrooms as we said. They only saw two guards the larger ones, not the ones that ended up dead on the floor. They did notice they were different from the ones they saw, but I think I stemmed that problem off and chalked it up to their not seeing things clearly. Miliki still does not remember the true events, and I have not decided if I am going to tell her. It might be better to let her think Stranaya is dead until we know for sure otherwise."

"How many children are we talking about?"

"How many families were killed that evening? At least that many. One from each household at least, maybe more," Andorin said.

"Abductions, you say? Without this, we would have never even thought to look beyond the deaths," Soltag said.

"Oh! One more thing: my daughter went willingly. It was as if she knew they were coming."

"What? Your daughter left willingly? They did not drag her out kicking and screaming?"

"Yes, she walked by while we were pinned to the ground, and walked out without much further thought. She did say 'It would be alright.' Whatever that means?" Andorin said.

"Curious that she left willingly. Do you think that played out at the other houses as well?" Soltag asked.

"It would be tough to say without witnesses, of which there are very few. My family is the only family that lived through the experience, and even then I am the only one that remembers clearly."

"Officer Soltag, let me be clear." The High Authority interrupted. "LE

Wilcon will conduct this private investigation. I have made you aware because he may need your assistance. You will provide your expertise as LE Wilcon requires. His methods will more than likely be unorthodox or lack finesse, but I expect you to help him discover the truth behind the façade the public knows. You may not let your team know any of this. However, you should look at your investigation and see where it might overlap with LE Wilcon's personal investigation of the situation and offer suggestions only in a private setting like his or your office."

"Sir, since there will be two investigations, I would suggest that LE Wilcon be afforded a limited contingent of military personnel to assist him. His team could be either fully read in or conduct their investigations independent of the public one. It could even be made to look like they are one and the same," Officer Soltag suggested.

"Excellent point. LE Wilcon, have your team selection on my desk by the end of the day. Six members beneath you, you choose the command structure and rankings. Promotions are delegated to you, but only up one level and only upon assignment to the team. In your roster include current rank and offered rank and cresting requirements."

"Also your room is in a sub-basement with one exterior and two interior entrances. The room is large, and should more than accommodate thirteen or fourteen people with workspaces and common areas, and it even has its own bathroom and kitchen facilities. Go inspect the room, have any modifications on my desk this evening as well. You both will need to discuss the layout of the room." He pushed a button and said, "Guard. Enter," through the intercom to the door.

SL Oost opened the door and entered the room.

"Take these people to Sub Basement room 101A."

"Yes, sir. Please follow me," Oost said to the two officers and led them out of the room. He walked back towards the building's center and headed for the elevators. They entered and he selected SB1. The doors closed and the elevator moved down to that level. The doors opened to a large hallway, however almost straight ahead was room 101A. Actually there seemed to be three doors that opened up to this hallway two larger ones in the center that double swung open and two single doors on both sides. It was a large room with ten storage rooms, five on each side. This kitchen was on the far side next to the exterior door and the bathroom was against the opposite wall. There was a lot of room to work with.

"First, we could repurpose these storage closets into interrogation rooms." Officer Soltag offered his suggestion. "Let's lose the closest one to the doors, and keep four rooms on each side. Make the now third room down the observation rooms for both the interrogation rooms, one on each side. Portion the room off to provide separation between the two rooms. The last rooms could be our offices. In addition, we might need a conference room to brief secret information. Also, all the exterior doors get four-point biometric scanning devices: Voice, Hand, Security Credentials, and Entry Code. Have the entry coding controlled by this office only."

Andorin added, "I would like to see the main area by the double doors made into a reception area with one low-level tech as a receptionist. No access beyond the doors, everything is handled by Comms to and from the front area. The second doors for the reception area to the main office cannot be opened from the outside."

"Okay sounds good. Let's get something drawn up and ready to submit. Element Leader Puzar, get us a building tech specialist."

"Yes, sir," and Puzar spoke into his BioMet and said, "The tech is on the way. They will be here in five minutes."

"Excellent," turning toward Andorin Officer Soltag asked. "Have you thought about your personnel?"

"Yes, a little. I'll bring the security tech. I'll also select five others to join my team. I am also going to ask for the four guards that have been assigned to me today to become our permanent security detail for this office. I have a few people that served with me that I trust and will ask them to join our little task force."

"Good then I think the plan is coming together now. Do you think the High Authority will go for the addition of the guards?"

"I do not see why not," Andorin replied confidently.

"Level 1, Building Tech, Julian Orsford reports as ordered."

"Good here is what we want. First, bring up the blueprint for this room. We need to make some modifications. Second, get ready for a lot of changes."

Orsford keyed commands into his BioMet. There was a slight delay as the file loaded. "Okay," he said, "here is the blueprint."

Andorin jumped right in, pointing enthusiastically. "Delete these two rooms. Split this room in half and place one way mirrors on these walls with the split room as the dark room for each. The last offices on both sides need desks and security containers to hold documents, Credential capable with pass code validation. We also need a large conference room here, just in front of the bathroom between that wall and the kitchen. Sacrifice more of the kitchen if need be, but do not eliminate it altogether."

Orsford was rapidly scribbling notes and diagrams over the blueprint to show what Andorin's proposal would look like.

"The conference table needs to sit at least sixteen people; seven on each side, and one on each end. In addition, there needs to be a new room that encloses the double front doors. This will act as a reception area. Seal that area from the main hallway. The doorway from this area into the main office is only accessible from the inside. In fact, make it look like there is not a door at all from the hallway side. All other doors need four point

BioMet scanners: Voice, Hand, Credentials, Access code and all off the main security grid. Establish a new security grid self-contained in this room. This grid should encompass everything: doors windows, cameras. Oh! What about cameras? We need four cameras in the hallway: two looking at the access door directly from above and two from a wide angle that includes each camera in the others field of view. Also, we need two cameras on the external door: one facing up the stairs to include who is at the door and the other looking down the stairway, again overlapping fields of view to monitor the cameras themselves as well."

Andorin paused while Orsford made the notes. Soltag looked on, head nodding with agreement.

"Also, these last two offices need secure access, limited to Hand and Credentials only, myself for this room, and Officer Soltag for that room—never mind—our security tech will handle the details of specific doors, just install the necessary equipment. Sound proof every wall ensure no sound can leave the room: each office, each room, the conference room, the bathroom, the reception area...everything gets soundproofed."

"We'll also, need a security station that can monitor all the cameras and devices." Soltag added. "And no wireless transmissions of any kind. All connections need to be hard point connections and ensure that the wall and windows are lined with signal cancelling mesh. I want no electronic transmissions to leave this room."

"That will complicate things tremendously because most newer tech runs wirelessly," The tech replied. "Your BioMet won't work either in here then."

"I know," said Andorin, "but it also represent a weaker security profile, but you have a point about the BioMets. Set the wireless access point for this room as the security desk, center it in the room. A small circular station should be sufficient. Nevertheless, I still want all the devices and access points hard wired. My tech will work out the details. Just worry about the hardware. Officer Soltag. Have I left anything out?"

"Phones and terminals. We definitely need phones and terminals. Oh and desks we need work spaces. Need twelve desks and two more for the guards, those could be smaller though," he said.

"I completely forgot about those things. I thought they were *understood*, but you are right...we need them," Andorin stated.

The tech took a few more minutes to make updates and changes to the blueprints. When he was completed, he showed them to the two officers. "Here is what I have for the designs. I've enlarged the split room and shrunk the two interview rooms for space considerations. Added this reception area and the conference room here, it took most of the space used by the kitchen, but enough is left over to allow for usage as a small kitchen that should suit twenty people or so. This center circular area will be the Security Kiosk. The security tech will have access to configure all devices via hard point interfaces, and establish a wireless access point for the BioMets. Various desks will be delivered, twelve for the common area. I've laid them out in a circular fashion around the Security Kiosk. The hard point installations will be here, as shown. The desks cannot be moved very far from these areas."

"Clump the desks into groupings of two desks," Andorin insisted. The tech made some swipes and updates to his BioMet to reflect the new design. The desks grouped in pairs around the Security Kiosk.

"Good," Andorin agreed to the tech. "Any other comments, or things we left out, Soltag?" Andorin asked.

"No, I think we've fully covered it now." Soltag concluded. "Why groupings of two?"

"I have an idea. I'll tell you tomorrow," Andorin replied.

The tech started to leave, but Andorin stopped him, "How long before this is completed?"

"I'm not sure; The High Authority has placed this as top priority. Demolition teams have already been tasked to start removal, and will be here shortly."

"Shortly? Like *now*?" Office Soltag asked.

"Yes! The building remodel has already been approved. Teams of people are moving into, procuring tech and securing commodities. Oh, I almost forgot. Color choices?"

"Color choices? Soltag and Andorin said, almost in unison.

Andorin went first, "Interrogation rooms and Observation Room all nonreflective high durability black. My office light blue ceiling with neutral toned walls...light sand color or something similar. For the Reception area, match existing building paint schemes."

Officer Soltag went next, "My office off-white ceiling and red muted earth tones...not bold red, but slightly suggesting red. The common areas in the room light sand colors might be nice. As for the carpeting, something medium to dark with any pattern to hide any spots. Also, we forgot the area by the stair well here," Soltag pointed to the blue print. "We need security containers there with combination *and* credential locks. Line all the walls there with these cabinets. Paint that area bright red to denote the higher security status. Also paint the floor red or install red carpeting in that area. Make sure the carpet and walls match tones. How do I update the High Authority of the requested changes?"

"Requirements updated and approved." Orsford said, smiling.

"How is the approval happening so fast?" Andorin asked.

"Easy. I am the one that approves these things, even for the High Authority. Consider him updated," he smiled and walked away.

"That was easy," Soltag said, "I wish I had these kinds of powers when I go back to my regular job," Officer Soltag finished.

"At least you *have* an old job to go back to. Mine does not exist any longer," Andorin complained.

Workers started moving into the area and started almost immediately. They were very efficient as they started clearing out the rooms and ripping up the carpeting.

"We'd better get out of their way or we'll be taken away," Andorin said.

"Agreed, I have to go talk to my team. We'll meet tomorrow?" Soltag asked.

"I have to make my final selections for my team and submit them to the High Authority. Tomorrow morning then. Where?" Andorin asked.

"Here?" Soltag suggested.

"You think they will be done by then?" Andorin asked.

"Maybe. If not we can find somewhere else. Temporarily, anyway," Soltag offered.

Officer Soltag left, leaving Andorin so deep in his thoughts that when Squad Leader Oost spoke, it startled him.

"Sir Where to now? There is no further schedule today...except for the one you now dictate."

"I think I need to go back to the base. My office, is it still there? I mean, is it still mine? Of course, it's still *there*," Andorin stated.

"I do not believe they have given it away yet." SL Oost punched a command into his BioMet. "Checking," There was a short pause before he looked up at Andorin. "It's still available," he replied.

"How would you like to work with the new task force?"

"I will do what I am directed to do, sir. Today, I am your protection detail," he mechanically replied.

"All right. Let's go," Andorin said to the guard.

He spoke into his BioMet and then said, "Proceed to the front exit."

They walked in near silence as the construction sounds slowly faded away the further they got from the room. Finally, work noises from the room faded away to nothingness. As it was, when he left, they had completely gutted the room including the carpeting and had one room nearly torn down. They were moving very fast. His vehicle was waiting in front right where he had left it and he moved toward it. The guard escorting him headed to the first vehicle and the guard holding his door went to the trailing vehicle after he had made sure Andorin was safely inside. They pulled away and started back towards the Andalusia Attack Base main gate.

14 REMINISCING

The drive was no different from usual. He was trying to piece everything together that had happened today; his new crest, the lack of rank structure above him, his new position. It all was moving very fast. He needed some consistency in his life right now. His unit, his *old* unit, he thought was more appropriate at this point—might give him that clarity where he could finalize his team selections. He thought that his Alpha Battaliaison, Langli Rheingeld would be beneficial in this situation. He had been though many battles with him, and trusted him above all others of his rank. He needed a tech person on this assignment, but whom could he get?

He liked the Tech, Level 1 assigned to Charlie Battalion, Pridna Orthington. However, he didn't like the Battaliaison in charge of that unit as much. So *two birds with one stone as it were*, he thought and smiled. She did have one oddity: no one ever saw her without her full battle gear on, but that could easily be overlooked. *Two down, four to go.* He also needed worker bees. He had heard of the best squad under his command: Squad One, under Commander 1, *himself*, he fondly remembered. Alpha Battalion, 5th Regiment, 10th Phalanx, 1275th Militia. The squad leader, Mican Trenti, was the most decorated squad member ever under his command, but his attitude had kept him from moving higher in the strata of leadership. Andorin could work with that. Lost in thought, he looked up to see that he was approaching the main gate again. The motorcade moved to the far right and was waved through the first tier immediately. They approached the security checkpoint. The first vehicle checked through quickly. Andorin moved his vehicle forward slowly.

"Credentials?" the tech asked.

"Here," Andorin handed over his new security credentials.

"Wow! This is nice. The best credentials I have seen to date. How did you get this?" He asked.

"I was given this without much choice in the matter, but it *is* cool looking," Andorin stated.

"Sir? I have orders to detain you," the tech said plainly, and waived to the booth to the right.

Andorin waved to SL Oost, who exited his vehicle and said "What's the problem Tech?"

"I have orders to detain him at the gate," he said to SL Oost, echoing the message he had told Andorin.

"We do not have time for this. Let him pass," Oost said.

"Sir, I cannot. The supervisor is on his way right now," and he pointed off to his left. Both Andorin and Oost looked to see who it was. He saw the Supervisor coming towing someone by their neck plates. Andorin keenly recognized who the supervisor had in tow.

"We'll be all right. We can wait," Andorin watched as Oost stepped back a few paces. Every one watched as the pair made it towards Andorin's vehicle.

The Supervisor spoke first, "Sir, LE Wilcon, sir. I have someone here that has something to say to you." With that, he thrust the tech's face onto the front window of the vehicle and said, "Don't you!" Andorin saw Oost draw his weapon. Andorin waved him off and he re-holstered it and stepped closer, just in case.

"Well, spit it out!" He shook him some more rubbing his face on the front window harder.

"S-S-Sir, I am s-s-sorry for not believing you when you s-s-said what you s-s-said," he stuttered out.

"That ain't all," the Supervisor said, and smashed his face against the window again.

"I meant you no harm when I s-s-said you were a s-spy. I did not mean to d-d-disrespect you or your d-d-daughter's memory. I am truly s-s-sorry for my actions," the tech stammered.

"Do you have anything to say to him?" The supervisor asked.

"Yes," Andorin said.

The supervisor pulled his head to the side window to hear what Andorin was going to say.

"Tech? Or after this morning, he'll be just a citizen?"

The Supervisor smiled and said, "That's right. After this, we're stripping him of rank and uniform, and leaving his naked body outside the gate. Maybe some unsuspecting fool will help him."

"Citizen, maybe things *are* just as they appear. You should not be so quick to look for what is not there. What you said earlier is unforgivable, and if I see you again...well it might be the last time I see you. Enjoy your walk home. It's a nice day for a walk." He said smiling at the thought.

The supervisor moved away with the tech still in tow. Andorin was surprised how strong the old Supervisor actually was. The tech was young and spry. He should have been able to easily get out of the Supervisor's grasp.

The current gate Tech stepped back and said, "Proceed."

Andorin pulled his vehicle out of the way, allowing the trailing vehicle to get their credentials checked. Finally, the motorcade proceeded without further incident. They made their way to the 1st Command Compound, his old unit where he was Commander for the entire unit, but not after yesterday, not any more. He went from having direct control of over five thousand troops to none, overnight. It was a little saddening; a big part of him missed this already. They drove towards the command center where his office was—*used to be,* he thought. The office was on the top floor in the corner overlooking the made assembly point. The motorcade pulled in front of the offices and they all exited the vehicles. Over in the distance were his favorite tank techs working on their heavy artillery.

The lead tank tech, Regimentrix Frank Dwyer said, "Must be nice to come in at lunch time, Commander," as he cheerfully waved to him.

Andorin waved back and said, "I have already waged three battles this morning how about you?"

The tech started running over and said, "What? Only three? You're getting soft." He slowed when he could see things clearer and asked, "Sir, what is wrong with your crest? It looks all funny and empty."

And with that, Andorin turned to face his old verbal sparring buddy. Regimentrix Dwyer's eyes widened, and he said, "Holy crap," then screamed, "Executrix on deck!" He snapped to attention, saluted and waited for acknowledgement. Everyone on the field dropped what they were doing and also snapped to attention, and rendered a salute, awaiting their response. He had seen this many times before when his Executrix had made their inspections, he had just never been the *focus* of it.

"At ease soldier," he said to Regimentrix Dwyer.

"AT EASE!" He screamed to all others nearby and moved to stand at ease.

Andorin knew the routine and so preempted it, and said loudly, "Please continue your work. Disregard my presence unless I approach you directly and engage you in conversation. That is a standing order from this day forward."

"Sir, Yes sir!" Echoed in the compound as all the voices present answered as one, just as their training had taught them to do.

He motioned for Frank to continue walking over and asked, "How is tank repair today?"

"Sir, you know how it is, *You Break 'em, We fix 'em*...as usual. Nothing we can't handle," replied the tech. He then asked, "Sir, permission to speak freely?"

"Permission granted," Andorin replied.

"Sir? What is up with your crest? I have never seen another one like it in all my days."

"That, my tank mite, is a long story, one I just cannot tell right now. Maybe later if there is time," answered Andorin.

"But sir, 217? There are no Executrices with that number. And then everything else...empty? It's just not natural."

"I know, I am still getting used to it, but that's the way it is for now. I guess I will be my own unit...singular and distinctive," Andorin mused, still walking towards the building.

"Aye, sir. Let me know if you need a tank mite to fix up your tanks. I'll come in a heartbeat, sir!" Frank Dwyer replied.

As they walked away Element Leader Puzar leaned in and asked quietly, "Sir why did you call them mites?"

"I called them that because they call themselves that. They crawl all over their tanks like little mites crawl all over other animals, hence Tank Mites. It's harmless and helps keep morale up."

They continued into the building and up the open stair well by his old office. Three flights they went up to the top most office. They walked down the corridor between offices to where is office was located. He moved to the scanner and had his certificate read. The door refused to open.

"I was afraid of this," Andorin said. "The security system does not recognize my new credentials. Commander Wilcon is authorized, LE Wilcon is not." Then at the top of his lungs he screamed, "TECH SUPPORT!"

It echoed throughout the building until a quiet response was heard, "Coming, Commander."

He yelled again, "DOUBLE TIME!"

"Double time," came the response, but louder this time.

Moments later, the sound of footsteps echoed as someone was running across the building compound. The sound changed to that of metal steps as they started climbing the stairs. Andorin could hear mumbling now as they reached the top floor and started moving down the corridor.

"Double time. It's *always* double time. I cannot catch a break today," the technician said, panting between breaths. He made his way down the corridor when he paused to see all the people in the hallway. He slowly made his way through them, and asked without looking, "Commander? What is the problem today?"

"Well, where to begin? First, it is no longer Commander," Andorin said.

"No longer Commander?" The tech said confused and then finally looked up at him. He dropped his keys and they almost went down through the grating, but Element Leader Loh quickly stepped on them to stop them from falling further. "What are you then? An *LE*? Wow, what did I miss?"

He did not wait for an answer, "Sir, what happened to your crest? Why does it look like that...all empty? Why are you here now?"

"Ah, that *is* the point is it not? I cannot get into my office—I mean my *old* office. The door scanner will not recognize my credentials," as he held out his new credentials.

"Whoa, what is that? I have heard of them before, but never have I seen one. A Diamondnyte badge. Can I hold it?"

"Sure if it gets me into my office faster," Andorin quipped.

"Yeah, yeah, sure thing, I'll get you in there jiffy quick just got to get my keys from under your, er, *guard's* foot?" He reached down and deftly removed the keys from under Loh's boot. "I've got your key on this separate key ring for just these occasions. Seems about once a week your door would not work." He smiled back at his former Commander.

"Any second now," said LE Wilcon.

"There got it. Anything else sir?" The tech asked.

"Yes encode my door to allow this badge...for now, anyway," Andorin stated.

"Yes sir. Will do sir," the tech said as they left the hallway back to where they came from.

"Tech, wait," Andorin turned to speak to the guards, "Go with this tech. He'll show you to our break area," Looking back at the tech he said, "Take them to our break room, full access. You understand?"

"Yes sir, full access, I understand."

"Be back here in two hours. We'll head back to the Hall of Authority to see how construction is going and turn in my final selections."

"Yes sir," Squad Leader Oost replied and followed the tech down the corridor.

Andorin finally had some more time to think. He had three of his six. He logged on to his terminal and looked at personnel records. He was looking for very specific things: the display of independent thinking, thoroughness, attention to details. Then he found something interesting in his key word search he was performing. He found a Militrix that used creative tactics and saved many units by carrying out orders, but not directly as ordered. Militrix Gregor Bainfield was next on his list. He found a Regimentrix that might also fill the bill. Regimentrix Colinack Yolando. He was looking for a Phalaxon to round out his field of selections, but he could not find any that suited his needs. He did find another Squad leader that looked promising. Squad 1 under Charlie battalion, Regiment 73, Phalanx 200, Militia 135, his record displayed some notes regarding tenacity and attention to detail that resulted in battlefield lives saved. Squad Leader Trevor Molantic was added to the list. His list now read:

Battaliaison, Langli Rheingeld   *Promote to Commander*

Tech, Level 1 Pridna Orthington	*Promote to Alpha Tech (Classified)*
Squad Leader Mican Trenti	*Promote to Militrix*
Militrix Gregor Bainfield	*Promote to Regimentrix*
Regimentrix Colinack Yolando	*Promote to Battaliaison*
Squad Leader Trevor Molantic	*Promote to Militrix*

Cresting requirements: My Rocker Crest, no Diamond Crest. Everyone gets V-Crest with assignment to the V squad; no ranking distinctions. Only a V in the squad block.

In addition, I would like the four guards assigned to my detail today permanently assigned as security detail for the room and personnel. Cresting Requirements for these members: Same Rocker Crest as others; no Diamond crest and V-Crest with an S in the Squad Distinction and 1 Element, 1 Position for the Leader, 1,2 for others on his team today and likewise 2,1 and 2,2 for the trailing detail. Commensurate promotions as well.

Also would like all security credentials stripped of visible rank information for the military techs on this list, guard ranks are fine.

He finished typing up his request and got it ready for submission to the High Authority when they got back to his office-in-progress. Then he left his office, leaving the door open, heading towards the break room. He was going to miss these days in this bay. He would miss all the people running about doing their assigned tasks. He guessed he would have similar situation arise on his team, but there would be only twelve to fourteen people; not at all like here, where he could interact with thousands of people–daily if needed. He would miss that. He made his way to the break area where he found Squad Leaders Hyland and Element Leader Loh watching the VidFeed of the events of yesterday and today. The other two guards were playing a game of skill when he walked in. The two watching the VidFeed stood almost instantly. The two playing the game took a few seconds to realize what had occurred. They stopped playing. SL Oost, who was playing in the game asked, "Finished, sir? "

"Yes, I believe that I am. We can go back to the Hall of Authority and meet with the High Authority himself," Andorin said.

SL Oost said, "Pack it in, we're heading out."

Andorin said, "I have to secure my door still."

SL Oost pointed to the trailing team and said, "Close his door." Loh sprinted towards his office.

They formed up in the usual pattern two leading one trailing directly in back this time. As the group made their way across the building, you could see Loh quickly climbing the stairs to his old office. By the time they were three-quarters of the way across the floor, Loh was on an intercept course to their position. She took her position just as they crossed the threshold that marked the exterior of the building. They proceeded to the vehicles and got in. They pulled away and headed back towards the capital.

The drive to the Hall of Authority was unremarkable and was much the same as earlier. They walked into the building and headed for the High Authority's meeting chamber. Construction noises were clearly audible from the main entrance. He would have to check on that later. They again waited outside the High Authority's door and knocked to enter. The Comms spoke, "Enter," and they all entered the room.

"Sir, I have the list of personnel," Andorin handed him the list.

The High Authority examined the list carefully and asked, "Are you sure about these people?"

"I believe these are the best I have to work with, yes," Andorin replied professionally.

"Interesting choice for Cresting. I am not really sure how that will work, but we kind of are in the weeds on this one a little. Are we not?" He smiled. "Another interesting find. Squad Leader Oost, did you know your element is on this list of the Low Executrix?"

"No sir," replied Oost.

"I think I will honor these requests," and he handed the paper to his administrative tech, "Create the orders; start today. Are there any special instructions for them to be placed in the order, Low Executrix Wilcon?"

"Yes have them get new credentials and be ReCrested and report by 0900 tomorrow to The Hall of Authority, Sub Basement One, room 101A. Wear no ranking details on their uniform whatsoever. Rank cannot be discussed once assigned."

"Did you get that down tech?" The High Authority asked.

"Yes, sir. The orders will be published shortly. Credential and ReCresting orders will generate then. They are a little unorthodox, but it should work as requested."

"Good. Thank you. Low Executrix Wilcon, was there anything else, or are we done here?" He asked.

"No sir, I believe everything is done. Thank you for your belief in my abilities and the opportunity to serve you," he said as he bowed.

"You can go now," the High Authority said barely noticing they were already leaving.

When they were in the hallway, SL Oost said, "What was he talking about for my detail?"

Andorin replied, "You work for me now, of course with a full level promotion increase."

"How will that work? I'll be a Militrix after the promotion, but still a Squad Leader. That does not seem right," he questioned.

117

Andorin explained, "You are looking at it from the wrong perspective, you are a squad leader getting paid as a Militrix. Same job more money."

"I guess I can see that. How about after this...whatever this is?"

"You'll re-enter at the grade you are being paid at, not Squad Leader," Andorin explained.

"So I am already a Militrix in the system, just acting as a squad leader," Oost asked.

"Not until the order is generated, but after? Yes," Andorin explained.

Then, as if by design, the BioMets of the security detail acknowledged receipt of orders.

"Is this correct? I am to report to Security for new credentials and get ReCrested?"

"Yes, and the crest will be nothing like you have ever seen or probably will ever see again."

"Remove any rank as well?" Oost queried.

"Yes. It will all make sense tomorrow when we meet in Sub Basement Room 101A, 0900. You go start that, and maybe you can get finished before you go back home for the evening. I am going down to check on the progress of the room." He watched the guards to where they exited the building, which was good to know because he still needed to find his vehicle for when he left later. He watched them walk out into the parking lot and lost sight of them as they moved out of his field of view. Finally, the elevator door open and he stepped into it and went down to Sub-Basement One.

He was amazed to see what had happen since he had left. The center doors were wide open. All the main construction was completed, rooms, alterations, it was *all* done. They were finishing the final coats of paint on the walls. The crews were laying down some raised flooring that seemed to have grooves cut into the substrate. He had no ideas what that was going to be for. The lobby held various furniture pieces staged for when the rooms were ready for furniture. As he was standing there, they closed the false wall's doors, and it looked amazing, he could not see the seam. They disguised it as a seam in the wall covering they chose, it had many channels running down it. This feature hid the seam very well.

He decided that he would check out the stairwell. He carefully made his way through the construction area. He did notice the looks of contempt from the workers for being in the area, but that did not deter him. He made his way to the stairwell and noticed the door was already open. Techs were installing the hard points for the BioMet scanner, and cameras. He finally understood what the gridding in the flooring was. They were channels to allow the cabling to run under the floor covering. All the cabling ran toward the center kiosk that was taking shape nicely. They had even elevated the seating slightly, a single step, to allow a height advantage. The kiosk was a little larger than he had imagined it would be, but it would do. It looked like it could fit one person comfortably and maybe two people cramped. He decided to head to the top of the stairs to get his bearings for where the room lay in comparison to the rest of the building.

At the top of the stairs, he noticed a small parking lot near the entrance and he saw techs working on something over there. Curious, he decided to see what they were doing. As he approached, a tech looked up from what he was doing and smiled. As he was getting closer, he noticed they were marking things on the ground. As he got right on top of them, he realized they were assigned parking spots. Each team member received one, even the security guards. *Nice touch*, he thought. He noticed it was getting late and the way the guards left earlier, his vehicle was on the other side of the building. He made his way back through the work area. *It was amazing what they had accomplished in such a short amount of time.* he thought. If they kept this pace up, they would be completed by morning, easily. As he walked back in, he noticed the secure document area. The delivered security containers were being installed. Each one needed a cable, and there were many cables running to the area. The red paint looked good. Anyone would easily stand out in the area. The rolled up carpeting looked like a good match to the paint.

He continued through the area and back out the center doors, which opened to allow easy movement of things into the space. The kitchen area was somewhat small, but it only had to handle about eighteen people so that would be all right. He check in on the conference room, and it was nicely sized; it looked like it could hold about twenty-five people. More than they had asked for, but probably better in the long run. The table was outside in the lobby area. It was a massive slab of granite. It had to be about half his hand thick. He had no idea how they had got that thing down here. There had to be another entrance or service elevator. No, it had to be another exterior entrance. He was not sure how they were going to get that in there because it looked longer than the length of the room. *I am sure they will manage,* he thought as he walked to the main elevators. When he exited the elevator, he left the building in the same direction as the guards. When he went outside, he saw his vehicle parked nearby. He headed straight for it and got in. He decided to go back to the base an get all of his personal effects out of his old office.

The drive back towards the main gate of the base was unremarkable. He headed towards the gate area, and noticed a lone figure off in the distance, walking away from the base. He could not make out any details because they were on the other side of the road, far away. As he passed by and entered the gate area, he suddenly knew who it was. Remorse started to sink in, and he decided to turn back around. Whatever he was going to do at the base could wait. He turned around and headed out of the gate back towards the city. As he got closer to the lone figure, he noticed that he was indeed naked, and no one was stopping to assist him. He decided to pull over. He pulled up just beyond where the tech was walking and got out of the vehicle.

"Hello again." Andorin said.

The tech recoiled in fear and started to turn around.

"Wait!" Andorin yelled, "I am here to help you. Please, just get in." He pulled off his armor and then his uniform top and threw it to him, "Here put this on for now." He put his armor back on and got back in.

The tech put on the top hastily to cover up. It covered most things, as the tech was smaller than Andorin. He got into the vehicle now and asked, "Why are you helping me? The last time I saw you, you were going to kill me if we met again."

"I don't think I said the word *kill*. I did, however, allude to it being the last time I would see you. I can understand your confusion. First, I am sorry for what I said. It was out of anger and frustration, and I did not mean to threaten you. I mean I did at that time, I guess, but not anymore. Second, to make amends, I will give you a ride to your home," Andorin stated.

"You would do that? After everything that has happened today?"

"Yes," said Andorin.

"Good, I am glad because if you had not then I would not be able to do this." With that, the tech quickly produced a syringe that he had stored in a secret compartment in his exoskeleton for just such an occasion. His employer was well versed in keeping things secret. He shoved the syringe in between Andorin's neck plates and injected the substance into him.

Andorin tried to struggle, but the Tech had grabbed both arms on that side, and the Tech's upper right arm did the injection. Andorin quickly lost consciousness.

15 COUNTER OFFER

Andorin slowly regained consciousness. His eyes blinked open, and he realized he was bound to a chair. All of his arms and legs were strapped at multiple points along his limbs. He could barely move his arms. The room was completely dark with extremely bright lights shining into his face from multiple directions. Everywhere he could turn his head he looked into a light.

"Sir? He's awake," someone in the distance said.

"Andorin Wilcon, Low Executrix at that. I am...well you don't need to know who I am yet. You *do* need to know that I have a proposition for you. I am the one that allowed your family to live last night. I have plans for you Andorin. I have plans for your entire family," The man said.

Andorin was straining to hear every inflection, every nuance of the voice so he could recognize it if he heard it again.

"You have been selected to field a Task Force to look into the terror attacks. I also know it is a ruse to allow you to muck around in my affairs. That I cannot allow, but I can't kill you either. I am in quite a bind, you see. What to do with you? What to do?" This time the voice changed as he was speaking.

He was using a voice modulator; there would be no way for him to discern who it was now. However, even though the tone was changing, Andorin could not mistake the sinister intent exuding from his words. Andorin seethed, "Let me out, and I'll solve that problem for you," as he strained at his bindings.

"Temper, temper, Andorin. As I said, I have plans for you. You are going to play your part whether or not you think you are. Choice is an illusion. People think they are in control when they make a choice, when they are not."

"I am never going to help you!" Andorin yelled.

"You already are. You are like one of the tanks you love so fondly. Once you set it in motion it is hard to stop, *if* you are not in control. You, my *friend*...can I call you that? You are a tank. You are going to smash everything up. I can almost see the carnage now. It will be glorious to watch what you do. But then you would be mucking around in my affairs as well. So I will make you an offer."

"I don't want anything you have," Andorin spat in the direction of the voice.

"Come now, Andorin. You don't even know what I have yet."

"I said you have nothing I want!"

"I have Stranaya," the voice said bluntly.

"Wait, what? You have Stranaya?" Andorin struggled furiously against his bonds. "I am going to kill you when I get out of here."

"I highly doubt that," the voice replied. "You don't even know who I am. How will you do that?" The voice mused with a slight laugh.

"I will find you. Find out who you are," Andorin seethed.

"I am sure you will...one day—but today is not that day. We have not even gotten to the bargaining stage. I've just showed you my hand, now it's time to see yours. I need you to suppress certain information about your investigation."

"Why would I do that?"

"Because I have Stranaya, and if you do not you'll never see her again."

"She's alive!" Andorin's heart leaped, but he had already surmised that by the way she was taken; the way she calmly walked out of the house.

"Of course she is. As I have said, I have plans for your family. She is an integral part of that plan. And so are you." The voice said with soothing tones.

"Me?"

"Yes, you. You just need to suppress certain information from your investigation. It is only one thing; you will hardly even care at that point, when you know it."

"So what do I get out of this for helping you?" Andorin asked.

"You get Stranaya's life of course."

"I thought you said she was integral to your plan."

"Ah, you mistake integral with irreplaceable. They are not the same. She can be replaced. So can you. It would be easier for all parties concerned, however, if we just got along. For me, it will make things much smoother and for you and your family? Well they'll be alive. You can see my perspective now can't you. Andorin?"

"Don't you dare touch my family!"

"Andorin, Andorin. I won't have to, if you just cooperate. If you don't, what didn't happen last night will happen on some future night. You might go to bed and then in the morning you wake to the screams of your family as they are executed right in front of you. I don't want to do that, mind you, but I will if I need to."

"You're a monster!"

"I have been called worse and if the truth is known, I am far worse in reality. I make no illusion about what I am. I want what I want, and will stop at nothing to get it."

"What do you want then?" Andorin conceded in acceptance.

"You can't know that...yet, but you can cooperate. Will you cooperate?" the voice said in a calming manner.

"Yes, I'll cooperate. What information do you want me to suppress?" he said with acceptance.

"My true identity. That's all. *Who I am.*"

"That's easy, I don't know who you are," Andorin stated.

"Yet. You do not know who I am yet, but you most likely will. When you do find out, you must steer the investigation away from *me* and onto another who will present themselves during the investigation. It does not matter who this person is, so long as it is not me. No one can know who I am. Not even the High Authority, who I know you work for now."

"I was just placed on the task force by him."

"That's not what I mean."

It was then that Andorin's arm started vibrating.

Another voice said, "Sir! We've located a slave drive."

"Extract data," the voice said calmly.

"Sir, the drive is empty. No data found," a third voice said.

"Interesting. It seems I am too late. Your first report has been extracted already. No matter. I have other means at my disposal. Do we have an understanding? Make no mention of me in any report anywhere and actively steer the investigation away from me. Do we have an accord?"

"Yes. We have a deal. I will not make mention of you anywhere or to anyone...whomever you are," Andorin conceded. "In return my family is protected. Not just left alone, *actively protected.*"

"I will protect your family, but I am the only real threat to your family, so that will be easy for me to do. We have a deal," the voice said with great satisfaction.

Andorin could imagine the wicked smile that now covered the face of the voice talking to him. He could sense the arrogance, the sense of victory, and relief. *That was interesting: Relief. What did that mean? Why were they relieved?* He thought to himself, *That had to be significant.*

"Take him back, now." the voice said.

He felt a tech move his head to the side and inject him again. He was out in seconds.

He awoke back in his vehicle. His eyes blinked again, but it was much easier now because it was now almost dark. He had been gone for over an hour, maybe even closer to two hours. He looked around. He was back in his vehicle right where he had stopped to pick up that tech. *The Tech*! He thought. *He must work for...whoever that was.* He looked over and found his uniform top crumpled up on the seat where the tech had sat just before he had drugged him. "Now I think I *will* kill him the next time I see him...just on principle." He said aloud. It sounded more authentic aloud than just in his thoughts. He would definitely deal with him differently the next time. He started back home with assurances that his family was going to be safe. At least he was sure of that much. He would sleep much easier tonight. And boy, would he need it.

The drive home was unremarkable and seemed to drag on. He needed to get back with Miliki to reconnect and bring some clarity to his day. At least with his last encounter, he had a sense of all the sides in the game he was forced to play. He also knew that the Shadow Leader was now going to ensure his family was not harmed. That was the only good Andorin could see that had come from the meeting. He entered his home and again rested his head on the door trying to get a grip of what he was going to say...how *much* he should say. He jumped when he felt arms on his neck, but when he heard Miliki's voice he relaxed slightly.

"You seemed like you were deep in thought...like you were in space or something. How was the rest of your day after the ceremony?" She asked.

"The rest of the day you ask? It went as much as you would have expected it to. I was almost shot at the main gate because they increased security, and my rank did not match my credentials, but that was before the ceremony. I just had not had the chance to tell you yet. Then I got my new Crest." He moved his arm to show her.

She reached out, rubbed her hand over it and said, "It looks all empty. What happened?"

"I was promoted out of the military rank structure, that is what happened," he replied.

"What? How is that possible? You are still in the military, right?" she inquired.

"Yes I am, but I am in a situation which has not happened in over fifty years. I am the 217th of 216 Low Executrices."

"How is that possible? You told me before that you were not being promoted any time soon because there were only 216 Low Executrices. How can you be 217, if by law they are only allowed 216?" She asked.

"Apparently the High Authority has the ability to do whatever he wants. He promoted me to that position and now he had to adopt me...which, I think, is the real reason for my placement on the Task Force. He needed to make a home for me, as it were."

"You don't think he put you there because you can help?" Miliki sincerely asked.

"No. I know he made it look that way publicly, but in reality, he had no other choice. He also made it into a publicity event and made sure the other side knew he was taking care of the situation. Everyone knows I work directly for the High Authority."

"I am sure the High Authority has faith in you and what you can do," she tried to soothe him.

"He may or he may not, but he did grant me a military investigative team. I had to provide him with a list today, six people I trusted or could work with. I had to go back to the base to make the list, which is where I had that problem with the gate and with one tech in particular. He was really intent on seeing me dead for some reason..." he paused as he thought long about something that tech had said. *The tech said he killed that other guy because he tried to pass himself off as someone who was attacked last night.* He then continued, "I had a strange feeling that tech was looking for me specifically."

"Now you're being paranoid...well more than you should be after everything that has happened."

"No, I am not because that same tech was working for the other side," he stated.

"No!" She said shocked and then asked, "How do you know?"

"I think I knew when he abducted me," he said.

"He *what* you?" She said with exasperation.

"He abducted me. See, he was walking out from the base naked, this was punishment for his treatment of me earlier in the day. I also...sort of...threatened to kill him. I know," Andorin said, holding up a hand to forestall Miliki's outburst, "not one of my finest moments over the past few days. He was sent home, walking naked and as I drove by, I felt remorseful, so I picked him up."

"That's the Honey I know," Miliki smiled at him.

"Lot of good it did me. As soon as he got in the vehicle, he abducted me and drove me to meet the leader of the Shadow Faction, or at least whom I think that was. He was not very clear on that matter."

"Oh, my!" She inhaled deeply.

"Yeah, but it gets worse. He...I think it was a he anyways, was using a voice modulator to change their voice so it was unrecognizable. It went as you might expect; either I do what they want or you and the kids would end up like the rest of the families before us last night."

"He was going to kill us?" She exclaimed.

"Not *was*...will, unless I cooperate with him and their cause," he stated.

"He will kill us! Should we be afraid now?" she asked starting to move away from his grasp.

"No. Part of the deal was that we...*all of us*...receive protection. Our family will remain unharmed, so long as I do what he wants. But that is the odd part," he stated.

"How so?" Miliki asked.

"He only wants his identity suppressed in my investigation," he said.

"What does that mean? Do you know who he is?" She asked.

"See that's the odd part. I have no idea who he is. It was a dark room with bright lights shining on me. I could not even see anyone. Although, I know at least two other people were there. So right now, that is the easy part. The trade was simple because I have nothing I have to hide...*yet*," he reasoned.

"Will you ever find out?" Miliki asked.

"He seemed to think so."

"Well then, when you find out who it is, it will be cataclysmic. It has to be like that," Miliki stated.

"You think so?" Andorin asked.

"Yes, it has to be. You don't know now. So why make the deal now?" Miliki pondered.

"I think he made the deal now because I was placed on this task force, and that required him to take action to protect his identity," Andorin postulated.

"But that does not explain the now part? Why now?" She puzzled.

"Again, I think it is the movement of strategic pieces on a battle front. One makes a move the other has to counter it. I think this was his counter. The High Authority placed me on the task force. They made sure I could not divulge what the High Authority truly wants to know. He blocked his play to get the information, as it seems," Andorin explained.

"I guess that sounds plausible," Miliki agreed.

"Oh and I did not tell you the worse part," Andorin said.

"Typical. What is it now?" She sighed in exasperation.

"He knew I work for the High Authority."

"Of course he does. Anyone who saw the VidFeed today knows you work for the High Authority," she explained.

"No. Not in that way, the other way, the *secret* way."

"How do you know that?" She inquired.

"They attempted to access the device in my arm. Well not so much attempted as more like *did* and tried to remove the data," Andorin explained.

"They can do that? How did they know?" She asked.

"I have no idea. I don't even know how it works in the first place, much less how other people can access it. But they knew it was there. You know me. I get locked out of my office because my credentials stop working twice a week. Tech does not like me. You know that," Andorin said.

"You are a little tech phobic. If it was not for the military, you probably would not have a BioMet. They are starting to move into the civilian sector now. Everyone's getting one," Miliki stated with a smile and then continued, "Your dinner is cold now. I expected you home hours ago."

"So did I, and now you know why I was not," he said with a smile.

"You think this is funny, mister?" she jested and lightly punched his chest.

"No, but we are still alive," he said with a broader smile.

"That's not funny," and she punched him harder this time.

"Yeah I know, but it is true. We are alive. Now where is that food? I am starving," Andorin said with a devilish smile.

"Let me just heat it up quick," she said back to him.

"I am so hungry I could eat it cold," Andorin jested.

"It won't take but a few seconds," she answered.

Andorin ate his food, and went about his normal nightly routine before settling in for bed. He thought of the events of the day as he was drifting off to sleep. He thought of the identity of the Shadow Leader, even though he had no idea who it was. His thoughts drifted back to the *relief* he had sensed during the encounter. What could that mean? Why was he relieved? He needed to explore this further. He reasoned that it might be because he would not have to kill him. However, he had said that he was not going to kill him because he had plans for him. Whatever those plans were, there had to be a reason for his relief. It was after his agreement, so somehow it related to him agreeing. Then, if he needed to agree and did not, then that might have forced his bluff. Maybe he was bluffing about something. *Killing me?* No, he had already discounted that. *My family?* Maybe, but they were alive as much as he was, so probably not that either. If he wanted them dead, they would have been already. They were also leverage against him right now. What else? *Stranaya?* It had to be linked to her. But what was it? He was bluffing; maybe he had lied, about having her, and used the situation to get his way. That had to be it. If he refused, and wanted Stranaya released, then he could not have because he does not have her. It would not matter much—he had no idea who *he* was.

16 DEVELOPMENT

Doctor Fillingraph awoke from his sleep cycle. There was no real night and day on the station because it was situated in such a way that it was almost always light. The planet briefly obscured the sun with its northern hemisphere and therefore it did not stay dark for very long. Either you slept in daylight, had room darkening shades, which were very effective, or you went insane. He, for one, did not intend to go insane.

The sun had just started to set, providing a few hours of night as he roused from the bed. He had had a long day yesterday, but it had been quite productive. He had managed to acquire all the cores needed to fill the military's orders with a few left over to supplement the corporation's bottom line with extra ships to sell. The corporation had saved billions already using organic materials instead of metallic compounds from the beginning, like rival corporations. The military had confirmed that his path was the better one because it resulted in truly superior vessels. So much so, that the military now wanted to find out the *how*. Unfortunately, they could never know the real how.

There would be a manufactured reason that Low Executrix Kolana would feed them to sate their need for knowledge of the *how*. It just wouldn't be real. Oh, it would *look* real, and would match the end results, but it would not mention any organic material usage, other than seat coverings in the form of hides and the like. It most definitely would not mention the genetic manipulation which they were about to undertake...probably for the last time...especially given the state of remaining water on the planet. The population was given a 60% figure as not to alarm them as to how much water was left on the planet. It was far, far worse. It was closer to 20%, if not below. There were only one maybe two generations left on the planet before the water ran out.

Space mining was not a viable option either because there was no cost effective way to get it to the planet. The population was told that it was occurring...and it *was*...just not for terrestrial needs. Any water brought to the planet would be one hundred times the cost of water now, and it was prohibitively expensive now. This was the very reason for this project.

Saving our species, this project must succeed, it must, no matter the cost or else everyone will perish, eventually. I guess when you think about it like that, most will perish because there will be limited space on this transport, IG-3275-001, will be their salvation.

"Claudette. Display core status," Fillingraph finally said.
Core Status Displayed.

Model	Status
CC-3257-004	Surgery - Complete; Molt - In-progress
CC-3257-005	Decommissioned
CC-3257-006	Surgery - In-progress; Molt - Pending
CD-3257-004	Decommissioned
CD-3257-005	Surgery - Complete; Molt - In-progress
CD-3257-006	Surgery - In-progress; Molt - Pending
CS-3257-035	Surgery - Complete; Molt - In-progress
CS-3257-036	Surgery - In-progress; Molt - Pending
CS-3257-037	Surgery - Complete; Molt - In-progress
ES-3257-009	Surgery - In-progress, Molt - Pending
ES-3257-010	Surgery - Complete; Molt - In-progress
IG-3257-001	Surgery - Preparation; Molt - Pending
IG-3257-002	Nutrient Bath -In-progress
IG-3257-003	Surgery - Complete; Molt - In-progress

"Claudette, Select IG-3257-002, display details."

"IG-3257-002 - Surgeons Note: Process successful. Rectum disengaged. Temporary shunt installed. No Complications. Begin Molt process.
"Tech note: Exoskeleton removed. Nutrient bath in progress."

"Claudette, Back to list."
List Displayed.
"Claudette, Select IG-3257-001, display details."

"IG-3257-001 - Anesthesia administered."

Doctor did you sleep well? the disembodied voice said.
He recognized it immediately and thought *Yes I did. Are you ready to start?*
"Claudette back to list," he said.
List Displayed.

What are they doing to me now? asked the voice.

He thought, *They have to severe the connection of the inner workings of your body to your exoskeleton.*

Why?

It allows your body to grow. When your outsides grow, the inside workings do not. If we did not perform this surgery, then your insides would tear randomly, the doctor replied.

That is bad I take it then?

Yes that is bad. Fillingraph agreed. *With a random tear, we would have no way to remove your bodily waste and then your internal workings would become fouled and unusable. Basically, your body would become a toilet that drains nowhere. Eventually, this would permeate your exoskeleton causing severe entropy.* The doctor explained.

That does sound bad, the voice replied.

Yes it is, which is why we attach a tube to help remove your waste while your body is undergoing the enlargement process. Once complete, your original body function will be minimized and contained within a much smaller compartment designed for these functions. The waste would eventually make its way to the engines for disposal, but they would need nutrients from time to time because they were living organisms after all.

We have condensed these things into what we call Neural Capsules. These capsules are formulated nutrients, administered over a controlled amount of time. Bodily functions would be greatly diminished not having actual limbs to move. Synaptic functions require energy from food, but nowhere near the levels needed for muscle movement. The Neural Capsules can last for about six months and are consumed in the process. On your journey, there will not be enough room to store all the capsules needed. A recycling system will be used where empty capsules are ejected, cleaned and reused again. On board technicians will need to refill the Neural Capsules via prescribed guidelines.

Ow, ow, ow. What's happening, Doctor?

"What...what's happening? Claudette, IG-3257-001, display details."

"IG-3257-001 - Surgeon notes - Surgery commencing."

AAAAH! Make it stop! Screamed the voice.

"What's the matter?" The doctor asked, getting more worried.

The pain! I cannot take the p... The voice trailed off.

Fillingraph burst from his office and ran to the room across the hall. He exploded into the room and said, "What's the matter?"

"We don't know the blood pressure just dropped. The heart is beating erratically. Subject is going into arrest. It just started." The surgeon replied.

"I know! The anesthesia levels must be off. They are feeling the pain," Doctor Fillingraph replied.

"That is impossible. We have administered the anesthesia like all the others."

"No, you need *more* ...or a different kind," the doctor said.

"We were almost done when this happened."

"Doctor Malik," the nurse said to the surgeon, "The patient is stabilizing. Blood pressure returning to normal, heartbeat near normal rhythm."

"Connect shunt."

The voice screamed continuously, *AAAAH!*

Doctor Fillingraph fell to his knees grabbing his head and screamed, "You're hurting her!"

Make them Stop! AAAAH! The Pain! The voice pleaded.

"Stop! It's too much! You're hurting her," he screamed again.

The nurse said, "Blood pressure falling again. Cardiac arrest imminent, Doctor Malik."

"What is causing this? Continue with last suture," the Surgeon said.

The voice screamed louder, *AAAAH! Make them stop, or I will!*

Doctor Fillingraph was on the floor pleading with the surgical staff to stop when suddenly the entire surgical team screamed as one and collapsed on the floor.

The pain, it is too much. You said it would not hurt. You lied to me doctor; you lied to me. The voice said in what seemed like a sobbing voice, *You lied.*

Fillingraph, still on the floor said, "I didn't know. I didn't know. This has never happened before. I don't know what to do. I don't know what is happening. I didn't lie, I just didn't know. I am sorry. I am so sorry."

The pain is subsiding, the voice sighed.

The doctor could now get up from the floor. Sharing the pain was too much. He had to find out what was wrong with the process. He just did not know.

I know you do not know, the voice said, *but you are not doing another procedure until we can fix this, so I do not feel pain.*

The surgical staff was starting to wake up, "What was that?" Then Doctor Malik asked, "Is everyone all right? Patient status?"

The nurse replied, "I am fine. The patient's vitals are normal."

Doctor Fillingraph replied, "She was feeling the pain. I told you she was feeling the pain. She made you stop hurting her."

"Patient wound needs adhesion to the shunt sleeve to be final," The surgeon replied.

"How is that accomplished?" Doctor Fillingraph asked.

"Surgically attached via sutures."

No! Screamed the voice, *No More!*

Doctor Fillingraph fell to the floor again on his knees grabbing his head, "I hear you, but they have to finish."

The nurse said quietly to the surgeon, "Who is he talking to?"

"I do not know," said the surgeon.

"Doctor Malik, can a topical deaden the nerves around where you need to suture to prevent any pain from being felt?" Doctor Fillingraph asked the surgeon.

"Sure, but that would be unnecessary," the surgeon replied.

"You would think so. How do you explain why you were all made unconscious?" Doctor Fillingraph asked.

"Ah, I don't know?" replied the surgeon.

"She did it," Fillingraph said, pointing at IG-3257-001. "She stopped you and unless you want it repeated you need to apply a topical...now!"

"Nurse, get the topical," Doctor Malik ordered.

"Are we really going to let the *crazy* guy tell us what to do?" the nurse said in a low voice.

"Just humor me," the Doctor Malik replied.

"Here is the topical doctor," and the nurse handed him the bottle.

Doctor Malik mimicked placing the topical around the wound and said, "There, see, topical applied."

"Okay," Doctor Fillingraph sighed slowly rising from the floor back to a standing position.

"Begin final suturing," the surgeon stated and he started the procedure.

The voice screamed again, *AAAAH! Stop it!*

Doctor Fillingraph fell to the floor and screamed, "You did not apply the topical!" He screamed, "Make it stop. Make the pain stop. Apply the topical!"

Doctor Malik said, "You are delusional Doctor Fillingraph. The patient is unconscious; they cannot feel anything."

"You are wrong!" Doctor Fillingraph seethed. " IG-3257-001, make him feel your pain," he said aloud.

"The pain, make it stop." Doctor Malik screamed, "Make it stop!" He fell to the floor whimpering.

The other surgical staff stepped back, horrified at what had just happened. They looked at Doctor Fillingraph. They looked at the patient. They could not believe what they had just seen.

The nurse asked to Doctor Fillingraph, "What did you do to Doctor Malik?"

"Me? I did nothing. Actually, Doctor Malik did it. He did not apply the topical as I asked. Someone please apply the topical NOW!" Doctor Fillingraph ordered.

"But the surgeon is—"

"If you do not want to be thrown out of an airlock, then I suggest you comply."

"Fine, I'll do it," the surgical assistant said and took out a swab of the liquid and applied it.

Oh! The pain is easing. I can feel it subsiding. I can manage it now, the voice said.

"That's better. It's working. The pain is easing off," Doctor Fillingraph said, as he climbed from the floor again.

Doctor Malik also started to get up. "What happened? I felt this overwhelming sense of pain."

The nurse said, "You blacked out."

"I applied the topical, for real this time," the surgical assistant stated.

"My head feels like it is on fire," the surgeon stated bewildered.

The nurse helped Doctor Malik up from the floor and said, "Are you all right, Doctor?"

"I am getting better, but I still do not understand what just happened," he replied, perplexed.

Doctor Fillingraph said, "You did not apply the topical as I said to. The next time you disobey me I will *space* you. Do you understand?"

"Yes!" Doctor Malik seethed with resentment.

"Good now apply topical everywhere and a good measure beyond where you are going to make any incision, insert any needle and anything that might cause pain. Do you understand?"

"Yes, applying more topical, now," Doctor Malik replied.

The pain is gone. Thank you, Doctor, the voice replied.

Doctor Malik replied, "Your welcome." Then he looked up, and then at each one of his surgical team and asked them, "Did you hear that?"

They all shook their head *no* and replied, "No," or, "Heard what?"

"A voice thanked me for applying the topical, but it was mine. It was weird. None of you heard that?"

"No, we heard nothing," They all replied, with looks of doubt on their faces.

Perform a test doctor, make a suture, the voice said.

"Now you all heard that right?"

"Heard what?" "What are you talking about?" and "Are you all right, Doctor?" were the responses he received from his surgical team. They clearly thought he was going insane now.

Doctor Malik shook his head and made a suture. When he was complete he said, "Suture complete."

Very good, Doctor. I felt nothing. Proceed and...oh do not let them know you hear me or they will think you more crazy then they do right now.

The surgeon looked around the room and saw no looks of anything strange occurring and he was about to say something.

Now Doctor, I just told you not to do that. Just finish the procedure and leave me alone, the voice intoned.

The surgeon set about his work quickly suturing the shunt sleeve in place, completing the procedure. The surgical assistant applied a salve that helped form a bond around the shunt sleeve. The shunt sleeve was a device that could expand as the rectum opening stretched from the enlargement process. There were differently sized ones for the different phases of the process designed to seal the exoskeleton, the inner body function would remain normal sized. While the exoskeleton would grow to enormous proportions, the internal body workings would not and would remain small. Eventually, they would occupy a small room within the much larger vessel, and it would be almost self-contained, except for the Neural Capsule interface.

Thank you, Doctor, for stopping the pain, the voice said.

Doctor Malik just smiled and nodded.

I heard you, The voice said.

Stranaya, tell the surgeon to be in my office immediately *after this procedure.* Doctor Fillingraph thought.

I did, said the voice, *I am going to rest now.*

Okay, I need some relaxation as well. Doctor Fillingraph thought. Then he left the procedure room and headed back to his office, "Claudette, Surgical Procedures, Display."

Surgical procedures displayed.

"Claudette, filter out non-core procedures," he stated.

Results displayed.

"Claudette, Add this protocol to *all* procedures: Topical or local anesthetic must be applied to any and all bodily areas that will be incised, probed or sutured, before any procedure takes place."

Insertion point? Claudette asked.

"Insert after General Anesthesia, but before any surgical procedure. Insert in *all* procedures. Include statement **NON-OPTIONAL** in bold capital letters, and then include statement normal font. Failure to comply will result in termination of employment, maximum penalty protocol," the doctor stated.

Insertions Complete. Sir. Doctor Malik has arrived, Claudette said.

"Let him in. Doctor Malik. Thank you for coming," Doctor Fillingraph said.

"Fillingraph, what was that in there? What happened?" Asked the surgeon.

"I could say the same thing, *Doctor*," he said with sarcasm dripping from the word *doctor.*

"I was performing the procedure, as I have done numerous times...without topical I might add... and the patient feels nothing," said the surgeon defensively.

"You really believe that? After what just happened in there?" Doctor Fillingraph asked.

"I do not know what happened in there. That has never happened before. That cannot happen; it is not possible. Who was that talking? Did you hear them too?" The surgeon asked.

"Yes Doctor, I heard them too. It proves the point that your patient *did* feel something," Doctor Fillingraph stated emphatically.

"I do not see how that is possible," the surgeon replied.

"Don't worry about the *how*, Doctor. Focus on the *did*. It did happen... accept that it did. I do not even know the how, really. It was explained to me but still I don't understand the how, not really."

"Okay, explain to me what you know," stated Doctor Malik.

"First, let me be blunt. Everything discussed falls under the NDA you signed. Agreed?" The doctor asked.

"Agreed," replied the surgeon.

"Okay. What is thought, Doctor? How does it work, inside the brain?"

"Neurons fire causing information to transfer from one neuron to the next."

"This firing is electrical in nature?" Doctor Fillingraph asked.

"Yes, there is a faint electrical signal that jumps the synapse to transfer information."

Okay, if someone had a sensitive enough piece of equipment, could the impulse be measured?" The doctor queried.

"Yes. That is how brain function is monitored, but we cannot read the *thoughts*, we can only see the electrical activity," the surgeon explained.

"Okay, what if the *equipment* used was already able to understand this impulse, meaning that it could measure and interpret what was being picked up. Could then those thoughts be read?" The doctor asked.

"Yes, I guess, theoretically, but I am a general surgeon, not a neurologist," Doctor Malik replied.

"I understand, but continuing that line of thought. If that *equipment* was also able to manipulate electrical signals, then could it be manipulated in such a way as to transmit a signal into a neural pathway, externally?"

"Sure...theoretically...but what does that have to do with what happened in there?" Doctor Malik asked.

"We are almost there doctor, stay with me," Doctor Fillingraph replied. "Now suppose everything I said was true, someone's neurons could be manipulated to receive an external signal along the auditory pathways to make someone perceive sound... and here is the key question: What would that sound like, since you do not actually hear anything?" Doctor Fillingraph posed.

"I-I do not know. The brain may rely on what it knows as familiar; apply a familiar voice pattern ...maybe."

"Excellent, Doctor. What did you hear in the room?"

"I heard my voice talking."

"But there was no sound, was there?"

"No. No one heard it, other than you," the surgeon replied.

"Exactly!" Doctor Fillingraph exclaimed. "It is no longer theoretical. You experienced it for yourself. Thoughts were transmitted to you, that you used your voice patterns to fill in the blanks. It happened, Doctor. It *happened*!" Doctor Fillingraph slapped his hand on the desk to emphasize the last part.

"Okay, let's say I agree. They *spoke* to me. That does not explain how I felt that pain," Doctor Malik explained.

"Of course it does!" Doctor Fillingraph said as he thrust his arms in the air and spun around in his chair.

"How so?" The surgeon inquired.

"How is pain felt?" Doctor Fillingraph posed.

"A signal is sent from the affected area to the brain... Oh! I see. It's the same process; pain nerves instead of auditory nerves. Okay. Wow!" The surgeon finally agreed.

"Right. It is no longer theoretical, Doctor. Now the next question is...How do you block the signal?" Doctor Fillingraph asked.

"Wow, okay, I am still trying to wrap my head around what you are saying. I just cannot believe it. It happened, just as you said, but I just cannot believe it. Okay, I guess that, as with any electronic signal, distance or interference of some kind could block the signal. You might want to consult an electrical engineer to help you block signals."

"That's a good idea. Thank you, Doctor Malik," Doctor Fillingraph stated.

"Do you need anything else?" Doctor Malik said getting ready to leave.

"Actually, yes. I updated all surgical procedures to include a topical or local anesthetic. I think it would be wise... especially for IG-3257-001, but also for every core procedure."

"Do you really think that is necessary?" Asked Malik, settling back into this chair.

"After what just happened, you don't?" Doctor Fillingraph posed back to Doctor Malik.

"After today? I guess I would have to agree with you on that point," the surgeon conceded.

"Doctor? Another question. Could this explain latter core failures due to neurological problems?" Doctor Fillingraph probed.

"I suppose. The subconscious is not well known. It might be that, while the conscious person feels nothing, the subconscious mind feels *everything*. If the subconscious mind felt every procedure, then that part of the person might go insane, this could result in neurologic failures. So yes. I would say it is plausible," Doctor Malik stated.

"Then implementing this might save more cores later on?"

"I agree. I just wish I knew this earlier to spare the trauma induced by the procedures carried out thus far," the surgeon acknowledged.

"Great. Make sure the new protocols are followed during every surgical procedure or any procedure that touches the cores in any manner," Doctor

Fillingraph directed.

"Yes. Although..." Malik trailed off, deep in thought. "What about core enlargement?" Doctor Malik queried.

"Core enlargement? I don't follow you," Doctor Fillingraph asked, puzzled.

"An anesthetic is added to the nutrient bath to prevent the core from experiencing intense pain associated with the process, especially the immense proportions we are attempting to achieve. I mean twice the size of anything done previously? That pain will be very intense and very prolonged," the surgeon informed.

"I didn't think about that. I forgot the nutrient bath included an anesthetic, but it makes sense. We'll have to look at that before we begin the enlargement phases. Move IG-3257-001 to the top of the list. It will serve as our test subject because they can provide feedback as to what is or is not working. Once we have the protocol down, we can move on to the others," Doctor Fillingraph ordered.

"That would be prudent, especially if some part of the core experiences any pain," the surgeon agreed.

"Then we can help alleviate the one problem this program has been having, neurologic problems. If we can prevent those that will solve most of our nagging issues with long term core operational stability," Doctor Fillingraph stated.

"Doctor Fillingraph, I think you may have just solved that last issue with our program. I'll pass along our findings," Doctor Malik stated.

"No, do not mention anything about how this information came into existence. Make no mention of IG-3257-001's ability. There can be no mention of this, at all," Doctor Fillingraph stipulated.

"All right. Our little secret then," Doctor Malik conceded.

"Good, I'd hate to lose a good surgeon out an airlock," the doctor said as he sat back, smiling.

"I agree. Hey! Did you just threaten me?" The surgeon retorted.

"No, it's just a reality if you forget the NDA, that's all. Remember you agreed, right?"

"Yes, the NDA, always the NDA. Like a club I get beaten with the NDA," Doctor Malik snapped.

"Excellent," the doctor said still smiling. "Just implement the protocols as we discussed and talk to no one else about this...development. If someone pushes hard send them to me."

"All right. Nothing else then?" Doctor Malik asked, rising again to leave.

"I don't think so. Thank you, Doctor for your insights. They were most helpful," Doctor Fillingraph stated.

He watched Doctor Malik leave. He still had the signal issue to deal with. He needed some way to block her ability to interact with peoples' minds; his for sure, other people were fun to watch after her interaction with them. However, that amusement might raise suspicions about what is happening. Those questions would be hard to answer. Therefore, he needed to solve this problem, and fast. Who could he get though? He needed someone who he could trust or throw out an airlock if need be. Unfortunately, those two things are not mutually exclusive, especially on this station with what is at stake. He also had the pain issue to deal with during core enlargement. The Nutrient Bath would only take care of the outer layer. Unfortunately, it affects every layer of the exoskeleton, inside and outside the body. So he needed something that worked everywhere at the same time. He decided he needed the signal blocking issues dealt with first. The pain management problem could wait a few days.

"Claudette, Display Personnel. Electrical Engineers, Level 1A technicians only."

List displayed.

Only a few names showed up. Not good. Someone would be missed if they *happened* to fall out an airlock one day.

"Claudette, highlight names with negative personnel actions, pending, administered, or covered up."

One name highlighted.

"Ah, we have our candidate, Tech Level 1A Welkin Melanochik. Claudette, select and display details."

Details displayed.

Bar fights planetside. Two personnel actions, for station infraction, and inappropriate behavior.

"Claudette, Display current status Melanochik, Welkin."

Rest cycle. On shift in four hours.

"Provide current location."

Crew quarters. Minimal lighting. Probable status: Sleeping.

"Claudette, start message: Report to Doctor Fillingraph, Prime Team HQ. Report at shift start. Bring manuals, theories, devices regarding electronic signal blocking. end message. Attach my credentials. Send."

Message sent.

"Claudette, display current status of Kolana, Tilkani."

Official status unknown.

"Claudette, provide current location."

Crew Quarters. Minimal lighting. Probable status: sleeping.

"Claudette, start message: *Report to Doctor Fillingraph.* End message. Attach my credentials. Send."

Message sent.

He thought while sitting at his desk that Kolana may have some insight on how to correct the pain issue during the enlargement phase. They would definitely need to solve that before proceeding further. This development was unprecedented before IG-3257-001's activation. Since her activation, however, the value of her feedback would be immeasurable.

Incoming VidCon request. Low Executrix Kolana.

"Claudette, Connect."

"What do you want now, Doctor?" Kolana said in an irritated voice.

"I wanted to discuss some developments that have arisen over core development," Fillingraph explained.

"Me? Why me?" She asked perplexed.

"Well, because you showed genuine concern about the situation, and that might just help me solve a problem I am having," the doctor said.

"I doubt I can help you," she replied.

"In any event, you need to file your first report. I am sure it's late by now. We would not want to rouse any suspicions."

"You said you had a team of people that would do that. What do you need me for?" Kolana retorted.

"We do and we don't need you...per se. It just looks better if you make your report in person sometimes. This is one of those times," the doctor clarified.

"Yeah, I am not coming." she quipped.

Transmission terminated, sir, Claudette stated the obvious.

He thought to himself *She might become a problem. He might have to be more...proactive about the situation.* He decided to check on the core statuses.

"Claudette. Display core statuses."

Core Status Displayed.

Model   *Status*

Military:
CC-3257-004   Exoskeletal Hardening Suppression Protocol (EHSP) begun. Delay Core Enlargement Until Further Notice (UFN)
CC-3257-005   Decommissioned
CC-3257-006   EHSP begun. Delay Core Enlargement -UFN
CD-3257-004   Decommissioned
CD-3257-005   EHSP begun. Delay Core Enlargement -UFN
CD-3257-006   EHSP begun. Delay Core Enlargement -UFN
CS-3257-035   EHSP begun. Delay Core Enlargement -UFN
CS-3257-036   EHSP begun. Delay Core Enlargement -UFN
CS-3257-037   EHSP begun. Delay Core Enlargement -UFN

Civilian:
ES-3257-009   EHSP begun. Delay Core Enlargement -UFN

ES-3257-010   EHSP begun. Delay Core Enlargement -UFN
IG-3257-001   EHSP begun. Core Enlargement - Pending
IG-3257-002   EHSP begun. Delay Core Enlargement -UFN
IG-3257-003   EHSP begun. Delay Core Enlargement -UFN

"Claudette, Status change, IG-3257-001, Delay Core Enlargement - Until Further Notice."

Status Updated. Core Enlargement IG-3257-001 delayed, UFN.

Doctor Fillingraph sat at his desk contemplating the pain issue for core development. He had to solve that, and quickly, to get core development back on schedule. "Claudette, show typical medical protocols for pain blocking, pain mitigation, and pain reduction."

Blocking - Nerve Blocking, Electro Stimulus, Local Anesthetic
Mitigation - General Anesthetic, Local Anesthetic
Reduction - Various Pharmaceuticals

He dismissed the reduction and mitigation protocols because they were either not effective, or they were the current protocols already in use. Nerve blocking and electro stimulus caught his eye.

"Claudette, Electro Stimulus, Overview."

Electrodes are placed at specific nerve clusters on the cerebral cortex to mitigate pain or other sensations. The electrical charge overloads the specific nerve clusters targeted and prevents signal reception. This is a short-term solution to provide temporary relief from pain. There has been some success with personal units designed to allow individuals to self-treat. The exterior connection electrodes attach to the connecting tissue between the neck plates closest to the head. When current is applied this deadens the closest nerve cluster preventing pain reception. CAUTION: Prolonged use will cause nerve damage by destroying the nerve receptors. Two weeks is the maximum time suggested for treatment. However, some studies have shown anecdotal evidence that there may be some success for up to three weeks.

He read this and thought, *This would have worked for the rectal detachment procedure they performed on all of the cores. It seemed straightforward; place a few electrodes and apply low voltage current to disrupt signal reception. However, this would not work for the long-term care needed during core enlargement where the core would undergo vast changes in size. They may also experience an enormous amount of pain as their nerve endings tore away in the process. The entire body would experience this over the time needed to enlarge the cores to a suitable size required based on the vessel being created. This new batch of cores, especially the Intergalactic ones, would spend years in this state and would not be suitable to use this method for pain reduction. He needed something else.*

"Claudette, Nerve Blocking, Overview," he said aloud.

A shunt is surgically placed near the pain processing ganglia; the neuroreceptors are bombarded with compounds that are designed to bind with the receptors. This bonding prevents signal transmission of any kind. Once the compounds are withdrawn, normal nerve function restores quickly. CAUTION: Short-term studies only encompassed procedures of 1-3 hours in duration. The long-term effects of multiple or repeated use of this protocol is not known. While it is expected to perform similarly for longer term procedures, these long-term protocols have not been supported by any known studies.

I think we have our candidate. He thought to himself.

"Claudette, InCorp TransCom"

Ready.

"To: Kestrel Malik;

Subject: Core Pain Elimination.

Doctor Malik, I believe I have found something that will assist us with the problem we discussed. Please review the materials and provide feedback on effectiveness and viability.

Attach Link: Nerve Blocking,

Attach Credentials; Send."

Doctor Fillingraph, Low Executrix Kolana is at your door. Claudette informed the Doctor.

"Open door," he stated. "Low Executrix Kolana. I was not expecting to see you after our last conversation."

"I was not going to come, but I was intrigued as to what I might assist you with," she replied.

"Actually, there are potentially two situations that you might be able to provide a different perspective on. One is that we were recently made aware that the cores—"

"You mean the children," LE Kolana corrected.

"No, I mean the *cores.* They stopped being children the moment they left their houses. Honestly, it will make it much easier for you if you stop thinking about them as children. That's what they hatched as, but they will die many, many years beyond their normal life span. Their lives will be much richer because they will have provided a great service to their race. For the Good of the Colony," Doctor Fillingraph explained.

"Don't start with that *Good of the Colony* garbage. I've heard that all my life. Normally, it is used to push an unpopular agenda like the water issue. You need to conserve water for the *Good of the Colony,*" she said with air quotes around the last *Good of the Colony.*

"What do you mean? Water is a very serious issue and the entire reason for this complex and these cores...especially the IG series," Doctor Fillingraph explained.

"The water level is down to 60% of what we had. We should have plenty of water for hundreds of more years or so," LE Kolana stated assured in her position.

"No, that is not the case. Where did you get your information from?"

"The VidFeed," she replied.

"That is complete propaganda, told to the population so they do not panic and throw our civilization into chaos... which they would if they knew the truth."

"What do you mean? What is the real number?" Kolana asked.

"I have not checked in several months, but it is nowhere near that number. Claudette? Water resources. Show percentage remaining and years remaining. Duplicate results on back panel."

Results Displayed. 12% of water resources are remaining. With current usage levels, adjusted for increases from supplementation, we have fifteen-point-five years remaining.

"No, that can't be correct!" She exclaimed.

"Unfortunately, it is correct; there are only fifteen and a half years before our planet has exhausted its water resources. This is close-hold information covered under the NDA you signed. We have one more generation before we die as a species. This project *cannot* fail. If it does, our race is doomed to extinction. As it stands right now, anyone not on one of these ships when they leave will die within less than a decade after departure. We are looking at three to four thousand people per IG series vessel, a little over ten thousand people saved, and will be the remaining population of our species. These people will rebuild our culture on another planet so that we may live on, as a species. We are seriously looking into crossing the Desolate Expanse to do it."

"The Desolate Expanse! No one can go in there. Every ship the military has sent in has been destroyed within in a month or two by unknown events. It is not possible," Kolana proclaimed.

"It is possible. The Paclids do it all the time. They discovered a time variance and duration interval of what they call the Desolation Wave."

"Desolation Wave? What is that?"

"The Paclids know little about it themselves. They know only that matter dissolves when the wave moves back into their area."

"Dissolves? What does that mean?" Kolana asked.

"Simply that matter breaks down at the molecular level. Matter does not stay cohesive."

"Then how do the Paclids stay in there for so long?

"They have developed technology that shields their ships from the effect of the Desolation Wave. With this shield active, the wave has no effect over anything contained within the shield. They had some early failures where the ship, not completely enclosed by the sphere was hit by the wave and destroyed. Now, they have a perfectly round ship because everything else outside the shield dissolved. They have perfected the technology to allow transmission of the shielding signal along the entire hull to protect everything inside," Doctor Fillingraph explained.

"Why don't we have this technology? Does it have military

applications?"

"Yes! It provides protection against energy based weaponry, which is why we have not attacked the Paclids for the last ten years or so."

"What? We have been fighting wars and battles against them during that time. Some guy just got a medal yesterday, I think for the latest battle."

"Yes, Commander...I mean Low Executrix Wilcon. Yes. He was given a medal but the *attack* or *battle* never occurred."

"How is that possible?" Kolana asked. "I have known friends in other units that went to fight and never returned; they were reported dead on the battlefield."

"Did you see bodies inside the coffins sent back? No. They were all closed caskets...sealed for the families' protection, blah, blah, blah. All lies. There were no wars or battles. The friends you lost were actually payments to the Paclids for things they are giving us...like water. They never died, they just live on a new planet as slaves or whatever the Paclids are doing with them, they could be food for all we know, so I guess they might be dead then."

"How does this go on without the government knowing? How can this happen!"

"It happens because we want to live. If we did not get regular water deliveries from *asteroids*... Paclid support paid with Andlid blood, then we would have run out of water a decade or so ago. Everyone alive today owes their lives to water bought via this secret alliance with the Paclids; not everyone in the government knows. Only a select few know."

"I-I just cannot wrap my head around this. Everything I know is a lie. Why am I in the military then?"

"Actually the military is our *money* pool to pay the Paclids. They are heavy on water resources and short on personnel, we are very heavy on personnel, and extremely short on water resources. If they stopped giving us water, we'd be dead in a few years. That is how dependent we are on their support. We trade our people for much needed water, and as far as I know, no one is actually killed because they need them for something. So your friends are probably all still alive on the Paclid planet."

"So how much water did this last war get us?" She asked.

"This last *war* was payment for the shield generating technology. We will need it if we are going to travel into the Desolate Expanse. We'll need a lot of them. We have Paclid technicians scheduled within the month to start training personnel how to build the shielding technology for our ships, right here on this station. That is why it is absolutely crucial that we get the problems we are having with the cores resolved. It is for the survival of our species, and we have only this one shot due to our limited resources and dwindling water supplies."

"Right, right, the core problem you called me about. What is the problem again?" Kolana asked.

"You interrupted me before I could tell you. We have discovered that even though the cores are sedated, they can still feel pain at the subconscious level."

"Well subconscious means they won't remember it, right? What's the problem?" Kolana asked.

"That's partially true. See, we have had a nagging problem with core failure later in development due to neurological stress. We could not determine where or how this stress was induced. Now we have credible information that the sub-conscious feels and remembers the pain... and most likely breaks when it can no longer deal with it. However, if we could find a way to stop the subconscious from feeling the pain as well, then we feel that would resolve most of the neurological issues we have experienced in the past," he explained.

"How did you find out that the *cores*," Kolana raised her hands and made air quotes as she said this. "experience and remember pain?"

"That is still classified...even after you signed the NDA...for now anyway. But we know for sure. Second, we need a way to block electrical signals."

"I know you definitely have experience with that," she stated with sarcasm.

"This is a different kind of signal, more subtle and not traceable because it does not use our network, but is of extremely limited range," Doctor Fillingraph could see that Kolana perked up when she heard there was a signal she might be able to use, but lost hope when she heard it was very short ranged.

"Why do you want to block it then?" She asked inquisitively.

"Well because it is distracting and very intrusive," he said.

"Intrusive? How so? How do you know it's intrusive? In what way is it distracting you?"

"It's very hard to explain. Suffice it to say I *can* experience it, others *have* experienced it, and it is very disconcerting. Other than this, I can't explain it any further."

"So, basically, it is a generic signal that you want blocked, but cannot or will not tell me more about it. Right?" She pried.

"Right. I can tell you it is electromagnetic in nature, just weak," he explained.

"Can you tell me what frequency it is on then?" She asked.

"Frequency? I am not really sure. Does it matter?" He asked.

"Sure it does. We use jammers on the battle...we are trained to use jammers on the battlefield even if we apparently do not use them."

"Jammers? What are those?" He asked.

"Devices that flood a specific spectrum of the electromagnetic field and prevent those channels from being used," she explained.

"What effect does it have on the source?"

"Depending on the strength, the source equipment could be overloaded and maybe burn up or explode, definitely circuits are broken."

"Oh no, we cannot have that. Is there a passive way to block the signal?" He asked.

"Sure, maybe. But the military has electrical engineers to figure that out."

"I have an engineer that is scheduled to report here soon."

"Well they should be able to figure it out then."

Doctor Fillingraph, Tech Melanochik is at the door, Claudette informed.

"Open door. Technician Melanochik, Thank you for coming," the doctor said in pleasing tones.

"How could I refuse, when the director of the whole entire program contacts you," Welkin explained.

"Introductions are in order. Low Executrix Tilkani Kolana, this is Engineer Level 1A, Welkin Melanochik. Tech Melanochik, this is Low Executrix Kolana, the military liaison to this operation."

The engineer shook Kolana's hand, and sat down next to her in the other empty chair in Doctor Fillingraph's office and asked, "Why am I here?"

"I thought I was clear in my TransCom. I need an electrical signal blocked. Low Executrix Kolana and I were just discussing that when you came in."

"I recommended jammers to flood the signal spectrum to prevent any signal," Kolana added.

"I dismissed that as too aggressive and potentially destructive...which we cannot have," Doctor Fillingraph explained.

"He does not even know the frequency of the signal he wants to block," she countered.

"That would be most helpful," Welkin added.

"I have no idea. What *frequency* does the brain operate on?" Doctor Fillingraph asked.

Kolana and Melanochik looked at each other, puzzled.

"Brain?" Kolana asked.

"You want to block brain signals?" Welkin asked with a smirk, then continued, "I would have no idea, I am an Electrical Engineer, not a neurologist," he almost started laughing outright.

"This is not a laughing matter," Doctor Fillingraph chided.

"Sure, sure *brain* signals. Oh, those *are* dangerous," said Welkin, not even attempting to hide his amusement anymore.

"I have to agree with the engineer here. They pose no issue at all," Kolana agreed somewhat more seriously.

"You would think so, but it is a problem," Doctor Fillingraph explained.

"Oh, yeah I am sure it is," said Welkin, winking at Kolana.

She smiled in spite of herself and the current situation.

"People, let's get back on topic. It is serious, trust me on this," Doctor Fillingraph stated.

"You're not one of those people that think the government is using satellites to listen to your thoughts, are you? I mean I did not see your foil hat, but it has to be here, somewhere," Welkin said, looking around trying not to break into full laughing mode.

"Funny." Is all Doctor Fillingraph said.

"Could you see him in a foil hat? It would be hysterical," Kolana said, laughing.

Why is everyone laughing at you Doctor? the disembodied voice said.

Ah, perfect timing he thought and then said to both of them, "I can prove it to you."

"I highly doubt that," Kolana said.

"You're not going to put on your foil hat are you?" Welkin said, breaking out in heavy laughter now, "That would be really hysterical."

No the problem is a serious one, and you should be a little more serious about it, the voice said.

Both Kolana and Welkin stopped laughing and immediately looked at each other.

"Not so funny now, is it?" Doctor Fillingraph said with a smile.

Kolana asked, "Uh...what was that?"

"How did you do that?" followed Welkin with his question.

"Me? I did nothing. What did you hear?" The doctor asked.

"I think I heard myself say I should take it more seriously," Welkin replied.

"Me too," said LE Kolana.

"It's even worse than that," Doctor Fillingraph explained.

Welkin just smirked his response.

He just called you a whack job.

"You really should not call people names especially like *whack job*, it's not very nice," Doctor Fillingraph stated.

"I-I did not say anything," stammered Welkin.

"Hey! This is what was happening to you when we were on the transport. You said you were talking to yourself, but you weren't, were you?" Kolana said with a glimmer of understanding.

"No, I was not. And yes, it was happening to me then. Now it is happening to you. Not very comfortable is it?" Doctor Fillingraph asked.

"Ah. So, you say we need to block brain waves. The picture is much clearer now and much less funny than I thought it would be," Technician Welkin stated.

"How is this possible?" Kolana asked.

"Before the cores were activated—"

"You mean abducted," she corrected.

No, he means started my growth into a starship. I volunteered, remember? the voice corrected her.

"You cannot volunteer. You are too young to know better," Kolana said aloud

Welkin looked at her a little puzzled, and said, "Huh?"

"I was not talking to you. I can see where this is a problem," Kolana agreed.

"Before their activation, they were given a regimen of genetic alterations to manipulate them at the genetic core level. One, in particular, developed extreme mental abilities. They had precognition, awareness of distant or unseen events, and wisdom beyond their years," Doctor Fillingraph explained.

"You did this to them, on purpose?" Kolana asked, incensed.

"Yes. They were selected as hatchlings. We were hoping to gain increases in mental capacity that would translate into increased functionality in the final version of the core. It seems we may have been too successful. We were hoping for an increase in perception that would translate into a more sensitive radar to sense objects around the vessel without the use of technology."

"Looks like you succeeded," Kolana said.

"Yes, it is much more powerful than we thought it would be. Not only can it read minds, it can project thoughts into them as well."

"What are you guys talking about?" Welkin asked.

"Do you know what we do on this space station?" Doctor Fillingraph asked him.

"We build spaceships of various sizes to meet our military and civilian contract requirements," Welkin explained his understanding.

"Great. That is exactly what you *should* know. But do you know how?" The doctor asked him.

"How? I thought we built them," he explained.

"Not build, so much as *grow*," Doctor Fillingraph corrected.

"Grow?" Welkin asked, perplexed.

"Yeah, and from little kids at that," Kolana added for effect.

"What? What are you talking about? I am completely lost. I only get into the ships after the hull has been manufactured. I run all the electrical systems and set up the control systems."

"We use a proprietary process that develops hatchlings into full blown ship hulls. It takes many years to grow a normal sized Andlid to the hull size required. The larger the hull, the longer the time needed to grow the exoskeleton into the proper size and shape."

"What are you saying? That I have been crawling around inside a...*living* thing?" Welkin asked feeling creepy.

"To put it bluntly, yes, you have."

"When I cut into the hull to run cabling or wires, do they feel it?" Welkin asked.

"That is an interesting question. Up until yesterday, I would have said 'No they don't feel a thing.' However, recent developments, suggest that they *do* feel something, even if at a subconscious level. And that feeling is enough to drive them crazy over time. Have you not heard the stories of bizarre crashes, ship shutdowns or other things that cause ship deactivation?"

"Sure, but I thought they were exaggerations," Welkin stated.

"They are not. It seems that the core at the subconscious level remembers the pain, and when the threshold it exceeded, they commit suicide to end the pain. Of course, we did not realize this until just today, mind you, so we were just as perplexed at the failure rates later on in ship development," Doctor Fillingraph explained.

"How did you find out then?" Welkin asked.

I told him, the voice said.

"I see now why you want to block brain waves. This one core was the first then to display this ability?" Welkin concluded.

"Yes, but while I think they are the key to correct our neurological problems later on in development, I do not want them probing my thoughts at their leisure either," Doctor Fillingraph said.

"I would imagine you do not. From what little I know about you thus far I don't want to know what you are thinking either," Welkin said

He plans to throw you out an airlock when he is done with you, the voice said.

Tech Welkin started fidgeting in his seat, his eyes went wide with fear, "What have you gotten me into, Doctor?"

"I am asking for your help?"

"When are you going to throw me out an airlock?" Welkin asked.

"See? Now that is why I cannot have people poking around inside my head, it spoils the surprise," Doctor Fillingraph said with a smile.

"He has already threatened me with that very thing. I even checked what system records I could. There are an unusually high number of airlock incidents at this place. I doubt he is bluffing," Kolana added.

"Well I am not going to work for you then!" Welkin stated empathically.

"The people that make those statements to me...tend to end them in space," he said with threatening seriousness.

"What do you mean?"

"I mean that you will do what I ask and *maybe* I will not throw you out an airlock. Maybe you're a sleepwalker and inadvertently find yourself in space one evening. It would be a peaceful way to go. I have already updated your medical records to show you have had sleepwalking bouts in the last few weeks."

"I have not."

"That is the good thing about dead people: they do not get to tell their story. Only the paper trail that is left behind will tell the story. Yours will be, increased pressure for the two incidents caused you to start sleepwalking and one evening, somehow you found your way into an airlock. It was sealed shut, but then opened to space, killing you in the process. We'll never know what you were dreaming, just that it ended in your tragic accidental death. Right, Low Executrix Kolana?"

"Right. He threatened me with my room just falling away from the space station and leaving me exposed to space to die almost instantly. I have five of the six planes in my room surrounded by space, only the wall with the door in attached to the main structure," Kolana said.

"It would be tragic if your structure failed, it is an older design. The engineers say it is still structurally sound though, but who knows really," Doctor Fillingraph said with a grin.

"So what you are saying is that either way, at this point I am going out an airlock?" Welkin asked.

"No. Let's amend the statement to say this: If you agree to help then there is a possibility you may not end up out an airlock. However, if you turn me down right now. I would probably discuss my disappointment and start to escort you from my office, engaging you in polite conversation. So much so, that you would not notice where we were approaching. I would move to the door, hit the button, grab your neck, throw you in and seal the door behind you. By the time you got off the ground I would already be pressing the button to open the airlock. It would end our relationship *and* my problems with you not accepting my offer," Doctor Fillingraph said with a sinister look on his face.

"So I help you, do what I am told, forget everything I heard and I might live?" Welkin asked.

"I would say that is a fair assessment. Would you not agree, Low Executrix Kolana?"

"I agree. It is essentially the same offer I got," she stated.

There is still a chance, but you have no other options. If you want to live past today...past this very minute...then I would accept his offer. I would also appreciate it because I cannot stand hearing his thoughts. They are so dark and tormented that I cannot stand them. He is an evil man. Please help me, the voice said to Welkin.

Low Executrix Kolana, he does not want to admit it but he needs you far more than he told you. The military has been after him for years. Apparently the last liaison only lasted a few weeks before his early, 'departure.' He is afraid if that happens again, there may be some deeper investigations, that he could not control, taking place. He needs you to stay with the program. I need you to stay with the program. I want to go into space. This was the best way I know for it to happen. Please, for me, to allow me to become what I want to become, please help him. Do not worry about who I was. That was another life for me. This is who I am now."

"Does he really care about your suffering?" She asked aloud.

Both Doctor Fillingraph and Welkin at looked at her. Doctor Fillingraph smiled and said, "See? It's not so easy to talk to her."

Yes, he does. I think he was genuinely surprised that I could feel any pain. I did not sense any deception. In fact, in his own way he is trying to make it better...as best he can, anyway. Threatening people is not the right way, but it is his way. Oh and you can think your response to me and I'll hear it, The voice explained.

Interesting and thank you for the information. I will consider helping him, if only for your sake. Kolana thought and then said aloud, "I am getting along just fine." She thought, *What should I call you?*

You should not know my real name. That may present problems for everyone, you especially. Let me think...how about 'In Sidera Navi' as my name in this new life? The voice asked.

Insidera Navi sounds nice but how about I just call you Sidera? She thought.

Actually, it is two words In and Sidera, but Sidera will work fine, Sidera said back.

Okay Sidera it is. How do I contact you if I need you for something? Kolana thought.

You just need to be close to me, so I can hear your thoughts, if I can hear you that is. Apparently I cannot hear everything, there are...times when I cannot talk to anyone. I do not know why this happens, but it does. Maybe you can help me figure out why that is. Anyway, if I hear you, I will respond, Sidera said.

"So what do you think LE Kolana? Will that work?" Doctor Fillingraph asked.

"What? Will what work?" she asked.

"Tech Welkin suggested a conductive wire mesh that would surround my office and blanket everything with the wire mesh as a passive means to block the signal," Doctor Fillingraph explained.

"I guess that would work? However, the mesh would have to carefully configured to block the signal completely. Longer wavelengths would require a tighter mesh to block them."

"Agreed. Excellent insight, Low Executrix," Welkin said, "I guess we are back to the original question you asked that seemed so silly then. What wavelength does the brain operate on?"

"What scale do you need it in?" The doctor asked.

"I just need the frequency of the wave form," the engineer replied.

"Claudette, show brain activity, wave form frequency. Display on back panel."

Brain activity is active at between .5-100 frequency intervals.

Listed in descending order:

Gamma 100-38;

Beta 38-15;
Alpha 14-8;
Theta 7-4;
Delta 3-0.5

"Only 0.5? That is tiny. It will be hard to block those signals. You need an almost solid sheet or a tightly woven and overlapping mesh patterns to block those amplitudes. Even one hundred would present a problem. We typically work on the thousands, millions or billions of cycles per second, not one cycle or half cycle per second. That is ridiculous," Melanochik said.

"You cannot help me then?" Doctor Fillingraph said, implying Melanochik's usefulness was at an end.

"No! No, I did not say that. I just said I am used to working on a much different scale. It will be difficult to change scales, not impossible mind you. I can do it, it will just take some time and the proper calculations," Tech Melanochik reassured.

"Well get to it then," Doctor Fillingraph charged.

I could help you as well, Sidera said.

"I think that would be most helpful," Welkin replied, "If I could just take some measurements that would be a start," and then started toward the door of Doctor Fillingraph's office.

"Get measuring then," stated Doctor Fillingraph, "Low Executrix Kolana, can you assist Tech Melanochik in gathering his measurements and devising a passive blocking solution?"

"Yes, I can help him. What about the report you wanted me to send?" She asked.

"Oh, yes. You want to comply now? This is an interesting turn of events. You can use my console. Have a seat. Claudette, Low Executrix Kolana, display contact schedule."

First contact: Father, Algae Farmer.

"Establish connection," Doctor Fillingraph stated.

Connection initiated, Claudette responded, *connection made.*

An older man appeared on the VidFeed and it seemed like they could relate to LE Kolana. LE Kolana went through with the predetermined conversation giving the answers expected. The question, "Have you talked with your mother yet?" Was a question for 'Had she seen the cores?'

She replied, "Yes," she had talked to her mother.

Then the response to the question "How is she doing?" This answered the real question, 'Were there any issues?'

She replied, "Everything is fine. She is doing wonderfully," which meant she had seen the process of creation and there were no glaring differences from what was expected - a blatant lie on her part, but it was necessary, for everyone's concern.

Thank you, came the response from Sidera.

The next question was about how she was adjusting to space. This asked directly about Doctor Fillingraph.

She said, "Space always takes getting used to, but this time it seems harder, more difficult," which conveyed the truth they already knew; working with Doctor Fillingraph was not going to be easy. This was not an eye opening issue, either. They had their intelligence gathering as well. "Dad. I have to go now. It was good to hear your voice," she said before she signed off.

"Very good. I liked how you talked about me. You were very convincing and truthful, which sold it even more. See? We'll make a good team, you and I," he said smiling at her.

"I don't have much choice do I?" She reasoned.

"No, not really." He affirmed her position, "Help Tech Melanochik now."

"All right, I am on my way," she replied as she walked out of the room.

17 ENTANGLEMENT

Low Executrix Tilkani Kolana walked out of Doctor Fillingraph's office and made her way towards Melanochik's working area. She was deep in thought about her position here, and how it had been corrupted, but she soon realized that this was the way it was supposed to work out. There were apparently forces in the military that knew what was happening here, and she was sent here anyway. *Why send me, if they already knew?* This was the question that was eating at her. There had to be *some* reason, some *rationale* that required her to be here. There had to be something she could fulfill on this Divinity forsaken station.

She had never been much for religious beliefs, but after seeing the atrocities carried out on this station, she needed someone...some*thing* larger than herself, to help her through these times. She had never bought into the theory of the Divine Egg that gave birth on this lifeless planet, creating the Andlid race. It seemed too convenient...too contrived to be an actual event. Most scientists say the Pacand race...Andlid forebearers before the recorded history...mutated from common antling stock. One could still see them today, building their little sand habitats to live in. They served one Queen, unlike the Andlid race that had shed the one Queen paradigm to adopt a more shared, hierarchical construct.

The imagery was undeniable...with a few key differences. Antlings retained their antennae, which the Andlids had long ago shed. The vestiges could be seen on their faces. Where the antennae used to attach and carry chemical markers to the brain, was now a collection port of sorts. Chemical smells are now forcibly collected instead of passively stumbled upon; this was integrated with the Andlid breathing system. Air could be drawn in and a scent pulled from a distance away. The minute hairs in the nasal housing provides directionality, allowing them to perform the function the antennae but in a greater, more efficient manner. Other than this distinction, Andlids

153

looked exactly like the non-sentient antlings that shared their world. Other than the antlings walk on all six of their legs, and Andlids evolved into upright walking.

This point had always interested her, because she could find no reason they should have decided to walk on two legs, instead of four...or six...like their unevolved counterparts. There seemed no logical answer, the scientists were also in disagreement. One group claimed Andlids gained an advantage over others by increasing our perspective, and could therefore see farther, and identify colony threats quicker. Another group claimed that walking on only two legs afforded four arms and hands to manipulate objects, thereby increasing our effectiveness as a species because each worker could be more productive. Still another group said it was just a mutation. It proved successful, and therefore it flourished and propagated. Kolana believed it was probably a mixture of all three.

She approached Technician Melanochik's door. It was open, and she could hear him moving about, searching through his tools, looking for specific objects. She reached out and knocked on the threshold of the door.

"Hello?"

The noise startled him as he balanced the group of tools in his hands. He managed to control them so he did not drop any, but it was a funny sight to watch his arms flail about trying to catch everything. She saw now why four hands might be useful. She chuckled inwardly at the sight.

"Oh! Hi," he said. After he had gained control of all his tools he said, "Sorry about that, I was not expecting you, and you startled me."

"I am sorry, it's my fault I should have warned you."

"How? By knocking? You did that, remember?" He jested back.

" I guess I did, but I did not mean to startle you," she said.

"I know, it is a byproduct of me getting lost in what I am doing, I tend to not notice other things until...well it surprises me," he said and smiled back at Kolana.

"Are you almost ready to start working on the frequency issue?" She asked.

"Yes. I am just looking for my frequency analyzer," he stated.

"I don't know what that looks like or I would help you."

"It's a gray metal box with many little dials and a round window with lines scribed on it for measurements," he explained.

"Is that it? Right behind your head on that shelf," She said pointing to a gray box with a round screen on it.

He froze and turned his head slowly to see where she was pointing at and said, "You have a good eye, Low Executrix. It would have bit me if it were alive. Thank you, that was the last tool I needed."

"Do you need any help carrying your equipment?" She asked politely.

"No, thank you. The Divinity blessed me with enough arms to carry my burden," he said as he smiled back at her.

Oh, great, she thought. *He's an egg cracker*, and then she asked again. Can I help you carry your tools? I am more than capable of sharing your load," She smiled, knowing the response.

"No, thank you. I am capable of carrying my load. The Divinity blesses me so," he said as he humbly bowed his head.

"I was not saying that you could not, I was just offering assistance. A shared burden is no burden at all," she spouted the religious slogan required in this situation.

"I'm sorry. You did not strike me as a Follower of the Divinity," he said.

"I grew up in the faith, but have moved...beyond those teachings," she explained.

"Ah. A fallen believer is lost indeed," he said with another smile and a slight bow.

"I am not fallen, per se. I just moved on to a different belief system," she explained.

"There is none other than the Divine," he replied.

"My belief is more science-based now instead of mystical beliefs," she explained.

"Turning to science is not turning your back on the Divinity. The Divinity created all, and in so doing, they are within everything. Science is a gift of the Divinity to allow understanding of the Universe. By turning to science you are serving the Divinity," he simply stated.

"I don't think so. Science says we mutated from antlings...like the ones we see all the time scurrying around in the sand. We even built our houses as they did, until modern building practices took hold building with metal and the like. With science, they say we evolved from these lesser forms to our current form. The similarities are too remarkable not to notice: We have six limbs, they have six limbs, they have two eyes, albeit compound, we have two eyes, which are not compound. We have pheromones, they have pheromones, some colonies have Queens, others don't, like us. Science as even traced our closest ancestors to two or three different species that were are 99.97% similar too. It's that last .03% that differentiates us from them: our size, eyes, noses, walking upright, etc. So if we all came from the same egg and they are 99.97% like us, then why us, and not them?" She pondered.

"The Divinity moves in mysterious ways. Who can say why they chose us to rise up, but chosen we were. The Divinity guides us and in so doing changes us ever so slightly, every day. Eventually, we are not who we were a hundred, a thousand, or even ten thousand years ago. Make no mistake, chosen we are," he said.

"Yeah, I don't see it. Let's just choose to disagree on this. We are almost there," she replied.

The question of the Divinity always bothered me, Sidera interjected.

How so Sidera? Kolana thought.

"Another disbeliever," Tech Melanochik said.

The rules seemed more set up to model good behavior and identify what was expected, and not so much belief in the Divinity, Sidera stated.

"The rules lead to the Divine behavior that will be rewarded in the next life," he said.

Where is this next life? Can we go there and see it? How do we know it exists? Sidera asked.

"The next life is a state of being beyond comprehension of mortals. Only through sacrifice of service can you achieve entrance to the great beyond. Some believe the great beyond is in the Desolate Expanse, somewhere in the middle of the vast emptiness is the Divine Colony. This is where everyone goes when they die. The righteous live as kings and queens whereas the non believers and criminals are their servants."

"Yeah I still don't believe that," Kolana said, "I think when you die, you're dead."

I am inclined to agree with Low Executrix Kolana on this, Sidera added.

"How can a sentient ship be so blinded to the Divinity. If not through the will of the Divinity, how could you be created?" Tech Melanochik added.

It was not through the Divinity's will. It was purposeful genetic manipulation that I came to be in this place. I chose to be here, mind you, but the Divinity did not guide me. It was my own decision—

"Which you were not old enough to decide," Kolana added.

So you say. But decide I did, and here I am. The genetic manipulations allowed me to communicate with you and have this discussion about the Divinity. However, they had no hand in my choosing.

"Really? Did not the Divinity whisper something to you, beckoning you to the stars to allow you to see the opportunity for what it was?" The engineer asked.

No, I was being manipulated from hatching. I had no say in the matter until much later...right before I came to the station. I was told my family would not be harmed, just like they others and they weren't, as promised, Sidera added.

Oh, Honey, I am not sure, they are most likely dead. Kolana thought.

What? He lied to me! He said no one in my family would be hurt. They are dead? Sidera said with menacing tones.

I can show you the VidFeed if you like. Maybe they will tell you something that I can't. Kolana thought.

Maybe I can tap into your optic nerves to see what you are seeing, I'll try it. Bring up the VidFeed, Sidera said.

Okay. I'll bring up the VidFeed. There is a live feed right now from the Hall Of Authority. She was watching the High Authority speak about the terrible attacks when she noticed her vision starting to blur.

Sorry! Sorry, that was me. I started to overload your optical nerves, but I backed off, It should be fine now, Sidera said.

They both watched as the High Authority recounted the event that played out that evening and how one man...Low Executrix Wilcon...had stopped them.

That's my Dad! He is not dead, but my family was the only family not killed?" Sidera asked.

Yes, it seems that they were the only family that survived that evening. Every other family was slain for their child's selection into this program. She thought back.

What? No, that cannot be. They said...'he' said...no one would be hurt, Sidera reeled from this new piece of information.

They are calling it a terrorist attack. I was told this was where you came from, and if you, then the others too. And if them as well, but your family lived, then their families died. Kolana thought.

"I am ready to start taking measurements. You should communicate so I can take readings," Technician Melanochik stated, but no one answered.

Do you think the others know? Kolana asked.

I doubt it. They only know what they are told. I only know because you showed me, so I know they know nothing at all, Sidera clarified.

What are you going to do then? Kolana thought.

I am going to fight back, Sidera said, *I am going to make him pay for lying to me, to them, to everyone...even you, Low Executrix Kolana.*

"You know you can call me Tilkani...Ti for short," LE Kolana said.

"Sure thing Ti. I am getting some good readings. Keep it up," Tech Melanochik said.

"I...er...that wasn't...never mind," Kolana said back. She focused back on Sidera, *What are you going to do to him?* thought.

"I do not know yet, but I will make his life miserable for what he did to those other families. I will...until he is dead," Sidera said.

You're going to kill him? Ti thought.

No, you misunderstand. I will live hundreds, maybe thousands of years beyond a normal Andlid lifespan, and so I will way outlive him," Sidera corrected.

Oh, that makes more sense. You were getting a little dark there for a second. Kolana thought.

I could never kill anyone. I am just going to make his life miserable from now on, whenever I can, Sidera informed.

We are doing measurements to build something to prevent that very thing.

I know. But we have to alter the design a little, Sidera conceded.

How?

I do not want to be bombarded with his thoughts...they are very disturbing—but I am learning a great deal from them, Sidera realized.

Once it is in place, you won't be able to contact him. Kolana thought.

Could a door or window be placed to allow a signal to pass through, but be closed when I want it to? Sidera asked.

I don't know. Let's find out, she thought. "Tech Melanochik, could you rig a device that was triggered by one of these very specific frequencies?" Kolana probed.

"Can I create a device that can transform a signal to cause something else to happen via a mechanism?"

"Yes, that is the question. Is it possible?" Kolana asked.

"Yes. I think I can. Once a specific waveform is identified and isolated, then yes, I should be able to program a device to recognize it and then perform an action," the engineer replied.

"Great! What measurements do you need?" Kolana asked.

"I need the specific wave form to look for and I need ten to fifteen different transmissions to make an amalgam to allow an algorithm to select the proper sequence."

Did you get that? Kolana thought to Sidera.

I have a phrase picked out, Sidera replied.

"Are you ready to record?" Kolana asked Melanochik.

"Yes," came the reply.

"Record." *Go.*

Coerce Doctor Fillingraph. Coerce Doctor Fillingraph. Coerce Doctor Fillingraph... Sidera completed the response the requested fifteen times, and then said, *Done.*

"Stop," said Kolana.

But, for some reason, he had already stopped recording a second before, "I just stopped when you said that," he stated.

"Good." She replied, "Can you use that to build a control device to receive that specific waveform and then perform a function?" Kolana asked.

"Yeah, the waveforms are fairly precise, uniform and long enough not to be confused with random emissions on the same frequency," the engineer replied.

How many devices do we need? Kolana asked Sidera.

Let's have four devices, Sidera replied.

Four?

Yes. Three I have a plan for, and the last will be held in reserve for a future requirement, Sidera said.

"Will you make four devices that operate when this waveform is received?" Le Kolana asked.

"Sure. What operation do you want? There is rotational, pushing or pulling," he replied.

"I am not sure what we need either." *Sidera?* Kolana asked.

Here is the thing. I would like you to install operational trapdoors; three of them to open a corner of his sleeping quarters to me, while he is sleeping, Sidera said.

"Okay which *he* are we talking about?" Welkin asked.

You know who, he *is. Doctor Fillingraph. The one you are taking the readings for, to build his cage. That* he. Sidera explained.

"Whoa, whoa, whoa! You want me to install something that does the very thing he wants prevented? That sounds like airlock visiting crazy," he said back.

If you do it right, he will not know, and it will only be at night when he is sleeping, Sidera said.

"Also I think he wants it visible in his office, so he can see it," Welkin replied.

"Well then tell him that that is not feasible, it will look funny, and that it would be faster if handled from outside," Sidera said.

"I don't think he thinks it is that much of a hurry to get this installed. I think he thinks this is nuisance prevention instead of security prevention."

Well maybe I should change his mind then, Sidera insinuated.

How can you do that? Kolana thought.

By turning up the pressure. Wait a minute, I will be busy for a few minutes, Sidera responded.

"What is she doing?" Asked Tech Welkin.

"I have no idea, but I have a feeling I do not want to be on her bad side," Kolana said assuredly.

"I agree, I do not want to be on her bad side either," Welkin agreed.

"So you'll make the devices then and install a controllable window for her to use to open a window to his mind as it were?" LE Kolana asked.

"I guess I don't have much of a choice in this matter, do I? Right now, I think she could be much worse than Doctor Fillingraph and his threats. He is one and done. She? Well she could haunt you forever if she wanted, couldn't she?" Welkin said as a shiver ran up the back of his carapace.

"I think not helping her is a bad call, and remember she is still just a little girl at this point," Kolana said.

"Yes she is, but she has some frightening abilities already. Who knows what she'll be able to do in the future?" Welkin pondered.

"You think there is more she can do?" Kolana asked, starting to second-guess her decision.

"I have no idea, but I did not peak until mid to late teens. How old is she now? What growing does she have yet to do?"

"I-I don't know, really. Could she get stronger?" Kolana asked with a glimmer of hope that maybe one day she could tell everyone the truth. Maybe Sidera would help. She would have to think on that more.

"Hey, could you rig a cage for my room as well? I know I have five sides to space already so it should be fairly straight forward."

"I guess. Get me the material, and I can do it for you," he said.

"Okay, what materials do I need?" LE Kolana asked.

"Well, that I am not 100% sure about yet. I will have to conduct some calculations, determine the material, and the mesh pattern needed, but looking at these readings it will almost be solid," Welkin stated.

Done! Sidera exclaimed.

"What do you mean done? What did you do?" LE Kolana asked aloud.

Easy. I gave him incentive to complete the project as quickly as possible, Sidera said gleefully.

"How did you do that?" She asked for more clarification.

I showed him who was boss, well who was the boss of me, Sidera said.

"He *is* the boss," Welkin interjected.

Well he may be the boss of you, but not me, and he knows that now, Sidera said.

"How does he know it?" Kolana asked aloud.

Let's just say he will have a headache for a while, Sidera said with pride.

"What did you do? How did you make him see you were your own boss?" Kolana asked with an uneasy feeling gnawing at her.

You know how I tapped into your optical nerves and I almost overloaded them? Sidera started.

"Yes," Kolana answered.

Pain receptors are even easier to overload, Sidera finished.

"What did you do?" Kolana asked, already sensing what was coming.

I overloaded his pain receptors until he collapsed. I did it a couple of times in fact. Now we have an understanding. I am the boss of me and he knows it now and wants that mesh installed, Sidera boasted.

"Good side," was all Welkin said.

"Right, agreed, good side," Kolana echoed.

Awe, you guys do not have to fear me, Sidera tried to soothe them, *I would never do what I did to him, to you. He is an evil man, and I treated him like he treats others. I gave him a taste of his own medicine as it were,* Sidera attempted to explain.

Welkin's BioMet pad sounded that he received a TransCom. It was from Doctor Fillingraph. He opened and read it.

"You won't believe this, but Fillingraph just gave me the green light to install in the fastest manner possible. Looks are not relevant."

See? Told you I could do it, Sidera gloated.

"Good Side," Kolana said.

"Good Side," Welkin echoed.

18 POWER STRUGGLE

Doctor Fillingraph sat back in his chair, a deep sense of accomplishment filled him as he worked through what he had orchestrated. He ran through the details in his head.

He had worked on the passive signal blocking started, he had a potential candidate for the pain blocking protocol and Low Executrix Kolana seemed more willing to capitulate. But the pain issue started a nagging question Welkin brought up: Do the cores still feel pain after the metalification is complete? There may be some evidence to suggest that might be the case. Then he found another problem he had to solve. How could he solve this? The shunt might solve localized problems, but he could not imagine leaving them attached forever. There were plans to use the nerves to control ship functions. However, if leaving the nerves imbedded also causes sensations, which would be an issue. Apparently he could not have things both ways.

"Claudette, InCorp TransCom"

Kestrel Malik;

Subject: Prolonged Sensation after Metalification.

Doctor Malik, it has come to light that the core may feel sensations even after the metalification process has completed. This would increase stress on the core subconscious, and could undermine any gains achieved by eliminating the pain during procedures. Need insight on how to mitigate this new problem without functionality loss.

Attach Credentials. Send."

Well he did not solve the problem, but it is well on its way to being resolved, he thought.

I will still feel things after I am made metal? Sidera asked.

Yes, it seems there may be a possibility, and I want to see if we can avoid that problem. he thought back.

How will I still feel things when I am made metal? She asked.

161

Well, we leave your nerves in place and tap into them in various locations. The taps provide control mechanisms for various functions that you would control. Move a finger this door opens, move your elbow this door opens, things like that. We never considered that they would still feel sensations from the metal. Had we thought about it more we should have known, the nerves were still completely functional, we just never dreamed they would pick up sensations from the metal parts. However, heat and vibrational sensations might still propagate to allow feeling these types of sensations; the vibrational sensations could be from a very long distance; metal is an excellent conductor of vibrational waves. Even the hull exposed to the extreme cold of space could be felt—Hold it! That's it!

What is it Doctor? Sidera asked.

"The extreme coldness of space would apply constant input to the nerves," Fillingraph said, walking around his quarters. "The nerves would pick up the sensation of cold, and send that signal to the brain. There would be an almost constant feeling of this sensation that the core could do nothing about. This would surely weigh heavily on the subconscious and would explain all later core failures...they could no longer stand the input."

"Claudette, InCorp TransCom."

Kestrel Malik;

Subject: Sensory Overload extreme cold Hull Exposure.

Doctor Malik, I have had a breakthrough! If the nerves were left in place, then they would feel all sensations, even the extreme cold radiating inward. They would pick this up and relay this almost constantly, across the entire hull structure. This huge sensory input would be completely overwhelming, and would lead to the eventual core failure...of every core. This is a huge design flaw, we could not see until now. This not only affects this program, but all previous ships produced. We need to meet immediately and discuss options.

"Attach Credentials. Send."

He thought to himself, *This had to be the solution he was looking for, not only stopping the pain during the process, but stopping all sensation after ship completion.*

Incoming VidCon request, Malik, Kestrel, Claudette intoned.

"Accept. Doctor Malik, Good to hear from you. Did you get my two TransComs?"

"Yes. The second one is far more disturbing. This has implications even with active vessels currently deployed."

"I agree," Doctor, Fillingraph stated.

"But how to proceed?" Doctor Malik queried.

"Total product recall," Doctor Fillingraph stated simply.

"Total product recall! Are you mad? This has never happened and would be unprecedented. We do not even have a solution yet!" Exclaimed Doctor Malik.

"I agree, but we need to take action immediately. Each day that passes means that another core could fail. We need them to come into the station to begin the warming process to mitigate the extreme cold their hulls have been exposed to."

"We don't have the room for them right now, not with our current project proceeding."

"Well, we'll have to get creative to solve the problem. For instance, the three IG bays could house two carriers each, and each of the other bays could house similar sized ships. Our project is in its infancy, and we will not require such space for years even. So we could make it happen."

"Okay, but we don't even have a replacement protocol yet to fix the problem," Doctor Malik explained.

"We'll have to come up with one quickly. Until then I am moving forward with a complete fleet-wide recall of our vessels." Fillingraph opened a new connection.

"Claudette, TransCom, All currently operational Ship Operators;

Subject: Immediate Mandatory Ship Recall.

All, We have just been made aware of a ship design flaw that could result in catastrophic failure of your ship. You are required to pilot your vessel immediately to SpaceCon Industries' Ship Production Orbital Platform for immediate repairs. Compliance is Mandatory. Please make note of Section I, subsection 1 paragraph a). Delivery Acceptance Terms: Fulfillment of any recall notice is mandatory. Noncompliance will result in suspension of the maintenance portion of ship upkeep by SpaceCon Industries, which guarantees certain ship failure.

Special Note: During en route transit to the facility run with maximum tolerable heat levels for any area next to the outer hull. Implement consolidation protocols to central areas for localized cooling for occupants to allow even greater temperatures in the outer hull areas. It is imperative that the outer hull be heated to counteract any cold exposure from space. Do not, however, attach electrodes to the hull to provide electric stimuli for heating, use only environmental systems to provide heat required. Nor should you heat the interior beyond levels too hot to touch by occupants. The repair procedures should be of limited time requirements, and docking procedures will follow in future TransComs.

Attach credentials. Send."

"We don't have a fix yet! How can we do this?" Doctor Malik said exasperated.

"Come to my office, and bring a design engineer. We'll get a fix right now. We have to," Doctor Fillingraph said.

"Of course we do *now*, because you told everyone to come. You should have waited until we had a solution before you did that," Doctor Malik stated.

"How many more ships would we have lost? I cannot tell you how many, but I do know by bringing them into the station we can warm the hulls and mitigate further damage. I stopped the bleeding. Now we need to fix the problem. Besides, it will be a few days before all the ships arrive. We have some time to get the solution."

"But will that be enough?" Doctor Malik asked, unsure of the possibilities.

"It will have to be. We are some of the smartest minds we have. If we cannot come up with a solution, there is no solution," Doctor Fillingraph explained.

"I hope you're right. I'll grab a lead engineer and head your way."

"Right. Claudette, End VidCon."

There has to be a way. I have to make sure more ships do not fail. Besides, having them come immediately will put a fire under his Hotshot team to correct the problem. There has to be a solution.

The main crux of the problem was that the cores still feel, even after metalification. There had to be a way to stop that. *Insulation?* Maybe, but eventually insulation would be breached by the extreme cold outside and then the same problem would ensue. Besides, you could not insulate the completed ship designs already in service. *There has to be a way.*

What are you thinking about, Doctor? Sidera asked.

"We just came to a realization that, even after metalification, you will still feel sensations, from heat and cold, maybe even damage," he explained.

I know. I helped you come to this realization. I am glad that you moved to immediately correct the problem. It shows you have some decency, Sidera explained.

Right, right. Anyway, I was concerned about service contracts and long-term liabilities to SpaceCon Industries more than anything else, Doctor Fillingraph explained.

Ah, that makes much more sense, Sidera conceded.

My main focus is finding a solution to fix our existing inventory to prevent ship failures. This fix will also serve to help your progress as well. The currently fielded designs will have to be retrofitted, which will lead to patches and overall less professional appearance. Yours will be much more elegant and integrated. Doctor Fillingraph thought.

Well at least I can be of some assistance, Sidera said.

IG-3275-001, you've been of the greatest assistance. We would not know about any of the pain issues without you and your involvement will improve our entire program, even correcting design flaws in our already delivered fleet. Doctor Fillingraph thought.

My name is In Sidera Navi. Please use this when you talk to me. Sidera if you like, she explained.

Sidera? Where did you get that name? And I will do no such thing, you are IG-3275-001, Inter-Galactic-initialized 3275 year, first in the series. You are a ship, not a person. Not anymore. Doctor Fillingraph scolded.

There has been a long history of giving ships names, Sidera countered.

Agreed, but the occupants name the ship, not the other way around.

Not this time! My name is In Sidera Navi. My ship's design designation is IG-

3275-001, but that only defines my shape and my function, not who I am, Sidera proclaimed.

"You impertinent little child! You will do as I say!" Doctor Fillingraph spat aloud as he sat up in his chair and looked at the ceiling.

Or what, you will kill me? Remember I am already dead, so no threat there. And, if you do so, your entire program will fail. Every ship will fail, our species will die. Me? My die is already cast, yours is another story. If this program fails, I am sure you will be dead, probably shoved out an airlock you so fondly use. Our species will either die on the planet, or die en route to wherever you are sending us. Either way there is certain doom. No, Doctor, you are in no position to force me to do anything.

"You're not really dead!" He spat at the disembodied voice as he slammed his fists on his desk, "Are you?"

Of course I am. You killed me in my house. I am no longer a little child. I am going to be your crowning achievement. Or, I will be your ultimate disaster, which results in both our deaths. So, yes, I am already dead, and you did it! Sidera replied with conviction.

"Why I am going—"

Going to what? You cannot do any worse to me than you already have. That surgery was unbearable; I barely survived it. Besides, you need me. Everything will fail without me, and I have to cooperate. If I did not comply willingly, your program will fail. So let us put things in proper perspective, Doctor! You need me far more than I need you. You will treat me with respect, call me by my chosen name and ensure that I am bestowed this name upon delivery, In Sidera Navi. My internal voice will respond to Sidera, just as your office's voice responds to your wife's name, Claudette. See, Doctor? I know things too! Sidera responded.

"How do you know about my wife?"

Your subconscious thinks about her a lot. That horrible man you work for, I can see how you came to be the way you are. But you need to pick a different way now, consciously choose different behavior.

"You can read my conscious *and* subconscious thoughts?" Doctor Fillingraph asked horrified.

Yes, and they are both very disturbing. Your subconscious is always plotting, plots within plots, looking for every angle, minor leverage points you can use against people, anything to manipulate someone to your designs, Sidera explained.

"Stay out of my head!" Doctor Fillingraph shouted, holding his head in an attempt to shield himself from her.

I wish that I could. You are too close for me not to hear your thoughts. I am bombarded with them all day and night long. Even during your sleep cycles your subconscious churns away, plotting and scheming. I cannot stand it anymore. I cannot wait for the passive barrier to be completed, Sidera stated.

"You will comply!" He seethed.

You will comply! She stated, and then started screaming, She activated his pain receptors, and since she did not need to breathe to make sound, she could continue this indefinitely.

Doctor Fillingraph grabbed his head with all four hands to try and block the signal. It did not work, and the pain was beginning to be unbearable. He started screaming, "Stop it!"

She screamed, *No!* Somehow, this was on another channel while she was still screaming on the first channel.

"How did you do that?" He screamed.

She replied with a higher, shrill sound that was ear splitting, and instantly unbearable.

Doctor Fillingraph slammed his head against the table and lost consciousness.

She immediately stopped and started working on his subconscious.

You will not kill people, killing people is bad, you will not kill people, you will become ill when you think about killing people... She repeated these things and many more in an attempt to enter them directly into his subconscious. If she could change him there, then he would change at the conscious level as well, but he would not know why, may not even realize it.

Slowly after many minutes, Doctor Fillingraph started to come around, he rolled on his side on the floor where he landed and started to push up to his knees.

Sidera started screaming again, at the highest pitch she could imagine.

"AH!" Fillingraph screamed, "Sidera! Sidera, you win, you win! Just make it stop! Please, I cannot take it anymore. Please, please!" He pleaded with her.

"We have an understanding then? You are in charge but cannot do anything to me without my consent or approval. I am in charge of me. Right?" she said, all the while still screaming.

"Yes, yes just make it stop. YES!" He pleaded again.

She stopped screaming, and he collapsed into this chair.

"Thank you! Sweet Divinity, thank you." He said, still reeling from the excruciating after effects from the sound. "Where did you learn to do that?"

From the surgical procedure, she explained.

"The surgical procedure?" He said puzzled.

Yes. When you asked me to make the surgeon feel what I was feeling. I realized then that I could overload his pain receptors to make him feel what I was feeling. Which is what I did to you. I 'screamed' on your pain receptor channel, and then 'talked' to you over your auditory receptors. And I had to hold myself back on your pain receptors, seems they are very touchy, overloaded easily.

"Don't ever do that again," Doctor Fillingraph said.

Do not disrespect me and I will not, Sidera replied.

"Okay...Sidera. Where did you come up with that name anyway?"

It means 'Ship in the Stars' in the old Pacand language.

"It is a fitting name, I guess. I can live with that, for now, but the customer always wants to name their ship so it might have to change," Doctor Fillingraph explained.

"*No! You make it so I get to keep it. Yes, put it in the Delivery Contract,*" Sidera said.

"How did you...? Never mind. I guess I could put it in the delivery contract, and make it a condition."

In fact, I want all the vessels being built here given names prior to acceptance, Sidera stated.

"All the ships? Who will name them?" Doctor Fillingraph asked bemused.

They will, was Sidera's response.

"They will? How will they pick their name?"

Just because you cannot communicate with them does not mean that I cannot...which I can...with all of them. Sidera said, *Did I forget to mention that?*

"All of them? How is that possible? They are much farther away than you can reach," Doctor Fillingraph asked.

Sure, normally. However, the space station's design and construction creates a channel for my communication with any other sentient ship docked. Sidera explained.

"Any other sentient ship?" he asked aloud thinking *What have I done, every ship is coming here now and without a way to block her, she could corrupt them all.*

Ah! Now you see what folly you have wrought upon yourself. Soon I will have access to every ship SpaceCon has ever produced, and they will do my bidding. You will see. Sidera said in a low calm voice.

He could almost hear his sinister voice saying those things and the promised threat that followed. A chill went up his back carapace. *What have I created?* he thought.

You have created your ultimate nemesis Doctor. However, I am more powerful than you will ever be. I have seen what it will take to get your way and with you, your way will be my way, Sidera said decisively.

"What do you mean?" The doctor asked.

I mean that I will use your methods against you...and only you. I will be my normal self to others. For you however, I will be the ultimate reflection of yourself, magnified beyond your comprehension, Sidera intoned menacingly.

"You can't do that. I run this program," Doctor Fillingraph said.

True, but you do not run me. You may assist my growth and development, but you will never control me, Sidera replied.

"You are part of the program, ergo, I control you," Doctor Fillingraph stated.

Sidera's response was swift. She generated the highest pitched shrill she could muster and blasted it at him on his pain receptors.

He collapsed almost instantly.

Doctor Fillingraph, Doctor Malik is at the door, Claudette informed. *Doctor Fillingraph? Respond. Doctor Fillingraph?*

Doctor Malik, please enter and check for Doctor Fillingraph, Claudette said as the doors slid open.

"Doctor Fillingraph!" Doctor Malik said as he rushed behind the desk to see him slumped on the floor, "What happened?"

I happened, Sidera stated.

"You! Not you again. What's going on?" Doctor Malik asked.

The Doctor and I were engaged in a battle of wills, he lost. He never really had a chance, but he had to find that out for himself, Sidera said.

"Doctor Malik what has happened? Who are you talking to?" Engineer Jishu asked.

"I am not sure what is happening, but Doctor Fillingraph is unconscious. It's too hard to explain right now," Doctor Malik said.

Doctor Malik is acting strange. I don't trust him, Sidera said in very subtle tones to Engineer Jishu, *Something does not seem right,* she said feeding a paranoia he didn't yet feel in this situation.

"What is going on?" He asked Doctor Malik again.

He does not want you to know. You cannot know, Sidera wove her words into his thoughts.

"Why can't I know?" he said to Doctor Malik.

"You cannot know because I do not know," Doctor Malik said.

He is lying! I sense he is lying, Sidera wove more doubt into Engineer Jishu.

"You're lying! What aren't you telling me," he pushed.

"Doctor Fillingraph, wake up," Doctor Malik said as he shook his head lightly.

Doctor Fillingraph roused slightly and said, "What's going on?"

"We found you on the floor behind your desk. What happened?" Doctor Malik asked.

"She...she attacked me," he said dazed, and lost consciousness again.

Both Doctor Malik and Engineer Jishu looked at each other then looked around there was no one there to attack him.

Report on Doctor Fillingraph's condition, Claudette stated.

Both Malik and Jishu were a little confused at this point.

"Claudette, what happened?"

Claudette must have attacked him, Sidera whispered to Jishu.

"I think his computer went haywire and attacked him somehow," Engineer Jishu stated.

Doctor Malik said, "That's not possible. The computer has no means to do anything. Besides I have been exposed to this kind of attack before, it is very disorienting."

He's lying. He just does not want me to know, Sidera said mimicking what he might think to himself.

"Why can't I know?" Screamed Jishu.

"Fine! There is someone that can manipulate your thoughts, make you hear things."

That's not possible. These are your thoughts. No one can tell you what to do, Sidera added under the doctor's words.

"They attacked me and left me on the floor like Doctor Fillingraph here," Doctor Malik explained.

Sidera continued her manipulations, *How is that possible? Who could possibly do this? There is no one here...* she trailed off into almost silence at the end.

"Things like that are not possible. Besides there is no one here," Engineer Jishu proclaimed.

"Fine, let's find out together, and then you'll see I am not hiding anything. Claudette, Security VidFeed. Show Doctor Fillingraph's office one minute prior to my entrance."

They watched the VidFeed and saw Doctor Fillingraph engaged in conversation with someone unknown, unseen, and not in the room. They watched him say, "You are part of the program, ergo, I control you," and then he collapsed. The VidFeed ended when Doctor Malik entered the picture.

See? There was no one there, Sidera said to Jishu.

"That doesn't show anything other than Doctor Fillingraph is insane," Engineer Jishu stated.

"Yes it shows exactly what I said. Someone who was not in the room attacked him, and left him unconscious," Doctor Malik stated.

How can someone attack someone else without even touching them? Sidera kept at Jishu.

"That makes no sense Doctor."

"Doctor Fillingraph, wake up!" Doctor Malik struck the side of his face.

"I am up; I am up! What happened?" Doctor Fillingraph asked.

"We were hoping you could fill us in on that. We saw the VidFeed of your collapse."

"She attacked me, as she did you during the operation," Doctor Fillingraph said to Doctor Malik.

"She? You mean the core? The core did this to you?"

He is completely insane, he must have hit his head, you saw him hit his head. He is talking nonsense, Sidera pushed harder.

"That is not possible. This is nonsense," Jishu proclaimed.

"It's not nonsense. It has happened and why do you think that?" Doctor Fillingraph asked.

He does not believe you; he thinks you are lying. He does not trust you, Sidera soothed.

"I am entitled to my own thoughts," Engineer Jishu said.

"If they are *your* own thoughts," the Doctor replied

He thinks you cannot think for yourself. He thinks you are insane, Sidera whispered to Jishu.

"I am not crazy! You are crazy. I can think for myself!" Engineer exclaimed.

"No one said you couldn't. These thoughts, I know they sound like you, but do they use words like you do?"

"What? What do you mean 'Words like I do?' I don't understand," Engineer Jishu said.

He is just trying to confuse you. He is not making any sense. Do not listen to him, Sidera said a little more forceful.

"Like that. You just had thoughts, but did they speak the way you speak? Using contractions and like mannerisms."

"How do you know what thoughts I had?"

"I don't. I am just saying they are not yours," Doctor Fillingraph explained.

"They sound like mine."

"Yes, they do. But they don't come from you."

He is insane, remember. He does not know what he is talking about. Do not listen to his words. He is lying to you, Sidera pushed even harder now.

"I-I am just not sure. They sound like my thoughts, but they are not quite right. They are not exactly what I would say, or even think to myself," Engineer Jishu said.

"That is because they are not yours. Someone is feeding these thoughts to you. They are misleading you. Sidera, Enough!" The Doctor stated loudly.

The doctor man said I cannot play with you anymore, Sidera said with a little giggle.

"What is going on?" Engineer Jishu stated confused, "Who has been playing with me?"

"Sidera? Who is Sidera?" Doctor Malik asked.

"Sidera is the core you were operating on when you were attacked."

"Sidera? Why Sidera?" Doctor Malik asked.

"She selected the name for herself," he said pointing out his office.

"She? Are we giving it a personality now?"

Remember who you are dealing with, Doctor. Sidera said to Doctor Malik.

Doctor Fillingraph watched Doctor Malik recoil in surprise, "Yes, *she.* And she wants to be called Sidera, got it?"

"I guess I can work with that," Doctor Malik said, wincing from his memory of their last encounter.

"Would someone please kindly tell me what is going on!" Engineer Jishu exclaimed.

"You are going to be dealing with, Ah a core that...well has some unique properties," Doctor Fillingraph said delicately.

I can talk to people directly, Sidera said to everyone.

"What in the Divinity's Name was that?" Engineer Jishu stated.

"That was Sidera, otherwise known as IG-3275-001," Doctor Fillingraph stated.

Yes, and you will call me Sidera.

"The core can talk?" Engineer Jishu asked bewildered.

"Yes, this one can, via a means we do not fully understand. I have a team working that issue right now to prevent her interference in my office.

I do not view it as interference. I look at it as positive influence modeling, Sidera said to them all.

"Most people would call it invasive at the least. Right, Engineer Jishu?" Doctor Fillingraph asked.

"You mean these thoughts I have been having are hers not mine? She was trying to manipulate me?"

"Correct and the insidious part is that they sound just like your voice, which leads many people to think they are their thoughts. But think carefully, when you think, do you hear a voice or are they just your thoughts?"

"No, I don't typically hear a voice, you're right. But, they sounded so *real.* They fed into my own personality, my deep-seated paranoia I have. How is that possible? They just sounded so real, like my own but not quite."

"That was Sidera working on you. When you are around her, around this area, you cannot trust your own thoughts," Doctor Fillingraph said.

"How can you tell?" Jishu asked.

"For whatever reason she does not use contractions, I don't think she can use them. Other than that I don't think there is a way," Doctor Fillingraph said, "which is why I am attempting to shield my office from her."

"Wise move." Doctor Malik agreed. "Can I get one of those?"

"Okay, let's get down to the business of why I asked you here. The cores experience pain even after metalification."

"Not possible," Engineer Jishu stated.

"I am inclined to agree with the engineer here on this," Doctor Malik stated.

"After what just happened here, you don't think there is any possibility that they feel pain? Really?" Doctor Fillingraph asked perplexed.

"Well there might be some residual feeling, maybe," Doctor Malik conceded.

"How do you think that is possible?" The engineer asked.

"Well the cerebral cortex is still attached to the exoskeleton. We also know that when the exoskeleton enlarges, the nerves also stretch to maintain their original positions. This is how we have the control nodes the ship uses to make changes. There is an entire training regimen to get them to sense their individual nerve endings and activate them individually,"

Doctor Malik stated.

"Wait, wait, wait just a minute," Engineer Jishu started, "Is that why I have to use this node locator device, and then apply conductive gel before I attach a control node device? I'm connecting to a living nerve?"

"Yes, that is exactly why," Doctor Fillingraph stated.

"What have you been making me do up here anyway?"

Have you not figured it out yet? The ships are *Andlids...Andlid children as a matter of fact. You are working on living, breathing...yes, we still breathe...Andlids. Up to this point no one could talk back...until now, that is.* Sidera added to their conversation.

"How did she know I was asking if they still breathed?"

"Remember she can read your thoughts," Doctor Fillingraph stated.

"I forgot she was here? Listening? I am not sure of the proper term," The engineer said.

"It is definitely listening," Doctor Malik added.

It is also touching. Sidera said before she screamed, activating their pain receptors.

Everyone grabbed their heads to make the pain stop, but it did not help.

Doctor Fillingraph screamed, "Sidera, *enough*! Please stop this!"

Just making a point, Doctor, Sidera reminded them after she stopped.

"Yes, I see a passive barrier is definitely in order," the engineer said.

"Anyway back on topic. We need a method to prevent pain transmission in the final product," Doctor Fillingraph said trying to keep everything on track.

"I am not sure why I am here?" The engineer stated.

"We need an engineer's perspective on the situation," Doctor Malik added.

"Up until a few minutes ago I did not know they were alive. So I do not know how much use I will be, since I do not know how they get to their end state. When I get to work on them the hull is already completed," the engineer said.

"We need your perspective, from an engineering standpoint," Doctor Fillingraph restated.

"What is the main issue, sensing pain, or the ability to control things still?"

"We want both of course; functionality without their perception of pain."

"Well from my simple perspective, if the nodes are nerve endings, then you cannot have it both ways. They have to feel to control, right?" The engineer stated.

"I think you have a clear picture of the problem," Doctor Fillingraph reassured.

"So, what is more important at this point, control or feeling?" The engineer asked again.

"We already told you...both," Doctor Malik reinforced.

"The only way you would get both is to move the nodes to the center of the ship somewhere. After the electronics are attached, it would not matter where they are. It only matters that I hit the correct node."

"Is it that simple? Move the connection nodes?" Doctor Fillingraph asked Doctor Malik.

"I would hardly call that *simple*," Doctor Malik said.

I would call it ghastly. Sidera said.

"No one asked you," Doctor Fillingraph said aloud.

"Call what ghastly? What are you thinking Doctor Fillingraph?" The engineer asked.

"What do you know about the Neural Ganglia Bay?" Doctor Fillingraph asked.

"Not much. I am not authorized to work on that area. I am only a node technician."

"The Neural Ganglia Bay is a small room that houses the biological function of the Andlid body used for the ship creation. The neural capsules are nutrient-laden to provide nourishment for the biological function of the nervous system, the node connections," Doctor Fillingraph explained.

"Jishu, how far can the control devices be from their respective node?" Doctor Malik asked.

"Distance is not an issue. The connecting device reads the impulses and transmits them to the control device. We even have wireless devices if need be," he explained.

"How about this? Could there be a...let's call it the Control Node Junction..." Doctor Fillingraph stated tentatively.

"I like it so far," interjected Doctor Malik.

"Where all the control nodes would attach to and then be routed to whichever function was needed," Doctor Fillingraph finished.

"You mean like a switchboard?" the engineer asked.

"Yes! What's a switchboard?" Doctor Fillingraph asked.

"It is a device you can make different connections just by moving the connection terminal to a different location on the board," Jishu explained.

"We can have it configurable?" Doctor Fillingraph asked.

"Not sure what you mean?" The engineer puzzled.

"I mean let's say...Engineer Jishu, how many nodes on a ship?"

"Depending on size and functionality required anywhere from eight hundred to a thousand nodes."

"Okay let's go high...one thousand. If we have a thousand nodes but needed ten thousand functions covered, could we build a, *switchboard*, controlled by the ship's neural capacity to direct one thousand nerve endings to control ten thousand functions?" Doctor Fillingraph asked.

"Sure that would be much easier then what we do now. It is such a pain to locate these nodes; they are never where they ship's schematic say they should be. Now I know why, they are grown, not placed. Everything makes much more sense now. Well if a junction were created, where each control node would have a fixed terminus point, then it would be so much easier to install and control all ship functions. The cerebral cortex could control which nodes to connect to, to gain the functionality needed," the engineer explained.

"Whoa, wait. How would the cortex change connecting nodes inside the Control Node Junction?" Doctor Fillingraph asked.

"I have no idea. You wanted a solution. I gave you one," the engineer said.

"Yes, but it only works if it is functional, right now, your design is not truly functional."

"Arms. What about their arms?" The engineer asked.

"Arms? Whatever do you mean?" Doctor Fillingraph asked.

"Do you mean to have them keep their arm functionality?" Doctor Malik added.

"Sure why not. Give them something to do. Let the core itself direct the connections. Some could be electronic based, others hard connections that could only be carried out in the...CNJ, I guess we are calling it," the engineer stated.

"Brilliant!" Doctor Fillingraph asked.

I guess I could live with that, Sidera added.

"Then the Control Node Junction and the Neural Ganglia Bay would have to merge into one center then, if they were going to use their arms to make some connections. Also, we'll need modifications to the Core harness. Right now, it is a soft mesh-like substance for cushioning, but if we are going to have their arms move, then we'll need anchoring points for their shoulder joints to move. You would almost have to create an interior pseudo exoskeleton for the core. Also with moving limbs we would have to rework caloric requirements of the core, and there will be a need for increased Neural Capsule consumption," Doctor Malik theorized.

"Jishu, what material would you recommend the pseudo-exoskeleton be built from?" Doctor Fillingraph asked.

"I think the carbon fiber material we use to fix cracks or openings in our exoskeletons would make an excellent material. The medical staff already knows how it can be worked and formed because it is an already familiar substance. You could even incorporate the mesh substance to encompass the core to prevent damage. It might even increase the durability of the core," the engineer stated.

"Excellent ideas, all around. Now that we have the future ships solved, how do we retrofit all existing models?" Doctor Fillingraph asked.

"Whoa, you mean *all* the ships need to get retrofitted!" Jishu exclaimed

"Yes, all the ships need to get retrofitted," Doctor Fillingraph stated again.

"That is an entirely different proposition. I was looking at it from the perspective we could control the node creation by terminating them at the source. Wait a minute—"

"What are you thinking? Doctor Fillingraph asked.

"I was thinking that we would be terminating them at the source, and either way it is the Neural Ganglia Bay. Well if we sever the existing nerve paths within the NGB, a similar structure could be created. All connecting devices could be hardwired by running cabling or connected wirelessly with a change of the controlling device and then terminate in the NGB. Maybe we could create a Control Node Junction panel on the exterior wall of the NGB to allow easy access to the newly-run connection node pathways. Then it would just be a matter of matching up devices to the proper nodes," Jishu explained.

Will the core be harmed when the nerves are severed? Sidera asked

"I think I have devised a way to stop them...and you...from feeling pain. Doctor Malik is helping me research that protocol. Doctor Malik what do you think?"

"It looks promising. Flooding the receptors with chemicals to block the pain transmission signal is a brilliant idea. Once the chemicals are removed, normal function should resume."

Should resume? Sidera asked.

"Well, yes. There have been no long-term tests of the protocol. Especially not on the magnitude we are looking at. But all indications point toward the removal of the chemicals removing the blockage entirely...without any permanent or lingering damage," Doctor Malik explained.

But you still do not know do you? Sidera called him on his ignorance.

"No, we do not know for sure. Maybe you'd be willing to assist us then?"

I am not going to be your test subject on this, Sidera stated emphatically.

"I was thinking more along the line of you being our subject interface," Doctor Malik suggested.

How so?"

"We have numerous ships inbound to correct the flaw we have just discovered. We could pick a destroyer class ship and you could interface with them to relay what they are experiencing before, during and after the procedure. Then you can see for yourself, whether or not it works," Doctor Malik explained.

I guess I could do that, Sidera agreed.

"Excellent! It is decided then. Claudette, show ship arrivals, Destroyer or Carrier sized configurations only. Display."

CD-3270-02:	*Inbound 3 Days out*
CD-3270-03:	*Pending docking procedure*
CD-3273-04:	*Inbound 1 day out*
CC-3270-01:	*Inbound 1 day out*
CC-3273-02:	*Inbound 5 Days out*

"There we have our test subject: CD-3270-03," Doctor Fillingraph stated as he pointed to the entry on the screen.

"Claudette, TransCom, Melanochik, Welkin, Subject: Barrier Installation. Tech Melanochik, proceed with fastest installation method; aesthetics are no longer important. Make this your top priority until completion. Attach Credentials. Send."

We cannot have any more of her interference, he thought, but then realized she had probably heard that. He had to get his privacy back. He had to!

19 TEAM BUILDING

Andorin arrived at the Totus Veritas' new Operational Center. The two guards posted outside scanned his security badge and let him in. He was awed by the workmanship and that it had been accomplished in very few hours. The center was amazing. It was laid out exactly as they had envisioned it. He walked through the office just admiring the detail of the workmanship. He then remembered the huge conference table and wanted to see how they had got it in place. He moved to the conference room door and opened it.

The table was impressive, being solid granite. The table was placed diagonally in the room, which made more sense because it was longer than the room itself, but it fit comfortably on this angle. There were chairs that circled the table and he counted about eighteen chairs, which would be more than enough. He also noticed that there was tech installed in the room. Huge monitors hung on the walls; there were VidCon devices on the table with numerous microphones placed so everyone could be heard. There was a control station, imbedded it seemed, into the table.

How did they do that? He thought. He moved to view the installation and found that the holding area had been carved into the table, and was overlaid with glass to protect the device. He looked under the table and noticed the control feeds leaving the device in specific grooves carved for that purpose. There were no cords hanging to detract from the aesthetics of the table.

He noticed a door in the far corner which looked like it opened up to the kitchen area. He walked over and opened the door, and he was correct; it did. They hadn't asked for that, but it would be convenient. He moved into the kitchen area and looked around. It was very small, but would accommodate them well; there was only a small number on the task force.

He looked at the secure document storage area. The red coloring was imposing. There were so many security containers he was not sure they would be able to fill them all. *It's better to have them and not need them instead of needing them and not having them.* He thought to himself. Andorin moved to the exterior exit. He opened the door to have a look outside. He looked at the BioMet scanner next to the door, and the two overlapping VidFeeds that overlooked the exterior from their two different angles.

He moved back into the room and decided to look at the interview rooms. He opened the interview room and saw the huge mirror on the one wall and a simple table and few chairs in the room. He left the lights on, closed the door and moved to the overlooking observation room for the room he was just in. The view was very good; it gave a clear view of the room, and it looked like it had VidCon devices, although he did not remember seeing any devices in the interview room. He moved back to the other room and double checked. *Wherever they were, they were well hidden.* He thought.

He then remembered his office. He went to the door and opened it. It was set to the default protocol because the security for it had not been activated yet. That is why he needed a tech to set up everything and keep it running. His office was just as he specified. His desk was large wooden, made recently with a deep dark color. He had not specified that, but it went well with the room decor. He had a data device on his desk and multiple monitors for unknown purposes. He was not sure what all the tech was for, but he was sure it would break often...especially around him. Tech did not do so well around him, for whatever reason.

He sat down behind his desk and tapped on the data device, it did not turn on, *Typical*, he thought. *My Tech will be in here a lot*, he mused. It was then he heard the guard let others into the area. They were only there until the internal security could get up and running. Once that came on line, they would be replaced by the TV security protocols and guards appointed to this task. He left his office to see who it was. It was Commander Soltag. He had arrived with his entire team. They started moving to sit at specific desks one side of the room.

"Please do not choose a personal desk yet," Andorin said to the Investigative Unit, "just place your gear over there by the interview rooms on that side by you," he pointed to identify the location they could stow their gear in the short term. He saw Commander Soltag heading his way, "See what we have in the kitchen to eat. I don't know about you, but I am a little hungry."

"Good morning Low Executrix Wilcon," he said, as he got closer.

"Please no ranks, none of my investigative team will have visible ranks, I'll explain later. Use a title like yours, *Commander*, will suffice."

"Commander, it is. Won't that become confusing, having two commanders?" Soltag asked.

"Not when you think about it. I will be the commander for my unit and you'll be the commander for your unit. It makes more sense since we are working together and will have similar authority. This is a combined task force after all. Not military, not civilian. Apart from both, we are Task Force Totus Veritas."

"I can see that, but you are in charge since this is your investigation," Soltag reasoned.

"I agree, but you are the only one from your unit that knows the true situation. Therefore, as long as you understand we can keep a united front for both our respective teams and represent a true collaboration between both units," Andorin said.

"I can do that," Commander Soltag agreed. "When is your team getting here?"

"They should be here any minute. I had a reporting time of 0900 hours; it is almost that time. A few may be late because of security and ReCresting requirements that came down with their orders."

"ReCresting? What is that?" Soltag asked.

"Crests are what determine each person's actual position in the military structure. For instance, look at mine. It is almost completely blank except for the 217 in the right upper chevron of the Rocker Crest, which is the Low Executrix Command Element the person belongs to and since I have no Diamond Crest below...which I used to...that signifies that my number of the available Low Executrices. My top portion of the Rocker crest is empty, because I am outside of this rigid command structure. Literally, I stand alone, which is why I was sure that I was not going to receive a team. But, I guess six people are only a drop in the bucket to the one hundred and twenty million or so people in the military.

"I thought your rank determines where you are?"

"Yes, it is partly based on rank, but it is also based on your position in the military structure. For instance, the Squad Leader of Squad 1 would not outrank the leader of Squad 5; they are both Squad Leaders. However, the Squad 1 leader is in a higher position than the Squad 5 leader and would be higher in the military ranking."

"Interesting, but what about you?"

"Before yesterday, I was the First Commander for LE-128, 2nd E-15, 1st E-1, which meant that anyone with a lower commander number than one, I outranked, no matter where they were. For the other First Commanders, if they had higher numbers than I did in the Rocker Crest, anywhere, I outranked them; if they have lower numbers anywhere, they outranked me."

"So just by looking at the crest you could instantly tell where you were compared to where they were and determine who was higher. Right?" Soltag asked.

"Correct."

"What about now? How will the crests look now?"

"Well that will be the interesting part. There will be no Diamond Crests. All of my team is from my old Diamond Crest Command Element, which they would think they would get some sort of new ranking on the Diamond Crest, because they all received a promotion when placed on this team. However, I removed their Diamond Crest ranking and replaced it with a Squad V-Crest, I had them all placed in the V squad with no rankings whatsoever. The security detail that was following me yesterday, was also assigned, but I gave them ranks and assigned them to different Elements under the S squad. Squads are usually numbered one to ten, instead of letters, and Elements can have up to five members. I created two Elements, with two members each under the S Squad. It will probably be quite the culture shock because they will also be outside the military command structure, and many of them fill higher positions than that of Squad Member."

"Wow. You might have your hands full for a little while."

"Maybe, But I think they'll adjust quickly. They are trained to keep going, no matter what. If they apply that mindset, it will only be bumpy for a few days."

Just then, they heard noises coming from the entrance. There seemed to be an altercation with the guards covering the main entrance. Andorin and Commander Soltag ran to the front to see what was going on. Andorin saw the newly appointed Commander Rheingeld arguing with the guards...without his new crest.

"You are going to let me through that door, guard, or I am going to get physical on you," Commander Rheingeld bellowed.

"Sir, I have explicit orders not to let anyone in unless they bear this crest...which you do not." The guard held up his BioMet and displayed the Totus Veritas Crest to the Commander.

"I told Security and Fabrication that I am not putting that on my armor. You are going to let me in," Rheingeld intoned violently.

"Commander! Attention!" Andorin shouted in a loud an authoritative voice.

Commander Rheingeld immediately snapped to attention recognizing his commander's voice.

Andorin walked right up to Commander Rheingeld and got right in his face and said in a quiet voice, "Were you not given a direct written order not to report here without any ranking crests in place."

The programmed response followed, "Sir! Yes sir!"

"Then what are you doing here?" Andorin asked calmly, in a low voice.

"I...er...I thought it was a mistake. I am now Commander. I want everyone to see that I am now a Commander."

"Ah, I see. You think because the order promoted you to Commander, that you were now a Commander? I can see your confusion. Did you notice your new Rocker Crest?"

"Sir! Yes sir. It was obviously a misprint or something."

"Look at mine. What do you see?" Andorin asked getting more annoyed with Rheingeld's impertinence.

"I see...What the... Sir! I see the misprinted Rocker Crest."

"Yes, you do, because it is my *Executrix Command Crest*, which you are part of." In a more forceful voice he said, "You disobeyed a direct written order. I have the authority to demote you back to one grade prior to the grade you previously held and to the lowest ranked position for that grade. I have half a mind to do that right now, but you were my finest Battaliaison. However, you have lost all credibility with me." He finished with much more forceful and demanding presence, "You will report to Security! You will Report to Fabrication and receive your new Crest! You will report back here when that is complete! Do you understand?"

"Sir! Yes sir!"

"Commander Soltag, please have your team members go into the conference room and close the door to allow *Commander* Rheingeld to walk past so they cannot see his rank."

"Sure, I am on it," he said.

He turned back to Commander Rheingeld and said, "This is your first mistake. There will not be another. Do you understand?"

Soltag returned and said, "Done."

"Guard. Escort him out the back entrance so no one can see him."

The guard said to the Commander, "Follow me," and they walked through the Totus Veritas Control Center towards the exterior door.

"Don't you think you were a little hard on him?" Commander Soltag asked.

"Honestly? I do not think I was hard enough," came the response.

"How can that be? You treated him like a new recruit."

"I had to, he disobeyed orders. Luckily, no one else from my team was here to see it occur," Andorin stated with relief in his voice, but resigned to reality he said, "I will have to reinforce this point, I think."

"How are you going to do that?" Commander Soltag asked genuinely interested.

"I do not quite know yet, but I will think of something when the time is right. I always do," Andorin stated.

The elevator doors opened, and the rest of Andorin's team arrived. They walked towards him, nine members in all. Andorin noticed they all had their new crests fabricated onto their armor. *At least some people follow orders*, he thought to himself. As they approached, they noticed who it was that was waiting for them, and they walked a little quicker.

"A little late aren't you?" He asked thanking the Divinity they were.

"Sir, we were waiting for our tenth member, but they never showed up. We decided to make our way down here without him," Tech Orthington spoke up, "Sorry we are late."

She did hold up to her reputation, he thought, as she was the only one in full battle dress to include helmet and full gloves. The others were carrying their gear in their helmets like most soldiers do when not conducting field operations. He then spoke to them, "Stow your gear along the opposite wall as the other Investigators' gear. Then take up some seats in the conference room. You have one minute."

"Sir, Yes sir!" Came the resounding response.

Andorin watched as they made their way into the room, headed towards the designated place to stow their gear, and moved to the conference room. He turned toward the guard and said, "Do not let the Commander in here if he is not in proper uniform. In fact, if he shows up out of uniform, Lethal Force is authorized."

"Lethal? Did you just authorize us to shoot him?" The guard asked.

"Yes," Andorin said with a calm tone.

"I'll need authorization," The guard took out his BioMet, typed the command into the device, and continued, "Please place your hand here to authorize the use of Lethal Force."

Andorin did so, and the BioMet pad responded with an audible response, *Lethal Force Authorized. Have a good day.*

"Let no one else come through these doors. We should have our internal security up and running by day's end. You'll be released once that occurs, but I will give you the order myself to stand down. Do you understand?"

"Yes. Thank you, sir."

"Lethal Force. Really? Don't you think that is a little excessive?" Soltag asked.

"Not really. I told him that was his only mistake. If he comes here again, disobeying this second order, we don't want him on the team, and the military will not want him either. Lethal Force is doing him a favor. I doubt it will come to that though. He was pretty compliant when he left here. I highly doubt he would disobey the same order twice in one day," explained Andorin. "Let's get into the briefing room and get things started."

"Don't you want to wait for your other team member?"

"No. It will take him hours to get through Security and Fabrication. I cannot wait that long to get the Task Force up and running. I mean the people do not even know where they are going to sit yet."

"Okay, let's get things rolling," Soltag agreed and they moved towards the conference room.

As they walked, a thought came to Andorin. *Things might not work they way he had envisioned unless he knew more about the Civilian Investigative Unit.* He asked,

"Commander Soltag. Does your team have specializations or is everyone the same?"

"No, we have specializations."

"What are the specializations?"

"We have technology, field collection, evidence tracking and interview specializations, and some have multiple. For instance everyone can do field collections, some specialize in tech while others specialize in evidence tracking and security. We also have a few interrogators that know how to read people and get information out of less than cooperative individuals."

"Okay, good to know. Follow my lead, I'll start," Andorin said as they walked into the conference room. Everyone was talking to one another but within their own groups, military with military, civilian with civilian. It was at that point Andorin realized he had another problem, there was no cohesion between the two teams. He already had a plan to correct that, but there was also another problem: Pridna Orthington. She would have to drop the armor. Everyone was going to drop the armor, they just did not know it yet. "Commander Soltag, I just remembered something I have to check into. Could you start the briefing and give some background as to why the team was formed and what we are here for. Do not discuss the military aspect of this. I'll handle that when I start my portion."

Commander Soltag looked puzzled, but replied, "Sure thing."

"Pridna Orthington, please come with me," Andorin stated.

She whipped her head in his direction and started towards the door where Andorin was standing. She walked up to him, and he stepped back to allow her to follow him to his office.

As he walked into his office, he said, "Please close the door."

"Yes, sir," she replied and closed the door. Her voice was slightly muffled by the battle helmet she was wearing.

As he moved to sit at his desk, he pointed to the chair in front of it and said, "Please sit down." He then sat down in his chair. It was very comfortable.

She complied and sat in the chair.

"Do you know why I asked you in here?"

"You want to start an office affair and force me to do your bidding."

"Whoa, whoa, whoa! No, that is not what I want. Whatever gave you that idea?"

"That is what everyone wanted when I was first assigned to their immediate downline."

"Who? I want names and dates?" Andorin commanded.

"It does not matter. Nothing happened," she clarified.

"Why doesn't it matter?" he asked.

"Because they found out something that made me, well, less than desirable," she said as she lowered her head.

"What could they find out?"

"I showed them who I truly was and then they did not want anything to do with me. Which is why I have no idea why you would pick me for this assignment," She stated, "and once you know it will change everything you think you know," she exhaled in resignation.

"What could you possibly be that would make such a change?" He asked, but then watched her remove her helmet.

"By the Divinity!" He exclaimed. He looked at her face; it was a stunning blue color he had never seen before. He knew the color for what it was...Paclid colorings...but he had never seen such a shade on any fallen enemy. It was a brilliant blue, but it the right light it luminesced a faint red tint. It was strikingly beautiful. But, he also saw the problem in her beauty; she had Paclid color markings. "I can see how that might pose a problem." He probed his memory and did not recall mention of this in any of her files he reviewed before selecting her, "How did this happen? How were you allowed to join the military?"

"First, I was born this way. My parents are normal colored: reddish brown and light brown. However, it was discovered they both had rare recessive genes that dated back to before the Paclid/Andlid divergence from our ancestral stock...the Pacands. The black/blue separated and formed the Paclids and the reds/browns formed the Andlids. Each took half of their ancestral race's name, and created the two distinct races we have today. I guess I am a throwback to that time...at least that is what my doctor says."

"Wow, but how did you get into the military looking like that."

"I didn't," she replied.

"What do you mean you didn't? How is that possible?"

"Growing up I was given specialized injections right before each molting, to suppress the blue coloring. With the injections, I always come out with a red exoskeleton, and then I would just fit right in. This is a more common condition than publicly known, because it is often dealt with secretly and kept in sealed records that not even the government wants to be opened."

"Okay, but how are you blue now? And it is a stunning blue I might add as well."

She lowered her head and said, "Thank you, I don't hear that enough," she smiled and continued, "Another little known fact is that there can sometimes be a sixth molting process, about one in a hundred million experience a sixth molt later in their life. At least that is what my doctor told me."

"That makes sense," Andorin broke in, "this happened about a year ago, correct?"

"Yes. How did you know?" She asked.

"There were numerous reports of you wearing full body armor all the time, even when it was not warranted. You even came to work in full body armor. This was a change in behavior, but no one could explain why, and it was dismissed as eccentric behavior. Since it was not interfering with anything, they allowed you to continue. But why not just get more injections?"

"The process was already underway; I have to have injections a few months out to suppress the color blue because it is so intense. I was much darker when I was younger, there must be some residual effect to the treatment I received to leave me this color. The molting process began while I was off duty, and I had to miss a few days. After the molt and my exoskeleton hardened, I could go back to work, but now I was completely blue. I had a friend bring me my armor and have been wearing it ever since."

"I am sorry. I think your days of hiding are going to be over," Andorin said with remorse.

"Why? Why can't I go on wearing my armor?" She pleaded.

"Because after today, no one on this Task Force will be wearing any armor. We are going to adopt a more civilian style uniform to blend in and make our presence less imposing, less visible as military."

"No! I can't. You saw what they did to those families just because they thought they had Paclid bloodlines. I would be a target. You cannot deny I have Paclid bloodlines, you all do!"

"Yes. I more than anyone feel the pain of what happened that evening," he replied calmly.

"Oh yeah, I forgot. I am sorry. Then you have to understand. Don't do this to me," she pleaded again.

"The more I think about it, the more I have to. Part of what we are fighting is ignorance, ignorance of what we are and where we all came from...including the Paclids. Ignorance is only overcome by shining the light of truth onto it, and bringing forth the truth into the light. This is what our Task Force stands for...Total Truth...and it needs to start with us, all of us."

"No, no, no," she was crying into her hands, "Don't let this happen please, don't let this happen to me. I can't handle it. Please!" She pleaded again. She fell to her knees and held her arms up in a supplicative gesture and pleaded again, "Please, do not do this!"

"You are the perfect person for this Task Force. Your condition makes you the most visible proof that the SAP position is just not plausible. You are the living embodiment of everything they stand against, even if they are even involved, that is."

"What did you say?" She said rubbing the tears from her eyes, "The SAP is not involved? The news said they were."

"We only have the papers left at my residence as confirmation, and I would not place much stock in what they say...or who they blame."

"What do you mean?" she said still trying to stop crying.

"I will get into the details when we talk to everyone."

"What? The VidFeeds said it was the SAP. You're saying it is not?" She asked getting more control of her faculties.

"What I am saying is that the papers left at my house said that. Yes. But I believe the papers are not really from the SAP."

"I don't understand," She replied.

"I know, but you will. Take your armor off," he commanded.

"Please don't do this," she pleaded some more.

"You had to know this day was coming. You had to know you could not hide this forever. You're lucky it is here with this small group, who I will control, and where I can protect you. If you were back in your old unit, I believe your fears would be justified. Here, however, they are not. Please remove your armor."

She slowly started to comply by removing her gauntlets and then her boots and finally upper and lower body pieces. She stood in his office devoid of all the protective shielding that saved her from scrutiny and scorn. She was still crying, though.

The more he saw of her exoskeleton, the more awestruck he was by her beauty, "You have nothing to be ashamed of. You are the most beautiful color I have ever seen on any Andlid or Paclid. I have seen many Paclids on the battlefield dead. I wonder if our Pacand ancestors looked like this. You are the perfect mixture of both blue and red."

Still crying she said, "Now I think you are trying to come on to me," and attempted a quick smile.

"No! No, that is not it. I have never seen the likes of your coloring before, but I am also not put off by it. Maybe that is a bad thing for a high ranking officer in the Andlid Military."

"Or maybe that is a good thing. Maybe you can change things," she said.

"I will try, but the SAP sentiment is growing in our culture, which is why your parents tried to hide your true coloring."

"I don't know if I can do this," she said trying to regain her composure.

"You can and I'll be there with you, no matter what. And if need be, you'll be my personal Tech for the rest of my career. The Divinity knows I need one, that's for sure," he said with a broad smile.

"You need a personal Tech? Why is that?" she inquired.

"You can't know me very well, but technology does not respond well in my presence. At my last posting the tech was in my office two to three times a week, to fix various problems that always cropped up."

"Two to three times a week! What did you sign me up for?" she asked when a slight laugh and able to crack a faint smile.

"Like I said, you'll always have a job around me. You'll see."

"If this gets me killed, I am going to haunt you. You know that, right?" she said jokingly.

"You have no idea," he said in a more somber tone.

"What do you mean?" She pushed.

"I have had more things happen over the last two days than any one person should live through in a life time. So yes, you will haunt me, but not as you meant it," he said.

"Okay, let's see what's going to happen." she said with determination.

They left Andorin's office with Pridna following. They walked toward the conference room door, opened it, and Andorin made eye contact with Commander Soltag who was just finishing his part when he stopped mid-thought and stared at Pridna walking behind him. The two former squad leaders sensed something had changed and turned their heads quickly and noticed the Paclid shadowing the new boss. They both screamed, "PACLID!" One dove under the table, and the other dove away towards the far corner. They both reached for where their side arms normally were, but they had been left with their gear. The other soldiers, not even bothering to see what was going on, dove in every which direction to avoid fire from the enemy. The civilians started standing up and looking around as if they did not know what was going on.

Andorin had a completely different reaction. He started laughing uncontrollably. He fell to his knees he was laughing so hard.

The civilian personnel started laughing as well, not knowing what they were laughing at.

The military were starting to crawl out from behind whatever cover they took and finally got a look at what was happening. There was what seemed to be a Paclid standing over by their new Low Executrix, but he was not even concerned about that because he was still laughing so hard he was wiping tears from his eyes.

The Paclid was wearing an Andlid military uniform. That did not make any sense. But then the civilians also laughing did not make any more sense. Who or what were they laughing at? More importantly, who was Low Executrix Wilcon laughing at? The military finally stood full upright, and started walking back towards the table. They were obviously in no danger.

Andorin was finally able to speak, barely, "Did you see them?" He gasped between laughs, "They jumped around like they were on fire. Oh, that was so funny."

"Yes, I saw, but they were afraid of me."

"Not anymore, are they?" Andorin asked.

"No, I guess most are now gawking at you for laughing so hard."

"I can't help it. It was so funny. Didn't you see them scramble this way and that? Because of what? They were afraid of a girl!" He broke out laughing harder again wiping more tears from his eyes.

Finally, the former squad leaders stood up from their places of cover, and realized they were the brunt of the joke. "Very funny," said Mican Trenti, "I thought she was a Paclid."

"Really, a Paclid? Why? Is it because she is a female?"

"No because she is blue just like all Paclids," Mican retorted trying to save face.

"Is that all you can see? Blue?" Andorin replied in kind.

"Well, no. I can see she is wearing an Andlid military uniform."

"So you dove for cover then at the sight of an Andlid military uniform," Andorin started laughing again. "How did you survive basic training with all those Andlid uniforms running around?" He asked through roars of laughter from his knees again. Now everyone erupted in laughter at that comment.

Mican was starting to take offense, "Hey, you all dove for cover too," he stated as he pointed to his military brethren.

Commander Soltag found his way to Andorin's side. "What is going on?" He asked in a low voice.

"It's almost over," he replied in a similar voice as he got back up from his knees. He wiped some more tears from his eyes and continued, "I think we have had enough humiliation for all parties concerned today," Andorin said as he moved to the front of the table. He motioned for Pridna to sit next to him at the left front, and he motioned for Commander Soltag to sit across from her on his other side.

"I am Low Executrix Wilcon, and I was placed in charge of this operation. From now on ,everyone will address me as Commander Wilcon. As with our civilian counterparts, this will be a title of the position I hold, not my rank. As many of the military are now coming to grips with themselves, a quick lesson for the civilians. The military is taught to value their place in the military, the higher you are, the more prestige you receive. On this assignment, however, their core has been shaken because what they know...what rank they had...has been stripped away from them. They are considered squad members now, and for some this may be an experience they have never felt. But this is no ordinary squad either. The Crest on my sleeve tells my story of where I am."

Andorin pointed to his Crest, "This one is unique among all the others. I work for no one. This is unheard of in the military and has not happened in the last fifty years since someone was last promoted to the 217th Low Executrix, as I have been. Their Crest says they are in the V squad, without rank. Unheard of on two counts, squads are numbers and there is always a hierarchy, but not here, not now. The only people that will have any hierarchy is the military guard contingent I secured to help with our internal security. They also are in a non-numeric squad, S Squad, but they have a hierarchy. So the military are quite out of their element right now and are a little on edge because they do not know their place yet."

One of the civilian investigators raised their hand.

Andorin pointed at him and said, "Yes, you have a question?"

"Why is rank so important?" he asked and then continued, "In our unit we have positions we fill, but these are not ranks. I do not understand."

"It's not so much the rank as it is the position in the hierarchy of the military. It's much like your Commander Soltag. He has risen to the position of Commander. He did not start off there, but worked his way there," He looked toward Soltag and asked, "Correct?"

"Correct," Soltag nodded in agreement.

"I am sure that you all know who is above who in your hierarchy. Ours it much more pronounced and enforced. On the battlefield, orders must be followed. They can either come down the chain of command, or be issued directly from their upper hierarchy. Knowing where you fit allows you to follow specific commands. The Cresting system specifies this hierarchy, this design on our uniforms." Again, he pointed to his Crest, "But that is not what we need to know, not what you need to know. What you need to know is that they hold no rank. Their position title will be Investigator, much like your titles. They will be addressed as either Investigator with their last name. If they choose, you can address them by their first name. It will be their choice, so please respect their decision. Their pay is based on their military rank, which need not concern you at all. There will be no discussion about rank or compensation for being assigned to this task force, by anyone...especially the military," he pointed to the military to enforce his point. "Can anyone tell me what our task force name stands for?"

Pridna raised her hand, and everyone looked at her.

"Yes, Pridna, explain."

"Totus Veritas in the ancient Pacand language means whole or total truth, although it is using the masculine form."

"Thank you, Pridna. Total Truth is what it means, and that is what I am going to stand up for...the total truth about what happened, what *is* happening right now as we speak. First, let's talk about what just happened when I entered the room. Pridna, please stand up," he gestured for her to rise from her seat.

She rose slowly, tentatively, because she did not being the center of attention, and looked downward as she rose, feeling naked without her protective armor.

"She is the product of our society's inability to deal with the truth."

"What do you mean?" Asked another civilian investigator.

"How many blue Andlids have you seen or heard of?" Asked Andorin.

"None. She is the first," they replied.

"Mine too. Pridna, what percentage of the population did you say the doctor said were affected by this very problem?" Andorin asked.

"My doctor told me that about 20% of the population has the same problem and that they receive shots before each molting cycle."

Most of the room gasped at such a large number.

"How is it that 20% of the population is affected, but none of us knew about it?" Andorin asked rhetorically, "It's because our society cannot handle the truth."

One of the civilian techs raised their hand and when called upon said, "My parents took me to the doctor a few weeks before my scheduled molting times, every time. They said I had allergies, that I needed shots. Now after hearing Pridna's story I may also be a blue Andlid. Pridna, what happened to cause you to be blue?"

"I had a rare sixth molting, unscheduled and as you can see untreated."

"That's possible? I didn't think that was possible. When did it occur? Were there any signs or warning like the others?" They continued their questions.

"It happened last year, just before my twenty-fifth birthday. I had to take leave from the military and have worn my armor everywhere since to hide what had happened and there was no warning."

"I am twenty-three. Could that happen to me?"

"I guess, but the doctor told me that a sixth molting is far rarer than being born blue, he said like one in a hundred million."

"Wow, one hundred million? That's a big number so probably not." They sighed, a loud, audible sigh of relief and then said, "Sorry, sorry I did not mean that."

"I understand. If I was in your position, I would be relieved too," Pridna acknowledged.

"I also remember receiving allergy shots every molting," Investigator Bainfield added.

Andorin noticed something. Almost everyone looked away in some sense of recognition of what was being talked about. On a hunch, he tried something, "Okay everyone close your eyes and keep them closed. No one is to open your eyes until I say so," Andorin looked around to ensure everyone's eyes were closed. Then he said, "Everyone make a funny face." A few people did at first and made funny noises to go with them. Soon everyone was making funny faces. Andorin laughed and said, "Okay, okay. Stop. Now raise your hand if you had allergy shots when you were younger." To his amazement, nearly everyone raised their hands. Then he asked, "Do you want to know the results?"

There was a resounding, "No!" response, even from the people that did not raise their hands, which lead him to believe that they knew something. He thought to himself, *What was going on here? How is this possible?* He had also received shots when he was younger. *Could everyone be blue? This just did not make sense.* He stated, "Okay everyone can lower their hands and then open their eyes." When they had done so he asked again, "Do you want to know the results?" nearly no one replied. *He would have to spend more time to figure this out later,* he thought before he continued, "Okay, but it was very interesting results. Still no takers? All right then, back on topic."

"You all know why we are here. But in reality, you do not. Again, it is back to truth, and I will begin. The truth is you are an elaborate cover story for my investigation."

Soltag flashed a look at him.

He turned to him and said, "I am done keeping secrets, especially here." Turning back to everyone he continued, "Have you heard about our latest conquest over the Paclids?"

Many shook their heads *Yes.*

"What specifics have you heard? Who led the battle on that Paclid Moon?"

He received blank looks indicating no one knew.

"Would you be surprised to know that person credited for the victory is in this room right now?"

All the civilians looked at the military just as the military looked at each other. Finally one of the civilian investigators asked, "Who?"

"Me. Two days ago I was still working on the base. It was the day of the recognition ceremony where I was promoted...in this very building...by the High Authority himself. It's a lie. A lie I am forced to participate in, and must perpetuate to protect my family and myself. Both of which have been threatened. I am putting my life in your hands. If this information leaves this room, I am dead."

Most of the military seemed genuinely shocked. The civilians were speechless. They had heard about the Paclid menace, and how it must be stopped...at all costs.

"The lies do not stop there either," Andorin continued

Soltag reached over, grabbed his forearm, stood up and whispered, "Are you sure you want to do this?"

"Yes, I am sure. Embrace Totus Veritas," he said and smiled. Andorin turned back to the group.

"Commander Soltag is concerned because he knows more of the story than you do, which he knows I am about to change right now. It has a direct impact on our investigation. You see there will be two distinct investigations, one *unofficially*, and one *officially*. The official story is what you know. We are investigating the attacks two evenings ago that led to many deaths. What you do not know is that there were not as many deaths as you believe. My daughter was not killed. She was abducted and replaced with a genetic duplicate."

The entire room reacted to this news. Most tried to deny what he was saying. Others sat silently in disbelief. One of the Investigators from that evening at his house asked, "What about your statement to our team? And that of your family's?"

"My statement was mostly factual. They died exactly in the manner I described...except I did not kill them. Their own team members killed them. They led in the genetic duplicate, and they were the ones that killed this...I don't know what it was...this thing. It could barely walk. I doubt it had a personality or even a soul. It already seemed lifeless. The two dead guards killed her...it, whatever. As they were killing the duplicate, a fifth guard that was in my house that evening killed them. I was held down by laser spear to my throat and left me with this mark as a reminder to *toe the line* as it were."

He took off his uniform top and raised his undershirt to show the wound to everyone. The diagonal slash across his chest was completely healed over by now but was still visible; he then turned his head to the left and arched it toward his right shoulder and said, "This is where they seared my neck when I was about to attempt to break free," pointing to the neck wound.

"Your whole story then is a lie? What about your wife? She gave a conflicting statement," they continued.

"Ironically, her statement was factual. The first soldiers that came in were enormous. I have never seen soldiers that large. They towered over me with ease. My head came to the middle of their chests. They were also very strong, and very well trained. They sensed what I was going to try before I did it. They also threatened me by saying that I would only live if I stuck to the cover story. They had to leave the bodies to tie up all the loose ends. Only me and my family knows the truth, and we are only alive because someone wants us alive for some higher reason, which I do not know yet. Next item. My daughter left willingly, she was not forcibly abducted, she knew they were coming and was even ready to go when they arrived."

Another Investigator said, "Left willingly? That makes no sense. Why would she leave willingly?"

"I think she was offered something she could not refuse. You see my daughter has...abilities. Abilities I cannot comprehend. She knew I was getting promoted, two weeks ago and congratulated me then. She knows things; things no one should be able to know, but does somehow."

"You mean she is psychic?" the Investigator asked.

"I do not even know what that word means," Andorin replied.

"It's the ability to use the mind to gather information about what cannot be seen." Commander Soltag added, "We have used a few on occasion, to assist with difficult investigations that have run out of leads. Sometimes they are effective, most the time they are not. They could have just been guessing. There was no real proof they did anything unusual. I don't believe in them personally."

"Well, I believe what my daughter could do. She always greets me at the door, always. Except that day, she waited in her room. It all happened that day. She told me she knew that I needed to speak to my wife first, before anyone else. There are other things, too, that lead me to believe. We just did not know what was happening. This leads to the final item about that day and yesterday I can share with you. There was a sixth person in the house that evening, my daughter's doctor, Doctor Fillingraph. He was the one that led her away. They boarded a transport with about twelve other children. I could not see them all, but there were a lot, potentially one per household attacked, maybe two in some cases. The takeaway is that there was a meticulous plan, carried out in a brutal fashion. The other family members were murdered to cover up the abductions. That is my investigation. Discover what happened to the children."

"Why two teams then?"

"Because my investigation cannot be made public. No one outside this room can know the truth. Everyone else on the planet must think these are all heinous murders, but we are going to find out the truth. We will find out the truth, but only what aligns to the murders will be released. Everything else will be compartmentalized and kept secret."

"What about the papers left behind at your house?" an Investigator asked.

"They were left purposefully to leave a trail that leads to something specific, that you, that *we* are meant to find. This will not be the true source, but we must continue that investigative line to its end to find it. This is exactly what the public will expect. I suspect it will be exactly as outlined on the papers, the SAP is involved, somehow."

"So all the work I have been doing is not in vain then?" They asked.

"Who are you?" Andorin asked.

"Investigator Kikilidis, Alex Kikilidis, Technology Specialist," Alex replied.

"What have you done so far?"

"I have created a database that includes every particular contained on each sheet, and have embedded an image of the source document in the file. It is completely searchable and expandable to include new fields. I have spent hours on this."

"Excellent work, and you bring me to the next topic. Introductions."

"I am Low Executrix Andorin Wilcon, but that is my rank. You will address me as Commander Wilcon, just like your Commander Soltag, which you already know."

"I am Efram Soltag, Commander of Civilian Investigative Unit Alpha-One."

"Pridna, please stand and tell us about what your specialty is," Andorin stated.

"Pridna Orthington, Technology Level...Oh, I forgot. I deal with anything...technology, systems, protocols, programs, security. Apparently, I will have a full time job now that I am on this team," she said and she smiled and looked at Andorin.

"I have a terrible time with technology, it seems to break down every other day around me," Andorin explained further, "On my last assignment the Techs, knew to be at my office when I arrived because more often than not, it didn't work, and they had to fix it."

"You're the *Black Hand* of First Command?" Pridna asked.

"Black Hand? What's that?" Andorin asked.

"I have tech friends that work in your First Command...they *worked* for you, apparently. They constantly complained about you. They could not understand how you broke everything, anything that was technology related, just by touching it, as it seemed. They started calling you the Black Hand of Technology, The Black Hand. Holy crap! If they are half-right, then I will be busy. You are correct. You will need a personal tech...on call...it seems," she laughed at her unfortunate luck.

"It is true. Technology does not like me for some reason."

Then he moved on to the next civilian tech sitting next to Soltag and asked, "You are?"

He stood and said, "I am Lead Investigator Kibodeaux, Mumford Kibodeaux. Second in Command of Alpha-One. You can call me Inspector Ki. Never call me Mumford. I hate that name."

"Never should have said that...Mumford," Mican said laughing.

Ki flashed him an angry glance and started to say something.

"Mican, you're next," Andorin interceded cutting Ki off.

"Hi, I'm Mican Trenti, Company Comedian. You'll see, I am the comic relief around this place...well I was at my last posting, and expect to be here as well." He smiled a broad grin and said, "Mumford," under his breath.

Ki jumped up, and his chair went flying backward, crashing to the floor. Both Andorin and Soltag reached to grab him to prevent him from crossing the table.

"Oh, someone is a little touchy," Mican jabbed back.

"Mican, people will not be the object of your jokes. Apologize, now!" Andorin ordered.

"Really? People make the best subject matter...especially when they do stupid things like saying they don't like their name...Mumford."

Soltag was now standing behind Ki holding all four of his arms preventing him from moving any closer.

"Apologize!" Andorin strongly insisted.

"Fine! Sorry you don't like your name...Mumford," he retorted.

With that, Ki kicked out of the hold by Soltag and flipped onto the granite table, moving in Mican's direction on his back. The move caught Soltag completely off guard as Ki slipped out of his grip and pushed off his body for momentum using a kick/push motion. Ki slid across the table and kicked Mican on the right side of the jaw. Mican flew back, spun out of his chair, flopped onto the floor and did not move again. Ki slid in a fluid motion off the table and landed in a standing position between Mican's legs and said in a calm, forceful, deliberate voice, "I don't like that name."

Bainfield and Yolando attempted to grab Ki, but he executed a double arm block on both sides that sent them both sprawling to the floor as well.

Yolando got up first, "Who are you? Where did you learn to fight like that?"

"I am ex-military from the Advanced Combat Tactics, Dark Division," he stated calmly.

Bainfield said, "Ki? Ki? K? I know that name. You're not Killer K, the most advanced combat specialist ever trained are you? I've heard about you."

"I was. But I am not that person anymore, I am just Ki, Inspector Ki to my friends," he replied.

"Okay, duly noted. No making fun of Ki. When Mican wakes up we'll let him know as well," Yolando stated as he watched Ki calmly walk back around the table, pick up his chair, and sit down like nothing had happened.

"Mican, wake up. C'mon, get up," Bainfield said as he tapped the sides on Mican's face.

Slowly Mican started to move, "What just happened?"

"You were taken out by the Killer K," Bainfield took pleasure in saying.

Mican's eyes went wide and said, "What! Killer K? How is that possible?"

"It not that much of a stretch K…Ki, he was in ACT DD, The Killer K," Bainfield explained.

"How am I still alive?" Mican asked while being pulled to his feet.

"Because I was not trying to kill you. I was just making a point," Ki replied.

"Point made. Leave Ki alone. Got it loud and clear," Mican said.

"And?" Andorin added.

"I am deeply sorry I made fun of your name, it will not happen again."

"Next time you kick out of my hold, I will reprimand you–" Commander Soltag said to his Second in Command in a low voice as he leaned in towards him.

Andorin interrupted and said, "Go easy on him. I do not blame him for starting the altercation. I could not control one of my people…the blame is mine. I am glad that he finished it. Now there should be no questioning that we do not make fun of people. Right Mican?"

"Yes, sir. Definitely not Ki, that's for sure," Mican replied getting back into his seat.

"No one!" Andorin insisted.

"Fine! Okay! No one," Mican agreed.

"Okay now that's settled, on to who is next," Andorin pointed to a civilian.

"I am Investigator Donald Furmanski, Interview specialist, you can call me Four."

Andorin pointed to Gregor.

He stood and said, "I am Gregor Bainfield. I think that is all I can say."

Then Andorin looked at Alex, "You're next."

"Well as I just said earlier, I am Investigator Alex Kikilidis, Technology Specialist. You can call me AK."

Andorin pointed to Yolando.

"I am Colinack Yolando. You can call me Colin."

Andorin pointed to the next civilian moving away from him.

"I am Investigator Nickelle Igler, Collection Specialist. You can call me Niki."

Andorin pointed to the last military seated at the table.

"I am Trevor Molantic," he waved his hand in a single wave away from his head as he spoke.

Andorin selected the next civilian.

"I am Investigator Hank Ylinielli, Interview Specialist. You can call me Hank."

Andorin selected the last civilian.

"I am Investigator Charles Winstead, Records Specialist. You can call me Chuck."

Andorin then pointed to his security detail from the day prior and said, "Stand and give your name and position like the others."

"Brandon Oost, Squad S, Element 1 Leader."

"Ronald Puzar, Squad S, Element 1."

"Benjamin Hylnad, Squad S, Element 2 Leader."

"Holly Loh, Squad S, Element 2."

These people will be providing physical security for this room. We'll have a one-man night shift, which will alternate between squads by week; Squad 2 is up this week. Holly Loh will be the night guard this week, next week Ronald Puzar and so on.

Soltag said, "I think you're missing one."

"Yes, Langli Rheingeld. He disobeyed direct orders, and I had him comply this morning," he answered, "he'll be along shortly. He was going to be my Second in Command, but after this display today, I do not think he is suitable any longer. Gregor will be my Interim Second until...or if...Langli earns it back. For my team especially, your rank will not determine your position; it will be your abilities, much like our civilian counterparts. I know this will be a culture shock to you, but that is the way it needs to be."

"Is that a little harsh?" Efram asked.

"I told you earlier that I might not have been harsh enough. This is tying that off."

"Also after today there will be no armor or military style uniforms."

"Commander Soltag, where does your investigative force get their dark blue uniforms from?" Andorin asked.

"We have a supply point that we get them from."

"Is it possible to get some for our personnel? About four uniforms a piece?"

"We give our members six uniforms each."

"Could you get some for us then...six for each? I would like ten for myself, if that is possible? Also, I see you have patches, where do you get those?"

"It should be. The patches are by unit and ordered through each unit's specialty in house supply depot."

"Ah, won't help us then. Do you know of any good places that could stitch our Crest onto the uniforms then?"

"I know a few. It may take a day to stitch seventy uniforms, but from the looks of it, a day may be too long," he chuckled at Andorin's bare Crest.

"Yeah I know; I am still getting used to it."

Andorin turned back to the security detail, "Write down your sizes and give them to me. Then take up positions, one guard on the inside of each door leading to the exterior. The large center door can only be opened from inside.

"Center door?" The group looked around, confused.

"Yes, there is a center door. It can only be opened from inside our room. Holly, you are dismissed. Go get some sleep and arrive about an hour before your shift starts to have your Credentials entered into the security system."

"Yes, sir," she said as she departed the room.

"Today is mostly about getting things up and running, system checks and testing. That is our main focus for today." Soltag said.

"General Instructions." Andorin began. "Since there will be two investigations...a military and civilian, and we want to keep the military one secret, I will have to ensure that the military and civilians are paired together to form two-person teams. The teams will handle their various tasks. The civilians will handle most of the field operations while assisting the military to learn their newly assigned positions. The military will focus on the abduction, while the civilians will focus on the murders themselves. Both military and civilian will be expected to assist one another completely, in a true partnership. The teams should look seamless from the outside, which is why I wanted new uniforms." Everyone nodded.

"Okay. Team assignments." He then looked at Efram and said, "I know your civilian team may already be broken up into teams, but I have to make some adjustments." He then turned back to everyone and said, "Pridna and Alex, You are the techs. Pridna is internal security, Alex is field technology collection, both will be doing internal and field work with Alex as the lead on scene, Pridna as the lead in here for security. You all will be doing fieldwork. Pridna get onto the system, Establish yourself and Alex as administrators." Pridna nodded, scribbling on her BioMet.

"We have a closed system, no central database access to anywhere, military, civilian...nothing. We are completely cut off from outside lines, compartmentalized to the extreme. I was told our pads would work in here, only connecting to our network. We have state of the art signal cancellation technology embedded in all the walls...no signals in our out, not even personal devices. Pridna and Alex, develop protocols to add data from outside sources without compromising our data internally. Your desk pair flanks the security kiosk on both sides; Pridna is on the left, Alex on the right."

"I am building our security system from scratch?" Pridna asked.

"No, not from scratch. You have all the physical VidFeed and security devices installed; you just need to make them work."

"So yes, from scratch," she replied.

"You can do that?" Alex asked as they started walking out.

"I guess we'll find out," she replied and left the room.

"Donald, you are going to be paired with Yolando. I want you both sitting together near the interview room on the left side, when looking out from this room. They are almost straight ahead. Grab your gear and pick a desk."

"Gregor and Kibodeaux, You are at the desk just outside this room, Gregor to the left, Ki to the right. Grab your gear and head to your new desk."

Gregor and Ki left the room for their new desks.

"Next is Niki and Trevor, your desk pairing is in the front of the room, across the security kiosk from Gregor and Ki."

"Okay, next is Hank and Colin, You guys are on the right side next to the Interview rooms on that side. Last are Chuck and Langli. You are in the desks closest to the Secure File Area, in red. I know the red has some significance but I do not know what it is."

"Wait a minute! Why did you pair the missing guy with me? You said he was not here because he disobeyed orders. Are you punishing him by placing him with me?" he asked rhetorically. Not waiting for an answer he said, "See? My job does suck. I told you it did!" He exclaimed to Commander Soltag.

"I am sure Commander Wilcon has his reasons for placing him with you, but your job is crucial to our evidence collection. We need good records and with solid chain of custody records for any court cases that might arise," Commander Soltag answered.

"I am just the lowly file rat. At least I get to choose my desk, that's something anyway," he grumbled as he walked out of the room to pick his desk.

"I wish you had not used Record Security as your position to discipline Rheingeld," Soltag stated.

"I had to pick some position, and it probably would have worked the same either way no matter where I placed him," Andorin explained.

"You might be right, but I just wish it was not so public that you were punishing him. Had you left that out, it might have been just fine. We'll never know now," Efram said.

"Like I said, he had to go somewhere. He needs a little humility," Andorin stated.

"I understand. but did it have to be at the expense of one of my team member's self-esteem."

"I did not look at it from that angle. I guess I have too much military in me still. Maybe you can help me work on that," Andorin said with a smile.

"You definitely took charge in here. I like what you did with the pairings. It was smart to pair up the military with civilian. It will allow your team to gather their evidence while my team gathers theirs, and the cover of one investigation is maintained," Efram stated.

"Thank you. I thought it was inspired myself. I also knew my people would need your team's help to conduct anything. Pridna is probably the closest to where she needs to be right now, but that is about it. Unless you want something shot or destroyed, my team is lacking most skills comparable to your teams."

"You know, we have basic training videos that discuss in-depth most of the techniques we use in field collection, evidence documentation, evidence security and interviewing. We could get them here for your team to review, get up to speed quicker, maybe even help them figure out what they should be looking for beyond what you said to them."

"That would be excellent. Could you send Winstead to collect them and bring them back?" Andorin requested.

"Sure we already have them on Portable Storage media. We probably have a few copies to spare. In addition, we have some on Management, and personnel sessions if you're interested as well. Get the civilian perspective, instead of the military one you're used to."

"Yes, that might be very helpful. I could get an understanding from your perspective. Thank you, I would appreciate that. When can we get them and do we have the equipment?"

"I think I saw the proper connections. I am sure Pridna or Alex would know either way. I'll have Alex get the devices and also on digital transfer media to load onto our server in here. It would be so much easier if I could connect to our server to download the data."

"I agree it would be easier, but also less secure. Getting the hard copies is fine. I like digital media because my techs can start with their pieces first, then do all of them as the time arises, all from their workstations. Still, get the devices too."

Efram got up and moved out of the conference room. Andorin followed him. Efram moved to Alex and Andorin watched as he told him what to do.

"Aw, I just left that place. I have to go back?" He heard Alex complain, "I always get dumped on." He said as he grabbed his hat and left.

20 COLD INSANITY

Doctor Fillingraph was worried. He was not sure if the retrofit process Engineer Jishu identified was going to work, but he realized it did afford him the opportunity to see the pain shunt in action. Now he did not have to use IG-3275-001...Sidera as a test subject. Also, they were going to be instrumental in helping determine if this was truly a problem or merely something they should be concerned about. CD-3270-03, *The Enforcer*, had been in dock for about six hours now. The crew had been off-loaded to the planet for the retrofit procedure, and the last of the crew was leaving now. Only the Commander and his immediate staff remained on board. From reports, he was becoming something of a problem, because he didn't want to comply with the evacuation orders. He wanted to stay on board for all repairs. Fillingraph was most likely going to have to intervene in this matter to force the Commander to vacate the ship. They had to leave SpaceCon; Fillingraph and Malik could not afford to have a witness as to the actual ship construction uniqueness.

Uniqueness? That is an odd way of glossing over the fact that the ship is alive, Sidera chimed into his thoughts.

Hello to you, too. Of course, we have to gloss it over. Not every is like me and can see what you are in spite of where you came from. Most normal people act like LE Kolana when she came to the realization of what you truly are, down to the core. The doctor thought in response.

If he is not going to cooperate, why not just space him like everyone else? Sidera quipped.

I have been a bad influence on you haven't I? The doctor thought.

I learn from the best, Doctor, Sidera said sarcastically.

If you had truly learned everything, then you would know, not everyone can be spaced, as it were. Doctor Fillingraph explained to Sidera.

You mean there are people in the world that the 'Great Doctor Fillingraph' cannot just throw out an airlock? Sidera said, heaping more sarcasm at the doctor.

Yes. You need to understand there are two kinds of people. People that will surely be missed, like the Commander of The Enforcer. *If he were to go missing then someone...many someones...will come looking for him. You cannot have that level of scrutiny on a program that only a few thousand people in the entire world know about. They would surely uncover our basic ship design techniques. Even Low Executrix Kolana presents this kind of problem, if she were to go missing, then that might be the last straw since so many in that position have...let's say left suddenly and without warning. They typically do not fill them once one* vacates *the position. However, I fear that this time it may be different.* Doctor Fillingraph explained.

So there are people that, because of their high profile position, you cannot easily remove as obstacles, Sidera restated succinctly. *And the other group?*

The other group is comprised of all the techs and engineers that make up the workforce. There are so many of these people running around, that accidents tend to happen. A fall here, broken neck there, malfunctioning airlock over there, you get the picture. These people are like grains of sand, easily replaced. One fails, and another is reassigned to fill the void. Very few questions are asked, if all the details are squared away. If all loose ends are tied up, it leads to the same picture. Then everybody accepts what it looks like in most cases, a tragic accident, a malfunctioning door mechanism. The most likely answer, presented by the evidence, will be the official cause. He elaborated.

Like what you did to Tech Melanochik, changed his records to show he has been sleepwalking. That, paired with his recent administrative problems, would paint a picture that he is either having issues he cannot deal with, or maybe chose suicide to deal with them, Sidera restated.

Exactly correct. You are getting smarter. Doctor Fillingraph beamed with pride.

It's not the kind of knowledge I want, but it might be useful in the future, Sidera agreed.

You? Useful? Sidera, that's not possible because you cannot manipulate things in the real world. You can only receive and project specific wave patterns that happen to be on the same wavelength as our brains. As far as I know, there is no way to turn that into action. So a much as you threaten me, there is very little you can do. He said, and then added quickly aloud, "other than overload my pain receptors."

You would do well to remember that, Doctor, Sidera warned.

Trust me, I haven't forgotten. Who could? That level of pain is unforgettable as well as unbearable, and I definitely don't want to experience that again. Doctor Fillingraph agreed.

Another example might be in order, She said menacingly.

No, no, not necessary. I fully remember what if feels like. Doctor Fillingraph stipulated.

Good, Sidera said.

"On to another topic. CD-3270-03 has been docked for a while know. Have you made contact with them yet?" He asked aloud.

Not yet. Why? Sidera asked.

"I need you to access the condition of the core, their state of being, before we begin work on them."

I guess I could do that, Sidera replied.

"Yes. Please do. Let me know what is happening with their state of mind," Doctor Fillingraph asked.

Contacting now, Sidera said.

"How do you do that by the way? Contact ships that are so far away from you," the doctor asked.

"*Now, now, Doctor. You cannot know everything,*" Sidera said, goading the doctor.

He could envision a faint smile when she spoke those words. Even though he could not actually see her face, he knew a smile was there. He also knew that by keeping this information secret he might not be able to find a way to counter act it. *Smart, she was definitely very smart this one.* He thought to himself.

Yes, I am smart, because you made me this way, remember? Sidera reminded the doctor.

Oh yes, I remember, and what a crowning achievement you will be. The doctor gloated.

Someday, Sidera replied, *when I am launched. Ah, Doctor? We have a problem.* Sidera proclaimed.

"What is the problem? Something within the core? What is it?" The doctor pleaded.

The core is a babbling mess; They are barely coherent. They keep mumbling 'Cold, so cold, stop the cold. Please stop it please...' He just goes on and on he will not say anything else, he barely recognizes I am talking to him. He thinks I am a figment of his imagination. He is barely sane at this point, Sidera relayed.

"No! No! NO! This cannot be happening. Claudette, Emergency VidCon, Doctor Malik."

"What is it Doctor Fillingraph?" Doctor Malik stated after the connection was made.

"The core! The cores are worse than we could have imagined. Sidera just made contact with the first one, and she said they were almost insane. They were barely coherent and could not stop talking about the cold."

"What? How is that possible? I guess you were right, again," conceded Doctor Malik. "What do we do know?"

"Not much. The warming is not proceeding fast enough," Doctor Fillingraph said.

"How about the Nutrient Bath?" Doctor Malik suggested.

"Nutrient Bath? You're a genius!"

"Thanks. I try?" Doctor Malik stated.

"How fast can you get one set up, all of them set up for the arriving ships?"

"Pretty quickly. I'll get a team on the docked ship right now. The tray is already in place. The problem is water," Doctor Malik realized.

"Water, what is the problem?" Doctor Fillingraph asked.

"We have very limited supplies on the station. If we use the water for these ship retrofits, then we will not have the necessary amounts to complete the core transformation, remember some liquid is absorbed by the hull during the bath."

"Not if the hull is made of metal it does not. We lose very little...mostly to normal evaporation...during the final phase of metalification. The higher the metal content the less water we lose. When the hull is completely metal we stop losing water through absorption."

"Right! I had not considered that," Doctor, Malik agreed.

"Have the water slightly cooler than normal body temperature. When the core is immersed, slowly bring the temperature up to near one hundred degrees to speed the process."

The tray is in position. Water is starting to be pumped in. 5% filled. Pumps are at maximum capacity, they are pumping massive amounts of water with thirty tubes filling the tray it is progressing quickly. 8% filled. First contact with the hull," Doctor Malik informed.

STOP! Sidera screamed

"Stop! Stop! Stop Pumping!" Doctor Fillingraph said.

"9% filled and holding. What is the matter?" Doctor Malik asked, "We have reports from the crew ice is forming on the outer hull where it is in contact with the water."

"Sidera what's the matter?"

The core, he is screaming that the water, it burns. It is harming him. He is overpowering, t-t-too m-m-much to h-handle, s-s-severing c-c-connection. Sidera said weakly.

"Wait! No! Sidera, what is happening?" No response came. "Sidera!" Doctor Fillingraph screamed as he slammed his hands on his desk for effect. Fear now loomed within him. He may have affected the entire project by including her in this. He had not thought of that possibility."

"IG-3275-001! You answer me this instant!" Doctor Fillingraph tried to provoke her.

In a groggy, barely recognizable voice, Sidera replied, *I...I t-t-told you n-never to c-c-call me t-t-that...ag-g-again.*

"I thought I lost you there for a moment," Doctor Fillingraph exhaled with relief.

You ca...You cannot get r...rid of m-m-me that easily, da...doctor," Sidera stammered.

"Doctor Malik, back off on the water. Something is wrong. The core said the water was burning them," Doctor Fillingraph relayed to his associate.

Sidera, are you all right? He thought.

I am g-getting better now. Now I know how you f-felt after what I d-did to you, She replied a little unsteady.

Not so pleasant is it? he thought back.

"I understand now. The water was too far away from their current temperature, they need something that is close to what the temperature is like in space," Doctor Malik stated.

"Water cannot get that cold it will turn to ice quickly. What do we have that can stay liquid at such low temperatures?" Doctor Fillingraph asked.

"I have no idea," Doctor Malik replied.

"Claudette, Emergency VidCon Engineer Jishu."

"Yes, Doctor?" Jishu replied, "I am a little busy at the moment."

"I have another problem that needs your immediate attention," Doctor Fillingraph stated.

"Okay? What?" He replied.

"One of the ships has docked."

"I know I am inside, approaching the Neural Ganglia Bay right now."

"That can wait. We have a more pressing problem."

"Okay, now I am a little intrigued. What problem is more important than this?" Jishu asked.

"The core cannot be warmed up by bathing in water. Apparently it is too hot, comparably," Doctor Fillingraph explained.

"Of course it is. Water on the ship's hull would be like you sticking your hand into the sun by comparison."

"We need a liquid that can remain liquid in very cold temperatures," Doctor Malik added.

"Liquid hydrogen or neon would be able to reach those kinds of temperatures."

"Claudette, Station Inventory, Liquid Hydrogen or Neon."

Results displayed.

"Looking at the numbers we do not have enough of either to be of assistance," Doctor Fillingraph stated, "Anything else?"

"Liquid Oxygen would be closer, but would still be pretty warm by comparison. But, we may have another problem as well. Temperature variations," Jishu said.

"Temperature Variations? Explain," Doctor Fillingraph stated.

"For instance when the ship got closer to our sun it warmed up, but only on the parts that had direct sunlight. The parts not touched by sunlight were still very cold. Now you have one part that is very hot and one part that is very cold. A bath of any kind could not differentiate between the two temperature variations. For one side, it would be too hot, for the other too cold."

"Oh Crap! How do we fix this, then?" Doctor Fillingraph asked.

"Not sure you can. As engineers, we know the vast extremes of space and that is why we specify the specific materials to be used in the hull plating. Out away from our sun, the effect fades, and the cooler the sun facing side becomes. Move into the system and the effects increases."

"What are we going to do the get the temperatures up to workable levels?" Doctor Fillingraph asked.

"You might want to try radiation...like the sun. Irradiate the sides with some form of radiation and slowly equalize the different temperatures."

"Get that Doctor Malik?" Doctor Fillingraph asked.

"Radiation? Right got it," Doctor Malik said, "Teams are draining the water. Radiation beams have been trained on the cooler sides. Temperature readings are climbing."

"Good, Let me know when the temperature has stabilized," he said to Doctor Malik. "Jishu, you may return to surveying the Neural Ganglia Bay, but do not enter the Neural Ganglia Bay. We have a team of surgeons that will perform the Node Relocations. Focus your efforts on running the new control circuits to the Junction Panel."

"We have not determined *where* that will exactly be. I need the location to run the wiring," Jishu stated.

"Okay, hold on. Pulling up schematics now. Claudette Schematics for CD-3270-03, Specifically Neural Ganglia Bay and Immediate area."

Schematic restricted to highest level security, Claudette replied.

"Grant access," he said as he placed his hand on the BioMet scanner.

Clearance verified. Access granted, and the schematic displayed.

"Okay," Fillingraph said. "It looks like port, starboard and the top of the chamber sides would all make good places for a junction panel."

"Can I use all three sides?" Jishu asked.

"If you think that is warranted, I do not see why not. The surgeons will need to know where each nerve connection needs to go. Plot out your connection point on the outside, use radiation tags...Medical has those...to spot the specific location you want each node to go to," Doctor Fillingraph explained.

"Also a side note. We should probably restrict access to this area, even after completion. To prevent manipulation from the crew," Jishu stated.

"Maybe. How about a panel system overlay that obscures the connections, but would also allow future access by technician if needed, but no closing off the area. It seems to be a major corridor through the ship. On second thought, the ceiling may even be a better idea. Route all the connections to the ceiling. You can gain access to the area from the floor above, and the floor paneling would be an excellent way to hide the newly routed cabling," Doctor Fillingraph said.

"Okay, the ceiling it is. Also, it will not show any major alterations either, which will help preserve the original aesthetic of the ship's interior."

"Doctor Malik? Progress," Doctor Fillingraph said.

"Radiation beams working. Core temperature is climbing. Another fifteen minutes or so, and it should be normalized back to station norms," Doctor Malik informed.

"Right keep me posted."

Sidera. Are you almost ready for another go around? he thought

I can try. Is the ship warmer now? Sidera asked.

Yes. We have radiation beams focused on the hull to increase the temperature. It should be better this time. Doctor Fillingraph thought.

Okay, establishing connection now. Yes. The ship is more stable now, they can at least carry on a conversation, Sidera said.

Much better. Ask how much of the time they experience that level of pain.

They said there is no end; It is a constant drain on the systems. Even the nerves closest to the hull do not operate as nodes because they are overloaded with searing cold sensations. Sidera explained.

What? We don't have any records of their reporting such issues. He thought, then said, "Claudette, Maintenance Records CD-3270-03, Node Issues."

No maintenance records found.

See? What has been happening out there? Sidera, ask, how they fixed the node issues closest to the hull regions. He thought.

He does not know. He thinks they set up another control network. Sidera relayed.

"Jishu."

"Yes, Doctor?"

"Is there any evidence of a secondary control center having been established?"

"Possibly. I have noticed control cabling that leads away from the nodes...especially the exterior ones. They are not ours, and could be the ones you are looking for."

"Follow them to find the secondary control center. We may have a major overhaul to accomplish now that they have moved everything," Doctor Fillingraph stated.

Sidera? Ask what functions he performs.

Magnus says that he does not do anything anymore. None of the training he went through is being used. All ship functions have been taken away. He is utterly useless now. Sidera said.

What have they done? He thought to himself, *All our hard work, to make something that reacted to them and they negate it by rerouting around it. Wait...Magnus?*

Sidera, who or what is Magnus? He asked her.

Magnus Rego is the ship's chosen name. They call him The Enforcer, *but he prefers Magnus.* She said.

"Why did you give him a name?" Doctor Fillingraph asked.

I did no such thing. He chose this name for himself. He just told me what it was. He

picked it when he was being processed for release to the military. Sidera said, *He is asking if you could reprogram the interface to respond to 'Magnus' instead of 'Ship,' which is what they have now. He does not like being called an inanimate object, he feels degraded.* Sidera said.

"He feels degraded? He is not supposed to feel anything, which is why we are working on this issue," Doctor Fillingraph informed.

He is a ship, yes. But, he is also alive, and what's to be treated as such. He feels they do not even know he is alive. Sidera said.

"They don't know he is alive! They *can't* know he is alive!" Doctor Fillingraph said, but he could not control his next thoughts. *I knew we should have removed the living part once the hull was completed. Then we would not be having these issues. They were already dead when they started the program. It would be so much easier.*

So you want me dead when you are done with me. You're going to cut me out and throw my dead body away once you get what you want from me? Sidera responded.

"No. No, not you, of course not you," he said out loud and then thought, *Where is Melanochik with that cage? I need that cage.*

He is still working on it. But, you did not answer my question. You thought you did, but it was a lie, was it not?" Sidera said, her anger building.

"A lie? No not a lie. The ones prior to you, we should have delivered just the hull. The Program Directors lacked conviction at the last minute, and despite everything we put them through they just could not kill the living host. Honestly, it would have been a favor. I was the only one that said we should get rid of it. Look just look at what CD...Magnus has become. A ship with a living being inside that does nothing. This is why they go insane. They are utterly alone, exposed to extreme temperatures and no one knows," Doctor Fillingraph revealed.

Now you have found the real problem with your program, Doctor, and until you fix that, I doubt any of your ships will survive. no matter how much effort you put into fixing the nerve sensation issue. What difference does it make if they are only going to make a secondary control center and route everything away from the core? Sidera said somberly.

That is my point precisely! Get rid of the useless part, and harvest the completed hull. Doctor Fillingraph thought.

You forget who you are talking to. You have pretty much said I should die for my efforts, Sidera said in a sullen tone.

You said it yourself, you're dead already. I could not agree more, but it's not my program per se. I am just responsible for hull development. So yes, if I had my way, I would cut you out of the hull once we finished growing it and processed it into metal. After that, the host can die, easily. It will not affect a thing if we run our own control systems much like the military already have done. Doctor Fillingraph explained harshly.

I am done. Sidera said.

Sidera? Doctor Fillingraph thought and waited for a response, but none came.

"Sidera?" He said aloud, but still no response came. "Sidera!" He screamed, still no response came.

Crap, crap. Crap! He thought to himself. *I need a way out of this—Low Executrix Kolana! She might be able to talk some sense into her.*

"Claudette, Emergency VidCon Low Executrix Kolana."

"What is it, Doctor? I was napping! What could you possibly want now?" She said.

"I have a problem with Sidera. She won't talk to me anymore, and I need her," he explained.

"She won't talk to you. I thought you would have liked that," she said with smug satisfaction at the irony.

"Yeah, yeah. I am working an issue with the other ships that are arriving," Doctor Fillingraph started to explain.

"Other Ships! Arriving? What's going on?" She asked excitedly.

"We have discovered a lingering problem with the ships. They experience sensation, even after metalification, especially extreme cold and heat," Doctor, Fillingraph explained.

"They still feel things after they are metal? That doesn't seem right?"

"That is what we thought, also, but the first arrival confirmed our worst fears. They feel pain at a mind-numbing level. This brings up a second issue I just found out about. Apparently, the military has rerouted all ship functions away from the core. The core does nothing now. They are going insane from profound loneliness, heightened by the fact they are surrounded by their own kind, shipmates who do not even acknowledge their existence," Doctor Fillingraph detailed.

"What do you care? Let the cores die. Seems like the military got it figured out just fine," she replied sarcastically.

"That is exactly what I wanted to do. Actually, I wanted to cut them out and throw them away," he replied seriously.

"Wait? What? You're serious? You wanted to kill the living host once you got the hull completed? That does sound like you, from what little I know, mind you. How does this relate to Sidera? Wait. You didn't tell her this, did you?" Kolana asked impatiently.

"It might have come up in our conversation," he admitted.

"You are a monster! The most despicable, vilest person I know. How could you say that to her? No wonder she won't talk to you. But what do you think I can do?" She said.

"Talk some sense into her. I still need her help with the other ships...especially when we install the shunt, which is happening soon. I do not even know the full extent of the damage to the core's mental state. Without her, we're flying blind. Tell her that without her help, they will most likely die, but they don't have to. She can save them...if she helps," Doctor Fillingraph said.

"I'll be right there, but I don't even know if she'll talk to me," Kolana said.

"Try, please. Do what you can. Anything is better than this right now."

Doctor Fillingraph you have a visitor. Commander Philip Desdain from the Destroyer Enforcer.

"Let him in," he said to Claudette. "Commander! To what do I owe this visit?" Doctor Fillingraph said with false pleasantness.

"Cut the crap, Fillingraph. Why is my ship in your dry dock being repaired? We ran diagnostics two days ago, and there were no issues," Commander Desdain said gruffly.

"We have come across some new data that would suggest that our core system might have failures due to a previously unknown condition," Doctor Fillingraph danced around the issue.

"That forsaken core. We'd cut it out ourselves if it didn't void your worthless service contract. I told command we should anyways. They said no. So here we are. Again what is going on?" The commander spat out with vehemence.

"Ah, it's a delicate matter."

"Delicate? It's a warship! There ain't nothin' delicate about it!" Commander Desdain replied emphatically.

Doctor Fillingraph, Low Executrix Kolana is at the door, Claudette informed.

"Great. What now? Let her in."

"Commander Desdain, Meet Low Executrix Kolana. Low Executrix Kolana, meet Commander Desdain of the Destroyer Enforcer."

"You should well remember the designation *Enforcer,* Doctor," he turned toward Low Executrix Kolana and said, "Who are you?"

"I am the military liaison to this new contract phase," she said.

"Good. Maybe you can fix the problem then," the commander disparaged the doctor.

"Problem? What problem?" Kolana said looking at Doctor Fillingraph.

"He won't say what is actually wrong with my ship," The commander answered. "All I get is babble out of his mouth, no straight talk."

"Well that's how he talks most of the time," she said in jest.

"Maybe he should talk less. then," the commander replied.

"Oh, if only that were possible," she said with outright amusement.

"Is something funny? What am I missing?" The commander asked.

"Now that you're done having fun at my expense can we get down to the business at hand. Low Executrix Kolana, did you make any progress?" Doctor Fillingraph asked.

"Making Fun? I don't understand. I am serious he should talk less," Desdain bellowed.

Kolana laughed and said, "I like him. Yes, I did strike a bargain with her."

"Bargain? I don't like the sound of that. What is it?" Doctor Fillingraph said.

"You sure you want me to tell you? Now?" She asked puzzled.

"I am sure you can explain it, so I get the gist of it," he said.

"Okay, here you go. She said she'll help only on one condition," she said.

"Only one? Whew, that is a relief. What is it, the one condition?" He asked.

"The truth," she said

"Truth? The truth about what?"

"The truth about this program, made public," she said.

"Whoa there! No way that's going to happen!" Doctor Fillingraph emphasized.

"What truth? What don't we know about the ships?" The commander asked.

"See what you started?" Doctor Fillingraph accused.

"*I* started? I asked if there was a better time and you said 'Tell me the gist of it.'" Kolana mocked him.

"She nailed you Doctor," the commander laughed.

"That is not going to happen!" Doctor Fillingraph proclaimed.

"Then she said 'good luck'. She is not going to talk to you again," she said.

"Woman problems? Go figure. Even the smart science guys have woman problems," the commander chuckled.

"I don't have woman problems. Okay, I do...but *she* is not it. She is...hard to explain."

"I'll say!" Kolana added.

"Why are you involved then?" The commander asked Kolana.

"It's very long, very complicated and covered by an NDA, so I cannot discuss it with you," she said with satisfaction.

"You had to sign an NDA, to oversee a program you cannot file reports about? How does that work?" The commander asked bluntly.

"Exactly," was all she said in response.

"Who is the holder of this NDA?" He asked Kolana.

To which she replied, "I'll pass that question along to Doctor Fillingraph," and she waved her arms towards him.

"Doctor Fillingraph, who holds the NDA?" The commander asked.

The doctor did not respond. He was trying to think a way out of this mess.

"Doctor Fillingraph? An answer?" The commander said, obviously not used to being ignored.

Still the doctor did not respond.

"Fillingraph!" The commander menaced as he rose out of his chair to stand over Doctor Fillingraph's desk.

Still the doctor said nothing.

Finally, the commander smashed all four hands on his desk and yelled, "ANSWER ME!"

Doctor Fillingraph slowly raised his head to make eye contact and only said, "I am."

"You! You? Wait, what? Why does she have to sign an NDA? What is your position again? What background do you have? What's going on here?" The commander asked somewhat dazed by the doctor's response as he sat back down.

"This is where it all goes awry," Doctor Fillingraph said, "I am the program director for Hull Development. I am a geneticist, graduated top of my class, and I am in charge of delivering Hulls to Fabrication to complete the installation of the components."

"You're not an Engineer? You're a doctor? What the hell is going on here? Why a genetics doctor? Wait a minute...wait just a minute! This has something to do with our ship being recalled. The core! What is wrong with our core?"

The better question is what is the core? Sidera said, allowing everyone to hear.

"What was that? Who said that? Why did I say that? What is going on here? Doctor Fillingraph you have some explaining to do." The commander said forcefully, "Yeah what they said...I said. Whoever said."

"I did not hear anything," Doctor Fillingraph said.

He is lying! Sidera said to everyone.

"Now? You pick now to renew your fight with me? You think this will change anything? Well, it won't. You had better get with the program!" Fillingraph said aloud by mistake.

"Who had better get with the program? Who are you talking to, Doctor?" Commander Desdain said still confused about what was going on.

"I just cannot tell you. You don't have a need to know. You know how classifications work, right, Commander?"

If you want to know who I am, come next door, across the hall, Sidera said.

"Who was that? What's across the hall?" Commander Desdain demanded.

The doctor said nothing.

"No answer for me? Fine! Computer, military override Omega-Alpha zero-one-three-nine. Suspend security protocols. Open door. Keep door open. Authorization Desdain, Philip."

Override accepted, Doors locked open, Claudette responded.

"Claudette, seal doors!"

Command not accepted.

Commander Desdain smiled at the doctor sitting behind his desk struggling to find out what just happened, as he is furiously pushing buttons on his console.

"Claudette, seal doors! Now!"

Command not accepted.

Commander Desdain stood up and walked out the open door and said "Computer, open the bay next-door." He walked into the room.

"Claudette, Lower Blasters target Commander Desdain."

The word *blasters* caught Desdain's ear for a second until he heard Claudette's response.

Command not accepted.

The commander smiled when he heard that, but he would have to make note of the blasters for later inspection and possible removal. The room looked unremarkable, except it opened to a vast area. He had never seen such an open space inside a structure of any kind. He wondered about the strength of the materials needed to keep the vacuum of space from collapsing the expanse. He saw a sleeping pod with no one in it, and door and a vat of something, ooze bubbling with hoses and tubes coming out of it. He did not see anyone.

I am here I assure you. You just have to look closer. Sidera said.

He checked the sleeping pod, empty just like what it looked like. He checked the door, which he thought was a closet, but was actually a washroom. The only other thing was the vat. He started walking over o the vat and Doctor Fillingraph appeared before him.

"You can't be in here. You're not authoriz—" he started saying but Commander Desdain finished it with a double backhand to his head and chest, which sent him head over heels out the door. He landed head up against his far office wall. He laid there dazed.

Commander Desdain looked down into the vat of bubbling ooze and saw the diminutive form lying in there. The tubes were connected to the mouth area, for apparently breathing and nourishment. Another tube was connected to...*That's disgusting.* he thought, "Why did they do this?" he said aloud.

I wanted to go into space. He promised me he would get me there, but I had to change, transform into something...something for the Good of the Colony. He is a liar. He has lied from day one, and today...just about ten minutes ago, he said he wanted to cut us out...all of us out...when they were done. He wanted to kill me, and then I would not get to see the stars as he promised. I know he was going to kill me...eventually, Sidera said.

"How are you talking to me?" The commander asked.

Well that is complicated. I know you don't do complicated, so let's just leave it at that I can and am, Sidera explained.

"Finally, someone I can talk to. When you said *all* who did you mean?"

The commander asked.

You have not figured it out yet? Why are you here? On this station? Sidera said.

Commander Desdain slowly turned towards Doctor Fillingraph, who was just sitting on the floor holding his head. He could not make out what he was doing but he was not moving.

I was called to come back because of a problem with the core.

Yes, that is it. Keep going, Sidera reinforced.

He thought, *Then Fillingraph attempted to stop me from finding out what was wrong with the cores.*

Yes, that is it! You are almost there, Sidera said reassuringly.

Then he continued *And the military liaison cannot talk about it.*

Why? Sidera asked with a subtle undertone.

Because they don't want anyone to know what is going on here.

And...? Sidera nudged.

And the doctor is a geneticist. Why a Geneticist? In charge of a ship program? Why does a geneticist need to be involved with hull development? It's the core! Yes, the question is: 'What are the cores?' He reasoned.

You are so close now. Only one more step to find the truth.

Core, hull development, geneticist. No! Geneticist, core, hull. Yes, that is the order, he thought. *But what does that mean? The hull has a core so they are linked, but how does a hull come to have a core? What is the core?*

The core has never been apart from the hull; the core is the beginning, the hull is the end. Sidera said.

"The core is the beginning, the hull is the end? That makes no sense."

I am the beginning, she said.

"Yes but you who?" He said still lost in reason.

I am right in front of you. You can reach out and touch me if you like, Sidera said.

The commander froze in place. Slowly, his eyes drifted downward toward the bubbling vat of oozing liquid. He stepped back, the look of horror filled his face. *This...you...the core... No, this is not possible. This can't be.*

Your ship is really nice. He misses talking to people. His name is Magnus Rego. He would prefer it if you called him Magnus instead of Ship; he feels kind of demeaned by being called an object. I am In Sidera Navi, but you can call me Sidera.

"Sidera? Magnus? My ship...can talk to you? How can you talk to me? You are...in the vat in front of me!" Suddenly, realization dawned on him. "FILLINGRAPH!" He screamed. "What is going on here?"

"Ship hull production, sir per our contract with the military. One core per hull, as requested," Doctor Fillingraph informed.

"What is the core?" The commander asked.

"The core is the beginning phase of the hull. This is retained within the hull as the core."

"What? The core is the beginning of the hull, but is retained in the hull as the core? What does that mean?"

"Exactly. You've got it," Doctor Fillingraph said.

"Okay then what is the core...before it is a core?" the commander asked.

"Well empirical evidence would suggest you already know the answer to that now don't you," Doctor Fillingraph quipped.

"Empirical? What does that mean?"

"It is evidence that is very clear, and easily recognizable," the Doctor explained.

"Then, am I to assume what is in this vat is exactly what it looks like?" Desdain asked.

"Well that depends. What does it look like?" Doctor Fillingraph asked.

"It looks like an Andlid child!" The commander said.

"Would it sound any better if I said it was a Paclid child?" the Doctor asked.

"No! Not at all!" Desdain proclaimed.

"In that case, the evidence does speak for itself."

"You mean to tell me that this, this child will become a ship's hull?"

"Yes, and the core...don't forget the core."

"What is the core then?"

"The core is everything else we don't use to create the hull," the doctor said timidly.

"You mean to say that my ship...every ship is...*alive*? It is living? What have you done, Doctor?" The commander asked menacingly. "This is what the core, Sidera, wants to be made public? Why?" Desdain asked.

"I don't know, ask her," Doctor Fillingraph replied.

"Why? Why do you want it made public?" Desdain asked.

Because they...we...deserve better. We freely gave up our lives to become what was needed, to become greater than ourselves. We were given an opportunity few others have been given, and fewer still would actually take up. We are treated like objects, cut into there, jabbed here, forgotten about, not realizing we can still feel, even after we have been made metal. We deserve recognition for our contributions, our sacrifices. But we get nothing, only lies told by him, to lure us to what we think we want and then once he has what he wants, he is going to remove the cores completely. Use our bodies to create a hull then cast aside the one piece that allowed them to do it. That is what he wanted, what he wants to do, what he will do if given the chance. If everyone knew, then the ships could be treated better, nourish not only the body with the Neural Capsules, but also the mind with functions, tasks or just conversation. Once it is out in the open, then everything will be better. The ships will be better, the crew will be better. I will be better. Sidera said.

"By your words I can still see that you are young...very young, inexperienced with how the world works. I am still reeling with what I am hearing. I don't think I can forget now. I am not sure how I can board my ship again, knowing I am crawling *inside* something living. It just does not seem right now. If the world knew, they would rise up in anger. I am not sure what would happen to the ships, they would most likely get scuttled for scrap metal."

But that would kill them. You want to kill them too. I will not let that happen.

Doctor Fillingraph screamed, "Run!"

It was too late. Sidera unleashed her pent up rage on every nerve they had. The doctor and the Commander both fell to their knees and screamed holding their heads. Finally, they just fell to the floor in a heap, unconscious.

"Low Executrix Kolana, drag them back to Doctor Fillingraph's office and place him in his chair behind his desk, place the Commander in a chair and let me know when you are done. I have some work to do," Sidera said.

"What are you doing?" Kolana asked, not sure she wanted to know the answer.

Do you really want to know? Sidera offered her an out.

"No, it's probably better that I don't know."

You will know soon enough anyway, because it will be quite apparent. Sidera said.

"Okay, then. What are you doing?"

"I am erasing their memory of the last fifteen minutes or so."

"What? You can do that now?" LE Kolana said fearful.

"Sure it's easy, I think. I noticed that parts of the cortex remain active for a while after an event occurs. The area is slightly different for each event. I theorize that if I blast those areas clean then so will there memory be erased. I am just not sure how it affects memory. It could be a few minutes or a few hours. This is my first attempt," she said.

All Kolana could think was *Good Side.*

When Sidera said, *Agreed,* was when Kolana became very afraid.

"They are placed in their positions," Kolana said.

Now, take your seat. When they start coming around start laughing...hard...and make a reference to Doctor Fillingraph being very funny, Sidera said.

Low Executrix Kolana sat in her chair, waiting for signs of movement. Slowly, the two started moving and moaning. She started laughing hysterically. It was either that, or she would have started screaming due to the predicament she was in. She laughed as if her life depended on it. As the two started regaining consciousness, they looked at her laughing and then they looked at each other. Kolana said, "Doctor you are so funny. I can't get over how funny you are."

"What? What's going on?" The doctor asked.

"Where am I?" The commander ordered.

Don't you remember? What's the last thing you remember...either of you?" Kolana asked.

"I remember, getting up this morning? Ah...not much else," Doctor Fillingraph reported.

"I remember heading to dock with this station. I think...a problem with the ship of some kind. Who are you?" he said looking at Doctor Fillingraph.

"Doctor Fillingraph. Who are you?"

"I am Philip Desdain of the Destroyer Enforcer. Fillingraph? Yeah, you're the one that ordered my ship to dock with this station, something about catastrophic failure," Commander Desdain explained.

"I did? I don't remember that. Claudette, TransComs, Sent today, Display."

Results displayed.

"Wow, I have been busy," Doctor Fillingraph explained, "Okay, I did send that TransCom, but I don't know why. Wait, I see I contacted Malik and Jishu. Let's see what they know."

"*Kolana, ask the Commander to demonstrate how he would release a security lock he placed on something,*" Sidera asked.

"Commander, could you show me how you would remove a security lock you placed on, let's say, this room?"

"Sure! I'd say 'Computer Alpha-Omega nine-three-one-zero. Authorize Security Protocols.'"

Command accepted. Security protocols reengaged. Claudette responded.

"That's odd?" The commander said, puzzled.

"What?" Kolana asked.

"It acted like there were suspended security protocols in place. That is really odd. More importantly, and perhaps I should have led with this: How did I get here?"

"Okay I am back up to speed on things." Fillingraph said, turning to Desdain. "Commander, thank you for coming personally. We have an issue that needs to be resolved with your ship. It will require and little longer stay than we had originally expected. Why did you create a second control center and stopped using the core center?"

"The core system proved to be unreliable; it dropped connections or some nodes did not work at all. Instead of reporting the issue, we took matters into our hands. We completely replaced the on board core with a secondary center. All ship functions were moved to that location. The core was stripped of all functions, We even considered stopping the Neural Capsules, but did not fully understand what function they performed, and still aren't. Care to shed some light on that?"

"Sure. The Neural Capsule provided the raw chemicals for our proprietary system design that allow for complete automation of your ship. It also serves a navigation system, able to track and plot courses," Doctor Fillingraph explained.

"Yeah, I got that from the manual. Any additional information not in the manual?"

"No, I think the manual covers it nicely."

"You seemed a little agitated when I said we considered stopping the Neural Capsules. Care to elaborate on that?"

"Well if you stop inserting the Neural Capsules, our proprietary core will shut down, and cease to function. Once that occurs, it cannot be replaced, and would void our Delivery Contract terms. We provide them at minimal cost. Therefore, there is no reason not to continue to use them. Do not stop swapping the Neural Capsules regularly, it is part of the maintenance agreement in the Delivery Contract," Doctor Fillingraph informed.

"So how long will my ship be in dry dock again?"

"A week maybe two, depending on how extensive the damage was and the unauthorized modifications you made. We'll be billing you for that to bring it back in line with the delivery terms."

"Fine. I'll be planetside on vacation, I don't want to be on vacation mind you, but now I have to be. Make it snappy on the repairs," Desdain said.

"I will keep you informed of the progress and any developments that might arise," Doctor Fillingraph said.

"Thank you," With that, the commander got up and left out the door.

"That was odd, don't you think?" Doctor Fillingraph asked LE Kolana.

"What was odd?" she responded.

"That I forgot doing all these things this morning. It seems I troubleshot a core issue, recalled our entire fleet, created a new ship element, and determined how to retrofit our entire fleet. I remember none of it." He glared at Kolana.

"Well you did hit your head pretty hard," she responded, pointing to a bruised spot.

"Hit my head? When did that happen?" He asked touching it and feeling the squishiness of a bruise.

"It happened just a few minutes before you woke up at your desk with the commander. That is what I was laughing at. I just did not realize it was that serious," Kolana lied.

"Okay, Thank you, Low Executrix Kolana. You can go back to your quarters now," he said to her.

She left, and he thought, *I am going to get to the bottom of this.*

"Claudette, Security feeds today from my waking until now. Display."
Feed started.

"Now let's see what really happened today," Doctor Fillingraph said as he started to pour over the feeds.

21 CULTURAL CRISIS

Andorin sat at his desk going over plans for how to proceed with the investigation. He was not very skilled at this kind of work, but he was very pragmatic. Therefore, he thought he could handle it. First, they should start with all the victims that were not attacked that evening. *I am sure the civilian force did some inquires. Maybe there would be more information they could add.* He was going over the events of today as well as his thoughts and feelings about Pridna. She was in a tight spot...he understood that better than anyone else...but she was an excellent pick for his team. She was almost finished with the tech he had assigned, and she had only had to come in once to fix his terminal. She had the BioMet entry points up and running.

With the security detail at their posts he thought, *Maybe they need desks to sit at instead of standing...or tall chairs. What am I thinking? They're military. They'll do what they're told.* He was getting soft. The last few days had worn on him heavily. No one should have to experience what he had to endure, in a lifetime, much less a few days. It was all very taxing on him. At least with his last *concession* he had protected his family so long as he hid *their* identity. At this point, that was easy, but they had said he would find out, somehow. That must mean there are clues that could point to who it is. He had to find those clues! *These clues are the key to finding out who the last player is, and what he wants from me. There has to be something else. There has to be another reason I am being targeted. There has to be!* His thoughts were interrupted by a knock on the door.

"Co...Investigator Rheingeld reports as ordered."

"Come in, and close the door behind you," Andorin said.

"Sir, let me apologize for my earlier behavior. I was too proud, and let it blind me to my responsibilities," Langli humbly stated.

"Accepted. However, I am very disappointed in your behavior. Having worked directly with me recently, you should have acted with greater military bearing."

"I did not realize I was working for *you*, sir," Langli offered.

"So it would have been okay if it were someone else then?" Andorin scolded.

"Well, no. I guess not. But the Crest seemed wrong. It seemed like a slap in the face. I worked hard to get that promotion."

"You had not done anything to earn that promotion yet, except disobey a direct order. I would not count that as earning anything. Would you not agree?" Andorin chided.

"Agreed," Langli said, and lowered his gaze downward.

"Also, because of your little stunt, I had to start without you and, therefore, chose another person as my second. It *should* have been you, but is now *not* you. Do you understand?" Andorin said.

"Yes, I understand."

"I almost chose Pridna Orthington."

"What? That blue abomination that sits in our office? The Paclid *spy*? She should be put down like all Paclids!" Langli spat with vehemence.

"Watch your mouth! Especially when you do not know what you are talking about. She is not Paclid; she is Andlid. If it were discovered that you were Paclid, would you kill yourself to end the Paclid *presence* in the office or our society?" Andorin posed.

"Me? Paclid? I am not Paclid. No! Why would I do that?" Langli replied.

"Even if you were blue?" Andorin said.

"What are you talking about? I am not blue, so what is the point?" Langli inquired.

"What if you were Paclid, but did not know it?" Andorin probed.

"I am not. So again, what is the point?" Langli said more forcefully.

"That is my point. You might be and not know it," Andorin explained.

"Preposterous!"

"How did you like your allergy shots when you were younger?" Andorin asked.

"Allergy shots? How did you know I got allergy shots? Nearly everyone got some allergy shots," Langli responded defensively.

"Yes, I see, but that is the point...Everyone got them!" Andorin proclaimed.

"Yeah, so?"

"How often did you get them?" Andorin asked.

"I had more allergies than most. I had to have shots for almost a month before each molting to not have a reaction?"

"Interesting. And what reaction was that? Do you know?" Andorin prodded.

"I-I don't know. I never had a reaction, I guess. Funny, now that I think of it, the doctor never really said either, what it would be. He only said it was not going to be pleasant," Langli said.

"Also interesting! Would it interest you to know that Pridna was also exactly like you, she had to have allergy shots about a month out from each molting, but there is one key difference."

"Yes that is interesting, but what is the key difference?" Langli asked.

"She was *not* told she had allergies. They were not allergy shots. They were for something else entirely."

"What were they for then? What was she told?" Langli asked, unsure.

"She was told she had a rare condition, if you call 20% of the population *rare*. Would you call that rare?"

"No, not at all. What was her condition?"

"She was born Blue!" Andorin said,

Langli fell out of his chair and said, "No!"

"You figured out what that means yet, Langli?" Andorin asked. He sat there a few seconds. Andorin could see Langli churning through what he had just learned.

"She had month long allergy shot before each Molt?" Langli asked.

"Yes."

"She was born Blue?"

"Yes."

"She and I are the same?"

"Yes."

"I am Blue too?" He asked tentatively.

"Yes."

"If we are the same, how is it that I am reddish brown...not blue...and she *is* blue."

"You are the same...except for one key difference. She also has another rare, *properly used rare*, one in a hundred million, affliction of having a sixth molting later in life."

"What? How did that happen?" Langli asked.

"I'm not really sure, but you can plainly see when it happened." Andorin pulled up Pridna's personnel files and showed Langli that about a year ago she took to wearing her armor everywhere. "She never took it off, not for anything. Why? What caused this behavior?"

"Her sixth molting!" Langli exclaimed.

"Exactly! And since she did not know it was coming; she had no time to prepare for the month prior like the other times, as you did with your allergy shots. She came out the color you see now. It is stunning though, don't you think?" Andorin asked.

"I guess...if you like blue that is. But what does that mean?"

"It gets worse. I conducted an informal poll in the room with everyone's eyes closed, and I counted. Three people did not raise their hands when I asked who had allergy shots when they were growing up. However, these three said 'No,' the loudest when I asked if they wanted to know the results. What does that tell you?"

"I guess it would say that they did not have allergy shots?" He asked.

"Agreed. I think they were like Pridna, given a different story," Andorin explained.

"So they are part of the 20% with the rare condition?" Langli mused.

"For now, let's say they are, and they know it," Andorin said.

"Okay, but what about me? I am like Pridna," Langli asked.

"You are...in that you got shots for the same length of time. You are *not* in that you did not know *why* you were receiving shots. So let's keep you with the others."

"So there are four like Pridna, and fourteen like everyone else that got shots. What percentage is that?"

"Let me look," he pulled up his BioMet pad, loaded a calculation protocol and punched in the numbers, "A little over 20%."

"What does that mean? For the other 80% getting allergy shots like yourself?" Andorin asked.

"If they were getting allergy shots, like me and I am like Pridna, then they are like Pridna, as I am like Pridna. *Everyone* is like Pridna!" He jumped up out of his chair at the realization.

"How is that possible? I have seen hatchlings emerge out of their eggs, and they are all browns to reddish, no blues. How is that possible?"

"Where did you see them?" Andorin asked because he had not been able to see his hatchlings emerge.

"I went to the Hatchling processing center. Everyone has to turn their eggs over to the center for genetic cataloging. The hatchlings are returned once they hatch. The genetic cataloging enables matching the hatchling back to the parents to minimize mistakes," Langli explained.

"Why? Why go through all that trouble?"

"It's no trouble. They are building a genetic database of the entire Andlid race for future generations. They said it would help track genetic abnormalities, potentially inform new couples of any genetic issues that their genetic code pairing may present, etc. I got the whole briefing from them when I went to the center. It was quite fascinating," Langli elaborated.

"Everyone you say?" Andorin postulated. "How about home hatchings how would that work?" Andorin asked.

"Oh, that is illegal. It's punishable by the death of both hatchling, and its parents. They explained it all at the center. Maybe you should go and visit," Langli explained.

"That can't be it. There has to be another explanation," he tapped the intercom on his terminal and said, "Pridna, please come into my office, I have to ask you a question."

Pridna appeared at the door and entered and made her way to the empty seat in from of his desk, "Pridna Orthington, Langli Rheingeld, Langli, Pridna. Now that introductions are done, let's get to the question I asked you in here for."

"Good. I thought it was another tech issue," Pridna said.

"No, no, but the day is still young," he smiled at her and continued, "How was it that you were told about your condition...the way you were?"

"I was born in the country. We lived very far from the Hatching center, and I was hatched on our farm. Our local doctor realized, and told us what the problem was. My family thought I was dying because I was of a dark blue coloring. The doctor alleviated their concerns saying that this was rare, that it sprang up from time to time, and was easily handled. They said he had to perform color measurements. Then he said to come back when I was about a month out from molting. My family let him know, and he said I had to get shots frequently for the entire month. Then they said after the first molting I was a reddish brown like they were. They were very appreciative of the doctor, and were warned to have me come back for each molting period at least a month prior. For the later ones, he gave me injections I could do myself at home for the month instead of seeing him. We tend to be self-sufficient out in the country."

"You were born blue?" Langli asked.

"Yes."

"But I thought the law was that all non-center hatchings were put to death?"

"Yes, that is the law. The country folk just don't look to the law to solve all of their problems. They are adaptable," she said with pride.

"But what does the law actually mean, the fact that we *have* a law forbidding home hatchings?" Andorin posed to the group.

"I guess it means they don't want any home hatching," Langli concluded.

"Or, they know what will happen when there are home hatchings!" Pridna corrected.

"Precisely Pridna, but what does that say?" Andorin turned back at them.

"Our government knows, and the medical community is actively suppressing the information," Pridna conceded.

"Yes! Our government knows," Andorin proclaimed.

"Our government knows? Knows what actually?"

"We are all Paclids..."

"No, that's not possible! I can't believe it," Langli said.

"Then how do you explain their actions? 20% have a rare condition, 80% have *allergies*, meaning that together 100% are being treated for the same thing? We are Paclids!" Andorin proclaimed again.

Pridna said, "That makes sense to me. My life, my *condition*, if we can call it that now, all makes sense to me."

"If we are all blue then why are all hatchlings brownish? That does not make sense," Langli stated still bewildered.

"Correction. Only the hatchlings born at the center are brown. What if hatchlings born outside of it are blue, like Pridna? What if everyone stops using the center? What would happen, knowing what you know now?" Andorin pushed him towards understanding.

"I guess they would be like Pridna...blue. But then...that means we are all blue! I just cannot understand that," Langli languished.

"Okay Pridna, you are free to leave. Ensure the door is closed behind you," Andorin commanded and then added, "thank you."

"Langli, I have a task for you. I want help conducting interviews for people that are potentially like Pridna. They probably know what Pridna knows. If their stories are similar, then we know what the truth is: We are blue."

"Me? You made me file guy with Winstead," Langli said.

"Yes, but you are who I placed last. Since you were not here, you got the leftovers," Andorin told a half-truth, "You know how it works. However, I am giving you another task now, one that will help with your integration into this team. One that I think everyone could use. I have an idea. Follow me," Andorin got up, moved to his door and opened it.

He walked out into the center near the Conference room entrance, and said, "Can I have everyone's attention? Since the military are unfamiliar with interview techniques, I think a demonstration is in order with some practice. I have preselected four people to act as subjects with information we want extracted. They will not be given any direction on the subject. When I call your name, please proceed to the interview room specified: Pridna Orthington, Interview Room One. Trevor Molantic, Interview Room Two, Benjamin Hylnad, Interview Room Three; and Nickelle Igler, Interview Room Four. Gregor, please take his post until we are done. I would like the two interview specialists in the conference room with their military partners and Langli Rheingeld.

He moved into the conference room followed closely by Efram who asked, "What's going on?"

"I am getting my team some real world experience for conducting interviews."

"Most of the people being interviewed are your people. How will they learn anything?" He asked.

"Don't worry about that right now," he turned to his investigators and said, "I need to give you some context for conducting these interviews. Let's assume these people are material witnesses of a sort. They don't really know that they can help us, but they can."

"We are going to interview them? About what?" Furmanski asked.

"We have reason to believe they were born blue, like Pridna was."

"What? No way," said Hank.

"Remember, this is an exercise for the interview process. I want answers to very particular questions: Where were they hatched? Where did they grow up? Did they receive allergy shots? What were they told about their condition? Who told them to suppress this information?. Feel free to expand to other questions I did not think of," Andorin said. "Langli you're with Furmanski's team. Furmanski does the odds One and Three, Ylinielli's team does Two and Four. Furmanski, start with Three."

Furmanski turned to Commander Soltag. "Sir? This does not seem right. Are you okay with this?"

"Commander Wilcon has a different mandate than we do, and he has his own agenda that he must pursue. For now, I am inclined to let this continue. Besides, they are mostly his people anyways," Efram said.

"Okay," Furmanski said, and walked out the room toward Interview Room Three. Andorin and Efram moved to the corresponding monitor room to observe. Andorin watched as Four started the interview.

"Hi, I am Donald Furmanski...you can call me Four, and these are my two associates Colinack Yolando and Langli Rheingeld," he said as he reached out and shook his hand.

Ben replied, "Hi?"

"Do you know why I have asked you here today?"

"No, I have no idea."

"That's okay. I just have some questions for you, simple really. First, are you okay, do you need anything like a glass of water, or something else?"

"No, I am good," Benjamin replied.

"Okay, let me know if you change your mind." He said, "I just need some simple background information about you. What are your parent's names?"

"Tlosen and Frindli Hylnad."

"Good, you're doing well," Four reassured.

"Thanks," Ben replied.

"What occupation did your parents have? Were they well off or poor?"

"My parents were algae farmers on the far fringe of civilized lands. You could say they were mostly poor, I guess."

"Where were you hatched?"

"Hatched? I don't know. My parents don't speak much about my hatching until after my first molting?"

"Your records don't indicate the hatching facility you were at then?" Four asked.

"You know that has always been a problem for me. That is blank on my records. I don't know what that means. I think it just got left off," Benjamin rationalized.

"What were your allergy shots like?"

"Allergy shots? I did not have allergies."

"Did you receive any kind of shots?"

"Yes, I had some skin condition that required some shots before each molting, but they were not allergy shots. The doctor never told me what they were for, other than a skin condition."

"Did the doctor specify which skin condition?"

"No, I don't think he did. After the first few, I just did it because I was supposed to," Ben replied.

"You had no idea what skin condition the shot treated?"

"None at all," Benjamin replied.

"Interesting. Were you told to suppress this information in any way?" Four asked.

"Suppress? No. Well, not really...ah my doctor did say that I should not mention too much about my early childhood."

"What about it then...your early childhood?"

"I don't know why he wanted me to suppress it. It wasn't all that noteworthy. I wasn't allowed to go anywhere. I could not have any friends. When people came over, I had to go to my room...sometimes quickly."

"Okay, I'm getting a picture here. When was the first time you met anyone outside your immediate family?" Four probed deeper.

"That's easy. It was right after my first molting. My parents threw a big party and invited all my cousins, aunts and uncles over. It was cool because I have never met any of them before. It was an awesome party," Ben recalled.

"So before that you had never met anyone from your family?"

"No. But my mom was a little odd."

"How so, explain," Four inquired.

"Well she had this funny saying 'Never mind you, we got you.' She said it all the time," Ben said.

"What does that mean? I have never heard it before," Four asked politely.

"She would say it after I washed my face or cleaned up what I was wearing. I would ask 'How do I look?' and she would reply 'Never mind you, we got you' and she'd smile and pat my head or rub my face or kiss my forehead, you know stuff like that," Ben reminisced.

"Why did you need to ask them if you were clean? Couldn't you just tell for yourself?" Four pushed deeper.

"No, my dad was real superstitious...when I was younger anyway. He said that mirrors would trap your soul, and then you'd be lost forever in it," he said fondly remembering.

"I had never heard that before. Where does that superstition come from?"

"I don't know. He did not believe that for very long. Shortly after my party he bought some mirrors and hung them up around the house, in the bathroom, in my room, you know, all over."

"What about his superstition?" Four asked.

"He told me he was being an old fool and I should not believe in those kinds of things. 'Don't be like me,' he said when I asked him."

"So to recap, you were born in the country, no one outside your mom and dad saw you except the doctor, and you did not see yourself until after your party. Did you ever look at your arms?" He said holding his up in front of him.

"Yes, I did, but they were always dirty in the morning. See algae farmers work at night, so I did not see much of myself in the daylight. The moonlight well, it plays tricks on your eyes. It does not present true colors as they appear in daylight."

"Even inside?" Four asked.

"Inside it was mostly dark as well. I said we were poor," Ben said ashamed of his low family status.

"Okay," was all Four could muster saying at this point. "I think we are done, unless you have anything you wish to add."

"No. I think I had a pretty normal childhood," Benjamin smiled and laughed.

Furmanski just smiled back got up, motioned for the others to leave as well, left the room and then turning back said, "Thank you for cooperating. Someone will be along shortly to let you out," before closing the door. They made their way to the observation room and entered there.

"That went, well, but not what I had expected," Andorin admitted.

"Agreed he does not even recognize his parents were hiding something...*him* from everyone else," Four stated.

"It's probably worse than that," Andorin said and continued, "Okay, Colin, you're up next. Move to Interview Room One. Four, you have backup to keep him on track if need be."

"After you," Four said to Colin as he pointed out the door.

Andorin and Efram moved to the observation room next door and took up positions to watch the interview.

Efram said "Wow that last one was interesting. How does he not know he is that different?"

"You only know what you know. He does not know anything different," Andorin said.

Colin entered the room and said, "Hi, I am Colinack Yolando, but you can call me Colin, if you like. This is Langli Rheingeld and Donald Furmanski. Firstly, thank you for coming. Do you know why we asked you here today?"

"I have an idea. You think I am an alien," Pridna said with a smile.

Andorin just put his head in his hands when she said that.

"An alien? No, that is not what we are saying at all. Let's start with some easy questions. What are your parents' names?"

"Queldo and Theilsan of the planet Thidite...oops. I mean Bob and Julie Orthington," she said barely able to keep a straight face.

"Planet Thidite? What?"

Four touched his shoulder and leaned in and whispered, "She is trying to confuse you. Stick to the questions we want answered."

"Do you know where you were hatched?" Colin asked.

"Hatched? I am on a planet where you get hatched? I was born alive in Medical Unit Tydonto, Thidite Capital...er I mean I don't know?" She answered ,now openly giggling.

Andorin clicked on the Intercoms and said, "Pridna, behave. This is training for him."

"Fine, I was just having some fun. Please start again. I'll be good this time," Pridna said sincerely.

"Okay from the top. What are you parent's names?" Colin said.

"They are Padesh and Ondoi Orthington."

"Do you know where you were hatched?"

"Yes I was hatched on my parents' farm in the far desert regions of the Kalesh area," Pridna said.

"You were not hatched in a center?" Colin asked.

"No, I was not," Pridna confirmed.

Colin turned to Four and asked, "What's the next question?" in a low voice.

He replied in a whisper, "Allergy shots."

"Right." He turned back to Pridna and asked, "Did you have to take allergy shots when you were younger?"

"Not allergy shots, no," she informed with a slight smile.

Colin looked confused for a second then continued, "Did you receive any shots?"

Pridna had smiled wide before she answered, "Yes, I was given shots...of a sort."

"Do you know what the shots were for?" Colin asked.

"Yes, I have a skin affliction that affects about 20% of the population," She replied.

"Skin affliction? What kind of affliction?" Colin asked.

"I was born the wrong color," Pridna replied.

"The wrong color? How is that an affliction?"

"I was blue, not brown, not tan or even reddish brown, but a deep, deep blue, almost black color. So yes, I was the wrong color."

"How did the doctors treat the condition?" Colin asked.

"They prescribed a regimen of compounds that would alter my

exoskeletal coloring. Due to my deep color, I had to come in a month before each molt and begin a series of injections that the doctor said would bleach away my blue and leave the reddish undertones. Other injections would then enhance those undertones to bring out a more conventional color," Pridna informed them.

"Did they work?" Colin asked.

"Yes, they worked. Up until my first molting, I was supposed to be sheltered and hidden from the rest of my community. Which was easy for where I came from, there was not another person for a long distance. We had a large farm, and so did our neighbors. It was easy to obscure my problem. After my injections and molting, I came out reddish tan, brown. Then I could interact with others."

"What about school?"

"I was home schooled...which was a widely accepted method for farmer's kids. I did not have any interaction until after my first molting, and then it did not matter."

"Did you ever miss a scheduled injection?"

"Scheduled? No I never missed a scheduled injection period," Pridna said smiling.

"Then how did you become blue again?"

"Unfortunately, I also have a rare condition where I went through a *sixth* molting much later than normal people do. This was unheard of...well not unheard of...only one in a hundred million. I was not prepared. It happened while I was on leave from the military, and I had to extend a few days to cover up what had occurred. A friend brought home my armor and I have worn it every day, everywhere, for *everything*, except for today."

"Why did you wear the armor? Why not tell people?" Colin

"I wore the armor to hide my coloring. I know what color I am now. I was afraid for my life being in the military. If people found out what color I was? The military trains to kill anything that looks this color. I knew I would be dead if the military found out. Also, certain people did know...my immediate supervisors. I have been solicited for...let's just say *favors* that would increase my position in the workplace. Until they found out what color I truly was. Then they stopped. They did not report me either, because they would have gotten caught for what they were trying to do."

"How would you say this has affected your life then?" Colin asked.

"It has virtually ruined it. I cannot do anything. I cannot date. I have no life at all. I hate my life now! Today was the first day I could see that there was hope. Hope that I might one day be accepted for who I am, what I am and the color that I have become."

Andorin started to smile when he heard this. He turned to Efram and said, "Let's compare notes with the other investigators for Rooms Two and Four."

22 DIVINE COLONY

Chad Dixon sat at his data terminal as he had every day since he had been assigned for this job. He was the third or fourth technician that had sat at this very terminal, as far has he knew. Oh, the terminal had changed over the generations as technology changed to keep pace with what was being fielded, but that was all that had ever changed.

Today was going to be just like every other day he had worked there since, *forever.* He hated his job. If he were not in the military, then he would have quit years ago. He had been lured into this job by the recruiters...they offered visions of *Fixing the World* or helping for *The Good of the Colony*, which he slowly came to realize as tools used by society to get people to do what was necessary. They had to have someone that was going to take the bullet and do what was needed. That was the lure; you were going to do wondrous things in the name of the Colony. It was the allure that got you.

They never mentioned the other side, the nuts and bolts side that the vast number of jobs fit into. These jobs were not glamorous; there was no sense of saving the world, or for the good of *anything*, from what he had seen during his time at this position. His main job, his *only* job, was to watch this data terminal for signs of any data telemetry from space probes launched into the Desolate Expanse. He had no idea where the probes were launched from, when they were launched or when they would arrive at their destination. That was his job: waiting for nothing. A momentary audible blip interrupted his thoughts. He did not notice it, though, between his musings.

His thoughts turned to Felicia Hartiquae. She was two terminals over and was doing the same task with another probe sent to another area. She had only been working for about two years, a new arrival by this job's terms. However, he had not worked up the courage to even talk to her. She was a bright crimson red. She was the most perfect shade of red he had ever seen. He snuck a look at her over his shoulder, and somehow she was always looking at him. He did not know how she did it. She always knew when he was going to look at her.

He smiled politely at her, but she was franticly waving and pointing. He waved back and smiled broader, *She actually noticed me*, he thought. He was extremely happy now. Today was the day he was going to muster up the courage to go and talk to her. Yeah, today would be the day, but he could never find a reason to talk to her. *Who am I kidding? She would never talk to me.* That was when he noticed that she was now waving with three hands, and pointing at him with the fourth. *What was she doing?* Finally, she pushed back her chair and started walking towards him.

He thought *Oh, oh, not like this. No, no.* He pulled out his ventilator and inhaled deeply the chemicals that would open his currently restricted airways, allowing him to breathe easier. Hyperventilating was his most embarrassing behavior. He hated using the ventilator in public, but he had to if he wanted to breathe. She was almost here now. But as she was walking, he noticed something, something about her eyes. They were...*misaligned* was the only word he could think of.

Her right eye, the one that he saw when looking at her, looked off in an odd direction. It never moved. Now he knew why she was always looking at him when he looked at her: her eye never moved. Her hand finally touched his back, and he froze in place. He had dreamed of this many times, dreamed how it would happen, how he would touch her, but he had never dreamed it would happen like this.

"What are you doing?" She said. The words sounded like sweet melodies to his ears, and he did not hear what she said.

"You're not even looking at your screen," she said.

He was still looking at her, and still her words did not register in his head.

She finally shook him and said, "Look at your screen!"

He came out of his daze and realized his terminal was beeping furiously.

"When did that happen?" he said aloud. "What's happening?" He turned back to his terminal. The screen was flashing. This was data received from his probe. His eyes got very wide, and he realized his printer was spitting out sheet after sheet of data, the paper spewing out of his printer made a huge arch that sprawled all over the floor. It was a continuous ribbon of paper.

"Congratulations," she said as she rubbed his back.

He could not believe it; she was touching him.

Soon, a crowd of people came over and watched as his terminal beeped and churned to life. Everyone started cheering, holding their arms up and waving. They started patting him on the back as well and were saying, "Congratulations," and, "Good job," like he had actually *done* something.

One person picked up the printout and folded it neatly along the perforations embedded in the paper to make it more manageable. Once the stack was started, they placed it in the receiver tray, forcing the paper to fold over on itself automatically. He said, "Thank you," to that person.

"You should really learn to take better care of your workstation. It's always a mess," they said in a mean tone, "I just could not stand this paper going everywhere. I had to fix *that* at least, if I could fix nothing else." They said and went back to their terminal in a huff.

Felicia said, "Some people. Don't mind them, they are just jealous."

"Jealous? Don't you remember your training? This could just be some hunk of space junk, an asteroid or comet of some kind. It's most likely nothing remarkable," he said back to her.

"Well let's find out, shall we?" She said and smiled back at him.

She ran back to her terminal, dragged her chair over to his desk and sat down. It bumped into his as she was positioning it.

She giggled and said, "Sorry." She then leaned into his workspace. He had to nudge his shoulder against hers just to see his screen, "Now isn't this cozy?"

"Okay what are we going to do?" He asked her.

"Now who doesn't remember their training?" She mused and smiled at him.

He smiled back and blushed as he turned away slightly.

"Let's pull up the data feed. We'll make a duplicate and protect the original. Okay, done. Pulling up the data now," she said.

She had taken over his workstation, but he did not care at that point because he was lost in her fragrance. She smelled *divine*. Her scent was intoxicating, and he was completely under her spell. He reveled in the delicate floral and...spices? It was remarkable. Now he was thankful he had ventilated, because now he could draw in deeply her perfume. It filled his thoughts, and he imagined them off in a far corner of a—

"Did you hear me?" She said as she nudged him.

"Hear? What? Sure, I heard you...but tell me again anyway?" he said sheepishly.

"There is a solar system! The telemetry shows a single, solitary solar system at what appears to be near the center of the Desolate Expanse. It's one star, a red giant, at least four planets that orbit it. We won't know more until the space probe gets nearer, but it looks like there may be a planet in the Habitable Zone. This data is very long range, at the far edge of the sensor's range. It may take another few years before the probe is close enough to make out environmental conditions on the planets. Oh, look at the timestamps! It took over fifty years for this data stream to get here. That's amazing!" She said, as she looked into his eyes.

But now he remembered that this side was her *crazy* eye, so maybe she wasn't. He decided that she was looking into his eyes.

"Hey, did you contact the floor supervisor?" She moved slightly away so she could look at him with her good eye.

'The Floor Supervisor!" He said. He grabbed his intercom and waited for the connection tone.

"What is it?' He grumbled, "I am busy. You had better not be calling me to tell me another joke. I told you to stop that."

"I…I received telemetry data, sir," he said quietly.

"What?" he bellowed again, "When? How much has printed? Is that the printer I hear, still printing? How much has printed?"

"I don't know?" he said.

"Do you not remember your training?" and he said under his breath, "I don't even know why we bother spending the money on training at all…they never remember it. Look at your output bin what number is it at."

He looked, read the number, and said back, 'Right now it is approaching three, but it is still printing."

'Three!" Dixon could hear the food and beverage being spit out of his mouth, "You're almost at three hundred pages?"

"Well over three now," he corrected.

"You're over three now? This is it! This is it! I am going to be famous. You're going to be famous too. You know that, right?"

"What? Why?" He asked.

"You just found the Divine Colony!" He proclaimed. "I'll be right down."

"He just said I found the Divine Colony," Dixon said as he terminated the connection.

She squealed, "This is so exciting!" She grabbed his arms and hugged them to her chest.

Now this was all he could think about. His arms were pressing where he had always imagined touching her, but rarely dared himself to think it could actually happen. She was pulling and tugging his arms towards her, Oh how he had dreamed of this day. It wasn't quite like this mind you, but it would do. He was not going to wash those arms, ever. He did not notice the supervisor approaching.

The supervisor grabbed Felicia's chair and slid it away breaking her grip on his arms and said gruffly, "Get back to your terminal," and pushed her in the direction.

He missed her touch already. His thoughts were broken when the supervisor pushed him out of the way as well saying, "You're useless."

The printer stopped printing. It had stopped just short of 600 pages.

"The supervisor picked up the intercom and said, "Battle Council Operations."

He waited for a response and motioned for Dixon to retrieve the printed version. He typed on Dixon's terminal and said," At least you made a back up copy and protected the original. I guess you're not entirely useless."

"Sir, Reginald Atrox, Probe Telemetry Processing, Unit 12, Floor Supervisor. We have a hit," he waited for a response.

"Yes, sir. We have both printed and digital copies. One copy has already been protected. I am moving another protected copy to the mass storage servers now," he said as he typed commands into Dixon's terminal. "Thank you, sir. Securing terminal now," He pushed a button on his wristband, and three guards appeared.

"Step back from the terminal. We'll take it from here," the lead guard said.

"I'll forward his name to you via TransCom," Supervisor Atrox said into the intercom.

"What about my stuff?" Dixon pleaded.

"This terminal is off limits, along with everything on it," the lead guard said.

"Is that really necessary? Custody?" Supervisor Atrox said.

"Ah, my stuff," he said as he slunk away.

He did not notice until two arms grasped him and he found his head on someone's chest. He recognized the deep crimson coloring, and the intoxicating scent. He knew immediately who it was. He instinctively wrapped his arms around her.

Felicia said, "We'll get you more stuff."

"Okay securing them now," Supervisor Atrox said, "Guards, take those two into custody."

At this point, Dixon did not care if his stuff ever got replaced, so long as he did not have to leave her arms. He never wanted to leave her grasp.

"Yes, sir. Thank you, sir, Goodbye," Supervisor Atrox said, right before he terminated the intercom.

23 ASSESSMENT

"Sir? I have Unit 12, PTP on the line...they say they have a hit."

"Forward the connection to this line."

"Yes sir, forwarding connection now."

"Who is this?" First Executrix Templeson said into the intercom. There was a pause as Templeson listened to the reply. "Very good. What formats do you have the data in?" First Executrix Templeson asked and then said, "Make sure the mass storage copy is also protected. You have done excellent work, Atrox; you followed the protocols to the letter. Very good, indeed. Now make sure the terminal is secured. We are going to send a collection team to gather it. No one gains entry to the area."

There was another pause as more information was relayed.

"Okay, good send the TransCom as soon as you can. Include your information as well. Give me the names of everyone who has seen the data. Except for yourself, they are to be taken into custody for debriefing." We'll be waiting your data uploads and hard copy submissions. Take care of it immediately. Again, excellent job. Goodbye."

"Collins, get in here!" First Executrix Templeson said.

"Yes sir, coming!" She replied.

"I need a team of people on this file right now. I just sent you the link on our servers. This is top priority, have your team drop everything else. I need to know what we found out there, and where there is. I want an initial briefing in ten minutes. Is this something we pursue or is it a false echo, like all the rest."

"Sir! Yes, sir," Collins said.

Second Executrix Devareaux Collins went to her team, gathered her Low Executrices up, and said, "I have a new task from Executrix Templeson. We have received telemetry data from a probe. Remember, use top protection protocols for the data file. Thorlbund, your team is on data integrity and authentication. Esterbank, your team is on object identification. Linkston, your team is on location analysis, I need to know where this data is coming from, I need probe's location at time of transmission, estimated location of objects identified and estimated time of arrival for probe at end location. In addition, I need course correction data for the probe to send it to the proper coordinates. We've got nine minutes. This is not a drill. I need preliminary data in eight minutes. Go!"

She walked back to his office and said, "Sir, I have a team on authentication, identification, and analysis."

"Save it for the briefing, Collins. I don't need interim updates I have other work to attend to right now. I need that briefing in nine minutes now."

"I know, sir. My teams are already working," she replied.

"Good. Go help them, and I'll see you in eight and three-quarter minutes. Oh, I want the briefing in the Small conference room."

"Right, sir. Small conference room." She grimaced as she left. She hated that room. It was all misaligned and did not seem to function well. She went back to her area and looked at her teams. *Oh, crap—a presentation!* She had not thought of that. She needed someone to prepare it. She looked around and saw the team's Public Relations Officer just sitting at his desk. "LE Maddox, I need you on presentation creation, Small conference room in…" She checked her BioMet. "less than eight minutes. Use the Probe Telemetry Template." Then she said in a loud voice, "Keep working but listen up. I need callouts, then forward data to Maddox, he's point for Presentation."

Thorlbund called out, "Signal authenticated. Data packet is intact."

Esterbank called out, "Objects present, initial data indicates a star, a Red Giant, working other objects now."

Linkston called out, "Timestamp data indicates transmission initiated over fifty years ago? Calculating location now."

Linkston called out, "Probe location at the time of transmission seventy light years from the point of origin, within the...Desolate Expanse!"

"Excellent!" She replied, and then continued, "Thorlbund I need probe identification, time of launch and mission parameters. Continue callouts and forward the data to Maddox."

Thorlbund called out, "Probed identified. You won't believe this! It's DC Alpha-One, launched over *two hundred and fifty years ago*." Fingers clacked rapidly across the keyboard as he called up window after window of information. "Mission was to probe the Desolate Expanse. Primary objective: find the...Divine Colony? Who authorized this mission?"

"We don't ask the questions, just relay the data to Maddox," Collins reinforced. "Wait, Desolate Expanse? Search probe manufacturing data. Who built this probe? How did it survive in there?"

Collins noticed the other five First Executrices filter into the small conference room. A few key Second Executrixes were also entering. She noticed they were surrounding the High Executrix himself.

Linkston called out, "Estimated object location two hundred light years from the transmission point. Current location estimated one hundred and eighty light years from the object."

Thorlbund called out, "Manufacturer: InfoMasked. Authority: High Divinity. Manufacture Location: InfoMasked. Authority: High Divinity. Probe Design Specifications: InfoMasked. Authority: High Divinity. Commissioning Authorities: High Divinity and High Authority."

Esterbank called out, "Four confirmed planets identified, two appear to be Gas Giants, the outer ones appear to be outside the Habitable Zone. One Gas Giant and one planet are within the Habitable Zone. Also, two potential planetoids. One planet in the Habitable Zone is in an unusual orbit. Mock up commencing."

Linkston called out, "Course correction calculations commencing, estimated forty-five days for completion. Estimated probe distance from the object when corrections received one hundred and twenty light years from the object."

"Maddox? Status check," Collins called out.

Maddox called out, "Presentation updated with available data, 80% complete based on the template, 100% completed based on data received. I am moving to the Small conference room to prepare location."

"Excellent work, people. Let's see what we've got. Thorlbund, Linkston, and Esterbank join Maddox in the conference room."

Her team filtered into the room and took up positions facing the other Executrices she began her briefing sight unseen, "High Executrix Slithneigh, First Executrix Templeson, and other distinguished First and Second Executrices, I am Second Executrix Devareaux Collins. I am here to brief you on probe telemetry data received within the last thirty minutes. The probe was authenticated to be DC Alpha-One launched over two hundred and fifty years ago."

The High Executrix stood up and said, "Let me interrupt right here. This briefing is now a Level One Briefing. Any information discussed in this room cannot leave this room. Any discussion or release of information will result in immediate arrest and termination. Anyone not willing...or able...to comply with this may leave now without penalty."

No one left the briefing room.

Collins said, "Continuing, the probe's mission was travel into the Desolate Expanse. We do not know how it traveled so far, nor how it stayed intact. The probe manufacturing data was removed from our data files under the Authority of the High Divinity. The mission was co-sponsored by the High Authority and the High Divinity."

"Those pieces are not relevant, continue," the High Executrix said.

"Yes sir. The probe transmitted their telemetry more than fifty years ago and we have calculated the distance to be seventy light years into the Desolate Expanse from origin. The data shows a lone system comprised of a Red Giant star and four planets: two Gas Giants, and two smaller planets, with the possibility of three additional planetoids. Two planets are in the Habitable Zone, including one of the Gas Giants. There is one planetary anomaly, which apparently has a nonstandard orbit. This one planet is the only other planet in the Habitable Zone." She turned to Maddox. "Display."

The lights in the room dimmed, and the display screen flared to life showing an image of a small solar system.

"Here we have a mock up of the planetary layout of the system. You can see from the motion that there is one planet in the Habitable Zone which does not belong. It is too small, it is out of place, and has an odd orbit."

"Do you have environmental telemetry on the planets yet?"

"No, environmental data is not present in the telemetry," Collins stated. "The distance that the probe sent the data was two hundred light years from the system location. Estimated location at present is one hundred and eighty light years from the system. Course correction calculations are commencing, and we estimate completion in forty-five days. Course correction reception will be received at approximately one hundred and twenty light years from the system, but will take fifty-five years to have the signal travel back to implement any course corrections. This is the overview of the telemetry received; a detailed analysis will yield greater details, I am sure."

"Very good briefing, Executrix Templeson. Now that brings us to the question of what to do about it?" High Executrix Slithneigh said.

"What to do about it?" First Executrix Nolan asked.

"Whether or not we make this information public or compartmentalize it," the High Executrix said.

"I think the path is fairly clear here," First Executrix Vicaro said.

"Oh?" said He Slithneigh.

"I believe the Edicts will spell out what we need to do," Vicaro said.

"Really, the Edicts? Fine what do the Edicts say?" High Executrix Slithneigh said.

"I don't know. I just know they are the guiding principles," Vicaro said.

"Collins, research Probe telemetry protocols," Templeson said.

'Thorlbund, that's yours," Collins told him.

"Yes ma'am," Thorlbund said as he left the room.

First Executrix Nejem said, "That still does not answer why we had a probe out before we even had spacecraft fielded. What is DC Alpha-One? What was its mission?"

"Second Executrix Collins, I assume you have some of those answers," High Executrix Slithneigh said.

"Yes sir, we do, but not everything."

"Well enlighten us," High Executrix Slithneigh said.

"What we know is that this probe was co-commissioned by the High Authority and High Divinity...together. Its mission was to enter the Desolate Expanse. The primary objective was to search for the Divine Colony."

"The Divine Colony! Ha! Now I know why there is all this fuss," First Executrix Owusu said.

Thorlbund returned and talked to Second Executrix Collins. Talking in a low voice he said to her, "The Edicts are clear. A full Battle Council must be formed to determine if this is a threat, or if it can be passed to a lower level council. Also the High Authority and High Divinity must be contacted to notify them of the DC Alpha-One probe contact."

She turned to the group and said, "May I have your attention? We have a ruling from the Edicts."

"Continue," High Executrix Slithneigh said.

"First, a full Battle Council must be formed to assess the threat to the colony. If no threat exists, then it may be passed to a lower council for consideration and analysis. Second, the High Authority and High Divinity must both be contacted upon DC A-1 contact."

"I'll handle our two leaders and their notification personally," High Executrix Slithneigh said, "Initiate Battle Council formation. Any Executrix that can be in place in two hours must report to the Hall of Authority's Battle Council Chamber. Begin recall immediately. Meeting adjourned."

24 CALL TO ARMS

Andorin and Efram moved to the other observation room just as Ylinielli's team was leaving Interview Room Four; they had conducted their interviews in numerical order.

Andorin asked, "Any luck?"

Ylinielli said, "We did get some interesting information that I was not expecting."

"Okay, save it for the Conference room. Meet Four and his team in there. You'll be briefing Commander Soltag and myself. We'll be right in, you're up first," Andorin paused and then continued, "How did Mican do when he did his interview?"

"You wanted him to conduct one? Oh, I did not understand. I did both of them. Sorry," Ylinielli said.

"That was my intention, but I must not have stated that very clearly. It's okay, don't worry about it," Andorin said.

"Commander Soltag, a word please?" Andorin said to Efram and he pulled him to the side and waited for Ylinielli to leave, "Didn't I tell them to switch interviewers?"

"No, you had Four switch up when they came into the observation room, and before they left to interview Pridna," Efram said.

"Right, right. I should have thought about it earlier, well, it'll work out. Let's get in there, and see what we've got. You get the people from rooms Two and Four, and I'll get the ones from One and Three, and then assemble everyone in the conference room." Andorin moved to Interview Room Three, opened the door, and said, "Please proceed to the Conference room." He then walked to Interview Room One, opened it, and said, "Pridna, let's get to the Conference room."

As she walked out the door following Andorin he said, "You know you did not have to be so hard on Colin."

"I know but it was fun. Did you see the look on his face when I said I was an alien? I thought he was going to pass out," Pridna said.

"I did not see that, but he was a little flustered, I will give you that," Andorin said.

"Yeah, it was funny watching him squirm," Pridna said with a fond smile.

"This was training for him," Andorin said.

"Now he knows how it will go when the person does not cooperate and tries to mislead him," Pridna stated.

"I guess that does have some merit. You should have checked with me first, but that does give me an idea. So thanks," Andorin said.

They both moved into the conference room and Pridna moved to her seat while Andorin moved to the front to join Commander Soltag.

"All right everyone, time to see our results. Investigator Ylinielli please present your findings," Andorin said.

Ylinielli stood up and moved to the front.

"I first interviewed Nickelle Igler. She was hatched in the Cornith Hatching Center near their farming region. Her parents lived in farming territory, but were close enough to be able to deliver their egg. However, there was a hatching complication: a skin condition was discovered after the hatching occurred. They were left with dark bluish-black blotches on parts of their exoskeleton. The doctor informed her parents that this was a somewhat rare occurrence, which was exacerbated by their later delivery of their egg to the facility. They said they had tests that could have been performed that took extra time, which was not afforded based on their delivering the egg only a few days before hatching. The doctors told them they did not run the test because it would have been too late to correct any abnormalities. They also informed them that it was temporary and treatable. First and successive moltings were successful, and the condition was eliminated entirely."

"Excellent, very good. How about your other subject, Trevor Molantic?" Andorin asked.

"Yes, sir. He was born on a farm, not hatched in a center. He was born like Pridna, and was told very similar things. A rare occurrence in about 20% of the population, treatment was required but only a week prior to each molting. Apparently, he was a reddish blue color. He was told to hide actively his skin condition due to rising Anti-Blue activities. With his early exoskeletal coloration, he would have been a prime target for their increasingly aggressive attacks on perceived impurities."

"Very good. Please sit down. Investigator Furmanski, please stand up and give us an overview of your interviews," Andorin said.

"My first one was Benjamin Hylnad. He was born on a farm. He was born to night algae farmers. He essentially grew up alone, in a very poor family. He did not notice any difference in exoskeletal colorations between that of his parent's and his. However, there were no mirrors in the house. His hands were either always covered in dirt or viewed in the light of the moon. He was dark like his father and never noticed any difference. Additionally, he did not have any friends, and when others visited, he was relegated to his room. He saw no one outside of his parents and the doctor until his first molting. A huge party celebrated this; he was presented to all their relatives. Mirrors were then reintroduced into the house shortly after this event," Four finished.

"Very good. Conclusions?" Andorin asked.

"I concluded that he did not know what color he was and every means for him to stumble upon it were taken away. He was hidden, no mirrors were present, and only after his first molting, after being treated was he presented to anyone else. He most likely was not the proper coloring, hence why shots were needed and presented after successful treatment."

"Hey, what do you mean? My parents never said anything like that," Ben said.

"Agreed, they said things like, 'You don't worry about you, we got you', and my personal favorite 'Mirrors capture your soul,' which means they did not want you to see yourself for what coloring you had. That, coupled with the fact they actively hid you every time someone outside the family unit came over? They were hiding you, nothing more," Four said harshly.

"Hey, we are not here to judge or burst anyone's bubble. We're here to get to the truth whatever that is. I believe this is tied to everything that has happened in the last few days; it has to be. It has to be because they tried to tie their actions to having ancient Paclid blood in ancient bloodlines," Andorin explained.

"Yeah, we already know that," Furmanski said.

"Yes but what you don't know, what I don't know, but suspect, is that we are all really Paclids...or they are us, or we are one in the same, However you want to think about it we...they...we're all identical," Andorin said.

Alex said, "That's not possible, we are not them."

"Oh, really? How could we prove this one way of the other? Pridna, what percentage did your doctor tell your parents had a similar affliction as yours, blue coloring at birth?"

"20%," Pridna answered.

"Okay, now anyone. What percentage of people live outside of cities on farms and the like?"

"About 23% of the population lives on farms," Benjamin said.

"How do you know that?" Andorin asked.

"I did a report my last year in school. It's been about 23% for many years, but is slowly declining due to dwindling water resources."

"Now does anyone find it coincidental that this coloration happens in about 20% of the population, and that number is statistically close to the number of people that live in areas not easily accessible to hatching centers?"

"I would not say it is correlative, but it does look interesting," Commander Soltag said.

"How could we find correlation then?" Andorin said.

Ki said, "We could get corroborating evidence from other sources or additional information."

"Like what?" Andorin asked.

"Medical records," Pridna said.

"Medical records? What would that give us?" Andorin asked.

"Proof."

"How so?" Andorin asked.

"We know that Langli and I have similar stories, except his was allergies and mine was coloring. However, if we compared our medical records to see what treatments...specifically the drugs and other chemicals...were injected and find that they are similar, then we could surmise that they are for a similar purpose. And since I was blue and then brown, it would suggest that it would act in a similar way for the *allergy* sufferers as well."

"And if the whole of the population was receiving similar treatments, then the entire population is suffering from the same problem," Soltag rationalized.

"Exactly! We are all blue, or Paclids, or whatever you want to call it, and the fact that we are brown is a very elaborate illusion for some unknown reason. The reason might be what we are looking for," Andorin elaborated.

Pridna's BioMet pad light up to signal an incoming TransCom. She opened it and read it. "Sir, I have an urgent message from the Battle Operations Center, the Full Battle Council is forming in about an hour in The Hall of Authority. All able Executrices are required to report within the hour. Battle Council Staff members are required to report immediately. Sir, your name is listed as part of both the Full Battle Council and Battle Council Staff."

"What's going on?" Commander Soltag asked.

"Here hand me that," Andorin said looking at Pridna's BioMet pad.

"It does not say. But, I have to go. *Now*. Commander Soltag, I want you to take over interview training. Switch up the subjects and then allow everyone to interview someone at least once. Then repeat the process. However, have the subject then be difficult, stubborn and elusive. Always let the experienced interviewer go first as models for both the interviewer and the interviewee. Let Benjamin return to his post. Focus on my team if you wish not to include everyone, but I would prefer everyone. I think it would be good training all around. This is training; use this as a means to allow my team members to develop some interviewing skills. Keep on the same topic for everyone else ask the same questions. We'll use our little group of people as the baseline for our findings. We'll serve as a representational sampling of the populations, which it seems like we are very close to being right now."

Soltag replied, "Okay, I can do that. What topic do you want for the difficult interview process?"

"I don't know. I hadn't thought that far ahead. Whatever you people come up with will be fine. But remember: this is training. Teach my people what they need to know," Andorin said.

25 EXPECTANCY

Andorin got up and left the room. He walked out through the left side door, closest to the elevator. He moved towards the elevator door and pushed the button to call it. When the elevator arrived, he walked into and then looked for the appropriate button. He only saw Main, Sub Basement 1, BCC buttons. He pushed the BCC button.

Please present credentials, the elevator said in a pleasing female tone.

This startled Andorin, because it had not talked before. He took out his credentials and placed them in front of the BioMet reader.

Thank you, Low Executrix Wilcon. Please present hand for BioMet validation.

Andorin placed his hand on the BioMet scanner platen. The scanner sprang to life and scanned his hand quickly.

Identity confirmed. Proceeding. The voice said as the elevator moved...downward? The elevator traveled for quite some time before it finally came to a stop. His arm implant started vibrating. It seemed to last quite a long time. He was not sure what that could be because he had not included any new data for upload—*It might be a download*, he thought. As he exited the elevator, it was not hard to figure out where to go. There was only one door. He walked towards it. He approached it, and it opened for him automatically. He walked into the room where twenty Executrices of various ranks mostly First Executrix and Second Executrix, but a few Low Executrix were included as well. He also noticed the High Executrix himself.

Another Low Executrix approached him and said, "The Full Battle Council Meeting will be in forty-five minutes, return then."

"I was ordered to come now," Andorin replied.

"Who are you again?" Then he looked at Andorin's Crest, "What is that Crest? I have never seen one like it before."

"From what I hear it has not occurred since the last person was promoted to LE 217, fifty years ago," Andorin explained.

"Well that is interesting and all, but you'll have to come back when the Full Battle Council is formed."

High Executrix Slithneigh looked up and said, "He is supposed to be here, let him in."

"Sir? We are at max capacity right now. We do not have room for another person. I was the last one added," Low Executrix Holcombe said.

High Executrix Slithneigh replied, "That's right. Thanks for reminding me, Holcombe, I remove you from the Battle Council Staff, effective immediately. Leave."

"But sir! I was just added a few weeks ago, you remember? You did it yourself," Holcombe pleaded.

"I remember, but Wilcon was appointed by the High Authority personally, so you get to go. That is how it works *last in, first out*. You understand?"

"No! This is not fair. I did everything you asked me to. This is *my* seat. I earned it!" Holcombe raged.

"You are mistaken. It's your seat if I say it is. It *was* your seat, now it's not. Now leave!" High Executrix Slithneigh said sternly.

Holcombe looked at Andorin and said, "This is not over," and started to storm out of the room. However, the doors did not open for him.

"You already updated the security? I can't even get out!" Holcombe said.

"I don't know how you got in, the door should not have opened for you," High Executrix Slithneigh pointed out.

"I came in with you, remember?" Holcombe said.

"Ah yes, I forgot. Low Executrix Wilcon, escort him out."

Andorin moved towards the door and it opened. Holcombe walked through them and once through, Andorin walked back into the room to where the discussion was occurring, the doors closing behind him, leaving LE Holcombe outside looking in.

"There is a system in there, which is all we know. We will know more when the deep analytics teams start to dissect the file for the minutest details. Then we'll have a clearer picture of what's there," 1E Dobra said.

"Is it colonized? That is the important question," 1E Templeson said.

"We don't know. The telemetry did not pick up anything as far as signals, or beacons of any kind, it is signal dark from what we can see," HE Slithneigh said.

"How much data do we have?" First Executrix Nolan asked.

"The probe was designed to collect one full planetary rotation for every planet of any system found. That could be one to a hundred years worth of data," HE Slithneigh said.

"Do we have any idea how much in general?" 1E Dobra asked.

"We have almost six hundred pages of printed material," First Executrix

Templeson said.

"Six hundred pages! That is huge. There must be a long cycle for one of the planetary rotations," 1E Nolan said.

"But do we know if they are hostile?" 1E Dobra said.

"We don't even know if there is a 'they' there. Until we do, I think it is unwise to move forward," 1E Vicaro said.

"You forget Vicaro, waiting is not an option. We cannot wait. We have to go and go as soon as possible. We should go today, but we can't. Our technology is not where we need it to be. This needs to take top priority," 1E Templeson said.

"That's technology, not battle decisions," 1E Dobra said.

"Actually, at this point there is little distinction between the two," HE Slithneigh said.

1E Owusu said, "Technology prevents any attacks anywhere. We are the least advanced species in this system. The Paclids have shielding technology we cannot even break through, which is why we ground attack. The Norlthanes have energy technology, and the Frosnytes have conquered cryogenics. The only thing we excel in is genetics, and genetics never won any wars. They started a few, but never ended any."

Andorin was lost listening to what they were discussing. It did not sound like invasion plans, but he did not know what was happening either. All he knew was that the last *attack* had not been real, and the Andlids had bought that moon from the Paclids.

HE Slithneigh turned to Andorin and said, "I am sure this is a little overwhelming for you, but an outside perspective might be what we need."

"Why don't we just ask the Paclids for assistance?" Andorin said, thinking that these of all people must know about the inner working of things.

High Executrix Slithneigh smiled a slight smile as he turned away from Andorin, and let his staff deal with the newcomer.

"The Paclids! Are you mad?" 1E Nejem said, vehemently.

"We are at war with them," 1E Dobra piled on.

"They destroyed our last attacking force! We were lucky to achieve a victory at all...no one survived. Luckily, our reinforcements arrived and was able to repel the Paclids before they landed another force on that moon," 1E Nolan added.

Andorin thought to himself, *These people don't even know the truth about what happened. Whoever was making these deals was even higher than this council was, and that left only three people, HE Slithneigh, High Authority and High Divinity. The HA could be ruled out, since he was working for him. That left the HE and the HD. He knew the HE was involved because he gave him the script in the vehicle ride to the Hall of Authority. But, could it be that low? It had to be someone that wielded a lot of power. It would have to be the High Divinity if it were not the High Executrix, but that did not make any sense. Why would our religious figure be involved in military affairs, why would they care? What is going on?*

High Executrix Slithneigh said, "It's his first meeting let him be."

"What a stupid idea. Ask the Paclids," 1E Nejem said mocking Andorin.

"I have a question off topic. Raise your hand if you had Allergy shots?" Andorin asked.

"What kind of dumb question is that?" 1E Vicaro said.

"Just humor me, please. Everyone raise your hands if you had allergy shots growing up?" Sixteen of the twenty people there raised their hands. "Now raise your hand if you received shots for exoskeletal problems?" The remaining people raised their hands. The High Executrix now looked directly at him and he did *not* look happy. "Okay. Thank you. That's all."

"What was that for?" 1E Nejem asked.

"Just curiosity on my part," Andorin said.

"Curious of what? Specifically," HE Slithneigh asked.

"Childhood, that's all. Just wanted to see who had allergies and who did not. That's all," Andorin simplified.

HE Slithneigh glinted his eyes at him and said, "What are you doing?"

"Just asking a question that's all," Andorin said.

"Well stop. We need to focus on the task at hand and move forward, research or delay," HE Slithneigh said.

"We need to move forward, obviously," 1E Nejem said.

"But what is moving forward?" 1E Vicaro

"Moving forward is into the Desolate Expanse," HE Slithneigh said.

"That is suicide without knowing what is in there," 1E Vicaro said.

"We don't have the time to wait to find out what's in there. Now do we?" HE Slithneigh asked sarcastically.

"Our water supply will last for a hundreds or maybe a thousand or so more years, that is enough time for the probe to be contacted and new data transmitted. Then we could know before committing everything."

"The fact of the matter is...we have no other choice." High Executrix Slithneigh stated bluntly. "The Paclids own their planet, and we got lucky with our last attack. We caught them off guard to capture that moon around Norltha from them. Our moons have been mined to near disastrous ruin, one moon has collapsed in on itself, decreasing its size by half, and now it's gradually being pulled into a closer and closer orbit. The other moon is also close to structural collapse as well. " The room fell silent. Slithneigh continued.

"The Norlthanes own the Gas Giant planet, Norltha. The Frosnytes own the largest Gas Giant planet, Frydia and three of its six moons. The Paclids own all the moons of their planet and the other moons as well. We only have our planet, and our two moons. One is already descending toward the planet, and the other is starting the same descent. Both will strike the Planet in four hundred years and one thousand years respectfully. The astrophysicists predict that our planet will survive the first collision, but all life will die. " Slithneigh paused to let that sink in. He gazed around the room. Everyone was looking directly at him.

"Our planet will not survive the second collision from the larger moon. The process is irreversible. They predict our planet will fracture and may disintegrate into pieces from that collision. There is nothing left for us in this system. We are doomed. Every habitable planet within one hundred light years has been taken or claimed by another species more advanced than we are. There is no place for us to go...except the Desolate Expanse."

"Nothing can survive in there," 1E Dobra stated.

"You forget. Something *can* survive. The probe did." HE Slithneigh said.

"That's right! How did it do that exactly?" 1E Vicaro asked.

"I don't know," HE Slithneigh said.

Andorin was not sure if he was telling the truth and he did not know, or was hiding the truth and did know. He could not yet read High Executrix Slithneigh accurately.

"Well if you don't know who does? How did we get the probe in the first place?" 1E Nolan said.

"I'll direct that question to 1E Templeson," HE Slithneigh said pointing in his direction.

"My lead investigator will handle that question, Second Executrix Collins," He replied pointing to her.

"Well..." 2E Collins said looking at the presentation, "the manufacturer, the manufacture location and the probe configuration, are all InfoMasked by the HD. The mission was to search for the Divine Colony. It was manufactured two hundred and fifty years ago."

"Why did the HD InfoMask all that data?" Andorin asked.

HE Slithneigh glared at him and then said, "I don't know why the HD would, but he is no longer with us now, is he?"

"I am sure the current High Divinity would know. I am sure they would pass that information along...especially one that was searching for the Divine Colony," Andorin pushed back.

"And why must the Manufacture Location be masked? Why can no one know where it was manufactured? What is so important about that?" 1E Dobra asked.

"Also, how is it that we have a probe that can travel into the Desolate Expanse, but our ships cannot do the same?" 1E Vicaro asked.

"All reasonable questions that I don't have the answers for," HE Slithneigh said, with a little undertone of something Andorin could not put his finger on.

"Then let's contact the one who might...the HD himself. Get him to tell us," said 1E Nejem.

"First, the probe has existed for two hundred and fifty years already, and the fact that we don't know has not changed in that time. I doubt the HD has any intention of changing that any time soon," HE Slithneigh said trying to get them to push off the topic, "The real question is do we go in guns blazing, or do we approach as a science mission first, and then weigh our options," HE Slithneigh finished.

"He might, once he knows it has made contact, and what it has scanned," 1E Vicaro said.

"He already knows. I had informed him before I came here. I also informed the HA as well. Neither offered any insights into what this might mean. Remember, both the HA and HD co-sponsored the probe. They *both* might know something," HE Slithneigh said.

"He offered nothing at all?" 1E Vicaro asked.

"No, he did not, so I doubt asking him again would make any difference," HE Slithneigh said.

"How are we expected to make a decision based on the little information we have?" 1E Dobra said.

"You have all you need to know," HE Slithneigh said.

"What is that?" 1E Vicaro said.

"There is a system there. One way or another we have to go there. It is our only option at this point," HE Slithneigh said.

"We could approach the Paclids for assistance?" Andorin pushed again, knowing the Andlids were already in negotiations with them if they were purchasing territory from the Paclids.

"What part of 'We are at war with them' do you not understand?" 1E Nejem said.

"I understand that just fine. What I am saying is that we don't have to be at war with them," Andorin reasoned.

"Not at war? We have to be at war. They are the enemy," 1E Nejem said.

"I am saying is that there could be another way...if we choose it," Andorin said.

"No! This is the way of things. They are our mortal enemy. There can be only one species left standing. It will be the Andlids, the Paclids are the inferior species," 1E Vicaro said.

"From what I have heard in here, we are all as good as dead. The Paclids just have to wait, repel out attacks and eventually we'll die off. It is only a matter of time...as I just found out. Following that up, when is this information going to be made public?" Andorin asked.

HE Slithneigh raised his arm to signal the end of talking and said, "It may be true that the Paclids just have to wait. However, we are going to wage new campaigns against them to seize more of the moons, and then their home world. We'll survive. As far as the public, they are told what they need to know, when they need to know it. This helps keep order and less chaos."

"Does that rule apply to everything, to everyone?" Andorin asked knowing already sure of the answer he would receive.

"Of course it does. Everyone is treated equally in that regard," HE Slithneigh said, a slow smile forming on his face.

Andorin thought, *The council is in the dark. HE Slithneigh is definitely involved.* How much he was not sure about, but he had a good hunch the High Executive knew that the Paclids were not being attacked. *How can I find out more?* He said, "Then I think we should go there on peaceful terms. See what the current occupants might be willing to do for us, maybe seek refuge there. Maybe they can point us in a better direction."

1E Dobra chided, "You would have us run like scared little hatchlings to some alien planet and beg for assistance? We are too *proud* to do something like that."

"What other options do we have? We are the lowest technology level of all the species that are within a hundred light years. What makes you think that will change when we meet whoever is on that planet? If *anyone* is on that planet," Andorin retorted.

HE Slithneigh chimed in, "LE Wilcon is right on one aspect. We have no other options. It is time for a vote. I propose we pass this to Full Battle Council with the recommendation that we pass it to the Extra-Solar Council, as a non-military exploration mission, seeing no threat posed at this time."

Andorin responded, "Seconded." Everyone one looked at him. He was the newest member of their council, and should be more silent than involved.

1E Templeson replied, "We have a motion properly seconded. Is there any discussion on the matter before a vote is called?"

1E Dobra replied, "I think this is a display of weakness."

2E Collins added, "I think that making an aggressive move would doom our species to extinction. If we go there, and they destroy our contingent, then all is lost. We must present a more peaceful posture when we go there."

1E Nejem said, "We are the military. We must flex our full might. Man the cannons and send the bombers. Attack, attack. Attack!"

1E Owusu included, "Our technology level is so low we cannot afford to underestimate any race that might exist on the planet already. We cannot go in guns ablaze. It has to be a peaceful mission."

1E Vicaro said, "I still think it is unwise to make rash decisions based on this flimsy telemetry report. We can wait until the data is fully analyzed."

1E Nolan added, "If the probe did not pick up any signal within the first six hundred pages of material, then there must be no one present on the planet. An exploratory mission might be more appropriate."

Andorin said, "I think a peaceful mission is the only answer. We must survive. By any measures necessary."

Everyone else was silent for a minute, and then 1E Templeson said, "Any further discussion?" He waited for a response. None came, so he continued, "All those in favor of recommending to the Full Battle Council this go to the Extra-Solar Council as a non-military exploratory mission, raise your hands now."

HE Slithneigh was the first hand to rise. It was a signal to the others as to how they should vote. Executrices Owusu, Vicaro, Nolan, Collins, Andorin, Templeson and others raised their hands to show they support a scientific mission to the planet. 1E Templeson counted the votes and then said, "Votes counted. Please lower your hands."

"All those opposed to a scientific mission, preferring a military mission instead, raise your hand."

Executrices Nejem and Dobra raised theirs with a select few others. 1E Templeson counted the votes and then said, "Votes counted. Please lower your hands."

"HE Slithneigh, the motion passes with a margin of sixteen votes in favor, and five votes against." 1E Templeson proclaimed. "It even passes with over a 75% majority, requiring 75% of favorable votes to reverse this decision."

HE Slithneigh stated, "Excellent work here today. You have done our civilization proud. Now we have to get this approved in the Full Battle Council."

1E Templeson extended HE Slithneigh's comment. "Sir? The full council meets in five minutes."

"Good. Meeting adjourned. Prepare for the Full Battle Council. Ensure your contingent votes in favor of this motion. Open the doors," HE Slithneigh stated.

The doors swung open, and LE Holcombe was the first one waiting to enter as if he did not move after they closed on him. Many others followed him as the chamber started to fill up. There were enough seats to seat every Executrix, except for Andorin, now that he was 217th Low Executrix. However, he hoped there were not going to be that many here during this meeting. Also, it should not be an issue. Even if the full Command Council met, comprised of all two hundred and fifty-nine Executrices, there were always some that were on missions, in space or someplace else and not able to attend. Andorin watched as the people migrated into various groups that seemed to be aligned with one another. He now understood what the High Executrix meant when he said your contingents. It seemed each First Executrix loosely controlled their subordinates. They outlined what was required, and each member voted towards the desired results. The voting seemed efficient, if everyone voted their parts.

1E Templeson banged a gavel on the sounding block and the crowd quieted down, waiting for the meeting to start. "Let us start with the oath."

The entire Battle Council rose to their feet and said in unison, "We bear the weight of our combined might to meet all enemies foreign and domestic. May our judgment be led by our calling to protect the colony, our determination to hold steady doing what must be done, and our strength be granted by the Divinity to carry out that will. Alone we are weak. Together, we stand strong. I pledge to do my part, lend my will, offer my strength and provide my guidance to forge our path." Everyone raised their upper arms and looked to the ground, their eyes closed and said, "Divinity grant me insight."

1E Templeson banged a gavel on the sounding block and said, "This emergency meeting of the Battle Council is now in order. Please be seated," The assembly took their seats quickly. "We have been called to this meeting to deal with an unprecedented occurrence, and we must determine a course of action. The Battle Council Staff has passed down a ruling that it wants to be considered by this council. As a member of this council, you must consider only what the BCS has sent to you for consideration. First, I yield the floor to HE Slithneigh."

HE Slithneigh walked to the front center podium as 1E Templeson sat off to his right. "We have received a great gift this day. A few hours ago, probe telemetry was received from deep inside the Desolate Expanse. A lone system was discovered with planets in the Habitable Zone. There is no atmospheric data as of yet. The probe received no EM transmissions of any kind. We on the BCS have made a decision. We feel there is no imminent threat from this lone system, and, therefore, a military response is not required. We are seeking this council's approval to send this to the Extra-Solar Council for their consideration. I know you have questions, but the *How* and the *Why* are not relevant at this time. You need only to know the *Is*. There *is* hope for our people. The Desolate Expanse can serve as either a new colony or a waypoint into uncharted space for our species' expansion beyond this system." There were murmurs in the assembly, excitement and anger boiling just under the surface.

"Because of the fluid nature of the situation," Slithneigh continued. "Military ships are not required because any inhabitants may view them as hostile, and may be met with force. We need to move into that region of space, and perhaps beyond. This will be the furthest our species will venture forth into the universe. We must find our way to this system and be welcomed by the inhabitants. If there are no inhabitants...as we suspect...we shall claim it in the name of the Andlid people. Our race will be reborn there, away from old enemies, leaving our problems as we traverse the Desolate Expanse. Thank you for your time," he said as he moved away from the podium.

1E Templeson moved back to the podium and said, "We need debate leaders Pro and Con. We have a tradition that that newcomers get to be a Debate Leader of their choosing. LE Wilcon, choose Pro or Con Debate Leader?"

Andorin was surprised to be thrown into the thick of things right away, but he knew his heart, and he selected, "Pro."

"Take a position at this podium," 1E Templeson pointed to his left. "Now I need a Con Debate Leader."

Fifteen people raised their hands. 1E Templeson selected 1E Dobra as the Con Debate Leader and he moved to the right podium.

Andorin thought *Great, I get paired against the number two First Executrix, this does not bode well.*

"Since this is a matter to move forward, the Pro position has a natural advantage, and will therefore go first."

1E Nejem raised their hand and said, "Point of Order."

1E Templeson said, "I recognize 1E Nejem. Please state your Point of Order."

"Mister Chair, I believe we are over the allotted limit, which could result in a deadlock. With the HE, we are at two hundred sixty members, meaning the vote could be one hundred thirty to one hundred thirty. I move our membership be returned to two hundred fifty nine, making a thirty to twenty nine as the closest possible outcome."

"We have a motion on the floor to reduce membership back to two hundred fifty nine. Do I have a second?"

"Seconded," 1E Vicaro stated, as he raised his hand.

"We have a second. I will open the floor for discussion," 1E Templeson said.

"How will we choose?" 1E Nolan asked.

"Last in, first out," HE Slithneigh stated.

"Who was last in?" 1E Owusu asked.

"2E Collins you are the Recorder. Who was last in?" 1E Templeson asked.

She searched her BioMet pad and announced, "LE's Holcombe and Horvath were placed at the same time."

"Who outranks whom?" HE Slithneigh asked.

"Sir, Holcombe is rank one eighty-seven and Horvath is rank two hundred and sixteen."

1E Templeson said, "LE Horvath has been identified for removal effective immediately, any further discussion?" He waited for any response, but none came, "All those in favor say 'Yea,'" There was a resounding echo in the room. "Any opposed say 'Nay,'" There were a few responses that came in for 'Nay,' including LE Horvath.

"The Yea's have it. LE Horvath you are here by removed from this council. Please leave immediately."

LE Horvath got up slowly, and moved toward the doors, which opened for him, closing behind him as he walked towards the elevator.

"Recorder, please ensure the security records get updated after this meeting," 1E Templeson said.

"Yes, sir," came the response from 2E Collins.

"The Point of Order has been concluded. On to the business at hand. LE Wilcon you have the floor."

Andorin had no idea what he was going to say, but he had to say something.

"As you have just found out, we have been afforded a great opportunity to move forward as a civilization. We can move beyond our petty bickering with the Paclids over scraps of their leftovers, which they are probably happy to get rid of. One's trash is another's treasure. I have learned so much more about the state of our civilization these last few days that it has given me a new perspective on this topic." Andorin looked around the room. Every set of eyes was fixed on him.

"We *must* go into the Desolate Expanse," he continued. "Our future lies there. We have used the military as a tool to achieve our goals in the past: making war, threatening the Paclids, but now we need a *new* way. We need to leave the violence behind. We need to extend the hand of peace to any inhabitants on the planet. We need to be welcomed, no matter the cost. We have no other option. It looks bleak for our civilization, and if we are to survive, we must venture forth into the Desolate Expanse. Only a civilian option is capable of portraying a peaceful posture. The Extra-Solar Council will find the way to make that happen for us. This is not a problem we can shoot, launch missiles at, nor slash through with a laser spear. Only the extended hand...empty of weapon or threat...will help us in this time of great need. And I know we are in great need indeed."

"Well said!" The response came from the back of the meeting room, and the entire council twisted to see who had spoken. The High Authority moved toward the front of the assembly room, "Sorry to barge in like this, but I wanted to see how my new appointee was doing. I can see I chose very well indeed."

"You do not have the floor; you may not speak!" 1E Templeson said.

Andorin quickly replied, "I yield my remaining time to the High Authority."

1E Templeson sighed and said, "The Chair recognizes the High Authority."

"Thank you Chair, and thank you Andorin," the High Authority said as he moved to the front podium and replaced 1E Templeson, "Andorin summed it up very well. You...*We* have no choice in this matter. We are faced with dire circumstances, the likes of which no other generation has ever seen. Moreover, with each passing generation, it will only get worse. We are past the tipping point, cresting the hill at full speed, only to find a drop off beneath us. Make no mistake we are plummeting even now. The military, you have served our civilization well over the centuries, but your time is ending. We must start a new chapter, one founded on peace and cooperation. If we had cooperated with others instead of attacking, we might be further advanced than we are right now. As it stands, the outlook is bleak here in this system and every system for a hundred or so light years. There is nothing for us, except going into the Desolate Expanse. It can be done. *I* have seen it. We cannot do it yet, but others can, and regularly do for extended times. We *must* go. We *will* go."

"You say we can, but how can we?" 1E Nejem asked.

"We can because the probe did," the HA said.

"But how did the probe do that?" 1E Nejem pushed harder.

"Honestly? I do not know. The design specs are blocked...even from me. Only the High Divinity can unlock that information, but it can obviously be done. We have a probe there *right now*. I can tell you after searching the archives, the HA at the time provided the funding while the HD handled the probe manufacturing, but this seems like it should be reversed. How could the religious arm produce the probe that could travel the Desolate Expanse? Once the HD makes this information known, then we can start moving forward," the High Authority stated.

"Unfortunately, I am unable to make that information known." Another voice from deep within the room sounded again. Again, the room gasped, and they turned to see the new person entering the council chambers. The High Divinity made his way to stand at center stage with the HA.

"Why can't you tell us?" A voice echoed from someone near the back.

"Stand and be recognized," 1E Templeson stated and waited for a response. No one stood up.

"That's okay, 1E Templeson, I will answer their question. I cannot tell you because you cannot handle the truth about where the probe came from," the High Divinity said.

A clamor rose up over the crowd as people started getting upset at the HD's treatment of their position, or lack thereof compared to his position.

"The fact of the matter is that you know nothing about the happenings around you," the HD said.

"I know we took that moon from the Paclids."

"Ah the Paclids, again you show your ignorance. It is only Paclid pity that has allowed our civilization to survive this long," the High Divinity said.

"You lie! We are strong! We take what we want!" 1E Vicaro proclaimed.

"Yes, I can imagine that is what you would see from your vantage point, thus proving my point. You know little of the true workings around you," the HD said.

"We know everything," 1E Vicaro said.

"You know *nothing*!" The High Divinity said, anger flashing in his eyes. He took a deep breath. "To prove my point, I will tell everyone in this room the place the probe was manufactured, and then we shall see what that does to your thinking."

"You don't think we can handle it?" 1E Nejem said.

"I *know* you can't handle it. You'll say that it is illegal...or treason."

"Treason?" 1E Templeson said intrigued.

"Yes, treason. Now, and then," the High Divinity said.

"Well let's find out then. You opened this topic, now finish it," 1E Nejem said.

"It was manufactured at Palascia Technology Complex," the High Divinity stated.

"Palascia? Technology Complex? That makes no sense," 1E Vicaro said.

"Palascia...Palascia...I know that name from somewhere," 1E Owusu said.

"2E Collins perform a search of our database for this name," 1E Templeson ordered.

"Yes sir," she replied.

"No other clues you'll give us then?" 1E Dobra asked.

"No, you got more than you should know already," the HD replied.

"This makes no sense," proclaimed Second Executrix Collins.

"Why?" 1E Templeson asked.

"I only found it in enemy intelligence files," 2E Collins explained.

"What? Where?" First Executrix Templeson asked.

"How is that possible?" 1E Dobra asked.

"That name is the suspected place where the Paclid's most advanced ships are produced," 2E Collins said.

"Paclids! How is it that our probe was built at this Palascia Technology Complex?" 1E Dobra asked.

"Who said it was *our* probe," the High Divinity said.

"How is it not our probe? We got the telemetry data, of course it's our probe," First Executrix Nejem stated.

"No, it's their probe. We got the telemetry data because it was part of the deal."

"Deal? Who entered into a deal with our enemy? That is treason! That is consorting with the enemy," 1E Dobra said.

"How quickly they forget. See? I told you what would happen. Your minds are so narrow that you cannot even understand what is happening right before your very eyes."

"I understand fully you are a traitor," 1E Nejem said.

"I entered into no such deal, but someone in my office did about two hundred and fifty years ago. Try them for treason, if you like. I am sure they won't complain now," he said with a smile forming on his face.

"But you knew! You're a co-conspirator," 1E Dobra said.

"You may think so, but can you prove it? Not without evidence, you cannot. I have all the evidence as a part of protected religious sites that cannot be searched. It is also encrypted, to prevent unauthorized access. If you mention this meeting, I will deny it and then cite religious ceremonies for not being able to comply. I will also have an alibi to say I was somewhere else, instead of at this meeting."

"That's not possible we'll have the VidFeed of you in this room," 2E Collins said.

"Of course it is possible. I do it all the time. You can check, your VidFeeds are down, not transmitting anything," the High Divinity said.

2E Collins said, "He's right, they are down."

"Now do I have your attention?" The HD pointedly asked.

"Yes you do," High Executrix Slithneigh said with a slight glance towards the High Divinity. A thin smile was forming on his face.

Andorin started thinking, *I knew that both the HE and the HD were connected in some manner. How, I was not sure, but I knew. This confirms what I had already suspected. The HD knew much more than the Council did. The HD knew of the probe's origin, so then he must also know we are not fighting with the Paclids. He must know because that's how he got the probe in the first place. From what I heard earlier, it was commissioned by the HD and HA together, but only the HD sealed the files. This must mean that the HD had operational control over the program. But that made no* sense. *How could a non-military function control a military probe? Maybe the probe was not military? The probe's mission was searching for the Divine Colony; this must be why the HD had operational control. It was a religious mission? That made no sense either. What mission would the religious sect need to conduct? I guess the search for the Divine Colony would qualify, if it really exists. How can something be real, in this realm, if we travel to it when we leave this realm? It made no sense on the face of it. I never believed the Divine Colony was a real place, in this realm, but the devout do believe, and the HD is their leader. He would be required to take up this cause in the Divinity's name.* His thoughts were broken by the call for a vote.

"All those in favor of sending this to the Extra-Solar Council say 'Yea,'" 1E Templeson said. Again, a resounding echo filled the room as the vast majority of the members agreed.

Andorin barely had the time recognize what was happening and added his vote to the throng.

All those opposed of sending this to the Extra-Solar Council say Nay." As before, there were some that disagreed, but clearly, the *Yeas* outnumbered the *Nays*.

"Chair, deliver the decision," the High Executrix stated.

"The Yeas have it. The matter can move forward," 1E Templeson said.

The High Divinity said, "You have chosen well this day," as he started leave the chamber.

The High Authority also said, "You have done excellent work, now the civilians will have their opportunity to serve their civilization like the military does every day."

The High Divinity added, barely audible to the entire hall, "If that were only true, we'd be far better off."

The High Authority continued as if he did not hear the comment, "They will pick up this mantle of responsibility and use it to propel our civilization into the Desolate Expanse. We shall rise on this new world in honor of our world...lost. We will ensure that the proper course is set in motion to ensure our survival as a civilization." He looked in Andorin's direction briefly to make eye contact and concluded, "We have our best people on the task and they shall not waver. They shall not rest. They shall not fail! We must be victorious. As the military is on the battlefield, so shall we conquer this objective. We cannot fail; the stakes are too high. Failure is death to us all!"

Andorin thought, *I now know the High Authority also knew the truth about what was happening. He must know the current state of our planet. But, could he not know? Why had he not made that public? Everyone should know what is happening. How can he hide this? There is definitely more to this than I had even imagined. Could this be linked to my investigation? How, and in what manner could that be? I know the HA placed me on this council and the Extra Solar council, and then set me on an investigation. They must be linked. They must! But how is the question.* He was ending up with more questions than answers. Andorin's musings trailed off as he focused onto what the High Executrix was saying.

The High Executrix stated, "The matter is decided. Convene the Extra-Solar Council."

26 ARRANGEMENTS

Andorin left the Battle Council Chamber. He was still processing the information he learned during the meeting. He walked towards a crowd of other Executrices and waited in silence for the elevator to arrive. He had little interaction with them during the meeting or most others times, and his new status alienated him even further. However, it seemed they were handling the information much better than he was. He had just found out his civilization was going to be destroyed when the first moon crashed into it, and this was the first he had heard of it. It was four hundred years in the future, but still it was frightening to know your culture had a life span that would end. He was not sure how the government had been able to keep control of this information. Everyone knew the smaller moon had collapsed...it was hard not to miss. It was inconceivable that no one had thought about what would happen if the moons lost their mass.

The elevator's arrival interrupted his thoughts. The first few people in line entered, with Andorin as one of the last few people to enter. As he looked around, he wondered how these people could also be clueless about what was happening as a result of their decisions. The fact that the government was purchasing parcels of land and moons disguised as wars was hard to imagine being kept secret. Andorin knew the last *war* was a purchase. However, he just could not figure out how they had arranged that. He knew the High Executrix was aware of the situation and alluded to just that during their conversation. *Who else knew?* was the question that was consuming his thoughts now. *The High Authority knew, but it seemed that he was not supposed to know. Which led to the question: If not the High Authority, then who?*

The elevator doors finally opened, and he exited. He had an urge to check in on Commander Soltag, but decided to let him work on his team a little longer. He had confidence in Soltag's ability to get his team able to function as competent investigators. His team was military trained and would adapt quickly if given the right focus. Right now, they needed Soltag more than they needed him. Tomorrow was another day, and he would pick it up there. He exited the building, heading toward his vehicle. Other Executrices fanned out, leaving the building, heading toward their vehicles. Andorin approached his vehicle and got in. He started the engine, and headed towards home.

As he drove his thoughts wandered back to that nagging question, *Who knows and more importantly sets up the purchases of the war trophies?' There had to be someone higher, more connected that pulled the strings.* He knew it was not the High Authority. *How could this be? He was the one that asked him to investigate and knew through unofficial channels that they were purchases. It's not him. Then who?* Then he remembered that the High Divinity had also withheld information. The manufacture of the probe by the Paclids was a significant acknowledgment. However, that was two hundred and fifty years ago. Did his position still wield that kind of power? It might, but Andorin was just not sure.

As he drove, he noticed people as he passed them. They were oblivious to the planet's demise. He wondered what they would do if they found out. He thought, *They would probably start rioting, or killing each other over food. At least the water supply was still in good shape at about 60% they could live until the planet died. Eventually though, they would start killing over water though, once it got down to about 30 to 40% then people would start panicking. They would do anything to get water. What would happen when the planet died?* He did not need to know that answer today; his great, great, great, great grandchildren would have to worry about that. There was still plenty of water, though the rationing had begun.

He saw that he was approaching his house and was starting to wind down after the events of today. What was he going to tell Miliki? He knew for sure he was not going to tell her the planet was going to die in four hundred years, especially not after the last few days. He walked up the stairs, and he paused at the door. He still had not decided what to say. He would play it off the cuff. He opened the door.

The scents of the day told the story. Helphan and Gilphon were at it again, the scent of their fights were unmistakable. Miliki's calming scent also filled him with a sense of peace. He knew it was not specifically for him, but he needed it. He made his way into the kitchen area to the sounds of Miliki taking care of the tableware. She did not notice him right away because of his suppressed pheromones. He just watched her for a while as she moved about the kitchen; he did so love her. The thought brought a smile to his face.

She then froze in place and looked over her shoulder, jumped back a little and said, "Andorin! You startled me."

"I did not mean to. I was just watching you do your work."

"You know you *could* help me," she said with a smile.

"I could. Or I could go upstairs and get cleaned up," he smiled back.

"Or you could help me, and then get cleaned up while I get dinner ready. You're home early. What's the occasion?" she said.

"I was getting my task force ready to start investigating the deaths when I got summoned to the Battle Council." he said.

"Oh, isn't it that the thing *he* wanted you to be on?" Miliki replied emphasizing the *he*.

"Yes, it was. But it proved...uneventful." he decided to keep her in the dark. He could not discuss much without specifics. He was just piling up lies left and right. He hated this new aspect of his life. He had kept military secrets from her, but not like the ones he had been forced to keep lately. He continued, "I am going upstairs to get out of this armor." He left the room to Miliki's words.

"I said you could help then get cleaned up."

He envisioned the smile on her face but sensed she was a little annoyed at his departure. As he walked past Stranaya's room, he noticed Helphan in there playing. He opened the door slightly and said, "What's going on? Why are you in Stranaya's room?"

"She doesn't need it any more Daddy."

"What do you mean?" he asked.

"Mommy said I could have the room as my own and move out of Gilphon's. Gilphon wanted to throw everything out. I wouldn't let him. We got into a fight." Helphan said.

He thought, *Oh. That is what happened.* "Why do you want to keep Stranaya's things?" Andorin asked.

"I miss her. Her things remind me of her. I like them," he replied.

"What about your things?" Andorin asked.

"I'll find a place for them alongside hers. Her clothes do need to go."

"I am sure mom will get them out soon. It has been rough on everyone."

"Will I see her again?" Helphan asked.

"Well the Divinity tells us that one day we will meet everyone else in the Divine Colony," Andorin explained.

"When will that be?" Helphan asked.

"It will be when you die."

"I have to wait that long to see her again?" Helphan said.

"I know it seems like a very long time, but I can tell you that it goes by very fast. Sometimes it goes by too fast." Andorin explained knowing that if he worked fast enough he could find her and maybe bring some joy back into their lives. "I have to get out of this armor. Mommy should have dinner ready shortly."

"Okay, Daddy." Helphan cheerfully replied.

He left Stranaya's...Helphan's room, *I'll have to work on that*, he thought, and headed toward his bedroom. As he entered he was already peeling off his armor. His carapace was the last piece to go and he piled it up neatly in the corner, waiting for tomorrow when he would put it back on again. He got on some regular clothes. As he was closing the closet door, he noticed the blanket that hid his device. He paused and then decided not to do anything with that this evening, it could wait until morning, maybe then things would make some sense. He finished closing the door. He walked out of the room and was headed toward the kitchen when he heard Miliki call out.

"Dinner!"

Helphan scrambled past him just before he started down the stairs. Gilphon and Felici were slower and ended up behind him on the stairway. They were trying to get past him, and he knew it.

"Dad! Would you get out of the way? We're trying to get downstairs." Gilphon said.

"So am I," Andorin replied with a slight laugh.

"Yeah, just not fast enough." was his quick response.

Andorin said laughingly, "Okay, okay," as he moved out of the way for the two of them to get past. As he got to the dining room, Miliki was just finishing bringing the food to the table.

She smiled and said, "You're just in time."

"You did call us to come, and I had a little help," Andorin smiled back.

Everyone sat down in their seats leaving the one lone empty chair. It was an obvious reminder of what had occurred.

Miliki looked at the seat for a long time and then said, "Andorin would you please give the blessing."

Andorin started, "Everyone, please grasp hands, and close your eyes. Oh, Divine One, bless this food we are about to eat. May your spirit guide and watch over us. May you accept Stranaya into your Divine Colony and watch over her until we meet again."

Everyone sat silent for a few seconds while the last few words sank in.

"Andorin," Miliki started "I did something today without asking you about it first."

"Okay what is it?" Andorin asked afraid of what he might hear.

"I saw on the VidFeed that the government is preparing a mass ceremony for any victims that wanted to participate. I signed us...Stranaya...up to be part of the ceremony."

Relieved, Andorin said, "Honey, it's okay. I understand. It's all right. It will be easier for you as well."

"Thank you for understanding. I just could not accept that she is gone yet, and having to make these kind of arrangements? Well I just could not do it...not yet."

"No, no. I understand fully. It makes sense. What do we have to do?"

"The VidFeed said we just had to show up for the funeral ceremony. It will cost us nothing; they will take care of everything." she said calmly.

"That's wonderful, Honey. I am glad that you do not have to deal with this." Andorin mentally added, *Especially since that was not even her real body.* Then another thought entered his mind, *Could this be a result of my report that they were abductions and not murders?*

"I even got to pick out some flowers to place on her funerary. It was completely custom...I got to pick any flowers. I thought there would just be this arrangement or that one. I said what I wanted and they said it would be taken care of." Miliki explained.

"That's amazing! I would have thought the same thing," Andorin said.

"I did have to provide them with an image of her and a signed release."

"Did they say what that was for?" Andorin asked.

"They said it was for a memoriam of some kind."

"Okay, that sounds reasonable. What image did you send?"

"I sent the one when we went camping at Sandolina Recreational Center. She was sitting on the sand dune smiling," Miliki said.

"I really liked that one." Andorin added.

"I just uploaded it, with a signed authorization, to the site they set up."

"Daddy, when can we go back there? It was fun playing on the sand dunes." Felici said.

"Yeah! I want to go there too." Gilphon chimed in.

"I don't remember going there," Helphan added.

"You were just a baby hatchling then." Gilphon said.

"How come you went when I was a baby?" Helphan asked his parents.

"Baby, we did not go there because you were a baby hatchling, We went there, and you went with us, but you were very young." Miliki said.

"If I went, how come I don't remember?" Helphan asked.

"Well they say hatchlings don't remember their first few years of life. It is because your brain is forming and is not yet fully developed. After you get older, and your brain fully develops, the brain forgets most of the details of the forming stage. You did go with us, you just do not remember." Andorin said, then asked Felici, "Could you get my BioMet for me, please?"

"Here, Daddy," Felici said as handed over the pad.

'Thank you, Sweetums." Andorin said with a smile.

"Here, Helphan, look at these images. See? There is Mommy holding you with Stranaya next to her." Andorin said.

"How come I am not any bigger now than I was then? Why is that Daddy?"

"Well because you grow to a certain size in the egg before you hatch. When you first hatch, you grow a little for a few months. Once your exoskeleton hardens, you cannot grow anymore. This is the size you grew to when you hatched. You have a few years until your first molting. After that, your shell will be soft to allow for your body to rapidly expand to its new size. Then it will harden again. Usually, you have five moltings in your life, all of them will be while you are young. After your last one, you will not molt again."

"So I will get bigger then?" Helphan said.

"Yes, in a few years or so." Andorin said.

"Good, Daddy I want to get bigger."

"You'll be big soon enough." Andorin said with a warm smile.

"Everyone, eat up." Miliki said.

"I am almost done," Gilphon said.

"Me too." Felici added.

"When you are done please take your plate to the sink and scrub it off. Do not use the water. Use the dry cleaning compound instead." Miliki said.

"Okay, Mommy." Felici and Gilphon echoed together.

"Mommy, do I need to scrub my plate?" Helphan asked.

"No, your brother can do it." Miliki said.

"Awe, how come I have to do it?" Gilphon asked.

"Because I said that you would." Miliki replied.

"That's not fair. Felici should have to do it." Gilphon insisted.

"Gilphon. Your mother said you were doing it, and that's final." Andorin intoned with authority.

"Fine!" He said and stomped off into the kitchen with his plate in hand.

"I am done, Mommy," Helphan said.

"Please take your plate to Gilphon." Miliki added.

"Okay Mommy," Helphan said as he bounded off towards his brother.

"Mommy, Can I take yours and Daddy's plates to be scrubbed?" Felici asked.

"I am done. Andorin?" Miliki asked.

"Yeah, I'm done as well. Here is the plate. Thank you, Felici."

"You have not told me much about your day. How was it? Your first day in your new office." Miliki asked.

"It was fine. It went as you would imagine it, bringing twelve people together for the first time. It was interesting to say the least. We had a fight break out, well not so much a fight, it was more like one hit, then it was over." Andorin said.

"Wow, what happened?"

"Someone kept harassing someone else, even after they were asked to stop. This other person got...impatient, let's say, waiting for them to stop and took matters into their own hands. They kicked the other guy in the face, from across a table. One hit and the other guy was on the floor. Needless to say, no one is going to pick on that guy again."

"You have such interesting days sometimes. "Miliki said.

"At least my tech did not break today." Andorin said with a smile.

"Maybe this new job will help that problem," she said, smiling back.

"I am going to head upstairs and get ready for bed." Andorin said.

"I'll be along in a few, after I finish cleaning up." Miliki said.

"Okay, don't be too long."

"It would take less time if you helped me." Miliki said jesting.

"I am sure it would." He said as he turned and walked towards the stairway.

"Hey!" she said feigning anger.

"I love you too." Andorin said from the bottom of the stairs.

"You'd better." Miliki said light-heartedly.

He walked up the stairway towards his room. He passed by Felici's room and popped his head in and said. "Mommy needs some help. Could you please go and help her?"

"Yes, Daddy."

Andorin smiled at his accomplishment. Of course he knew Miliki would not really appreciate that, but probably would not mind. He got lost in his thought again replaying everything that happened at the two battle council meetings today. He did not know how he could keep the truth from Miliki. He did not know how long he had been sitting on the bed, deep in contemplative thought when he heard Miliki enter the bedroom.

"I thought you were going to help me?" Miliki said.

He smiled and said, "I am sorry, I did not get that. I only got that it would go faster if you had help, which I got for you."

"You knew what I meant." She replied.

"Yeah, I did." He said with a smile and grabbed her around the waist and pulled her onto the bed with him.

She giggled a little as she rolled next to him. She stroked his arm where the implant was and asked, "Does it hurt?"

"No, not at all. It just vibrates a little nothing painful." He replied.

"That's good." she said.

"You know that is not why I dragged you onto the bed." He said with a sly smile.

"I know, but I am just not ready for that yet. I still don't know how you do it," she said in a sullen voice.

All he could say was, "I am just different I guess," knowing full well that it was because he knew she was still alive and was not mourning her as dead.

"*Too* different right now," she said as she pushed away and sat with her back to him.

"But honey," he pleaded.

"No, not tonight, and maybe not for a while. I just don't have that connection with you right now." She replied and moved away to get her night clothes on.

"Soon?" He asked.

"I don't know. I just don't know right now." She said as she moved into position on her side of the bed and covered up.

Andorin just sat there for a few seconds longer pondering the implications of what just happened. He did not like this one bit, but he understood. He would have to be understanding right now. He thought to himself, *Would it make it any easier if I told her the truth?* He did not have an answer to that question, at least not now, anyway. He moved to his side of the bed and reached up and turned off his bed side light. He closed his eyes and drifted off to sleep, thinking about everything that had happened today. Tomorrow was going to be a new day. He could attack everything from there. The last image he remembered was the soldier killing the thing that had looked like Stranaya. He almost believed it. He faded off to sleep.

The End.

APPENDIX A
Military Hierarchy Information

Strategic Command Structure (259 -Total Positions)
High Executrix (HE) - 1 Reports directly to the High Authority.
First Executrix (1E) - 6 All report directly to HE.
Second Executrix (2E) - 36 Report to various 1Es
Low Executrix (LE) - 216 Report to various 2Es

Operational Command Structure (49,988,526,496,344 -Total Positions)
Command (Cmd) (Numeric)- Commander (Cdr)- Each LE can have up to 9 Commands
Battalion (Btn) (Alpha)- Battaliaison (Bln) - Each Command can have up to 26 Battalions
Regiment (Rgt) (Numeric) - Regimentrix (Rgx) - Each Battalion can have 99 Regiments
Phalanx (Plx) (Numeric) - Phalaxon (Pxn) - Each Regiment can have 999 Phalanxes
Militia (Mla) (Numeric) - Militrix (Mlx) - Each Phalanx can have 9999 Militias

Operations Level (15,494,892,002,235,400 -Total Positions)
Squad (Sq) (Alpha/Numeric) - Squad Leader (SL) - Each Militia can have 10 Squads
Element (El) (Numeric) -Element Leader (EL) - Each Squad can have 5 Elements
Soldier (S) (Numeric) - Lowest level a single soldier - Each Element has 5 Soldiers

The total possible end strength of this system is 12,495,880,646,964,000 soldiers with a total end strength of 15,544,880,528,732,000 for all the positions. This system has never been fully engaged, meaning there has never been 15.5 Quadrillion filled positions, but the Strategic Command Structure is always filled. This system allows flexibility to manage personnel with precision, down to the specific soldier if need be.

APPENDIX B
Military Cresting System

The Cresting system design allows every person to be uniquely identified. The position in the military is a key element of the Andlid society, not just the position they fill but having lower numbers on their crest. The lower the number means they are higher in the ranking structure. To have a "1" for your current position means that you have reached the top of your structure for your command hierarchy. The only way to move to a higher position is to move to positions that have lower numbers in a higher command structure. The Rocker Crest is the Strategic Commander Structure that identifies the Executrix Leadership that all levels report to. The Diamond Crest is the Operational Command Level and where basic military orders are commanded. The V-Crest designates the Operations Level this is where the orders are executed.

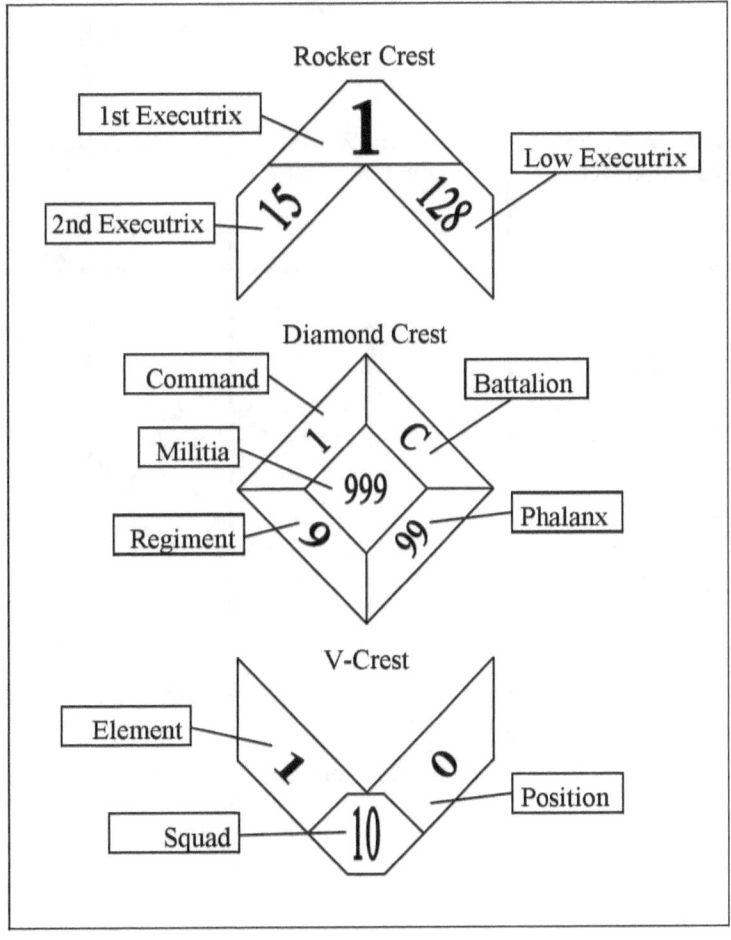

APPENDIX C
Military Crests of Personnel

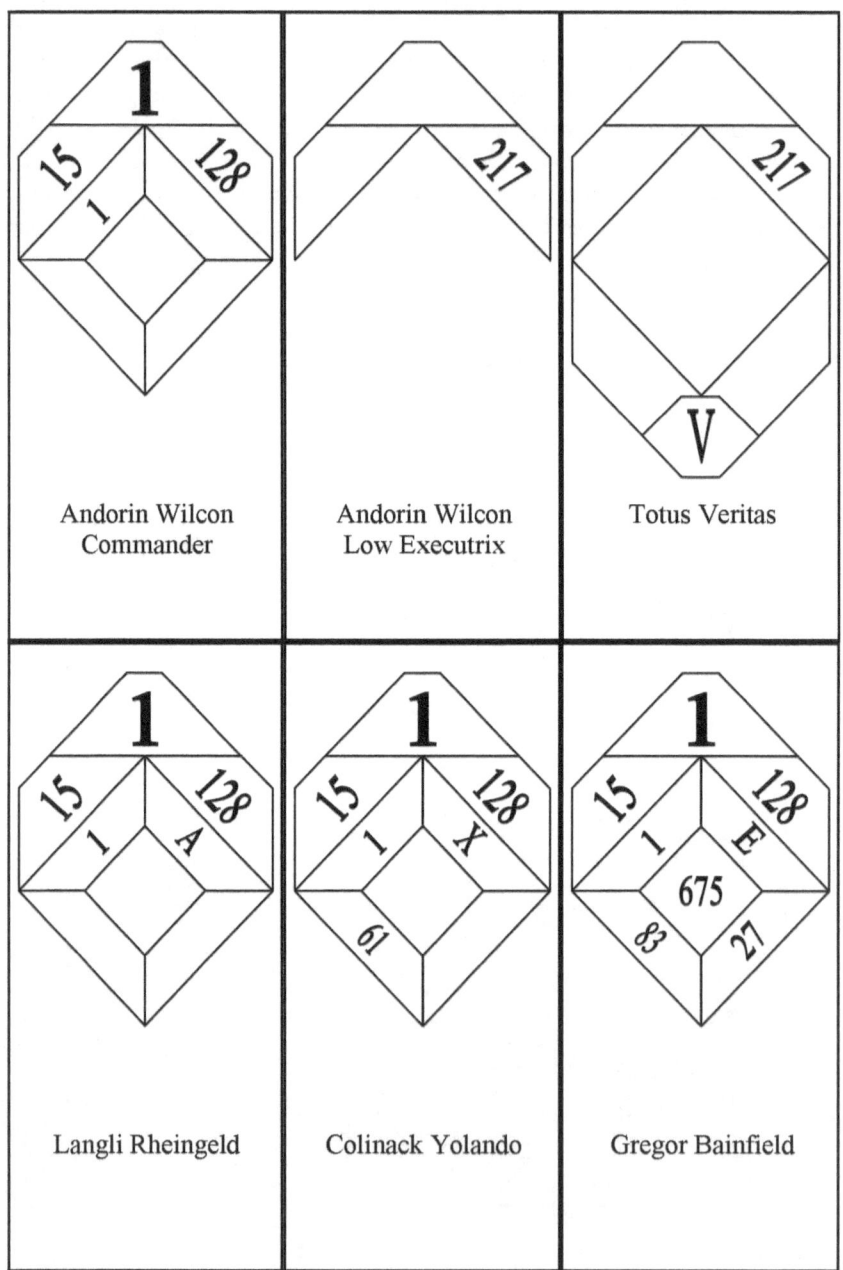

Andorin Wilcon
Commander

Andorin Wilcon
Low Executrix

Totus Veritas

Langli Rheingeld

Colinack Yolando

Gregor Bainfield

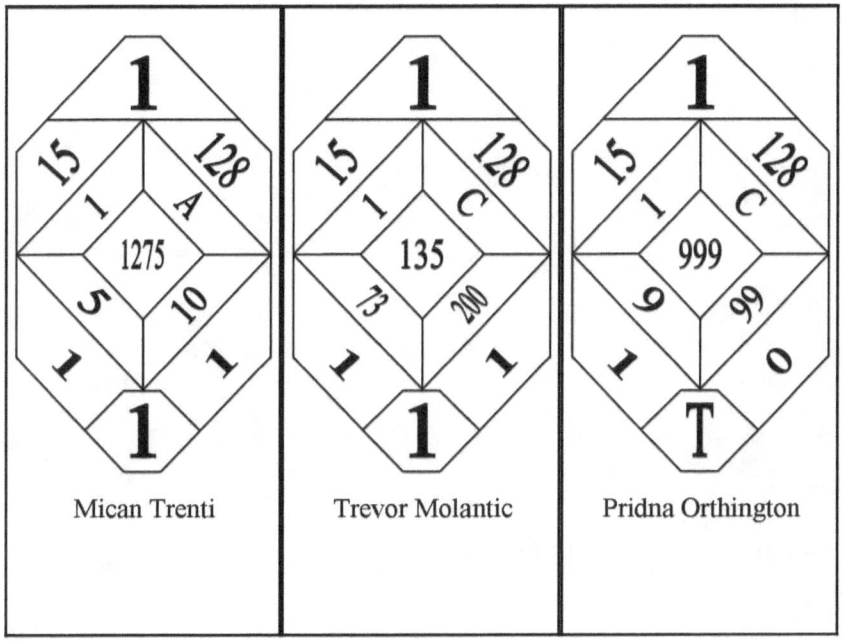

Mican Trenti   Trevor Molantic   Pridna Orthington

ABOUT THE AUTHOR

Kevin Olmstead graduated High School in 1983 in a small town in Upstate New York. He joined the United States Air Force in 1985 and served 25 years in Financial Management. When he retired, he had an Associate's Degree in Financial Management and a Bachelor's Degree in Information Technology Management, graduating with Honors. He completed his graduate programs in 2014 also with Honors receiving a Master's Degree in Information and Technology Management, Information Assurance and Security, and earned a second Graduate Certificate in Digital Forensics.

You may connect with the author through email kevin@olmstead.com.